D0032696

SEDUCTION AND SURRENDER

"I'm not some piece of property to be decorated and displayed for you and your men," Jana said angrily.

"Careful, little moonbeam," Varian warned. "You are what I say you are." He flashed a devastating smile.

Her heart fluttered wildly. "And what am I, Commander?"

"Fishing for compliments, Jana?"

She ran her finger over his sensual lower lip with provocative slowness, then lowered her hand to rest casually upon his muscular chest. "Compliments aren't necessary. The fact that I'm your elite prisoner is proof of your high opinion of me. Is that not so?" she challenged.

Her tone was seductive. Her eyes held a hint of mystery and promise. She felt his heartbeat quicken beneath her hand.

Without warning, he seized her in his powerful arms and covered her mouth with his. His lips were warm and persistent. Caught totally unprepared, she helplessly melted into his embrace and surrendered her kisses. At her response, his arms tightened around her.

Suddenly, nothing but this moment mattered to Jana. Varian had been transformed from her captor and tormentor into a man—a man she desperately wanted . . .

PINNACLE'S PASSIONATE AUTHOR—

PATRICIA MATTHEWS

EXPERIENCE *LOVE'S* PROMISE

LOVE'S AVENGING HEART   (302-1, $3.95/$4.95)
Red-haired Hannah, sold into servitude as an innkeeper's
barmaiden, must survive the illicit passions of many men,
until love comes to free her questing heart.

LOVE'S BOLD JOURNEY   (421-4, $4.50/$5.50)
Innocent Rachel, orphaned after the Civil War, travels out
West to start a new life, only to meet three bold men—two
she couldn't love and one she couldn't trust.

LOVE'S DARING DREAM   (372-2, $4.50/$5.50)
Proud Maggie must overcome the poverty and shame of
her family's bleak existence, encountering men of wealth,
power, and greed until her impassioned dreams of love are
answered.

LOVE'S GOLDEN DESTINY   (393-5, $4.50/$5.50)
Lovely Belinda Lee follows her gold-seeking father to the
Alaskan Yukon where danger and love are waiting in the
wilderness.

LOVE'S MAGIC MOMENT   (409-5, $4.50/$5.50)
Sensuous Meredith boldly undertakes her father's lifework
to search for a fabled treasure in Mexico, where she must
learn to distinguish between the sweet truth of love and the
seduction of greed and lust.

*Available wherever paperbacks are sold, or order direct from the
Publisher. Send cover price plus 50¢ per copy for mailing and
handling to Pinnacle Books, Dept. 659, 475 Park Avenue South,
New York, N.Y. 10016. Residents of New York and Tennessee
must include sales tax. DO NOT SEND CASH. For a free Zebra/
Pinnacle catalog please write to the above address.*

JANELLE TAYLOR

MOONDUST AND MADNESS

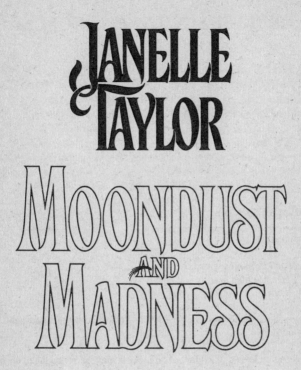

PINNACLE BOOKS
WINDSOR PUBLISHING CORP.

PINNACLE BOOKS

are published by

Windsor Publishing Corp.
475 Park Avenue South
New York, NY 10016

Copyright © 1986 by Janelle Taylor. Published by arrangement
with author.

All rights reserved. No part of this book may be reproduced in any
form or by any means without the prior written consent of the
Publisher, excepting brief quotes used in reviews.

Pinnacle and the P logo are trademarks of Windsor Publishing
Corp.

If you purchased this book without a cover you should be aware
that this book is stolen property. It was reported as "unsold and
destroyed" to the Publisher and neither the Author nor the
Publisher has received any payment for this "stripped book."

First Pinnacle Books Printing: November 1992

Printed in the United States of America

*To Sheila Taylor and Deeny Alford who never
stopped believing this book would see print.*

*And to Michael Taylor, husband, lover, best friend,
and indispensable helper. He gave so much to
this book, and adds even more to my life.*

Acknowledgments

To Linda Grey, Publisher of Bantam Books, who was willing to buy something "different"; my agent Adele Leone-Monaco, who made my fantasy become a reality and worked as hard as I did on it; Coleen O'Shea, a super editor with talent and patience; Richard McEnroe, who is very creative and most helpful; and Dr. James Matheny, whose transfer from MCG to UKY evoked my writing career. Thanks for all you taught me.

Prologue

It was a splendid night for a special party. A fun moon was rising over the treetops and the sky was sprinkled liberally with tiny points of light. An evocative breeze which wandered over the shadowy landscape was as gentle as a lover's caress and the heady fragrance of gardenias and tea olives joined those of honeysuckle and sweet shrubs to scent the night air. Jana Greyson had always loved the many large gardens on the McKay estate. She could hear the rippling water of several fountains in the midst of lily pools. Cicadas, tiny tree frogs, and night birds pierced the silence. Muffled sounds of merriment reached her ears.

Jana hastened to the nearest garden walkway, which led to the rear of Andrea McKay's family mansion. The enormous gardens were artistically designed in several tiers, downplaying the distance of the tennis courts from the terrace. She hurried through the hedgerows on two lower levels until she reached the first decorative pool. As she halted to catch her breath, her gaze flickered over neatly tended beds of roses, camellias, and pansies which offered a vision of beauty and symmetry.

Jana frowned as the moonlit yellow roses and purple pansies reminded her of the two beautifully gift-wrapped packages, Andrea's graduation present, which she had forgotten in her car trunk! Since there were no parking spaces when Jana arrived at the private entrance and she didn't want to walk from the road, she had parked in the service area.

Now she grumbled to herself as she retraced her steps. A few moments later, a curious shiver ran through her body. She halted to check her surroundings. In front of her was the McKay home, a beautiful and elegant Greek Revival plantation built in 1835, and Jana imagined it filled with lively music and glittering lights from numerous candles and chandeliers. She knew that Andrea—her closest friend since age twelve—had spared no expense or effort to make this, their graduation celebration, perfect. The circular driveway lined with oaks and magnolias was filled with Jaguars, Mercedes, Cadillacs, Porsches, Corvettes, and limousines. As was the custom, chauffeurs would await their employers in the pool house to the far left of the mansion. Yet she was filled with a weird sensation, as if a potent force were bearing down on her. She shrugged, dismissed the feeling, and continued.

Maybe her nerves were taut because she didn't want to see Alex McKenzie, tonight or ever. She and Alex had dated during high school and college. Following the completion of her dissertation in January and during the first three months of her part-time work at the medical center in Houston, they had become almost inseparable as a couple. Had she been too distracted by studies and work to see the real man, or was she too naïve and gullible?

It had not been easy to graduate from the University of Texas with a major in biochemistry, to do graduate work in microbiology and chemistry, and to earn a Ph.D. before turning twenty-four.

Alex had graduated last June and now had a law practice in Houston. During the last few months, Alex had not been the same man who had attracted her time and attention. Their last date had ended with bitter words. Defiance and resentment flooded her anew as she recalled their final quarrel. Alex had made demands, or more accurately ultimatums, she could not meet. She could see his handsome features set in angry lines as they were when she had challenged his demand that she forget her career dreams and move in with him in Houston! *If* their arrangement worked out satisfactorily, he had stated imperiously, they would marry in a year or two. The startling truth had struck Jana one night in May; she didn't love Alex and she owed him nothing! Her only regret was in taking so long to make the decision to push him out of her life and thoughts forever.

And so tonight she would congratulate herself and her friends

8

and celebrate, just as soon as she retrieved the gifts for Andrea from her car.

Jana reached her car, unlocked the trunk, removed two oblong boxes, then closed it. That eerie sensation washed over her again; she shuddered as if very cold, causing her to drop her keys and purse.

"Need any help?" a raspy voice asked from the darkness behind her.

Startled, Jana whirled, tossing her possessions in several directions. One hand flew to her chest where her heart was hammering. Her eyes searched the black shadows. Then she saw him. The stranger was outfitted in black leather pants, boots, and jacket. Moonlight danced off the shiny bill of his captain's cap. She eyed the patches and emblems sewn haphazardly to his jacket. His scraggly beard and leering grin added to his ominous appearance. She suddenly realized all the lights in this area were dark. The full moon had cast deceptive brightness and inspired a false sense of security.

Jana's mind worked swiftly. Whoever he was, this person was standing between her and the walkway. To her left, there was a thick hedgerow. To her right was a fence enclosing the tennis courts. Behind her, an open gate led to a dark road. She knew the tennis house was locked, just as she knew the landscaping smothered most of the noise in this area. She was trapped except for the darkness outside the gate.

"If it's money you're after, my purse is there." She pointed to the pavement where it had landed. Only a slight snickering reached her ears.

Ignoring the purse, he headed for Jana. She panicked. As she turned to run toward the gate, she was intercepted and her arms were seized. "Let me go! Help!" she screamed. As Jana kicked, clawed, threatened, and struggled, her gown was torn; her arms and chest were bruised and scratched.

"What a little she-cat! Wait till Deke sees what I've found for us," he said, sneering over her threats. "Just what we wuz lookin' fur, rich an' beautiful."

Hungrily scanning her face and partially exposed cleavage, he flamed with lust. "Damn if you ain't a beauty! I bet yore worth a fortune."

"I'll kill you if you touch me!" Jana yelled. Although she knew this distant area was well out of hearing range.

He laughed wickedly. "Me little angel, is that any way to be talking to Tully, yore new loverboy? Me an' you gonna spend a lot of time together."

Jana had to act quickly before "Deke" appeared and she would be faced with two thugs. She relaxed her body and lowered her head dejectedly as if giving up her fight. She sniffled as if she were about to burst into tears. These actions took him off guard momentarily. Without warning, Jana gritted her teeth and forcefully brought her knee up into his unprotected groin.

Tully released her and doubled over, retching and nearly fainting from the sudden and excruciating agony. Moaning raggedly through clenched teeth, he spouted terrifying threats.

Jana ran as fast as she could. Her escape was hindered by her evening shoes but she didn't dare take precious time to remove them. She kept silent, for she knew she still could not be heard over the loud music and party sounds which came from the house, and she did not want to lead her attacker to her.

The gardener's cottage was closest. Jana took the side path and headed that way. Burly Garcia could handle this hoodlum. Her legs were cramping and her lungs burning. She was breathing heavily and tiring too quickly. Where were her vitality and energy now when she needed them desperately? Terror drained her stamina. What if Garcia was not in his cottage?

Jana hurriedly rounded the bend in the hedged path and came to an abrupt halt. A tall, masculine body was positioned in the walkway, blocking her escape. She weighed her choices: fight this villain or the one behind her? Her first assailant was only a few inches taller than her five-eight frame, but this tower of muscles was an invincible barrier.

The man before her was dressed in what looked like a snug-fitting silvery jumpsuit. The iridescent glow from his garment flickered eerily in the opalescent moonlight. Jana's eyes hastily registered the triangular black medallion around his neck, and the wide black belt around his narrow waist from which several unfamiliar items were suspended. Her frightened gaze took in his silver helmet with its impenetrable vizard. Her gaze hesitated on that mirrorlike visor, but all she could see was her own terror-filled reflection.

Quivers of apprehension spread throughout her body as she

stood there. As confused as she was, Jana perceived immense power emanating from this man. Rape, ransom, and murder flashed across her mind. Could this be "Deke?" It was then something ordered, *Scream, Jana, scream!*

But Jana could not scream or speak. Her chest rose and fell rapidly in response to her lungs' demand for more oxygen. Fear raced in her mind and body as she began to back away from him. She wished she could find an opening in the hedge-row to escape this new threat but she knew there was none, for she had walked this garden path many times since childhood.

Jana swallowed hard, then moistened her dry lips. She jerked around as she heard footsteps behind her. Tully rushed into view, a knife in his hand and hatred on his face. Jana instinct-ively took a few steps backward, closer to the tall stranger.

Sighting the muscular man in the silvery suit, Tully halted. As he huffed and puffed through clenched teeth, a curious expression crossed his face, but Jana did not comprehend it at that time.

Her alarm mounted as two more silver-clad men appeared behind Tully. Four men now surrounded her: three dressed in shiny silver jumpsuits and one in black leather. She trembled visibly.

"Hey, you guys, I wuz only funning. I wasn't gonna hurt her." He lied badly, but nervously continued, "I only scared you, right?" Jana did not move or reply. "I'll be moving on. Okay?" he wheedled nervously.

No answers dispelled the weird silence and strange aura which surrounded the three strangers. Jana curiously eyed those three males whose disguises perplexed her. From her first at-tacker's fear and panic, it was clear they were not his friends. Who were they? What did they want? Their odd behavior still did not suggest help or safety from Tully.

Jana waited to see who would make the first move and what it would be. She was very much aware of one man's proximity to her. She half turned to study his arrogant, self-assured pos-ture. She surmised he was the one in control of this situation. He emanated an imposing aura of authority and raw power. He would be the one to appeal to or defeat when the time came, if it did. . . .

Her first attacker ended the impasse when he began hesitantly to head back along the pathway toward the other two men. The man to the left raised his arm and pointed an object at him. It was about the size of an oblong wallet. He pressed something on its side with his thumb. The object released a narrow ray of intense light.

It touched Tully, causing an iridescent glow to outline his body. He shuddered at first contact, then froze immobile like a statue. The deadly glow shimmered for a few seconds, then dissipated, leaving no trace of Tully. Jana shook her head and blinked in an attempt to clear her confusion. *People don't vanish before your very eyes*, she reasoned. Jana pinched her arm to test her alertness. The sudden pain told her she was awake. Was this a sick joke or sinister game someone was playing? If so, it was not funny.

"Tully, where the hell are you?" a second man in black leather called out as he came into view, a gun in his grip. Jana knew this was "Deke."

The men nodded a signal to each other. The one to her left raised his arm again and fired a beam at Deke. Deke shuddered, froze, and lit up with an evanescent glow. He shimmered, then disappeared completely. She gaped in disbelief and alarm. She was the only one left. A witness to murder?

The two men walked toward her. She was alone, at their mercy. If Jana could trust her senses, they had disintegrated two men in a mysterious way. She panicked. She turned to flee, but too late she recalled the muscular man's presence. She found herself trapped in the confines of his iron embrace. He held her forearms as securely as he held his silence.

His grip was like a steel band, yet painless. When Jana could not overcome his tremendous strength, she gazed up at the visored helmet of the man towering over her. His features were completely obscured from her wide, searching eyes. She begged her assailant, "Please, please let me go. . . ."

He neither spoke nor moved to comply. But she could tell from the angle of his head that he was looking at her, watching her. He was at least six feet four and well developed. He was strong and agile. She stared at her unseeable foe, then her eyes involuntarily traveled his body. His tight clothing revealed a very masculine physique beneath it.

Jana struggled wildly and briefly, but realized escape was impossible. Her voice quavered as she demanded with false courage, "What do you want? Ransom? Robbery? Answer

12

me!'' She angrily twisted against him, warning, ''Let go this instant or I'll scream until someone hears me!'' She glared up at him with fiery eyes, then she opened her mouth to scream, jerking on her arms to free them.

His hand covered her mouth, trapping the sound in her throat. His other arm immediately encircled her back and pulled her to his broad chest, with surprising gentleness and self-control. She could feel the rippling firmness of his body beneath her hands, which were pinned against him. They detected the steady beating of his heart. Jana knew she was defenseless. Was she their intended victim, or had she accidentally been ensnared in some other plot? She tensely awaited his demands.

One man approached and made several nods to the one who held her captive in his iron vise. She assumed they must have prearranged signals or voice communicators in those helmets, for she could hear no sounds.

Her captor tightened his steel-like grip while the other man firmly yet painlessly took her wrist in one of his hands. He touched her bare arm with a pencil-shaped tube; he pressed the other end with his thumb and she heard a soft hissing noise for a second. He stepped back to join the other man.

Jana felt a tingling sensation on the area he had touched with the strange object. She gazed up in confusion, then back at her arm. Almost immediately her vision began to blur. Her mouth was suddenly dry, with a minty taste to it. She felt weak and dizzy while a numbing sensation crept into her legs and arms. She had to fight to hold her eyelids open. She unknowingly leaned against her captor for support, gripping his shirt to keep from collapsing to the ground.

Her body felt light enough to float away if he released it. Jana tried to focus on the man who held her protectively, but his form wavered like a desert mirage. She tried to ask him what he was doing to her. Her brain refused to order her speech center to obey her mental commands.

Jana's head sank to his chest. She turned it slightly, resting her cheek against his firm torso. A steady heartbeat filtered into her buzzing ears, and a stirring male odor teased her nose and drugged senses. Immensely strong arms held her gently. His bearing, strength, scent, and physique mingled to conjure up intoxicating images. She inhaled deeply and sighed dreamily. Everything began to spin and fade as she went limp against him.

PART I
Moondust and Madness

As the playful Gods gather to watch mortals below,
The helpless Fates warn sadly, for only they know:
Careful of "Moondust" which captures a heart;
Beware of its "Madness" which tears lovers apart . . .

Chapter One

Commander Varian Saar lifted Jana Greyson in his strong arms. He shifted her body to afford himself a better look at her features, stunned to be looking at the Universe's most beautiful female. Two of his highest-ranking officers and best friends had suggested he capture this woman. Varian had read her file put together by First Officer and Lieutenant Commander Nigel Sanger and Dr. Tristan Zarcoff, the chief medical and scientific research officer; so Varian knew what had sparked their interest in this particular female.

Jana's dark blond hair was thick and long. It tumbled over his arm in a lush cascade of curls and waves which were streaked with a color as pale as a full moon. Her silky skin had been lovingly kissed by the sun to produce a surface of golden satin. Varian recalled the strange color of her eyes, which had varied with her emotions. They were neither blue, nor green, nor violet—but a coalescence of all three. Her gaze was like a kaleidoscope of magical allure and sweet mystery. He wondered how many times those unique eyes and their sensual hint of promise had been some man's undoing. Her pinkened lips almost boldly invited a man to taste them. Her nose, chin, and cheekbones increased her rare beauty. Never had he viewed such a harmonious blending of features. Jana appeared too perfect and beautiful to be real, but her steady respiration assured him she was very much alive.

Varian tensed at his line of thought and his rampant emotions. For him, this breath-stealing and loin-tightening vision was a forbidden fruit. Yet she had the unconscious power to pervade him without even trying. She evinced traits which ensnared his senses. Perhaps he had watched the tape which his men had made of her before her abduction once too often! Was that why he had captured her himself? With so many enemies after his life, how rash to become entangled with any special female.

Varian was displeased she had witnessed the deaths of the men who had attacked her. But when Jana's abduction came to light, he could not afford to have an account of their visit to Earth, even from unreliable witnesses. He was angered by her torn gown, bruises, and scratches. He had been unable to communicate with Jana and lessen her fear. She would never have understood his language without the aid of an audiotranslator.

"You and Tris were right, Nigel." Varian admitted. "She will bring the highest bid ever made for a captive mate."

They gazed appreciatively into the sleeping face of the most beautiful female they had seen in any galaxy. While scanning Houston's television signals one night in May, Nigel Sanger and Tristan Zarcoff had viewed the news story about how Dr. Jana Greyson—daughter of the late Temple Greyson, cattle baron and oil magnate, and the late Katrina Stacy Greyson, heiress to the prestigious and lucrative Stacy Aerospace Firm—had set up a foundation for terminally ill children. And even though her vast estate contained property and businesses and cattle and oil, she had completed her science studies and hoped to research childhood diseases. The news report had said that while Jana was waiting to assume a research position at the Johns Hopkins medical complex in August, she was working temporarily at the Baylor medical complex in Houston. And it had revealed that although she had finished her studies in January, she would attend the University of Texas graduation ceremony in Austin with her friends and classmates. Tonight they had tracked her to the graduation celebration in her hometown of West Columbia.

Second Officer and Security Control Chief Kyle Dykstra spoke up. "Too bad I couldn't just stun those things. Ready to return to the ship, sir?"

Varian shook his head of dark sable hair to clear it of rambling thoughts. "Affirmative, Kyle. Seems we have the treasure we came for."

The starship *Wanderlust* orbited high above Texas; it drifted silently in the vast and weightless ocean of space, undetected by all Earthly tracking systems. No one suspected the starship's presence or its primary and humanitarian purpose to gather data for studying the threat of awesome destruction in the Milky Way Galaxy and to see if such a disaster could be prevented. After their return to the *Wanderlust*, Varian issued the order to leave their present orbit around Earth.

"Yes, sir," replied Lieutenant Tesla Rilke, who had never enjoyed an assignment more than this one for the Maffei Interplanetary Alliance under Commander Varian Saar.

Varian smiled. Tesla Rilke had proven himself to be the best navigational officer to serve under his command. "I'll be in my quarters if anything unusual shows up on the scanner."

Tesla Rilke hastily checked his instrument panels, aware that Varian Saar had an uncanny ability to hone in on trouble before the panels displayed it. "All systems functioning at safety levels, sir. I'll keep you posted."

"Lay in a course for the planet Zamarra. We'll need the extra time to get our *charls* ready for sale," Varian stated, then sighed heavily, as he personally found this enthralling practice repulsive. Until this current mission, he had not given much thought to the existence of a *charl*: a captive female who would be auctioned to serve and live as a mate, companion, mother on one of the planets in the Maffeian Galaxy.

Varian sat at the desk in his private quarters and propped his chin on a balled fist. While he awaited his science officer's arrival and final report, his thoughts went to the female "cargo" which temporarily inhabited the lower decks during this unusual voyage. With only a skeleton crew and select technicians aboard, the large starship had seemed almost empty before taking on the women from Earth and Uranus. The remainder of his crew had been given leave on their home planets until his return because the fewer people involved in this distressing affair, the better chance of keeping the real motive for this trek a secret from enemies.

Only a few officers present knew the reason behind this assignment by the Supreme Council, the elite three-man ruling body of the Maffei Galaxy. An enormous meteor soon to enter the neighboring Milky Way Galaxy would gradually increase its speed due to the gravitational pull of the Sun and would head straight for a collision course with Jana's world.

From Varian's viewpoint, the fate of Earth looked grim. The meteor's size and composition made it impossible for the *Wanderlust* to destroy or to divert it. Because of the placements of nuclear weapons and reactors, Earth and its inhabitants would be doomed when the "fireball" struck and exploded.

By plotting the course and speed of the meteor, which would enter this solar system in nine weeks, decisions could be made by the Supreme Council on whether or not to interfere in this impending catastrophe, if intervention was even possible. The ship's primary mission was to collect and deliver firsthand information to the Maffei rulers, to suggest any possible solution to this imminent cataclysm, and to carry out the Council's final decision. This crucial mission had to remain a closely guarded secret to prevent rival galaxies from taking advantage of the tragic situation. The ship's cover mission was the capturing, training, and auctioning of *charls*. This was the first time that the *Wanderlust* was directly involved in the enthralling process and Varian wasn't happy about it.

The Maffei Galaxy had not recovered from a virulent plague fifty years ago which had greatly decreased the female population. Many females had been left sterile or were presently too young or too old for reproduction: a vital facet to race survival. Thus the Supreme Council had enacted the desperate policy of capturing alien females to become Maffeian mates and mothers, whether or not they agreed. Luckily most adjusted within a short period of time.

As he returned the *Wanderlust* to Star Fleet base on the capital planet of Rigel, Varian was to stop and hold an auction on each of the thirteen planets in his home galaxy. Varian pondered his orders to use the *charl* auctions as ruses to secretly pass a report tape of this mission to each of the thirteen avatars who comprised the Alliance Assembly and served under the Supreme Council of three men. Each avatar had been notified to watch for Varian's return from deep space and to attend the *charl* auction. The thirteen planetary rulers were to study the facts and meet with the Supreme Council on an agreed date to discuss the fate of the Milky Way Galaxy and any actions to be taken. Varian was under orders not to allow a single one of these tapes to fall into the wrong hands.

The entry buzzer sounded. Varian pressed the door- release switch on his desk panel to allow his science officer, First Officer Nigel Sanger, to enter. Varian swiveled in his chair and leaned back, locking his fingers behind his head.

As he seated himself on the divan, Nigel informed his superior officer and best friend, "Kyle has security under control and Baruch said all ship systems are functioning at peak levels. We're lucky no environmental alterations were required for any of the *charls*."

Varian murmured, "We could use some luck or even magic about now."

Varian had studied the reports compiled by the mass-memory computer, but he wanted to make certain he full understood this dire situation and its consequences. "I guess there's no stalling it. You'd best fill me in," he ordered resignedly. He settled back in his chair and rested a head of shiny sable hair against the headrest. He absently rubbed his left forefinger up and down the deep cleft in his chin. By anyone's measure, male or female, Varian Saar's physical appearance was matchless in its superiority.

Nigel was one inch shorter than Varian's six-feet-four frame. His hazel eyes could shade to brown or to green according to his emotions. A head of thick, curly brown hair gave him a carefree look. Tiny creases near his eyes and mouth came from laughter and concentration, not from his age of thirty-one, the same as Varian. Nigel had been one of Varian's closest friends and constant companions for the last twelve years.

Nigel handed Varian a binder. It contained the report which would be placed on tape and delivered to the three Supreme Council members and to each of the thirteen planetary leaders by Varian personally on the day of the auction on each planet, hopefully without arousing any undue suspicion. "I'm afraid it couldn't look worse," Nigel remarked sadly.

The science officer leaned forward and spread out a galactic map on Varian's desk. He traced the meteor's course with his finger and related the sudden calamitous event which would bring great damage, loss, and destruction to Earth by the end of October. "There's no mistake, Varian. The planet Earth is in grave danger." Nigel went on to explain details of a grim situation which Varian already seemed to know by heart.

"And it only takes a few pages to relate such havoc," Varian muttered, angered by this violent challenge by nature. "Is there anything we can do, Nigel? Which won't endanger our Star Fleet?"

Nigel witnessed the troubled look in those deep sapphire eyes which seemed to be begging him to give more favorable answers. Varian Saar was not a man acquainted with defeat or weakness, and this uncontrollable predicament was eating at him. "We have a few choices, but each one carries dangers. We can let nature take its course and see what happens. Perhaps fate will avert a catastrophe." Nigel could tell that Varian Saar did not approve of leaving such an awesome task in the hands of often cruel or mischievous fate.

Nigel listed the next choice. "We can use the time left before impact to rescue and relocate as many Earthlings as possible. But if we send enough starships to accomplish an evacuation of any consequence, it would leave our Star Fleet spread mighty thin for defense against our enemies."

"Maal Triloni and Jurad Tabriz would be thrilled with that error on our part," Varian said with a sneer, aware of the covetous dreams of the leaders of their two neighboring galaxies.

Varian looked at Nigel and concluded aloud, "I doubt there's time for a large-scale rescue attempt. It would require our whole Star Fleet to deliver food, supplies, and water. Such a movement of ships would not go unnoticed by Maal or Jurad. Our world would sit as a helpless prey to either beast. It's a shame the Earthlings aren't capable of space travel so they could relocate themselves. Can't you imagine the terror and disbelief those people would experience if we simply dropped in to warn them? We'd never win their trust and cooperation in time to help them. If we don't think of something clever, it's best to leave them in blissful ignorance. Do you have another suggestion?"

"We could try to either disintegrate or deflect the meteor."

Varian looked confused. "I thought you said we couldn't divert it or destroy it." he probed. "Have you come up with a new plan?"

"We can't carry out such a project alone, but a combined

force of at least five or more starships might succeed. If we could stack, so to speak, our starships on two sides of the meteor, we might be able to shatter it. Then our starships could attack the largest fragments. Even if we failed to handle the broken pieces, they would cause less damage to Earth than the whole meteor slamming to its surface. We'll need top specialists to locate the meteor's internal stress points and decide how much time and power would be required for such a task. We'd need to strike at her before Uranus or between Uranus and Jupiter at the latest, I would think. Either solution will require enormous firepower from many starships. Their energy banks would be drained by the expenditure. I would suggest a chemical laser beam, if you and the Council go for this plan.''

"We can't take multiple risks. Those ships could sustain debilitating damage, or be destroyed, or left defenseless for days. What would happen if Jurad or Maal appeared on the scene while most of our Star Fleet was crippled? Or what if they pulled a sneak attack on one of our planets or on our Alliance Force while so many of our starships are away on a possibly futile mission? Isn't that right, Nigel? You don't know if such a plan could work?''

"It sounds logical, but I can't promise our success," Nigel admitted.

"Why a chemical laser?" Varian inquired.

Nigel knew why his commander and friend was asking that question. Trilabs—the company which developed most of the drugs, chemicals, and weapons used by the Maffei Galaxy—was the sole owner of the chemical laser being discussed. The formula and design belonged to their creator, Ryker Triloni, Varian's evil half brother and most vicious enemy. Ryker Triloni . . . how different he was from Varian Saar, even if they did share blood from the same father.

Over the years since Prince Ryker Triloni had left the Androas Galaxy to live in the one dominated by Varian's grandfather *Kadim* Tirol Trygue, high ruler of the Supreme Council, Ryker had become an influential and wealthy man. Ryker's genius could not be argued. He was a matchless chemist and research scientist who owned his own impregnable planetoid, which was aptly called Darkar, for Ryker Triloni's heart and soul were as black as satanic evil itself. The Trilabs complex was located there. Everyone knew if Ryker ever defeated his half brother and Tirol, he would probably take over the Maffei Galaxy and fuse it to his grandfather *Kadim* Maal Triloni's Androas Galaxy to create an enormous and powerful empire. Yet, no one dared to defy the strength or to enflame the temper of the powerful bastard son of Galen Saar, except Varian and Tirol Trygue.

"A regular laser beam isn't strong enough." Nigel responded. "The chemical laser is the most powerful, the easiest to control, and the surest path to victory."

"You know where we would have to obtain the necessary gases?"

"Only Trilabs has what we need. Why not let the Council handle it?"

Varian stared into blank space as he moodily reflected on several dark episodes in the past which this conversation had recalled, as if they were poorly healed wounds which had been reopened. The blue-eyed man muttered cynically, "I still say *Kadim* Maal is biding his time until he has the power and courage to seek revenge for what he thinks my father did to his family."

As if needing to verbally purge himself for the first time in years, Varian somberly continued, "It's so tiring and infuriating to stay on constant guard, Nigel, to be helpless before enemies because you can't legally touch them without breaking the law yourself or injuring the people and world you love. I know the moment I weaken, one of those bastards will end it for me, or make me wish I were dead. You saw Ryker's last chemical tortures in use: those truth serums and agony inducers. Can you imagine the perils our world would face if Ryker openly sided with either Maal or Jurad? Or both! It scares me to know that bastard has such awesome secrets and talents."

Nigel's expression told Varian that he had those same fears. Varian scoffed bitterly, "I'm positive Princess Shara Triloni was a witch who taught her son all she knew before her suicide. I'd rather Ryker kill me than use his evil skills on me! If Jurad doesn't get me first. Or perhaps I'll get it in the back from one of their hired men or from another enemy. *Kahala* knows I've got plenty of them, too many to settle down and risk the lives of a wife and children. Every time I see Ryker, he refreshes his vow to slay any woman I marry and any child I have. He wants to make certain, once I'm dead, he'll be the only surviving Saar. Damn him, Nigel. What kind of life is this for either of us? I'm ready and willing to make peace, but Ryker will never allow it. Maybe the bastard is truly insane, and he can't rest until I'm dead. Or until he forces me to slay him to end his madness. If he's really crazy, maybe that's his diabolical scheme. I sometimes wish I could use Shara's magical potions to put a little love and peace in him. *Kahala* help us. Within a year, one of us will be happy and the other one will be dead.''

Varian's sapphire eyes revealed stormy lights. ''You'd think Ryker's appetite for revenge would be sated by now. How much misery and blood does he want from me? Shara murdered my parents seven years ago. I can't help it if she then killed herself. For certain, one day, Ryker and I will be forced to end this lingering war. Then I'll go to the Androas Empire and confront *Kadim* Maal and settle that old score. I need to get both of them off Grandfather's back. He's getting old, and he's suffered enough because of the Triloni family. He still talks about Mother every time I visit him. I know it must have been hard to lose his only child, my mother. Amaya Saar was so beautiful and gentle. Why do such tragedies happen, Nigel? And why do I have to be punished for them? I need to stop the *accidents* I've been having for years. I want to find a special woman, marry her, settle down on Altair, and raise sons.''

As Varian's mind dreamily roamed to his privately owned planetoid, Altair, which orbited the capital planet of Rigel where his citizenship rested, Nigel grimaced in shared anguish. Why were these memories plaguing his friend tonight? Because of their conversation over uncontrollable events? Or because of the beautiful, sunny-haired Earthling named Jana Greyson? If Nigel had ever seen or imagined a bewitching goddess, Jana was surely one. Still, Nigel was surprised that Jana inspired dreams of home, a wife, children, and military retirement in the adventurous and roguish Varian Saar. The starship commander had made no secret of his vow to never mate with an alien female and mix Saar blood in another half-alien bastard. And in Varian's eyes, children born of a union with a ''captive mate'' were not legitimate heirs. Besides, he could not imagine buying a mate!

It seemed obvious that Varian did not view Jana Greyson in the same light as he viewed Ryker's mother. Princess Shara Triloni had been an exquisite alien creature from another galaxy, a ravishing temptress who had nearly ripped apart Varian's world, a green-eyed blonde whose actions had provoked the fierce hatred and hostilities in Ryker and Maal Triloni. Now, her evil bastard son was in a position of great power and wealth, exceeded only by a few males in this sector of space. Ryker's private planetoid, Darkar, was beyond the authority or conquest of any galactic alliance, law, and power. Nigel knew Varian was not asking him questions he wanted answered, for most had no answers. He knew his friend needed to clear his head and appease his anguish. Nigel waited and listened patiently for Varian to finish his dark and painful trek into the past.

"It all seems so long ago, Nigel, yet almost like yesterday. If I had been at Grandfather's home on Eire that day, Shara would have slain me too. I'm glad he buried them before I returned home. I was told that Shara used a laser knife countless times on Mother. It seems Shara planned to kill Mother, then use her potions to entrap Father again. She even called her magical powder Moondust. He said when Father arrived and attempted to stop Shara, she went wild and slashed him numerous times. I suppose she decided to kill herself when she realized she had slain the man who had been the object of her obsession for twenty-three years. Even mad, Shara was clever. She took poison to prevent spoiling her beauty with bloody wounds. They should have cremated that alien witch's body before releasing it to be displayed in a glass case by her father! Eternal beauty and youth—she doesn't deserve them even in death! Would you believe Shara's note said it was all done for love of my father and her bastard son?"

Varian snarled coldly, "No Triloni knows the meaning of the word! I wish I could prove Ryker plotted and ordered my parents' deaths."

"Jana reminds you of Shara, doesn't she?" Nigel asked in dread. "They have the same colorings, and they're both from alien galaxies. Is it necessary to say Jana is nothing like that alien enchantress Princess Shara?"

She's enough like her to carry out my new scheme, Varian said to himself. Knowing how impressed Nigel was with Jana, he would not expose that plan to his science officer just yet. "Don't worry about Jana, Nigel. I'm concentrating on defeating Ryker and succeeding in this mission. If it's a lethal confrontation he wants, so be it."

"Until you obtain indisputable evidence that Ryker is plotting against you or our Alliance with his grandfather or Supreme Ruler Jurad Tabriz of the Pyropean Galaxy, your hands are bound," Nigel warned.

An ominous grin traveled Varian's face and settled in his rich blue gaze. "Not for long, old friend. I have two men secretly working for my brother on Darkar. All I need is to lure Ryker out of Trilabs and off his planetoid for a few days. Once my men have the facts, Ryker can be dealt with once and for all."

"How do you plan to lure him away from Trilabs and his work?" Nigel inquired skeptically. "It's rare for him to leave Darkar, or to trust anyone."

"My bait will be Jana Greyson," Varian replied. "Don't you see how clever my scheme is? Trap another Saar with another green-eyed alien enchantress. I'll order Martella to send out publicity on Jana's enormous talents, beauty, charms, and intelligence. Martella is the perfect trainer for the *charls*, and she's a member of the Elite Squad like myself. We report *only* to the Council. Besides, Grandfather personally selected and assigned her to this mission. She'll know how to handle this plan wisely and carefully, and she'll agree to help me capture Ryker."

Nigel wanted to refute Varian's impressions about the serious-minded First Lieutenant Martella Karsh. From talks with the sixty-year-old woman, Nigel knew that Martella did not approve of her part in the enthralling project and was actively seeking ways to change the *charl* laws. Also, Martella was greatly impressed by Jana Greyson and would surely resent being ordered to use the helpless woman in such a cruel manner. Although Martella's fiery hair was gradually turning gray, the superior officer had a temper and personality to match that once-flaming head of curly hair, and Martella wisely and skillfully kept them under control ninety-nine percent of the time.

Varian explained his ruse. "By the time we arrive at our first auction on Zamarra, Ryker should be consumed with curiosity about a unique alien enchantress who's not only ravishing but is also a research scientist like himself and holds the only elite position on my list of *charls*. When Ryker views Jana's pictures and reads about her many qualities—which I'll make certain

27

he does—he'll be forced to check her out. He'll want to see if Jana is another Shara who can be used against another Saar. This mission has been a gut-wrencher, Nigel, so we should make some valuable use of it. Maybe that will make up for our having to abduct and sell these women, and for having to kill those two villains when we captured Jana. If we can't save her world, maybe she can help us save our own galaxy.''

Nigel was stunned by this clever, but pernicious scheme. ''Is that why you captured her and agreed to her special training? Not because of me and Tris?'' he asked.

''As soon as you showed me her tapes and told me about her,'' Varian confessed, ''this plan came to me, but I rejected it. I decided to capture Jana and consented to her special training based on your and Tris's advice to use her as the focus for our cover mission. Displaying a rare goddess at each stop will provide a logical reason for *avatars* being drawn to our auctions so I can safely pass along those info tapes. Who would be watching me with a distraction like Jana Greyson nearby? I was going to rescue her from Earth's doom regardless of her appeal as bait for Ryker's defeat. But the more I watched those tapes and read her file, the more I realized my idea could succeed. You believe in fate. Maybe fate led Jana to us for several reasons. I hate to trick her, but any risk is worth taking to earn such a victory.''

''What if Ryker doesn't take your *bait*?'' Nigel inquired sullenly. He knew how desperately Varian wanted to defeat Ryker for himself and the Maffei Alliance, but this plot was dangerous for all concerned, especially for Jana.

Varian reasoned aloud, ''I've considered that angle too. As you and Tris suggested, Jana will be sold last on Rigel, but at a special auction befitting her superiority over most females in all galaxies combined. She'll accompany me at each planet and auction along the way. On my arm, she's the perfect lure. In fact, I think she's the only one who can draw Ryker into my trap. I'll see to it Jana isn't harmed. She's too rare, and I didn't rescue her from her world to let her die in mine. Ryker's sly and intelligent; this may be my only chance to defeat him.''

''I know what you've got in mind, Varian, don't do it,'' Nigel gravely beseeched. ''After you flaunt Jana for weeks, Ryker might take your bait and bid the highest for her. You know your behavior will snag his interest, not Jana's beauty or intelligence or science background. What then? Ryker legally qualifies as a bidder. Even if he is Maal's sole heir, he's become a citizen of Maffei and he's single. He's also very rich. If he purchased Jana, you couldn't refuse to hand her over to him. And he hates you. Don't let Ryker think he can make you suffer by injuring or destroying an innocent woman.''

Varian stressed, "I told you, I'll protect Jana from Ryker. But I must convince Ryker that I'm blindly fascinated by her—luring him away from Darkar so my agents can obtain the evidence and opportunity we need to arrest him. You think about the consequences of my failure, Nigel. You know Ryker's dark desires: my life, my holdings, the Saar name and rank. He also wants to hurt Grandfather for preventing Galen from marrying Shara and legitimizing him. You know our laws: a blood heir inherits everything, and there's no denying Ryker Triloni is Galen Saar's son and my half brother. If Tirol is slain or dies, I inherit the Trygue estate as I did the Saar estate. If I was killed, that would give Ryker the Saar, Trygue, and Triloni fortunes, powers, and positions. Can you envision that mad devil with such awesome wealth and strengths?''

Varian inhaled and exhaled heavily. He stood up and flexed his tall, supple body. He went to the servo for a refreshing drink for Nigel and himself, then he sat on the divan and propped up his feet. He slowly sipped the beverage as he reminisced about his stormy past.

There were episodes which he wished he could rewrite. In the midst of many had been the beautiful alien witch Shara. Now, fate had offered a path to equity through another alien beauty. "Poetic justice," he murmured to himself, then prayed he was making the right decision for all involved in his scheme.

Varian wondered if Ryker still carried the scar on his right shoulder and jawline from the knife wounds he had received during one of their worst fights. If Nigel had not intervened, Varian shuddered to think what might have happened. That had been long ago, and Varian had learned to conceal his warring emotions and to master his violent reactions to his nemesis.

A *nemesis?* his mind challenged. Besides Ryker, there was *Kadim* Maal Triloni of the Androas Galaxy, ruler of the Androas Empire, wanting revenge for his daughter's grim fate and his grandson's misery. Then there was Supreme Ruler Jurad

Tabriz of the Pyropean Federation, head of the Pyropean Galaxy. As with Maal, Jurad had been in on this twist of fate from the beginning.

The two neighboring rulers had requested permission for Princess Shara Triloni to be allowed to travel through the Maffei Galaxy from the Androas Empire to the Pyropean Federation, as the Maffei Alliance was positioned between them and the route around the Maffei Galaxy would add months to her journey. Naturally the Alliance Force had refused to permit alien starships to cross her territory, as neither ruler was trusted. But as a gesture of goodwill, *Kadim* Tirol Trygue had offered to deliver Jurad's promised consort to the edge of the Pyropean Galaxy. Tirol had given the weighty assignment to his much loved and respected son-in-law, Galen Saar: notable starship captain of the *Galactic Gem* and supreme commander of the Alliance Forces.

Trouble had struck almost immediately following the departure of Galen Saar and Shara Triloni. The ravishing and willful princess instantly decided she preferred the handsome and virile Galen to the "repulsive barbarian" Jurad. It was a known fact that Tirol was grooming Galen for a seat on the Supreme Council and eventually for the rank of *kadim*. Shara selfishly resolved to have all she wanted or needed through seducing Galen. During the first week of their ill-fated trek, Shara had gone to work on entrancing the mind and body of Galen with her hypnotic drugs. Neither Galen nor his crew realized what was happening to him until it was too late: Shara had brought him under her mesmerizing control and had seduced him. As days passed and it became noticeable that Galen was spending too much time with the alien princess who was betrothed to another man, Chief Medical Officer Tristan Zarcoff started an investigation into the matter.

Upon discovering the secret affair between Galen and Shara, Tristan realized that Galen was functioning in a near hypnotic state induced by a potion which had been outlawed. Tristan had formulated an antidote, and ended Shara's enslaving control.

Galen had been enraged by the woman's deceit and his uncontrollable submission to her plans and wanton desires. He had refused to complete the voyage, suspecting Shara would pull the same trick on Jurad, then take over his Pyropean Federation and join it to her father's Androas Empire, supplying them the power and means to crush Maffei between them. Galen and Tristan had no trouble convincing Tirol of Shara's treachery and possible future threat if she wed Jurad. Tirol was the one who met with Jurad and related Shara's evil to the supreme ruler, who refused to believe him, and accused Galen and Tirol and the Alliance Force of treachery.

Matters had become worse when Shara not only humiliated Jurad by refusing to marry him when she was brought back to her father but she also publicly announced she was pregnant by Galen Saar. Shara had proclaimed undying love for Galen and pride in bearing his child. But she had also vowed innocence in the drug charges against her; instead, she had sworn that Galen Saar had seduced her and had promised to marry her as soon as he could rid himself of Tirol's daughter, Amaya!

Kadim Maal Triloni had demanded that Galen divorce his beloved wife, Amaya, and marry his daughter Shara. Galen and Tirol had rejected such an incredible demand, and had raised countercharges of treachery. Maal would not believe the accusation against his daughter; or if he was a party to it, he would not admit it. The further her pregnancy progressed and the longer Galen refused to even speak to her, the deeper into madness she went. Until finally Maal was forced to confine her to prevent her from harming herself and the unborn Androas heir. The man's hatred increased over the years.

So had Jurad's, for he had lost his valuable bride to Galen Saar and his dream of obtaining the Androas Empire through her. Jurad had been forced to settle on a marriage to Brea Ylor, daughter of his most elite planetary ruler. Although beautiful and gentle, Brea had lacked the intelligence and strong character which Jurad had desired in a wife. Brea had died six years after her marriage while giving birth to their second child. Jurad had not mourned poor Brea for she had fulfilled his need for her—a male heir.

Both Jurad and Maal blamed and hated Tirol for believing Galen and protecting him from their vengeance. Seven years ago, the insane Androas princess had escaped her father's confinement and murdered Galen and Amaya Saar. Maal and Ryker had claimed innocence in aiding Shara's escape and grisly crimes.

Now, at every available opportunity, Ryker or Maal or Jurad took their hatred out on Galen's son and heir.

Silence filled the room while Varian reflected upon the twists of fate. Watching him, the ship's first officer was tense and troubled. Nigel wondered if Varian understood stood the perils and costs involved in recklessly creating another deadly triangle . . . involving another beautiful woman. . . .

Chapter Two

Varian was too keyed up to sleep after Nigel left. He decided to go to the gym and exercise. He changed into an ocean-blue T-back tank top and sweat pants. First, he wanted to check on Dr. Tristan Zarcoff's progress. He arrived at the medical laboratory to find Tristan at the data acquisition-input system entering the results of his examinations of captive females. Tristan glanced up and smiled at Varian, the son of his past commander, a very special man like Galen Saar had been.

Not wishing to interrupt Tristan's concentration, Varian nodded and entered the adjoining alcove. All alien females were kept sedated during this initial period of the capture process; it was easier on them and the medical staff. Varian ignored two forms sleeping on stretchers to concentrate on the lovely Earthling who was to unsuspectingly aid his mission and scheme. Varian smiled at the rangy doctor of fifty-eight who joined him.

"All finished?" Varian inquired, leaning against the wall. Varian had always admired and respected this man, with whom he shared an easy, warm rapport. Besides intelligence and loyalty, Tristan had a pleasing disposition and spotless character. Varian couldn't imagine his own character without the good and steady influences of Nigel Sanger and Tristan Zarcoff.

"They've all been through the decontamination process and initial testings. I have these three exams to complete," Tristan remarked. "I was about to return to the lab. Did you need to see me for something?"

"Just checking everything before I turn in." When Tristan eyed his outfit, Varian shrugged and clarified, "After a little exercise and a cool shower. How long will you be? I might check back after I visit the gym."

"An hour or so," Tristan informed him. When he saw Varian's gaze lingering on Jana, he concluded his friend wanted a closer look at the stunning creature now that she was within reach. He suggested, "Why not push that second stretcher into the lab for me? Then you can lock up here." He took one stretcher and ambled out of the room with Varian close behind pushing the other.

Varian returned to seal off the laboratory to unauthorized or accidental exits and entrances. He wanted one last peek at Jana, a private study, with no one observing him, for this woman had plagued his thoughts and dreams for weeks since her discovery by his friends in May. Perhaps her intimidating magnetism was the reason he had taken Tristan's advice to capture her last.

Varian Saar entered the room, pressing the lock switch behind him. He crossed to the alcove, pausing in the archway. Varian glanced at the examining table with an anticipatory gleam in his blue gaze which encompassed the magnificent creature who was sleeping so peacefully within his reach. Jana was almost like an enchanting illusion, a ravishing woman who was beyond the average man's ability to create in dreams. Yet, here she was in reality. At last he crossed the distance which separated him from the stunning goddess. His tension mounted as he reached her side and his eyes explored her seeming perfection.

His gaze hungrily absorbed every detail of her features. How had she been born so beautiful and perfect? Varian caressed the satiny texture of her face, its skin firm and smooth. He absently ran his fingertips over her high cheekbones and inviting lips. Her complexion was unmarred, as slick as a crystal goblet. Her flesh was of a shade which remained honey-colored all year long, perhaps deepening in the summer. He lightly fingered her dainty chin and pleasingly shaped nose.

Varian lifted an eyelid to study those unusually colored orbs. He had never seen anyone's eyes with this fusion of colors. Jana's eyes were a heavy dash of forest green, a sprinkle of deep blue, and a trace of rich violet, encased in a band of dark jade. Her lashes were thick; the edges were slightly curled upward like fluffy feathers. What beauty and bewitchment was displayed there, he mused to himself.

Varian's liquid blue gaze washed over her entire face. She

was wearing little makeup; and he realized that none was necessary. Jana possessed natural beauty, an enormous amount of it. Her mouth was a natural pink where she had licked off her lipstick. How fortunate to have beauty which didn't require cosmetics to provide looks or to hide nature's cruel flaws. "Oh, the envy you must have inspired in females and the lust in men," he murmured.

His hand reached out to stroke her tousled champagne tresses. It looked as if a magician had stolen color from the two moons of Zamarra and had painted her hair with the silver and gold mixture. He chuckled and warmed at the way the soft curls encircled his fingers. He was reminded of Mailiorcan silk, a sensuous and costly gold material shot with threads of expensive silver and which had the trait of clinging provocatively to the figure. Her hair was very long and wavy on the sides and back, but shorter on the crown. From the tapes he'd seen of her, he knew it could hang luxuriously in controlled curls, or it could fly wildly in the breeze. It was thick and lush, and enticed a hand to wander into it or a nose to bury itself in those fragrant tresses. Presently, Jana's hair was spread around her head like a radiant halo. Varian couldn't resist lifting a curl and teasing it beneath his nose. His pulse quickened.

Varian's hand traced Jana's throat to a softly inviting shoulder. Where did her magic cease? he wondered. Unable to stop himself, he lifted the sheet and tossed it aside. He inhaled at the sight of her stunning figure. Her bosom was ample and firm. Her slim waist drifted into a flat stomach between seductively rounded hips. Her shapely legs were little and smooth. Her ankles appeared both dainty and strong. Her body was taut and supple. How many men had she tempted beyond willpower and logic? Varian realized Jana put every lover he had known to shame. He chuckled wickedly as he imagined what Canissia Garthon's reaction might be to such incomparable beauty. No doubt Canissia would demand that her father, supreme Council member Segall Garthon, banish Jana to the edge of space! He could imagine the reactions of hopeful buyers from across the Maffei Galaxy when they gazed upon this perfection of intoxicating loveliness and purity. He wondered who would bid the most and carry this treasure home.

Clearly Jana Greyson evinced superb breeding and refinement. Her observation tapes showed her to be fresh, warm, unspoiled, and arresting. Despite her great wealth, matchless beauty, and elite social status, Jana had the courage and self-confidence to be herself and to pursue her dreams. Jana lived her life with a flair all her own, one which seemed to come as easily and naturally as breathing. "What an asset for your owner, a priceless treasure for some lucky male."

The rise and fall of her bare bosom caught his attention. His gaze drifted slowly over her frame, as if he were possessively branding each inch with his mark of ownership. Even her toenails were neatly trimmed and painted a soft rose color. His study of her ignited his senses and enflamed his body with intense desire. His manhood began to stir to life. Never had it flamed to life so hotly and urgently, simply from gazing upon a female! No female had denied him or resisted him. Yet his charms and skills could have no effect on this drugged angel.

He could not prevent himself from making contact with that enticing flesh. Varian negligently trailed his fingertips back and forth across her collarbone as his cobalt eyes feasted on her face. Craving to know how her supple skin would feel against his lips, he bent forward and brushed them over one shoulder, up her throat, and to her ear. He smiled and nibbled at it when she moaned softly and shifted her body. Her instinctive responses to his actions encouraged him. His respiration quickened even more as she seemed to nuzzle her face against his.

Varian straightened, but he continued to study her. His entranced mind now began to explore her body. He imagined the daring trek his fingers would take if he allowed himself more than a fantasy, something he could not and would not do to Jana or to any drugged or helpless female. As a daring explorer with a mind of its own, his left forefinger could begin such a trek over her appealing territory by slipping down the canyon between two fleshy mounds with twin brown peaks, then playfully circling her navel, which was positioned like a tiny dry pond on a flat track of arid land. He noticed how her ribs were displayed like soft ripples across desert sands. The adventurous appendage could then tease over hip-bones which jutted upward like smooth ridges on a grass-free prairie. Reaching a flat plain, the traveler could rest boldly on her taut stomach, without daring to venture into that compelling forest nearby.

In reality, the enchanted male lifted one of her hands and pressed it against his jawline, eager to feel her touch. He closed his eyes and shifted her palm over his lips. His tongue sampled its flavor, then traveled down her arm to steal a kiss in the hollow of her throat. His lips trailed feathery kisses over her face, then lightly brushed over her velvety lips. But his hands dared not encroach upon her satiny frame.

Intoxicated by this magnetic creature, Varian's mind returned to its fantasy. He saw his lips following the same path which his forefinger had fancifully traveled earlier. When another drowsy moan of undeniable passion passed between her lips, Varian was pressed beyond thinking clearly or wisely. His mouth captured Jana's and parted her lips. His persistent tongue invaded her warm and tasty recess, sending thrilling shocks of joy and bliss through him and her. His hands grasped her shoulders and pulled her pliant and susceptible body into his trembling arms.

The sedative was weakening just enough to slightly arouse Jana. Her lids fluttered, then opened. Jana had never experienced such wild and wonderful sensations as he was creating within her body. She moaned in rapturous delight and total contentment, and unknowingly returned his kiss.

Careful not to tangle her hair, Varian placed a palm on either side of Jana's head and awaited her reaction to him. Spellbound, he didn't realize Jana was too dazed to comprehend the reality of this situation. Varian leaned forward, bringing his face within range of Jana's partially cloudy vision. He watched an appreciative gaze slip over her face.

Jana tried to study the strikingly handsome face with molten blue eyes which hovered over her. She instinctively responded to this pinnacle of manhood with bronze skin, sable hair, rich sapphire eyes, a perfect smile, strong and compelling features, and a virile physique which was so boldly exposed in a snug and semibare outfit. He had a roguish gleam in his eyes and an enticing smile on his lips. His shoulders were broad, exuding an undeniable aura of strength. Crisp black hair peeked out around the edges of his tank top, hinting at a provocative chest. Muscles bulged in his taut arms. Her gaze helplessly and eagerly roved up and down his body as it worked its spell.

The smile which engulfed Jana enraptured her senses and claimed her heart. As if mesmerized, she dreamily watched his strong hand stroke her hair, then move over her parted lips. In her half-wakeful state, Jana made no attempt to stop Varian's attentions. Her breath was stolen as he bent forward and covered her mouth with his. A fiery explosion took place within her body, kindling and engulfing her with passion's flames.

Jana was adrift upon a sea of stormy waves which tugged at her body, threatening to drown her beneath its obscure surface. Her head spun in the whirlpool of feverish desire and staggering pleasure. There seemed no inch of her face which didn't glow from a kiss. When his powerful blue gaze fused with hers, she was drawn deeper and deeper into its pool of magic and mystery. Down she went into the all-consuming well of delight.

Jana's senses reeled, but not from the sedative. This perfect male was assailing her senses, enslaving her to his will. A warming glow pulsed through her womanhood. Her arms weakly but uncontrollably encircled his neck. She clung to him and returned his kisses.

Varian was tempted to undress, climb on the stretcher with her, and boldly take possession of this creature who was driving him mad with hunger. He groaned as flames licked unmercifully at his manhood. At the last moment for retreat before yielding to his cravings, a flash of reality jolted his senses. He couldn't believe he was trying to seduce a defenseless victim of fate, a partially drugged *charl*! Varian unconsciously mopped beads of perspiration from his brow and upper lip. His respiration was rapid and shallow. He could not permit his fantasy to become a reality! He covered Jana, lifted the side rails, and retreated. He dared not touch her again; her stimulating beauty was affecting his wits, will, and carnal desires! He was acting like a mindless fool, a rutting beast! Tremors of warning touched his mind and lodged there. Her feminine allure was powerful, mysterious, and magical. Beware the helpless male who fell prey to these abundant charms!

Varian observed the bewitching girl as she slowly relented to the call of narcotic slumber. He realized Jana's senses were still too imprisoned by the sedative to be responsible for her behavior, even if she was responding to him and enjoying their actions. He admonished his loss of control. What a distraction she could become if he did not watch himself carefully during her training period. Despite Jana's many physical qualities, Varian Saar could not envisage himself buying a mate, as he had never experienced a shortage of female companionship. More important, there was Ryker to remember.

Varian was distressed by his strong attraction to Jana, for no woman could enter his life and heart until his war with Ryker and his threat to the Universe were settled. Jana was like a deadly decoy beacon set out by the forces of evil fate to lure him into danger. If he was not careful, he could be destroyed. An obsession for this lovely alien could drive him to madness, as Shara had gone mad with her obsession for his father! Varian stepped to the stretcher and tightly grasped the protective rails. He stared down at Jana.

Varian accepted his duty to make Jana the pawn in his battle for victory over a powerful enemy, but his heartfelt emotions were already resisting that decision. But he promised himself that he would resist her. Not wishing to be discovered by anyone, Varian left. He went to the gym and exercised his body until he was positive it was too weary to be affected by Jana again tonight. To prove his self-control, he returned to the medical laboratory.

Varian arrived at a good and bad moment: Jana's examination was over and Tristan was replacing her gown. "Be with you in a moment."

Varian was forced to turn his back for fear his interest would become apparent. He picked up her chart to read it. "Jana Greyson; twenty-three; hair—pale and dark blond; eyes—*caritrary*." Varian frowned. Tristan hadn't said bluish-green. The softhearted doctor had used the color of one of their galaxy's most precious gems.

Varian read on: "Five feet eight inches; one hundred and twenty pounds; skin—golden glow; medical condition—excellent; scars—two; virgin."

Varian was amused and slightly annoyed by the descriptions of her physical appearance, but he understood Tristan's dilemma. Jana's coloring lacked the correct Maffeian word to identify it. With his ebony hair and dark blue eyes, his and Jana's only similarity was a golden tan, though his was darkest. He found himself wondering how their contrasting colorings would blend in a child. That thought troubled him, and he dismissed it.

"Kyle told me what happened during her capture. Those men's deaths will be hard for her to accept, even if they were trying to attack her."

Varian nodded agreement. "But he couldn't just stun them,

Tris. You know the amount of investigating and publicity her kidnapping will receive. Imagine the police finding those two thugs in the garden and questioning them. Panic would begin if sightings are made of men in shiny spacesuits and helmets at these women's abductions. It was unfortunate, but necessary.''

Tristan gazed at Jana, then at Varian. He remarked, ''She's quite a find. You'll have no trouble getting a buyer. A shame, she's too special for this fate. If her life hadn't been in peril, I wouldn't have persuaded you to capture Jana. Such a transition and existence will be hard for her.''

Varian consoled his friend. ''Don't worry about Jana Greyson, Tris. She's proud and intelligent and courageous. Give her time and good training. She'll make the adjustment to being an envied *charl* to some lucky citizen.''

''But she's a medical scientist, a doctor,'' Tristan said. ''She should be placed in one of our research centers. We could use talents like hers. Later, if necessary, she could be matched to a perfect male.''

''You're dreaming, Tris. The Supreme Council wouldn't allow an alien slave to run free. I doubt many Maffeians have forgotten it was an alien scientist who created that virus which nearly destroyed our female population. I can only promise to let the staff do all they can to aid her adjustment. As agreed, Jana will occupy the gold room on deck one.'' Varian reminded Tristan of placing her in quarters normally reserved for an elite guest and of supplying her with a special wardrobe which had been sized for her.

Tristan said the other two women were ready for their quarters, which were shared by many captives. What Tristan didn't tell Varian was that when he had begun Jana's examination he had noticed her rosy cheeks and passion-swollen lips, which were not the result of her struggles with the Earthling males. ''These are charts on the last five captives.'' Tristan lifted them to read Varian the information. When he finished, he asked, ''Any chance we'll have to use this despicable ruse again?''

''I certainly hope not,'' Varian replied instantly, scowling in disgust.

''Me, too,'' Tristan declared, sneaking a revealing look at Jana. ''We capture and enslave women, then expect them to calmly accept their new fates. I wonder what we would do if the tables were turned . . .''

"Certainly not adapt as well as most *charls* do. Have you implanted the microtranslators in their ear canals? I want to be certain these women understand us the moment they wake up. We don't want them any more frightened and confused than normal." His eyes lingered on Jana as he spoke.

"They'll hear us loud and clear. Once they learn the truth, I'm sure most of them would rather not understand our language," he responded.

At what would have been dawn had she not been in space, Jana began to stir in the guest quarters. Intense splotches of bronze, sapphire blue, cloud white, and rich ebony swirled and mingled and separated to paint an intoxicating image of a spellbinding creature upon the canvas in Jana's dreamy mind. The magnificent man was perfect in form. His smile and gaze tantalized and hypnotized her. His kisses sent her senses racing wildly like a runaway stallion. His caresses ignited flames in her mind and body, smoldering and burning until they fused into one roaring blaze of uncontrollable wildfire. His body was as sleek and smooth as the legs of a racehorse. His arms and shoulders evinced great power and prowess. Passion's hungers struck her like bolts of lightning, causing her to squirm and moan upon her bed. The fantasy became so vivid and unsettling that she was aroused from her sedated slumber.

Jana forced open her heavy lids and blinked as she yawned and stretched. Lying motionless to bring herself to full awareness, she inhaled and exhaled. Since she could never meet this provocative man whom she had conjured up in her dreams, Jana defensively pushed aside such disturbing feelings and desires. From past experiences, she doubted such a perfect and beguiling creature existed anywhere! Ready to begin a new day, she sat up.

Jana's roving gaze took in her unfamiliar surroundings. She was in an oblong room, about thirteen by sixteen feet. Her gaze scanned the luxurious decor in harmonizing shades of gold and ivory. She could not recall where she was or how she had gotten here. Jana's brain frantically sought its last remembrances. Who were those strange men? What did they want from her?

Should she assume from the lavish appearance of this setting that money had nothing to do with her kidnapping? She and her lawyers and guardian had always feared that something like this might happen, especially after the news coverage of her large grant to the foundation for terminally ill children. The furniture, fabrics, and accessories looked very expensive. Caution, patience, and observation were essential to survival, she cautioned herself.

Jana studied the golden cell. There was an ivory- colored étagère in one corner, filled with books and decorative art objects. Next, there was a pressurized sliding door, like one finds at a supermarket. Jana was positive it was locked, but she would check it. Positioned next to the door was a wall display with opaque windows, colored buttons, a small drawer, and a shelf. Before it was a low bar with two chairs. On the adjacent wall, another door caught her eye. There was a sofa in variegated tints of gold and cream. A raindrop swag lamp was suspended over a round, low table. She wondered why the owner of this elegant room, or its decorator, had selected a phantasmic painting to hang over the sofa. Her curious gaze continued to a square commode by the bed, which was an ivory shade like all the furniture but the bed. An octagon- shaped swag lamp was suspended over it. The bed she was lying in had sheets which were an unidentified silky golden fabric. She fingered the sensuous covers which exhibited an intricate creamy design on a gold background. Strange sensations washed over her.

Her prison walls appeared to be of a metal in an ivory hue. She touched the wall to her left and was surprised when it registered neither cold nor hot. The carpet was a deep coin gold. She glanced up at the diffused lighting panels which were very dim at this time. There appeared to be a night light over the main door. Seeing no switches, she reasoned the controls were outside this room. It was the same with the gilded lamp at her bedside. Light and dark were at the discretion of her abductor. Jana speculated it could be hours before anyone came to check on her. She allowed her bare feet to fondle the lush carpet appreciatively. She walked around the room, studying, touching, and observing her exquisite oubliette.

Varian's timbre voice ordered First Lieutenant Martella Karsh to take over the meeting. She had been a wise selection by his grandfather to head up this facet of their mission. Martella was more than qualified to train these aliens and to handle any difficult problem which might arise on the ship or at one of the thirteen auctions. As a brilliant psychologist, she had been in charge of similar tasks on other starships, though she had vowed this was the last time she would accept this repulsive task. Varian welcomed her leadership and talents.

Martella took the floor. The stately female with graying red hair and pale green eyes knew it was unnecessary to go over each person's duties. Varian's staff had been well versed on their training tasks. They were making excellent progress with the women from Uranus, and she expected them to do the same with the Earthlings. Her penetrating gaze slipped around the table. Despite her sterility from the plague which had inspired this enthralling custom, sixty-year-old Martella Karsh felt no envy or hostility toward these women who were heading for her world.

The head of the psychology department supplied reports which profiled each female and alerted the staff to possible troublemakers or nonadapters. Dr. Tristan Zarcoff was to be informed of anyone who seemed headed for mental depression. The historiographer gave a concise report on Earth and Uranus, relating any historical or political event which might play a pivotal role in the women's behaviors or personalities.

Lieutenant Kara Curri discussed her recreational and physical conditioning schedule, which was designed to improve figures, physical and emotional health, and to inspire relaxation and friendly attitudes.

Daxley Prada would use his data processing department to store all this individual information in his confidential computerized library banks. He would gather, analyze, correlate, and store all information concerning these women. A complete dossier would soon be available on every female.

Security Control Chief Kyle Dykstra would be responsible for monitoring the women's behavior from a central control room similar to closed-circuit television, from which instructions and announcements would be given.

Martella went over the schedules she had filled out for the staff. Group assignments were made for the captives. At the beginning, the females were to be informed of the staff's purpose and expectations. The Maffeian plight was to be explained in detail, with hopes of showing the *charls* they were needed and wanted. The females would discover they were to become mates to alien males whose appearances varied little, if any, from the males of their planet.

The relaxed tone of business and lively recreational schedule planned by the staff would help to dispel the captives' apprehensions. Within a reasonable length of time, most would adapt to their new fates. The captives' mates usually cooperated for there was no turning back. Females who were orphaned and unattached were most usually chosen, as they adjusted quicker and easier to their new lives.

The male officers played an important role in the forming of the *charls'* positive attitudes. Luckily, this crew consisted of numerous attractive, charming, polished men who revealed wit, intelligence, good breeding, and sex appeal.

There were matters concerning *charls* which angered and distressed Martella and many other Maffeians, including Tristan Zarcoff and the recent convert Varian Saar. Ever since this procedure began fifty years ago, the original laws and practices had remained intact. An alien mate had no rights under Maffeian law. As long as she was captured outside of any treaty territory and was sold to an unwed male citizen, she was the chattel of her buyer. Since there was no marriage involved, children of such a union belonged to the father, to his family in case of his death. In cases of owner death or displeasure, the mate could be sold to another male. This situation led to abuses of human rights. These women were not animals or objects. Marriage should be required. If it failed, divorce—not another sale—should end the matter. Changes were needed; these females deserved citizenship, protection, support, and basic freedoms and rights. Martella was working on bringing her views before the Supreme Council's eyes and vote.

Martella smiled as she realized there were many men in this very room who could make a woman's heart flutter. Too bad their charms and good looks were overshadowed by the matchless ones of Varian Saar. She could use the aid and support of a man of Varian's power and influence, a male surely destined to become the *kadim* one day. After taking part in this cruel practice during this mission, hopefully he would help her fight for the changes which were needed. If a female was good enough to sleep in a male's bed and bear his children, she was good enough to wed!

At the same time not far from the conference room, Jana couldn't decide what the furniture was made from for it neither felt nor appeared to be wood, or metal, or plastic. Jana went to the étagère. The books were in a foreign language and on a variety of subjects, as she could tell from the illustrations. Most of the *objets d'art* were statuettes of what she took to be imaginary creatures. The figurines appeared to be either brass or gold. The books were covered in aureate bindings with indecipherable lettering. Jana surmised they had been specially bound in matching covers. There was a striking model of a spaceship which was constructed with the finest details; clearly it was handmade and quite valuable. If she wasn't mistaken, that was gold trim on the ivory-colored ship! She dared not handle it. Her perceptive mind grasped several facts. Either her abductor was foreign, or he wanted her to believe he was. The various books suggested he had diverse interests. She returned each object to its place, noting there wasn't a speck of dust or a single stain on any item or furnishing in the room.

Jana moved to the first door. She promptly realized either it did not open by floor pressure or was locked. Since there were no buttons, knobs, or controls in sight, she was definitely sealed inside this golden room.

Jana entered the space between the eating bar and wall unit. There were recessed spaces, of which three contained units with smoky-glass doors. Two units resembled microwave ovens without controls. The top unit had one button beside it. To the left of the lower unit was a small drawer which contained numerous metal objects, the size and shape of a credit card. She wondered if the perforations on them were a computer code. Over the drawer was a narrow slit, the size of the metal cards. She was tempted to check out this conclusion, but changed her mind. It wasn't wise to tamper with unfamiliar equipment.

The next recessed unit opened like a laundry chute and made a *whoosh* when she closed it; it was perhaps a garbage disposal. In the niche above it, there was a device for dispensing liquids. She surmised that the row of four buttons by the door offered various selections. The surface of those buttons revealed foreign symbols which she couldn't read. Evidently this was some type of sophisticated, possibly experimental, food center. Only dishes and food were missing. She glanced under the bar and found nothing.

Perhaps she would be served through one of the devices. Perhaps she would be kept secluded until her captor's demands were met. Her hope for survival and release grew as she surmised he did not want her to be able to identify him. Jana eyed the other door, then gingerly approached it. The swishing sound and instant opening of the door startled her. She hastily backed up a few steps and the door closed. When the rapid pounding of her heart slowed to normal, she summoned her courage to continue her exploration, and she stepped to the door. It instantly slid open to reveal an elaborate bathroom. She ascended two steps, then the door closed automatically behind her.

To her left, there was a lengthy vanity with two gold-colored sinks and a row of buttons beside each one. The entire wall above it was a huge mirror. In her state of intrigue and astonishment, she failed to notice her scanty attire.

A gold or brass chair sat before the vanity. The floor was tiled in an artistic pattern of gold and ivory to form flowers, and the toilet and sunken tub matched the color of the double sinks. The end wall was spanned with closets. The gold and ivory color scheme exuded a powerful aura of wealth, beauty, and serenity. This boudoir was definitely designed to soothe the mind, body, and eye.

Jana wondered if she was the first prisoner to occupy this suite. It seemed illogical for a kidnapper to be concerned with his victim's comfort and fears. She rambled through the vanity drawers and cabinets for clues. Most of the products were from foreign markets; she could not read the wording on their packaging. Anything a female could need was there, along with her regular bath necessities. She questioned if this supply was intentional or coincidental. Jana's eyes narrowed in suspicion and her heart began to pound forcefully. Had her captor gone to such trouble to please her or to calm her fears? Did such accuracy in selecting her choice of products mean her captor had observed her for a long time? Did he know her other likes and dislikes?

She asked herself why she kept thinking "captor" and "he," not "they" or "captors"? Whatever instinct caused her to believe the towering man with a perfect physique was responsible for her abduction and imminent fate could not be ignored. She had sensed his raw power and authority. The other men were nothing more than friends or followers or paid assistants. These lush surroundings caused panic within Jana. A kidnapped victim wasn't usually handled this way, was she?

Her eyes caught sight of the closets. She went to them and threw the doors open wide. She stared at the wardrobe inside. It was very elegant and extremely feminine. Someone certainly had good, and expensive, taste. She could not help but notice the fabrics were very soft. Although there were outfits for any and every occasion, she instantly realized the majority of the clothing was for lounging, sleeping, or formal wear. When all she really needed were jeans and T-shirts for a short period of captivity. This observation panicked her. Surely these garments were not meant for her, or for a lengthy stay!

She hastily checked the sizes. Everything would fit her. She checked the shoes—her size. She pulled open the drawers, which were arranged in a vertical row to her right. Once more every single item of underclothing was in her size. She cringed in rising apprehension at this discovery.

Jana opened a small drawer and revealed numerous necklaces, pierced earrings, bracelets, and rings. She gaped in disbelief. She lifted several pieces and carefully studied them. If they were fakes, they were the best replicas she had ever seen. This gem collection was worth a large fortune! Jana dropped the expensive stones as if they had suddenly singed her fingers. She closed the doors and leaned against them, breathing rapidly. This situation was becoming more and more perplexing and alarming. What did such a wealthy man want from her? Why had he gone to such expense and trouble? Did he hope to assure a compliant prisoner? What kinky game or intricate scheme was he planning for her? White slavery? Jana scolded her wild imagination. Surely this room belonged to a female who was her size. It was all coincidence. Surely this man was only interested in ransom. There was no reason to harm her. He controlled her food, air, and light supplies. Her life was in his hands. Wasn't that enough power over her? They, she reminded herself; there were three to five men involved.

As her eyes darted frantically, they touched on the mirror and widened in horrified shock. She stared at the silky apricot nightgown she was wearing. Her face reddened, then paled, as she realized someone had placed this gown on her while she was unconscious. Had the leader done it? Had . . . The words "white slavery" and "kinky" thundered across her frightened mind again. Surely those hoodlums in black leather had been hired to abduct her. No doubt their incompetence had spurred their bosses into action. What secret and lewd game were these men playing?

Jana fumed in humiliation. She opened the closet doors to search for her own dress. As she pushed aside the garments in her vain search, she blushed in modesty at how provocative, romantic, and revealing many of the dresses were. Surely he— they didn't expect her to wear those clothes and . . . And what, she wondered fearfully. She selected and dressed in a soft brushed knit in ice blue. How long had she been here drugged?

Jana crossed the room, eager yet reluctant to learn her fate. The door automatically opened and she reentered her golden cell. She paced, trying to reason out this alarming puzzle. In turn, she sat on the sofa, the bed, the chairs, and ended up partially reclining on the sofa. She absently fingered the soft material of the dress she had put on. She toyed with her curls. She jumped up to pace again. She fretted, *How much longer will they ignore me? When will they tell me something?* She hated this frightening uncertainty and torturous waiting.

"Anything else?" Martella asked. She had hopes that Varian's high opinion of Jana would open his eyes and heart to changing the situation involving the *charls*.

Tristan stated, "I'm very impressed by their profiles and appearances."

"All, or one in particular?" Nigel jested with a smile so broad his dimples were vividly displayed. Now that they were heading home and trying to do something beneficial for the captives and Earth, moods were lightening.

Tristan's bright blue eyes twinkled with merriment and guilt. He shuffled the papers before him as he recovered his poise, relieved that Martella knew the truth, for they had become very close during this assignment.

Nigel couldn't resist another jest. "Why, Tris, I do believe I've touched a tender spot. For which girl, or need I even ask?"

"Come on, Nigel, you know me better than that."

"Sure I do," the first officer murmured playfully. "It wouldn't be for that medical research beauty by any chance, would it?"

A revealing sparkle lit Tristan's piercing eyes. "I'll admit Jana does impress me greatly—exceptional beauty and brains—a rare combination."

Varian spoke up for the first time. "Martella has already noted and planned for this special case. Do your best with her training. Besides being the focal point at our auctions, she's very special like Tris said."

Varian's apparent interest in this woman stilled any further chatter about her. He had been annoyed at having her openly and casually discussed. The mere mention of her name had sent warm tremors up his spine and reminded him of last night. But the viewing of her videotapes and pictures had been his undoing! Yet he was unaware of the heat in his voice and eyes as he had spoken of her.

The training staff found this development baffling and surprising. It registered in Tristan's mind that Varian was more than slightly intrigued by Jana. Martella was pleased by Varian's attitude and comments. Nigel thought he knew the reason behind them, his private scheme to defeat Ryker.

"Any more comments or questions?" Martella asked once more. She hoped the men would not spoil her plans by placing Varian on the defensive with their jokes about "an alien enchantress." She needed to provide Varian time and privacy with Jana. When no one spoke up, she dismissed them. Without defying orders, she had to figure out a way to thwart Jana's auction to an unworthy man. If only Varian would keep Jana, fall in love with her.

As each staff member departed to plan his schedule, Varian gathered his reports and tapes to head for the privacy of his quarters. But first, he would check out his "cargo" from the central monitors, and he intended to view one woman in particular. . . .

Once more Jana began to roam her prison. Why didn't someone come, at least to bring food and drink? She had been awake for hours and was hungry. Her rambling thoughts returned to the scene of her abduction. She wondered how they had pulled that vanishing trick with those two hoodlums. "A sly tactic to terrify me. Evaporate into thin air? Impossible! It was a controlled illusion."

Jana walked past the sofa and stopped to look at the painting above it. Suddenly Jana realized she was staring at a red light in the fake pond of the picture. She lifted her head and stared at a surveillance camera mounted in the corner. A glowing light indicated it was on. Was there a hidden microphone somewhere? Now she understood why they hadn't come to check on her! She went to see if a camera was mounted in the bathroom. No, at least they would allow her some privacy. A horrifying thought came to mind. What if this mirror was one of those two-way glasses? This new discovery was too much! It was time for some answers! At least time to learn how many captors were holding her.

She determinedly raised her chin and shoulders. She returned to the outer room and glared at the offensive camera. "I demand you tell me why I'm being held prisoner," Jana stated angrily. "Who are you? What do you want from me? You have no right to keep me here or to spy on me!" No one responded. Fear, panic, and anger gnawed at her.

Jana spat at the camera, again, "You'll be sorry when the police and FBI catch you! You'll rot in prison. How much ransom are you demanding from my lawyers? Tell them I said to pay you immediately so I can get out of here." Still no reaction.

Time moved on as Jana tried to show a brave mask of unconcern and contempt, but it kept slipping. She felt like a specimen under a microscope. Yet, strangely, she didn't feel in mortal danger.

On and on the impasse went until Jana thought she would scream from the mounting tension. How long had she been here? What was happening at home? What was stalling her release? Had Mr. Purvis, the executor of her father's estate, refused to pay him? If Purvis dared to do anything that foolish and dangerous for her, she would start legal action against him! Would her captors kill her, even if they received the money they demanded? Surely not, or they wouldn't be keeping her in seclusion! But how could she possibly guess what went on in the dark minds of criminals?

Jana sat on the sofa, her back to the camera. She was silent for a time, thinking. Perhaps they were enjoying her little display of temper or jeering at her total helplessness. Perhaps they derived some thrill from watching her fear and panic, or felt some surge of power at her vulnerability. Perhaps if she tried to reason with them . . . She went to stand before the camera. She looked directly into the lens. She struggled to speak calmly this time. "Please, if you're listening, tell me what you want from me. I'll order my lawyers to pay you any amount of ransom. You can have all the money. Whatever it takes for you to release me. . . ."

She waited. No response. "Please," she coaxed in desperation. "At least answer me!" Still nothing. Tears gathered in those beryl-colored eyes and slowly ran down her cheeks. In a quavering voice she asked, "Why are you doing this to me? Why won't you answer me?"

Security Chief Kyle Dykstra, who had returned to duty after the conference, sat watching the monitor and feeling remorse as he stared into her exquisite face. He was touched by her beauty and gentleness, her vulnerability and fear. He wished a thousand times he didn't have anything to do with this despicable mission. As with most males his age, he had not given *charls* much thought, until this voyage.

Being confronted by the realities made its cruelties and demands strike home. Kyle envisioned his mother or his sister or his beloved Karita as a captive mate to an alien stranger. Jana Greyson inspired anguish within him. He had made Jana's surveillance tapes and helped capture her. He was plagued by the unknown destiny she was racing toward, a fate which he was assisting. It seemed so cruel to watch her suffer, but his orders prevented him from offering solace. She was a magnificent creature. She would be an excellent mate for the right man.

Varian arrived to find Kyle staring moodily at Jana's distraught face as she pleaded for someone to speak to her. Varian moved closer to get a better view. Kyle glanced at him and forced a wry smile.

"She just wake up?" Varian inquired as he witnessed the trembling in Jana's body. He knew what she must be feeling, just as he knew he could not explain the truth to her about Earth's doom or his mission.

"My relief officer said she's been awake for hours. Sometimes those sedatives don't last as long as expected. She was investigating her surroundings and noticed the camera. It's natural to be frightened and to want answers in her situation," Kyle explained.

"Did you respond?" Varian felt a rush of desire as he watched Jana.

"My orders are to observe, not communicate," Kyle replied. "Her case is unlike the others. I wouldn't know what to tell her."

Jana turned away from the camera. She could sense a powerful gaze on her, that same potent gaze of the man who had prevented her escape. If he meant her no harm, he would alleviate her terror. When the tears lessened, resentment replaced her fear. She ran to the bookcase and snatched up several books. "Stop playing cruel games with me! I want to go home. I'm tired and I'm hungry. And yes, damn you, I'm scared too! How dare you kidnap me and treat me this way! The least you can do is feed me and give me some kind of explanation for this crime!" She furiously hurled the books at the camera.

Sparks flashed and a zinging sound filled her room as the books hit and deflected off some sort of invisible electrical field surrounding the camera. She gasped and moved back. One book was tossed against the lamp, shaking it. She had underestimated her perilous position and her foolish action had gained her nothing. Or so she momentarily thought. . . .

Varian watched her look of surprise at the effect of the books on the force shield around the monitor. Despite her fears, she revealed spirit, and he was impressed with the ravishing creature.

A deep, clear voice addressed her in a commanding tone. It startled Jana. She could not judge where it came from; it was as if the walls themselves spoke to her. Kyle moved aside and curiously watched as Varian wielded his power like an artful club over the defenseless woman. He watched Jana bow to the authoritative imposing tone.

Jana glanced all around her in bewilderment. Her gaze came back to rest upon the camera as if it were the speaker. Varian studied her expression as he spoke to her from the control room. "Calm yourself, Miss Greyson; you'll be told everything very soon. I'm sorry if you were allowed to go hungry. I'll have that error corrected immediately. I'm not playing games with you. Relax and rest." He couldn't resist teasing her. "If you behave yourself and do as you're told, I promise you won't be harmed. Do you understand me, Miss Greyson?" he pressed in a tantalizing tone.

Jana was staring at the camera as if hypnotized by it. She nodded her head and softly answered, "I understand you. But when will you release me? Has Mr. Purvis refused to pay my ransom?" she asked in concern.

"I'm not asking any ransom for you," he told her.

Her eyes blinked in confusion. "Then why am I here?" she asked.

"All your questions will be answered later," Varian calmly replied.

"I don't like being held prisoner by five men. Whose clothes and rooms are these? I want to be told the truth right now! I demand—" Rumbling, mocking laughter filled the room and silenced her.

"I'm in charge here, Jana," his firm voice countered. "You'll be given answers when I say the time is right, not before. You are *my* captive, not theirs or ours. It would be most wise to settle down and cooperate."

"Cooperate?" she echoed. "How so?"

"By obeying my orders, which I'll reveal later," he replied mysteriously. Varian was warmed by her reaction of relief to his claim of ownership.

Jana frowned and sighed heavily. She could not force information from him. She had to relent. He had said she would not be harmed. Could she trust him? Cooperate? No ransom? Obey his orders? What orders?

Varian noted reluctant acquiescence, but wariness was written on her face. "Relax, Jana. You're in strong, capable hands," his voice informed her. Yes, he had selected the right weapon and ruse. "You'll be quite safe and happy in your new home. Trust me, Jana; I won't let anyone or anything hurt you."

"Trust a kidnapper?" she scoffed, "Your words carry little comfort or credence." But they did carry intimidation. *New home?*

In that same lazy drawl which hinted of amusement, he roguishly jested, "So be it." He issued orders for Kyle to pass along to Jana, then left, grinning mischievously, pleased with her and himself.

Kyle watched his retreat and wondered at the odd scene he had just witnessed, Could it be possible that Varian was attracted to this beautiful alien? He chuckled, then scoffed at such an absurd idea.

"Wait!" Jana shrieked. "Who are you? What do you mean, my new home? Where are you taking me? Damn you! This is a mistake! You've abducted the wrong woman!" Silence greeted her ears. Jana vexingly realized that if she were to give a voice and laughter and enticing traits to her stunning dream man, they would match those of her captor!

Chapter Three

The red light stayed on, but Jana was no longer aware of that potent stare. She looked for clues in his mysterious words. Then a different voice spoke to her. It was gentle and kind, but firm. The man informed her that food would come through the servo. He told Jana to bathe and relax before her meal arrived. Jana fired questions at him.

Kyle refused to say more than, "Commander Varian Saar is in charge. He'll have to explain matters. Be patient; you're in no danger."

"Commander? Are we on a ship? Does this have anything to do with the government? Are you sure you have the right woman?" she probed.

"I'm sorry, Miss Greyson, but I can't respond to any more questions. Just follow his orders, and he'll see you soon," Kyle coaxed.

Surely a name which sounded like "Zar" had to be foreign. *Varian Saar*, she rolled and savored the romantic name on her mental tongue. Jana eyed the camera suspiciously. "Is the bathroom monitored by camera?"

Kyle grinned at her expression. "No, the bathroom is monitored only by a voice transmitter in case of an accident or problem.''

"Merci, mon spectre. And you had best be telling the truth!''

Kyle laughed easily and genuinely. "Call out if you need anything.''

Jana flashed a stony glare and hastily retorted, "I can manage alone, thank you." She went into the bathroom and studied the mirror with suspicion, finally deciding to test it just in case he had lied. She touched her forehead with the back of her hand and swayed slightly. She pretended to slide to the tiled floor in a faint. She lay completely motionless for a long time.

Nothing. . . . She called out, "Are you still there?''

A voice came back at her, "Any problems?''

Jana smiled to herself and sat up. "No, just checking—''

What kind of tub is this? Let's see if I can use this situation to my advantage. "Mister—'' she began hesitantly, then paused. "What do I call you?'' she asked, seeing if he would slip and give his name or a clue.

Jana was surprised when he immediately replied, "Lieutenant Kyle Dykstra.'' To avoid putting him on guard, she resisted more questions and stored his title and possibly foreign name for study later. "I don't know how to work the water controls on this kind of tub.''

"The buttons are temperature codes. The cold water starts with white and gets warmer as it deepens to gold. About button three is perfect. There's an automatic cut-off valve when the tub's three-fourths full.''

"How ingenious. I would love to have a tub like this when I go back home,'' she hinted to entice another clue, but Kyle commented no further.

Jana undressed and slipped into the water. It felt like silk to her touch. In spite of her dismay, she was impressed by the luxury flaunted here. So far she had not been harmed or mistreated. She lifted the washcloth and looked for soap. She called out, "Lieutenant Dykstra? Where is the soap hidden?'' she inquired, trying to sound friendly.

"There is a button on the left side of the tub. Press it.''

A panel opened to reveal soaps, bath oils and fragrances. She selected one which reminded her of a field of wildflowers in spring. She bathed and toweled off, then chose a mint-green caftan. As she brushed her tawny tresses, a low swirling sound pulled her gaze toward the sunken tub, which was automatically emptying and rinsing itself. She stared in amazement and remarked, "And I thought I had all the modern conveniences. . . ."

"Did you say something?" Kyle's voice rang out instantly.

"I was talking to myself. An old habit I'll have to break with someone listening all the time." She heard him chuckle. In the other room, she replaced the books she had thrown at the camera. All she could do was wait. At least she wasn't receiving the silent treatment anymore. A buzzer sounded. She curiously glanced at the wall unit, the origin of the noise.

"Your dinner is in the servo," Kyle politely instructed.

She removed her first meal. The main course was an individual casserole which looked and smelled like a ramekin—a dish of bread crumbs, eggs, and cheese, baked to perfection. There was a salad of strange-looking lettuce and odd vegetables and a small dish of reddish-colored pudding. She realized one apparatus had supplied hot food and the other had contained chilled items. She wondered how the foods had been passed to her, as the units appeared self-contained. Kyle instructed her how to retrieve her beverage from the other device while soothing music filtered softly into the room.

That feeling of otherworldliness touched her. Were these men foreigners? There was such a strangeness about them, and this place, this crime.

Her stomach rumbled hungrily at the sight and smell of the delectable dishes. She cautiously began to sample the unfamiliar food. Even if it was drugged, she wouldn't starve. It was marvelous and tasty; "a compliment to the palate" as Alex would say. Alex . . . Could he possibly . . . Surely not!

What were her friends thinking? They had to know by now she had been abducted. Was she a hostage in a political situation? Had Andrea or another guest been their target? No, the men knew her name. She must have been missed at the party and later at home. But if these men had not demanded any ransom, how would anyone guess what had happened to her or where to look. Perhaps they had left no clues. Would anyone be able to find her and rescue her? Jana pushed the tray back with a sudden loss of appetite. Her back obscured her face from the probing eye of the camera. For a very long time she sat staring at her tray.

Varian re-entered the control room and inquired, "Is something wrong with the food, Miss Greyson? I thought you were hungry." Either Jana did not hear him or was ignoring him. "Jana!" the timbre voice boomed over the strains of an unknown melody.

Startled, she turned and shrieked, "What?"

"Is the food not to your liking? Would you prefer another dish?"

Jana glanced at the half-empty tray and replied honestly, "No, it's fine. How much do you want to release me? You don't have to waste your time with this scare tactic to drive up the price. Two million? Five? Ten? Twenty million? When can I go home?"

The beseeching look in her eyes touched him. Twinges of compunction nipped at his mind. He might as well tell her now. "You can't ever go home."

Jana trembled visibly. "But you said I—"

He cut her off, knowing what she was about to say. "You would not be harmed, but I never said released. I said no ransom would be asked."

"Why? Am I a political hostage for some terrorist group? I have no enemies that I know of. Probably some people dislike me, but surely no one hates me or wants me dead. If not for money, then what?"

"You do not have enough money to buy your freedom from me. Besides, it's too late to return you to Earth." He ignored all misgivings as he spat out the brutal truth.

Jana did not catch his last word for she was concentrating on his first, incredible statement. "Surely you know my estate is worth over a billion dollars! You can name any amount. I can't identify any of you, so I'm no threat. Please . . . Anything . . ." she recklessly vowed in desperation.

"Anything" aroused Varian to forbidden thoughts and feelings which he quelled with great effort. "My answer is no ransom and no release."

Jana could not trust her ears. She stared at the camera in stunned silence. She needed her life and freedom, not wealth. Who and what was this man? Had he captured her to fulfill some wild or sexual fantasy?

A wealthy man often pursued for his fortune, he found Jana's attitude about money pleasing. She had or was all a man could

56

want or need from a woman. He wished he could explain about her planet's imminent doom and her capture. If she knew the truth, he would be her hero, not her enemy, her champion rather than her abductor. But she had no idea of the horrors from which he had rescued her. He certainly could not confide the truth about this mission to a captive when he couldn't even reveal it to most of his crew! Also, there was Ryker, always Ryker, breathing lethally over his shoulder. The evil bastard would slay this beauty with a smile on his face if Varian Saar dared to claim her!

"Are you there?" Jana inquired. "What will it take to buy my freedom?"

"This talk is futile, Jana. I will not release you. Don't beg. Take my word, you're heading for a safe and happy life."

Jana caught curious inflections on his words. Remorse? Anguish? Loneliness? Bitterness? Strangely, her heart went out to him. "Don't you realize you've made a terrible mistake?" she reasoned softly. "You've kidnapped the wrong woman. You don't want or need me for any reason."

"I don't make mistakes, Jana; I captured the right woman. You underestimate yourself. Your estate is worthless compared to your own value."

She wondered if she should be flattered or terrified. "What amount would you consider fair exchange for my *value*?" she pressed scornfully.

"There is none," Varian murmured. "You are a priceless treasure."

Fighting for some logical explanation to this mystery, she suddenly accused, "Is Alex paying you to frighten me? Is this a trick to change my mind about marrying him? When is he going to stage his gallant rescue?"

She heard laughter before her captor replied, "I assure you I am quite sane and this is no joke or mistake. As for *your Alex,* you've seen the last of him. You were smart to reject him, Jana. He didn't deserve you."

This conversation was disconcerning. She struggled to display false bravery as she stated, "You won't be so smug when the police find us."

Again he released that rich laughter which unnerved her. "Your police, FBI, CIA, and even your NASA are powerless against me, Jana. Don't count on any rescue; there will never be one. You're heading for a new home and life far away. Accept this fact now.''

Jana shook her head to dispel the image blocking her concentration, for she kept applying the face and body of her masculine fantasy to her captor! She reviewed his words. *NASA?* He must be a foreigner, for he had linked NASA with the police, FBI, and CIA. Was he taking her to another country? Did he deal in white slavery? In this day? Perhaps she was on a luxury ship. He had said, ''too late to return you to . . .'' *Earth?* His English was distinct, but perplexing. Did his voice carry a Welsh accent? Who was he? What new home and life?

Just to provoke him, she caustically questioned, ''And what does NASA have to do with kidnapping, and why can't I return to Earth?''

Varian easily saw through her questions. He was impressed with her intelligence, not to mention her courage. She was like a breath of fresh and intoxicating air on a stifling day. He hated to crush such spirit, but it was best to dispel her hopes for rescue right now.

His voice was cold, his words were cruel. ''We are four hundred million miles from Earth. We're presently nearing the planet Jupiter in your star system. Your world lacks the knowledge and skills to penetrate our force shield or to track us. Earthlings are a backward and inferior race, except for you of course,'' he taunted. He was trying to use an air of arrogance to inspire anger in Jana which might help to lessen her fears and doubts.

''That's impossible! You're playing games again!'' Jana said.

''Nothing is impossible,'' he disputed in a mellow tone. ''I'm Commander Varian Saar, and we're traveling on my starship the *Wanderlust*. I come from the planet Rigel in the Maffei Galaxy where I'm taking you. There's a model of my ship on your bookcase, if you care to examine it.''

There was something in his tone which distressed her. An undeniable ring of truth and finality? Did he think her fool enough to fall for such nonsense? Was this a psychological trick? ''Surely you don't expect me to believe I'm on—'' She paused and trembled as her eyes touched the model.

''On a starship heading out of your galaxy forever?'' he finished for her. ''Think about all you've seen and felt, Jana.

58

Is it really so impossible? Look around you. You're a scientist. Use that smart head on your beautiful shoulders. Don't be frightened, little Earthling; Maffeians aren't monsters; we look no different from you. Don't worry; I did not capture you for an alien zoo display or for any medical experiments.''

Jana presented her back to him. Her eyes darted around frantically as her mind reeled with his hateful words and mocking laughter. Yes, she had heard of UFO'S, but this . . . This just could not be real. Kidnapped by aliens? Spaceships? Leaving her world forever?

No, this could not be happening to her. But how could she intelligently discount the facts? Space travel was a reality: astronauts had been to the moon; shuttles and satellites orbited the Earth; scientific missions went to and past other planets; and space labs were already in use.

Jana's logic reasoned, why couldn't there be worlds that were more advanced than Earth was? Her heart and brain battled for the truth. Her mind said it was possible, but her heart refused to accept it just yet, could not accept it because of the obvious consequences if he spoke the full truth. . . .

If he did, there would never be any rescue or escape, ever. She faced the monitor and said, "I don't trust you, Commander Saar, if that's your name. I don't know what this deceit is all about, but you're lying.''

Varian read the doubt and panic in her expression. "Have it your way, Jana. But the time will come when you'll be forced to accept the truth.''

Jana boldly taunted, "The truth, or your so-called truth?''

"They are one and the same," he said politely. "If you cooperate, we can teach you all you need to know to live happily and safely in our world.''

Jana sought to trick him. "If we're traveling through open space and I cannot possibly escape, then why are you keeping me locked up?''

"Soon you'll be allowed partial freedom on your deck. Until then, you're confined to quarters," he told her. "You don't expect me to allow you to go running around my ship getting into mischief? Or distracting me and my crew?'' he added devilishly.

"If what you say is true, why did you capture me?''

"All in good time, Jana," was his reply. "Get some rest;

you have a busy schedule tomorrow and during the coming weeks. Later, there will be a meeting to tell you and the other women what you need to know.''

Again Jana's mind was playing that naughty trick where it fused her dream lover and this stranger into the same man. That must stop, for it might cause her to speak inappropriately in this grim situation! His last words registered. ''The other women?'' she questioned in surprise.

It was Kyle Dykstra who explained, ''There are many female captives onboard, women from Uranus and Earth. We'll tell you everything later. You have nothing to fear if you obey his orders.''

Uranus? She asked softly, ''Did be speak the truth?''

Kyle answered, ''Yes, it's all true, Jana.''

Tears filled her eyes and rolled down her cheeks. She lay down and buried her face in her pillow and wept. Either they were cruel jokesters, escapees from a mental asylum . . . or aliens from another world.

Varian returned to his quarters in a state of mingled dejection and elation. His thoughts were centered on Jana. Calling her vividly to mind, he flashed a smile which revealed even, white teeth and softened creases around his sapphire eyes and sensual mouth. He speculated on how pleasant it was going to be to help train that bewitching woman from Earth. After all, he was saving her from certain pain and death on a doomed planet. She would be thankful when she discovered the truth, even if that revelation wouldn't come for months or longer. The only fate worse than suffering and dying on her world was being sold to Ryker Triloni. Whatever it took, he would never allow his satanic half brother to get his vile hands on Jana Greyson.

Jana was his responsibility. Varian smiled again as he thought how he would definitely take a personal hand in her instructions. There were certain things he wanted to instill in her without altering her charm and personality too much, if any. He wanted to retain her spirit and courage, but teach her when to control them. He also wanted to retain that intrinsic air of gentility and innocence which were so compelling, which reminded Varian of his dead mother, Amaya Trygue Saar. Damn Shara Triloni and her son Ryker! Damn *Kadim* Maal Triloni for raising Ryker to be so evil and vengeful! Damn all three Trilonis for ruining his life, and for darkening his future. For a sunny-haired angel had come along who could brighten his gloomy heart, but could also increase his agony if he relented.

"Little moonbeam, you will shine as one of my greatest triumphs, my masterstroke of luck and genius, a jewel beyond comparison. Buyers will come from every sector just to peek at you. Not only will I be able to get my reports to the assemblymen and supreme councilmen about the grim fate of your world but, before we orbit Rigel on this infamous trek, Ryker will surely be enticed by your pictures and reports. I'm certain you'll provoke him to come and challenge me again," he said aloud.

Varian found himself speculating on her purity. *Perhaps you've not yet met a man who can stir that fiery passion which lies dormant within you. It would be a delight to teach you the joys of love.* He experienced a surge of jealousy and protectiveness toward her. He cringed at the thought of another introducing her to sex, then he tried to ignore the idea. What was it about this particular alien woman that caused him to experience this upheaval of emotions and to think such foolish and dangerous thoughts? Even if Jana had been a free woman or a Maffeian citizen, she was beyond his reach as long as Ryker lived and his satanic hatred existed.

He must choose his words and actions carefully in this scheme to entrap Ryker. It would elicit suspicion if he behaved too differently with Jana, considering she was an alien captive, soon to become a *charl*. He must move cautiously. He had to add all he could to Jana's appeal—as if she needed more allure! He would make the other *charls* envious of her, causing them to treat her in a manner which would hone her wits and courage. Since she must accompany him to the other planets and auctions to be displayed for prospective buyers, that mettlesome trait would help Jana survive the publicity for her own auction, and hopefully it would beguile Ryker. Varian realized he would have only eight weeks to train her and enjoy her company, for Jana's auction would be the last one; it would be held on Rigel, capital planet of the Maffei Galaxy, his native world and Star Fleet base.

*　*　*

61

Far away from the starship *Wanderlust*, on the planetoid called Darkar, which orbited the ninth planet Caguas in the Maffei Galaxy, Canissia Garthon had arrived in her luxury cruise ship the *Moonwind*. Presently she was visiting the handsome scientist and chemist with tawny hair and green eyes. The flaming-haired female eyed the virile physique of Ryker Triloni as she boasted of her cunning and daring across the galaxy. Her gaze caressed his striking features, even the knife scar on his right jawline from a fight with his half brother, Varian.

As if her concentration on the scar caused it to itch, Ryker absently rubbed it. While the obnoxious female chatted, he pretended to listen and to join in on her conversation and playful mood. He observed the ravishing creature sitting near him, uninvited and unwanted. Consistent with his reaction to most females, he was repulsed by her wanton behavior, repulsed by her very existence. He inwardly mocked her conceited opinion of herself and her wits. Yet outwardly Ryker was a pinnacle of charm and poise.

Ryker despised and detested Supreme Councilman Segall Garthon's daughter and Varian Saar's ex-whore, as he labeled her in his mind. But Canissia did have her value, for she often supplied him with secrets which she had stolen from her father or beguiled from one of her endless number of lovers. Until his dreams of slaying Varian Saar and assuming command of the Maffei Galaxy— and perhaps of the entire Universe— were realized, he would tolerate her. After she had served his purposes, he would slay her, or expose her criminal or wicked deeds to the "right" or "wrong" people and let one of them have that great pleasure. Canissia had made many enemies, male and female. He knew he could choose someone from that long list who would love to get vengeful hands on a captive Canissia.

Ryker laughed deceitfully at one of Canissia's vulgar jokes about a past lover. He decided that the woman had no morals, and no loyalties to anyone but herself. Of course, the same was true of him, he admitted. As he did, this evil bitch tried to keep a sharp eye and ear on Varian Saar, but never could she succeed to the extent he did. Ryker knew that Canissia craved his half brother and wanted to marry him. But Ryker also knew that Canissia would marry any man in one of the highest positions in galactic government, which included Supreme Councilman Draco Procyon. She hungered for matchless wealth, power, and status; and she would use any means possible or necessary to obtain her wishes. Canissia wanted Varian for his power and position and even more so because Varian was one of the few men who spurned her, like his half brother! Yes, Canissia Garthon would marry Prince Ryker Triloni in the flick of an eye if he agreed!

Ryker was clever and patient. Until he was sure he didn't need Canissia in some capacity to entrap Varian, he would let her visit Darkar and he would continue to supply her with the ''magic potions'' which sexually enslaved her many conquests for as long as she found them desirable. She thrived on her use of those powerful aphrodisiacs, for her sexual appetites were immense and varied. That was actually the reason for her visit today, to obtain more drugs, and perhaps to try once more to entice him into an affair with her. Never, he vowed disgustedly.

Ryker prepared two drinks as Canissia stretched her lithe body in an attempt to catch his eye and enflame a desire to bed her. He thought, *Poor Cass, what a fool you are. Your little spy on Varian's ship is actually working for me, not you. He tells you only what I want you to hear about my brother. You should know by now not to blackmail a desperate man. You should also know that your spy fears me far more than your threats of scandal, and death for him and his family. He'll never forgive you for using your love affair to steal Star Fleet secrets from him. Oh, yes, my greedy bitch, he'll enjoy your death and his freedom from your grip. I can offer him even more: the promise of fame and riches and command of the Star Fleet when I become ruler of this galaxy.*

A worker arrived to speak with Ryker, interrupting Canissia's talk. She watched the powerful and compelling prince before her, heir to the Androas throne and fortune upon *Kadim* Maal Triloni's death. And if anything happened to Varian, heir to the Saar estate as well. Like Varian, this man stirred to life wild desires within her. She knew Ryker did not like her, but she vainly believed she would eventually change his feelings. Few men could resist her beauty, erotic talents, or status; or defy her power to destroy them in one way or another. She had made friends and allies of people who could ''get things done secretly and lethally''; she could obtain items or secrets to sell or to trade to acquire her wishes; she could use blackmail or Ryker's drugs to handle difficult people. Yet, as with Commander Varian Saar and most high- ranking men in the government, Ryker was immune to mind-controlling drugs, thanks to a chemical process created by Ryker himself.

Canissia was angered and challenged by the rejections of both brothers. Somehow she would find a way to conquer and marry one of them, hopefully Varian because of his more favorable reputation. As soon as the *Wanderlust* returned to Maffei, and her contact covertly reported to her on Varian's mission and actions, she would generously reward her helpful spy by allowing him to enjoy her for a week in any way he desired. That should appease his anger at her vexing blackmail!

Canissia had decided not to reveal Varian's mission to Ryker, not just yet. She felt no loyalty to her father, his position, or to the Alliance Force. She felt as if she had already paid Ryker for a year's supply of aphrodisiacs with the information about Prince Taemin's plan to join forces with Ryker whereby the Androas Empire and Pyropean Federation could conquer and then divide the Maffei Galaxy! Prince Taemin, son of Supreme Ruler Jurad of the Pyropean Federation, wanted more than revenge on the Saars and Trygues for humiliating his father long ago; the alien prince wanted great power and wealth; he wanted a part if not all of the Maffei Galaxy under his leadership. When Canissia had secretly met with Prince Taemin, he had discussed his dreams of conquest with the hope she would deliver news of them to Ryker. Canissia had agreed to cooperate with the prince for the promise of becoming the new Maffeian *kadim*'s wife, no matter who the two conquering princes appointed. What an alliance, she thought, the three of them: Ryker, herself, and the evil prince who was magnificent in and out of bed and without any use of her drugs! Perhaps she would grow weary of being scorned and denied by both Saar heirs; she just might reject Ryker and Varian to marry Taemin! Obtaining the ruler of one galaxy was as good as another, especially when his dark and greedy appetites matched hers. Perhaps she and Taemin could form their own secret alliance and conquer Maffei for themselves! After all, she would be insane to trust Ryker Triloni!

For now, she wouldn't talk about the Alliance trek to that inferior Milky Way Galaxy. There was plenty of time to decide

64

how to use that secret which her father had let slip to her one night. Revealing it to Ryker would be more valuable and useful in a few weeks. . . .

"Is that vain whore well supplied again?" Ryker's assistant and mistress probed when he returned to his research complex, an impregnable structure which could be entered with a code known only by the handsome chemist. The female's green eyes watched his approach.

Galen Saar's bastard son never allowed anyone other than his mistress to work inside this private laboratory. Nor did he ever allow his adoring mistress to leave this complex. The formulas and genius of Ryker Triloni belonged here where no one could study or steal them. It was an enormous and unconquerable structure which contained five laboratories, many storage rooms, several botanical gardens, holding areas for rare or special animals and birds and insects, a communications room, recreational facilities, and living quarters for the golden-haired beauty who catered to Ryker's every whim. This was the place where Ryker did his creative—often evil—work, the place which held all of his awesome secrets and powers.

The numerous other structures on Darkar were used for growing exotic plants and animals which didn't need to be kept secret, for producing and storing chemicals and drugs, for making weapons, for packaging his products, for selling and showing his products and for meeting with clients, and for living and entertaining facilities for his employees. There were immense buildings which housed shuttlecrafts for delivery of items to orbiting ships, and there was a central control complex for communications and defense. Not far from this private structure was Ryker's palatial home, where he spent little time. There, as well as here in the private laboratory complex, robots performed household or menial tasks.

Ryker entered the main laboratory where he knew the inquisitive and jealous woman would be awaiting his return. "As usual, Precious, Cass left with plenty of drugs and hot lust in her eye," he remarked, then laughed wickedly. "What a stupid fool she is to try to dupe me. She didn't even hint at Varian's trek or his trusted lieutenant's betrayal. I can't wait until the day arrives when she learns her little spy aboard his ship actually works for me and tells her nothing I don't hear first. She should be glad my brother hasn't married her—and won't marry her! I'd kill her just like I'll slay any woman he marries. When I rid myself of that arrogant rogue of a brother, I'll be the only Saar alive, or Varian will pray I was. Of course, brother dear hasn't truly been denied a wife and children because of my threat; brother dear hasn't found a female worthy of him," Ryker said, sneering.

The beautiful woman poured her lover a drink and handed it to him. Ryker sat on a laboratory stool as he continued his threats concerning Varian. "I plan to take everything he has, Precious. It should all be mine."

While he spoke, Ryker observed his mistress drop to her knees between his spread thighs and unfasten his pants. She gently pulled his limp manhood into sight and spread kisses over its head. Her eagerness and excitement during this and other erotic actions never failed to amaze him, or to sate his *outré* urges, of which she was ignorant. He grinned and relaxed, allowing her to succeed with her sly test. As he grew hard and large and hot within her hands and mouth, her pleasure and feverish labors increased; for she always viewed his hasty response as proof of her erotic skills, and as proof of her power to arouse and to potently satisfy her deviant master.

As always after one of Canissia's visits, Precious tried to make certain the flaming-haired woman had become no threat to her position, or to make sure Canissia had not become a temptation to him for any reason. Little did his loving and pliant mistress know that her skills and sacrifices were nothing more to him than physical releases or sadistic thrills. Except for Canissia, his mistress feared no feminine rival, which was foolish; for he would never be tempted to make love to that ex-whore of Varian's! The ravishing blonde called "Precious" fretted each time Canissia returned to Darkar to see him. Ryker would laugh and tease Precious about her jealousy over the redhead, but he would cunningly let the exotic blonde retain her one insecurity which held her under control. As for Canissia, he would tolerate her a while longer, for she could present perilous obstacles to his plans if she vindictively revealed any of his secrets. Later, he would have no further use for either Canissia or Precious. . . .

His mistress stood, removed her silky garment, and let it

slide to the floor. "Think of more pleasant things, my love," she coaxed as she caressed her body and writhed seductively before him.

Ryker's impervious gaze moved up and down her naked body several times. In truth, she was very beautiful. But it was his twisted urges which had kept her around for years, for she unknowingly fed them. She was his property to use as he pleased, even if it did not please him as she imagined. For no physical pleasure was greater to him than feasting on his power over this greedy whore, than being able to take his hatred for women out on her and having her willingly submit to any and every perversion he ordered. The trusting bitch actually believed he loved her body and soul, beyond measure, loved her enough to keep her locked away from any foe who might try to capture her and use her to harm or destroy him. He could never allow Precious to leave this imprisoning complex for even a moment. . . .

When she tried to straddle his lap to encase his erect manhood, he shook his head. "Not yet, Precious, I still crave the stimulation of your sweet mouth. If Cass had only half your beauty and talent, I would be enjoying two mistresses. Show me how much you appreciate my rejecting her again," he commanded. "Down on your knees, Precious, and let me see the delight and hunger in your eyes."

His mistress complied instantly and skillfully. Ryker smiled as he witnessed his control over her. She would not halt her task until he changed his last command. He relished her blind obedience and this subservient position on her knees. He could tell when the flames of passion were scorching her body so urgently that he would be able to sate her quickly and easily. As he liked to degrade her, he ordered her to lie over a large and round barrel while he took her fiercely from behind like the demonic beast he was and the savage bitch he considered her to be.

Chapter Four

Jana was awakened the next morning by a series of brief, shrill buzzes. Startled, she struggled to a sitting position. She was not in her bedroom, and that was not a smoke detector or burglar alarm issuing a warning. She recalled this golden suite and her ominous predicament. The remainder of yesterday had passed slowly, with her time consumed by closer study of her "quarters." Neither of the two males had come to see her, nor had the "We'll tell you everything later" meeting taken place yet. She had been sent a delicious dinner through the servo unit; and before going to bed, she had received curious orders about today's business.

The monitor light came on and an unfamiliar voice instructed in a pleasing tone: "At the signal each morning, you will arise, bathe, dress, and eat. After sufficient time for these tasks, your door will open. You will be shown to a room where you will receive your daily instructions. Any questions will be answered at that time. Tardiness, absence, and defiance will not be permitted. Anyone practicing them will be dealt with severely. You will begin your tasks immediately. There will be a signal of three buzzes shortly before your door opens."

Jana was reminded of school bells, rules, teachers, and classes. Perhaps this routine was typical for prison or military life. A female had made the announcement, adding another person to this crime list. "Daily instructions, tardiness, absence . . ." sounded as if she would be performing a task. Despite trepidation, Jana was anxious to obtain clues. She quelled her anger and an urge for defiance which might prevent answers to her questions, as her captor had promised. She must solve this mystery: No ransom, rescue, or release . . . Aliens . . . Another galaxy . . . His captive . . . Starships . . . Forever . . . Could these claims be true?

Jana bathed and dressed. She brushed her hair until it glowed with a gold and silvery sheen. She applied a light touch of

68

makeup and a hint of fragrance. She was determined to look calm and attractive at this critical revelation of her fate. When she entered the other room, her meal was ready. All of the dishes were tasty, but again unfamiliar to her. That eerie feeling of uncanny reality touched her once more. She trembled visibly. She gently rubbed her hands up and down her arms to warm their sudden chill.

"Cold, Jana?" the now familiar masculine voice asked.

Jana half turned and gazed up at the camera. She shook her head. "I'm just anxious to get this over with," she replied in a cautious tone.

"Over?" Varian ruefully echoed. "It's just beginning," he corrected.

"Or so you claim," she bravely retorted. "I'll believe you when you've adequately proven your words. A scientist requires indisputable data."

"Have it your way. But don't say I didn't prepare you with the truth."

He was like an unknown chemical in a vital formula. She must test him gingerly and respectfully. To challenge him could prove a harmful error. Once she obtained all the information she could, she would evaluate it and come up with a method to neutralize him. Soon, they would meet. She didn't want him to think he had a timid, dull-witted coward on his hands. She must stand her ground bravely, but exercise caution. "Prepare me for your criminal character, or your ridiculous explanation?" she sparred.

"Oh, I'm certain you won't find my explanation ridiculous or boring. We'll see . . ."

"I'll await your proof with bated breath." She hoped her brave façade would make him think again before baiting her.

Her words drew a chuckle. "I'm afraid you might expire first. The meeting has been rescheduled for later today," he informed her.

"I suppose more stalling to increase my nervousness?" she taunted.

"I suppose," he agreed in a wickedly teasing tone.

Momentarily, the female's voice gave the announcement of the canceled meeting. The order came to relax until notification of a new time.

More tricks! I've got to know the truth. Damn that camera!

If I could only get out of this room and check out the rest of this place. . . .

Jana recalled how she had escaped that thug in Andrea's drive, giving her a risky idea. Jana stood and leisurely strolled around the room. She wanted to make certain she had her specter's attention. She halted near the bed and swayed slightly. Touching her fingers to her forehead, she gave a soft moan and gingerly collapsed to the floor.

A voice called out immediately, "Miss Greyson, are you all right?"

Jana remained still. If she failed to carry off this scheme, they would punish her greatly, or so they had threatened. Within minutes someone arrived. Opening her eyes very slightly, she could see the door remain open behind the black knee boots approaching her. She fought to master her rising fear, because she was terrified even though committed to her dangerous ruse. She closed her eyes and waited, dreading to learn if aliens existed.

A hand gently shook her shoulder as a strange masculine voice questioned, "Miss, are you sick or injured?" Jana moaned and stirred, as she decided this was the third male from her abduction. "Do you require medical assistance?" he inquired.

She asked in a small voice if he could assist her to the bed. He gripped her forearms and helped her to stand. She swayed against his chest and moaned. He released his grip on her arms to catch her sagging body.

Without delay, she forcefully kneed him in the groin. He doubled over and groaned in pain. Jana fled toward the door, slamming into a hard chest. She found herself imprisoned in the iron grip of another man whose entrance she had failed to notice. She struggled vainly to pull free. He gradually backed her up to the first man.

"Ferris, are you all right? It seems my little Earthling is bent on defiance and hostility," he stated. "I had believed her too smart for such conduct. Foolish and unnecessary, my rash alien," he scolded her. Her open rebellion and attack on Ferris Laus—his weapons chief and a security control officer under Kyle—caused Varian's concern over Jana's health to shift to anger.

Jana recognized the voice of the man who held her and had foiled her escape. Disheveled tawny hair settled wildly around

70

her flushed face and shoulders. His face was hidden behind a reflective vizard; but she guessed his identity from his virile physique, rich voice, a painlessly firm grip and his stirring smell. Her multicolored eyes displayed an array of warring emotions, whose mirrored image provoked recklessness.

"You beast!" she screamed at him. "Release me this instant! You have no right to keep me here!" She squirmed futilely in his strong grip, but did persuade him to shift his confining hands from her forearms to her wrists.

"Behave yourself, Jana. This conduct is silly and dangerous. Don't act like a spoiled brat!" He gently shook her like some naughty child. "Where is all that aristocratic breeding and intelligence I observed when I was watching you? Have you forgotten all of your manners in less than two days?"

As Jana struggled with Varian, she screamed at him, "You blasted animal! You vile demon! I will not become a docile prisoner or follow your stupid orders! And I will not be insulted or abused by perverted animals!" She rashly bit his hand to break its hold and to steal his attention from an action which she hoped would obtain her freedom instantly: she tried to knee him in the groin with all of her strength.

Commander Varian Saar was well trained and experienced, but Jana's surprise attack took him off guard. A combination of eye-blurring reactions took place swiftly, unthinking, instinctively: he agilely blocked her knee jab with his right thigh, he yanked his injured hand from her mouth as he yelled aloud in pain, and his highly developed reflexes sent Jana spinning from a stunning back-handed blow across her jawline.

She helplessly toppled and fell. Her scream silenced the heavy thud her forehead made upon impact with the bedside table. Dazed by the sharp blow, she could not make out his following words over the humming inside her ears. Her senses were reeling as she fought against the blackness which threatened to engulf her. Jana touched her throbbing temple. In hazy confusion, she gazed at the red liquid on her fingertips, as tousled hair shielded her face and the bloody injury from the two men. She could feel a warm, sticky substance slowly making a path down her right cheek and she sensed an urgent need to lie down. She gradually pulled herself up and reached for the bedpost for support, swaying slightly, but noticeably.

As Varian was not a man to strike a woman, this behavior

71

shocked both men because it was natural for a captive to attempt escape!

Varian felt remorse and shame as he watched her struggle to rise. He reached to aid her as he spoke her name tenderly. "Jana . . ."

She jerked her arm free. "Don't touch me! You animal—" She collapsed on her stomach on the bed, crying into her pillow.

"Are you all right, Ferris?" Varian asked his security guard to cover his anxiety. He didn't like to lose control, physically or emotionally, and he was distressed over his unintentionally violent response to her attack.

Ferris grinned sheepishly and nodded. "I guess she took me by surprise, sir. I'll be fine in a few minutes. You all right, sir?" he queried, noticing his commander's dismay and realizing the blow was unintentional.

Varian frowned, then nodded. He tried to lighten the mood by saying, "You better let Tris check you. Jana wields a mean right knee. I've seen it in action before." His comment was lost on Jana, as was his following apology: "I'm sorry, Jana. You caught me off guard. Please don't attempt similar stunts in the future." When she failed to respond, Varian accredited her silence to stubbornness and let it pass for now. Baffled by it all, he turned and hastily departed. What did he know about such assignments and females?

The bleeding continued and saturated her pillow. The laceration turned an angry red. As time passed, a bluish bruise began to form and swell. Jana was unable to hear the buzzer or announcement for lunch.

Ferris observed her on the monitor, then called out, "Miss Greyson, it's time to eat. No more games or defiance." Ferris was tempted to suspect trickery again, but he suddenly realized she had not moved or made any sound since her fall this morning.

"Miss Greyson, can you hear me? It's dangerous to persist in this rebellion. Will you answer me?" he asked, his concern and uncertainty growing.

This time, Ferris Laus approached her with caution. On entering her room, he coaxed, "No more tricks. The commander will be upset with both of us. We're not going to harm you. Don't you understand you provoked his anger. He didn't mean to hit you." But his words brought no response. Ferris gently shook her and called her name. He leaned over and pulled her long hair away from her face. He inhaled sharply as he saw the injury on her temple and her blood-soaked pillow.

Ferris put his ear to her back and sighed aloud in relief. There was a steady heartbeat. He shouted to his relief officer in security control, "You'd better alert Dr. Zarcoff and the commander. She's really hurt . . . and bad from the looks of it."

Tristan and Varian were rapidly at her bedside. As Tristan checked Jana, Varian said regretfully, "I didn't realize she was hurt. How is she?"

"Mild concussion with a large contusion. Sixteen-millimeter laceration," Tristan muttered as he examined her following Varian's dismissal of Ferris.

"Isn't that too much bleeding for a small cut? She's awfully pale."

"She burst a small vein on impact. It's clotted and sealed off now."

"But why has she been unconscious for so long?" Varian anxiously asked. "Why didn't she say anything to me at the time?"

"Pride. Shock from the blow. Surely you can imagine what she must have thought? You've studied her psychological profile."

Varian considered Tristan's theory for a minute. "She probably thinks she's in the hands of a brutal barbarian. How long will this state of shock last?"

Before Tristan could answer, a stretcher arrived and Jana was taken to sick bay where Tristan sedated her lightly during treatment. He cleaned the wound thoroughly and infused Clinitroid, a drug to reduce swelling an to extirpate fluid and blood from the surrounding damaged tissues. Tristan would seal the laceration after the medication had done its job.

While he waited, Tristan wondered at Varian's unusual cruelty to this woman. What had she done to provoke him so violently? Perhaps she would drop a clue when she awoke later. Tristan was infusing three more units of Clinitroid into Jana's wound when Varian entered the room.

Varian covered the short distance in a couple of long, easy strides. "How is our little patient doing, Tris? Any change?"

"Some," Tristan answered. Five hundred women aboard, and Varian could keep his distance and thoughts from all except Jana. Interesting . . .

Varian leaned forward to glance over Tristan's shoulder. He noted the steady decrease in swelling and discoloration in the surrounding area. He grinned and sighed loud with obvious relief.

As Tristan touched the tender area, Jana groaned and tried to brush away his hand. Tristan said, "Go to the other side and hold her still. We certainly don't want to risk further damage from interfering hands."

Tristan grinned slyly as he observed the gentle way Varian handled her. As he continued to attempt to soothe her, Jana arched her back and tried to pull her hands free in unknowing protest to his ministrations.

Tristan knew the area was still too swollen to effect a scarless sealing of the laceration. As he pushed on the two jagged sides to promote the body's natural effort at self-healing, she struggled weakly and cried out, "No-o-o . . ." The injury was still too sensitive to work with under this light sedation, and he could not risk a stronger narcotic with her concussion.

Varian held her hands firmly. Jana struggled for consciousness. Her eyelids fluttered as she tried to open them and focus on the dark form towering over her. For a brief period they cleared. She stared up into the face of the handsome and breathtaking man of her dreams who had come to save her from danger and pain. Feeling safe, she relaxed.

A soul-tingling voice tenderly commanded, "Relax, Jana. Everything's fine." When her dreamy gaze locked on his face, a charming smile settled on his mouth. He was warmed by the way she seemed mesmerized by him.

Tristan completed his work and turned to put away his instruments. He reflected on Jana's skills and training. With his regular staff on leave . . . Tristan glanced at Jana and smiled secretly. Varian wanted her happy and calm, didn't he? What better way to distract and relax her, to win her loyalty?

Varian released Jana's hands. He leaned forward, bringing their faces close. His blue gaze was tender. He stroked her hair and murmured softly, "That's all, Jana. Close those beautiful eyes and sleep."

Jana's left hand reached out to touch his sensual lips. Her

fingers traced the cleft in his chin and the smile creases near his mouth. She stared into his cobalt-blue eyes for a moment. Grasping his head between her hands, she pulled it down to join her lips to his. Jana relished the flavor and skill of his mouth as it responded to hers. She murmured, "I've waited for you all of my life." Her gaze melted into his as she fought the sedative. Her eyes closed and she lost her battle for consciousness.

Varian grabbed her hands as they were limply falling back to the table. He placed them at her sides. He caressed the soft skin of her arms as his wishful gaze roamed her face. "Sorry, little moonbeam, but I'm not your destiny."

Tristan observed the gleam of desire sparkling in Varian's eyes. He watched the way Varian fingered her golden hair and satiny skin and he caught the sultry tone in Varian's voice when his commander teased, "I see our little Earthling is a flirt when her wits are dulled. Her face will match the sunset when she recalls her wanton behavior toward me of all men."

Tristan dashed his hopes and pleasure. "I doubt she'll recall."

"Too bad. I would have enjoyed seeing her reaction when she realized she brazenly came on to the man she doubtless considers her worst enemy. Perhaps my appeal to her would have made her realize I'm not an evil monster," he stated with a humorous chuckle. "Carry on, Dr. Zarcoff; she's in capable hands now," he teased, then left.

It was past the dinner hour, and Jana was dreaming that she was dancing with the handsome stranger. His mocking sapphire eyes held her senses imprisoned in a world of romantic fantasy. She ran her fingers through the luxurious mane of wavy hair, as dark and shiny as an expensive Russian sable. She longed to taste those sensual lips again. Her fingers lovingly traced the strong angle of his jawline and wandered across his dented chin. His face came closer and closer to hers. As his manly scent teased her nose, she trembled in anticipation of his warm kiss. Just as he was about to press his lips to hers, his image faded and she was all alone—alone in a small, semidark room which glittered with golden shimmers. A minute red light gleamed. The sedative was wearing off. Jana opened her eyes.

She glared at the surveillance camera in angry resentment of its untimely intrusion. She tried to sit; the throbbing in her temple prevented it. Her fingers touched the tender spot on her forehead, then withdrew quickly as she gave a low moan.

Jana turned her head from side to side very slowly. Where was she? She gradually recalled what had happened in hazy detail. Escape was definitely impossible. She had underrated the evil of her captor and her situation. Next time, she must be more alert and careful. She would bide her time until she had a better perspective of him and her imprisonment.

Tristan came to check on her progress. He had looked forward to this encounter. "I see you're finally awake," he remarked cordially.

Jana glanced in the direction of the vaguely familiar voice and face of the man who was approaching her with what appeared to be a genuinely friendly smile and easy manner. Did she know this man? she wondered. He had spoken in a clear and precise tone which carried a noticeable hint of gentleness. Had she been rescued?

Tristan smiled as he carefully checked her injury. "It's doing just fine, Jana," he stated. "How do you feel? A headache? Dizziness? Nausea? Blurred vision?" His tone rang with more than professional concern.

Jana stared at his mouth in open bewilderment, warning him of a problem. "You look distressed. What's wrong?"

She hesitantly answered, "I don't know. . . . My eyes and brain aren't working in unison. Your lips move differently from what I'm hearing, like a movie with the sound and picture running at different speeds."

"No, problem, Jana. We speak different languages, that's all."

"But I can understand you perfectly," she argued, confused.

"Because I've implanted a microtranslator in your aural canal. It instantly translates my language or any language you may hear into yours."

"That's impossible." Jana said, fear teasing her mind.

"Perhaps on Earth, but not in our world. You see, the people of the Maffei Galaxy and our two adjoining galaxies are advanced a thousand years beyond your native planet. We all have embedded microtranslators. They're necessary when dealing with so many different languages. Don't let it confuse you or frighten you," he entreated.

He sounded as if . . . Dread filled her. "Who are you? Where am I?"

"I'm the chief medical officer and head of research on this starship. You're in my medical facility being treated for an injury. I'm from the capital planet Rigel in the Maffei Galaxy," he calmly explained.

"Come now, Doctor, surely you aren't going along with this ridiculous tale of my being abducted by aliens?" she challenged.

A troubled look touched his eyes. "It's true, Jana. You must accept it."

"And if I refuse to play along with this evil sport?"

"Your reason for being my patient should tell you how reckless that decision could be. Commander Saar is adamant about obedience."

"Obedience!" Jana scoffed in astonishment. "Why should I obey a brutal criminal? He said he won't release me. Why should I cooperate with him in any way? No!" she stated firmly.

A genuinely worried expression appeared on Tristan's face. "I hope you will comprehend the futility of such rebellion. I know a great deal about you, Jana. Don't make things rough on yourself by being reclassed as a disrupter." He flashed her a winning grin, "Please don't belie my high opinion of you."

"I suppose your *high opinion* of me is that I'd cower in fear, or become a submissive and timid prisoner," she said angrily.

"No, you're very wrong. I was under the impression you would find the courage and wisdom to accept a situation you can't alter. I expected your intelligence and curiosity to overrule any foolish pride."

"So I'll cower before that barbaric animal you call your leader? Grovel like some coward or simpleton?" Anger sparked in her eyes.

"Not grovel, Jana, merely accept his authority," he reasoned.

"Commander Saar is a ruthless tyrant, and you're all liars!" she cried.

"I understand your confusion and doubts, Jana, and even your anger. As incredible as it seems, it is true. If you'll allow me, I'd like to help you through this adjustment. I hope you can learn to trust me, and like me. I've great respect for you

77

and your abilities. I would give my retirement for a research assistant like you." Tristan smiled at Jana.

"He said I could never return home. Is that true?"

"Yes," Tristan reluctantly replied. "But you're in no danger."

"Then why am I treated so vilely?" she demanded.

"If I'm correct, you did provoke Commander Saar by attacking him and one of his men," he admonished her.

"I only tried to escape or learn the truth. Any captive would have done the same, including your savage leader."

Tristan again emphasized the facts. "You're on a starship in the middle of space, Jana, so escape is impossible. We are Maffeians and we're traveling back to our native galaxy. You must accept your fate and submit to Commander Saar's authority. I should think your curious, probing, scientific mind would find this adventure a little bit thrilling and intriguing," he suggested, trying another path to reach her.

"Thrilling to be a captive?" she protested. "You must be as insane as he is," she stated quietly. "Perhaps it's contagious madness, Doctor."

"Think of it, Jana—other worlds, other races, advanced technologies, the unknown. Doesn't that fascinate you at least a little?"

This man with his warm smile, gentle blue gaze, and sunny disposition affected her favorably. Jana pondered his words and reasoning. If he spoke the truth—but as a captive! Resentment flared anew within her. "Surely you jest, Doctor . . ."

"Zarcoff, Dr. Tristan Zarcoff, chief medical officer and chief research officer of the starship *Wanderlust,* at your service. Try to accept this situation, and work on adjusting, Jana, then you'll be happier. If you find yourself in need of a friend, I'll—" He halted and actually flushed and stammered in obvious embarrassment.

Seeing that blush, she warmed to him immediately. "You'll what, Dr. Tristan Zarcoff?" she prompted.

He recognized the change in her mood. "If you're not totally averse to the idea, I'll be honored to fill that position." His eyes twinkled with a merry gleam. He awaited her reply.

Jana thought of a sad-eyed but comforting hound dog. She smiled and answered, "As I find myself lacking friends at the present, I'll accept your kind offer if you are serious." Perhaps she would find a valuable ally in this genial man.

"Quite serious and delighted. Friends?" he offered.

"Friends," she readily agreed. She asked, "What will this Commander Saar have to say about your fraternizing with the enemy?"

"Hopefully nothing," he said, then laughed.

"And if he does?" Jana asked, pondering his motive.

Tristan lowered his voice to a secretive tone of conspiracy and replied, "We'll have to make sure he doesn't, won't we? Take this and get some rest."

Jana eyed the sleeping pill. "But I just woke up, Dr. Zarcoff."

"I know, but it's late. By morning, you'll be fine. Come on, Dr. Greyson, don't be a bad patient," he teased and waited for her to take the pill.

In the commander's quarters, a meeting was taking place between Varian and Martella Karsh. It was late, but the coordinator of the *charl* project was too distressed to sleep. Sensing a problem brewing, Varian had agreed to a private conference with Martella. He had assumed Martella was upset over Jana's absence in class today, or more accurately the reason for it.

"Commander Saar, are you sure you want to proceed with this scheme for Ryker? Do you thoroughly understand the ramifications of what you're doing, sir? If it suited his purpose, Ryker could slay Jana or a thousand women and feel no guilt. This plan to ensnare Ryker makes me nervous. So much deception for one delicate female and for one grim mission." Many times during the last six weeks Martella had seen Varian enter the control room, where surveillance tapes were being made of impending captives, just to watch Jana, before this "Ryker bait" ruse had entered his mind. Now, after the trouble today . . .

Varian leaned back in his chair and studied the obviously worried officer. He reiterated several points. "You know she was selected and captured to serve as our cover, Martella. The other females will only draw regular attention to the auctions; we needed a goddess to justify obtaining the attention and presence of planetary rulers. I scanned those promo tapes on Jana which you sent out today. No man, however powerful, could resist attending our auction when such an angel will be displayed. Luring Ryker off Darkar so we can simultaneously accomplish a second goal won't be an added burden to Jana's adjustment or her role in our mission. She won't even know she's our accomplice."

Varian shifted in his chair in an attempt to relax. "We've already discussed this with Nigel and Tris and Kyle. I thought everyone involved in this additional scheme was in full agreement, even if none of us likes using Jana for a dual ruse. But it's a perfect plan, Martella. Jana has all of us to protect her, she'll come to no harm from that demon. You're a member of the Elite Squad, Martella; surely you recognize the importance of defeating Ryker Triloni, who we know is somehow plotting the overthrow of the Maffei Interplanetary Alliance. The *Kadim* personally chose you for this assignment because he has faith in your skills and loyalty. I need your help on this." For the second time today, Varian was caught unprepared by a woman's conduct; this time it was by Martella's statements and turbulent emotions.

She did not back down from her sense of duty to Jana and herself. "Ever since our talk earlier, I've been worrying over this pit you're digging for Ryker. Like all men, Ryker needs heirs. A *charl* would probably suit his needs and character perfectly, especially one like Jana, and more so if he thought he was stealing the woman he thinks you love or desire. There are so many hazards in your plan, sir. We shouldn't do this to Jana; she's too special. Whether or not she knows she's helping us, we owe her."

"Relax, Martella. She's only a temptation, not a sacrifice," Varian asserted confidently, noting the woman's formality, as if she were registering an official protest against his offending order. He patiently went over the same ground he had covered in his talk with Nigel and during their joint conference this morning. He explained Jana's "accident." "She can help us accomplish two goals: defeat Ryker and execute our mission secretly. And if I can foil Ryker, I might find a way to encourage truces with Maal Triloni and Jurad Tabriz. As long as Ryker's around to keep their hatred and hostilities burning, our world is in danger. Don't fight me on this," he urged the disquieted woman. "Help me make it work for all of our sakes. In return, I'll help you any way I can with your pet project. Is that fair enough?"

"But not in time to save Jana from being sold like a piece of property. Isn't there some way to avoid auctioning her? She's such a valuable human. Can't we release her for aiding us? Or couldn't we pretend to sell her to someone who'll protect her until the laws are changed and she's freed? What about feigning a sale to Supreme Councilman Draco Procyon? She would be safe, and he wouldn't have to actually pay for her. Her living with Councilman Procyon would keep Ryker or one of your other enemies from getting to her. You haven't overlooked that possibility, have you?"

"No, Martella, I haven't," he confessed in a tone which unintentionally exposed his inner feelings. "If there's one thing I know, it's the effect of enemies on my life."

Martella wanted to make a wild suggestion about Varian buying this perfect mate; she decided it was too soon to risk putting him on the defensive. Yet, she quietly asked, "Varian, what happens if Jana falls for your ruse to fool Ryker? What if we can't change the *charl* laws in time to spare her or if we can't entice Draco's help?"

"Don't fret, Martella; I won't allow her to fall in love with me."

"How will you prevent it? When you feign interest in her to seize Ryker's attention, how do you think Jana's going to react to you? Like all women do. Despite your good intentions and cautions, she'll be hurt."

Varian hadn't wanted to think about this facet of his plan, for he knew how he would be compelled to deal with it. "I'll give her reasons to mistrust and dislike me. The pretense need only be mine. I can make other people think I'm enchanted by her without her assistance or knowledge. Perdition! I don't want her to fall in love with me! She doesn't need that complication in her new life. And I don't need it in mine. If Ryker suspected such feelings—"

"You know I trust you, and I wouldn't disobey orders. But this time, I think you're too close to the fire to see its flames. Look at her, Varian. Have you ever seen such a perfect specimen? This girl was born to mate with a very special man." Martella's gaze drilled into Varian's, as she unwittingly dropped a stunning clue to her thoughts.

"I hope you aren't insinuating what I think," Varian scolded. He didn't know why tremors swept over his muscular frame. "She's a *charl*. Varian Saar can't buy a mate! What about her alien blood in my sons?"

Having exposed her feelings, Martella did not back down. "What you really mean is you can't risk claiming a mate which your brother will try to slay, right?" she boldly quizzed this unique man who had shared many days and perils with her on this and other Elite Squad missions.

Varian scowled. "I'll reward Jana's help, but nothing more. Forget this nonsense about Draco and secret plots to save Jana. Hear me, Martella? Get these crazy ideas out of your head."

Martella eyed Varian intently. He was as brilliant and dangerous and powerful as a fiery comet, a man destined for even greater things than he had already accomplished. A man like Varian Saar attracted the attention and influenced the emotions and the fates of males and females, of friends and foes. Could Jana Greyson win this man's love and acceptance? If so, could she hold on to them? Could she hold on to a man who was a blazing comet speeding across destiny's heaven? Could she hold on without being burned painfully, or without being utterly consumed?

Chapter Five

Jana awoke early the following morning gazing up into the cheerful face of Tristan Zarcoff, who offered her a warm, "Good morning. How did you sleep last night? And how does my favorite patient feel today?"

"And how is my only friend?" she said, testing his sincerity of yesterday.

Tristan beamed with pleasure. "Excellent." He passed a black boxlike instrument over her body. It issued several clicks and bleeps. Tristan studied the digital readouts and grinned. "All vital signs are perfect."

Tristan held the medical analyzer out for her to read. "That modern technology I spoke of yesterday," he explained. "This little instrument is so sensitive it can accurately measure and record your blood pressure, heart rate, temperature, and respiration instantly. It can even detect mental and physical stress and report its findings in any language requested.''

Jana was impressed. "I'll show you another of our modern scientific advantages." He held up a mirror. "Look at your forehead."

She did as he suggested. She stared at her temple, which bore no sign of any previous injury. She touched it, then winced.

"It'll be tender another day or so. Tissues fuss about rapid healing."

"How?'" she asked in disbelief. "Have I been here longer than two days?"

"You came here yesterday. We have drugs that rapidly expel dead blood cells and fluid which cause the bruising and swelling. I returned while you were sleeping and sealed the laceration with a *latron* beam."

She was amazed by his advanced knowledge, if she could believe her eyes and his words. She was not sure what to think anymore.

Tristan observed her mingled look of doubt and admiration. "It'll take time to trust us and accept us, Jana. I knew you'd find this procedure interesting." He handed her a turquoise robe.

"Yes," she admitted as she slipped it over a matching gown.

"Walk around. I'd like to see if you've suffered any side effects from your injury or the drugs. I'm glad your chemistry varies little from ours."

After a few minutes of exercise, she remarked, "I feel fine."

"Let me show you something in my lab. I think you can be of some help to me for a change." Tristan was eager to learn if Jana was as skilled as he believed. Besides, he and Martella needed a way to help Jana avoid her impending fate. Jana obediently followed his lead.

He went to a surgical table and pointed to a small furry brown creature. "They're similar to Earth's spider monkeys. He's carrying a virus I need to cure. Problem is, I'm having trouble getting a veinal cannula inserted. These old hands aren't as steady as they used to be."

"Don't you have an assistant who can do a simple veinal cannula?"

"My staff is on leave," he answered, as feigned irritation

83

filled his tone. He sighed in mock exasperation. "I cannot seem to manage adroit microsurgery anymore. Nor can I seem to find a competent assistant. I may have to resort to euthanasia. He's a hazard to the other specimens." He watched to see what her reaction would be.

"You can't do that!" she shrieked in dismay. "I could easily insert the cannula for you. It would be cruel and unnecessary to destroy him." Jana eyed the little creature with pity. Her interest and attention were snagged. For a time, she ignored her predicament.

"You would do it for me?" he questioned slyly behind a pleased grin.

After sedating the animal, Tristan handed her a pair of surgical gloves and a lab coat. Jana seated herself and pulled them on. Depending on a power-lens magnifier to give a distinct and enlarged view of the working field, she worked quickly and skillfully with the scalpel.

"Do you infuse heparin to prevent clotting, Dr. Zarcoff?" she questioned, without looking up as she was totally immersed in her work.

"A similar drug, Jana. It's in the smaller syringe. The dextraphine for treatment is in the larger one."

She obeyed his instructions, pressing very slowly and evenly on the syringe. When three units had been given, she switched off the Y-connector. "Do you want me to infuse the dextraphine?"

"Yes, four hundred cc's." He was observing her work with intense pleasure. She was indeed highly talented. Even he could have done no better. What an assistant she would make. . . .

Twenty minutes later, Jana stated simply, "That's it. Will he require further infusions or do you want me to close him up?"

"He'll need one more dose in four hours. If I have any trouble, I'll send for you. That was excellent, Jana. You'd make a fine surgeon."

Jana flushed at his compliments. "I faint at the sight of human blood," she quipped, half in truth and half in jest. "I'm certain patients would not care for their surgeon passing out in the middle of delicate operations. I'll stick to research, my first love."

Tristan chuckled. "Too bad. I could use a good surgical assistant."

"I doubt I was abducted for my medical skills, Doctor." Jana removed the red-splotched gloves and lab coat. "What now?"

"After that beautiful piece of microsurgery, you must call me Tristan or Tris. All my friends do. You'll be returned to your quarters this morning. The rest is up to you and the commander." Tristan was eyeing her intently.

"I see, back into that tyrant's clutches?" she hinted coolly. How she wished she could remain in this research lab with this genial doctor.

"You rest until he sends someone for you," Tristan instructed.

Jana glanced at his medical equipment. Even if he had lied about the spaceship, she definitely was on some type of ship— very sophisticated, elaborate, and expensive. This mysterious commander was undeniably wealthy, powerful, and ruthless. Jana began, "I wish I could—"

A stirring voice which she could never forget cut into her wistful sentence and seemed to fill the entire room. "I see our capricious Earthling is better this morning. You can work miracles, Tris."

Varian crossed the room with grace and ease. Tristan noted the involuntary stiffening of Jana's body and the panic which flooded her features. She visibly paled at simply hearing Varian's voice behind her.

Jana turned to face her antagonist. Her startled eyes widened. Her mouth uncontrollably dropped open in disbelief. He was not wearing his concealing vizard this morning. She stared at the magnetic, handsome face of the man approaching her. Only in her dreams had she ever seen such overwhelming perfection. Jana's heart fluttered madly. He had the bluest eyes she had ever seen, the color of very expensive and precious sapphires. They glittered with vitality. His sensuous smile could have dispelled the darkest gloom of night. A lock of ebony hair fell casually over his left temple. He was very tall, for she had to look up at his face. Jana stared into his smiling eyes, which revealed a fiery passion for life. He was magnificent. Wits, fears, and reality momentarily fled her mind. Without realizing she was speaking aloud, she murmured in astonishment, "You're the man in my dreams . . ."

As his hand caressed her cheek, Varian's broad chest rumbled with zesty laughter. "I hate to disappoint and disillusion you, little moonbeam, but you saw me while you were semiconscious yesterday. I helped Tris with your injury, after I was rashly provoked into creating it."

"I don't recall seeing—" she halted as she comprehended what she had just said. Her face reddened and she hastily lowered her gaze to his firm, muscular chest. He wasn't a fantasy! If she had seen him twice while drugged, how much of her "dream" was real?

Jana flinched as Varian brushed her hair aside to check her forehead. "I see you've performed your usual excellent job, Tris." He secretly observed Jana as he took much longer than necessary to check her. "No sign of injury. No scar. Perfect . . ."

His touch burned like hypnotic fire. She trembled, bewildered and alarmed by her ridiculous behavior and wild thoughts. She hurriedly jerked away from him. "No thanks to your brutality!"

"Please don't provoke another show of my power and loss of temper."

Jana looked up at him. Despite his mellow voice, there was a warning gleam in his blue eyes. "Are you forbidding me to speak?" she asked curtly.

"Not at all. I'm only advising caution and temperance in speech and actions." Varian caught Tristan's humorous grin over Jana's shoulder.

"That will be all, Tris. I'll see to Jana," he said in a brisk tone.

Tristan's grin broadened. "Yes, sir, Commander Saar." As he passed Jana on his way out, he smiled and offered a warm and grateful "Thank you, Jana. I'll be seeing you very soon." To Varian he said, "She hasn't eaten yet. Will you have Kyle or Ferris see to it for me?"

Amid Varian's confusion at the doctor's order, Jana returned Tristan's friendly overture with a dazzling smile. "Anytime, Dr. Zarcoff. I really enjoyed it," she murmured as if speaking to a good friend.

Varian witnessed the transformation of bitterness and resentment into softness and charm which her smile so vividly revealed. She watched Tristan's departure with apprehension, as Varian watched her with new interest.

"Why won't you release me?" she asked. "What is it you want from me?"

"As soon as you've dressed, I'll escort you to your quarters," he casually announced, as his gaze engulfed her body.

"Dressed?" She glanced down, suddenly aware her robe was hanging free. "Oh-h-h," she cried. Her hands grasped the satiny material and overlapped it, trying to shield her half-exposed chest.

He chuckled. "You have absolutely nothing to hide from me, Jana. I am well acquainted with all of your numerous charms."

Her gaze flew up to his mocking eyes. Her frosty glare bored into his molten one. "You're despicable!" she said.

He sent her an engaging grin. "You're absolutely right. In fact, most people think I'm far worse. But you'll have to change; I'm afraid you'd prove too distracting to my crewmen attired in that flimsy gown."

He motioned to some clothing she had not noticed. She was begrudgingly grateful for this small concession to her dignity, wisely suppressing the surly words which threatened to spill forth. As she picked up the green caftan, she realized he made no move to leave. She cast suspicious eyes toward him. "Where do I change?" she demurely inquired.

"Here," he stated, a devilish half smile playing across his lips.

She paled. "H—here?" she stammered. "But surely you'll leave?"

"Why? I've seen you nude before." That piece of horrifying information came as an unexpected shock, even though it was something she should have realized sooner.

She flushed again, to her great dismay. "I will not undress in front of a total stranger. How dare you treat me in this vile manner."

"Either you do it, or I'll do it for you. And if I'm forced to rip that gown from your lovely body, you'll return to your quarters that way, regardless of the temptation to my men." He could see the fires of rebellion burning blightly in her eyes, fires he must extinguish.

Jana wisely decided not to provoke this man. She lowered her head in shame and started to undress. Varian seized the front of the dressing gown, his massive grasp rumpling and closing it. "It isn't necessary to finish this test, Jana. I simply needed to learn if you would now obey orders, no matter what they were. You have five minutes to change. I'll wait outside." When her head jerked upward to verbally assail him, he shook his head and warned, "Don't do it, little moonbeam. You just won my forgiveness for your defiance yesterday. Don't make a new strike against yourself. I don't want to hurt you, but I must have your obedience."

As Varian and Jana approached the elevator which would take them to deck one where her quarters were located, an intercom issued a call. As Varian answered the page, she eyed him intently. He commanded attention anywhere and anytime. Like her beautiful stallion Apache, he evinced power. Jana was alarmed by the strong and compelling attraction she was feeling. She was bedeviled by this mysterious and complex male.

"Sir, we've picked up a radiation belt in our path. It wasn't there on our way in. I advise a course change as soon as possible."

Varian was aware of Jana's gaze locked on him. He would give her the chance to learn firsthand of his command, the reality of her situation, and the impossibility of rescue or escape. He also felt a curious need to impress and disarm her. "I'll come to the bridge, Lieutenant Rilke."

Tesla Rilke's confusion at Varian's odd reaction was short-lived. Changing course to avoid peril was a common occurrence requiring merely the commander's permission and not his personal attention.

Varian headed for the elevator with Jana in tow. He issued a verbal order to the computerized panel: "Bridge." They moved sideways, then upward. Only a faint hum was detectable to her ears. The door opened and they stepped out into a huge, semicircular open area.

Jana took in sights and sounds which could stagger the imagination. She had never seen a more complex conglomeration of computers, panels, and instruments. Crew members were either concentrating on their individual tasks or chatting lightly in jovial tones with those nearby. She froze at the unbelievable sight before her.

The crew came to alert when Varian appeared. Jana instantly noticed the high esteem and admiration on the faces of the men and women before them. She was reluctantly impressed by his reception and rank.

"As you were," Varian cheerfully stated.

The crew returned to their prior tasks or conversations—all but one male who surreptitiously observed Jana and Varian. Varian headed toward a man standing next to a videoscreen. Jana mechanically followed, but Varian behaved as if she were not present. He pretended to study the screen before him as Tesla Rilke gave his report and suggestion in a muffled tone.

Jana was only half listening. Her attention had been captured by the large window spanning the front wall of the bridge. She went to it and stared outside. The panorama was breathtaking. The heavens were an intense blue-black with hints of indigo. Off in the distance, vivid and harmonious hues of blue, red, and green cloudlike formations dappled the skies. They seemed adrift in a dark sea filled with millions of glittering points of light. She was stunned and enthralled.

Jana remained motionless, as if hypnotized by the infinity before her. Space . . . that terrifying word drummed loudly inside her brain. This was not an elaborate and imaginary charade; it was all too real to be ignored. There were too many people and too much evidence for her to deny. She was being taken to God-knows-where by aliens, for some unknown reason. She trembled at the missing facts. A scientific study of human biology on Earth? Living specimens? Unless these aliens were disguised, they had been created in the same physical mold as Earthlings. But why capture her to study? *Why?* she wondered.

Varian joined her at the transascreen and stood very close to her, too enchanted by her to notice the probing gaze of one of his lieutenants on them. She would present no further problems, Varian decided. He relaxed. His ploy was working perfectly. "I see you find our view spellbinding, Jana." She instinctively nodded agreement. "Perhaps awesome and terrifying?" She only nodded again as she continued to stare at the vastness before them.

To emphasize his power over her, he lightly stated, "We are bound for the Maffei Galaxy where the Maffei Interplanetary Alliance consists of thirteen planets. Each planet is ruled by many *zartiffs*, much like your kings or presidents on Earth who govern certain areas. These men report to an *avatar*, the head ruler of each planet. Those thirteen men make up our Maffei Alliance Assembly, which answers to the Supreme Council of three men who rule our entire galaxy." He slipped his arm around her waist as he continued relating facts to her. "The Supreme Council is all-powerful, especially its leader, the *kadim*. You have no one on earth to compare our Supreme Council or *kadim* with; those three males are feared and envied and their word is law or death. Right now, the Supreme Council consists of Councilman Segall Garthon, Councilman Draco Procyon, and *Kadim* Tirol Trygue." Although he knew she could not absorb so much information at a time like this, he went on casually to list the planets and their *avatars*.

He took a deep breath. His tone lowered as he revealed, "I've lived in space much of my life. Yet I always find it mysterious, overpowering, and exhilarating. I can imagine how it must affect someone who's never seen it beyond the surface of her world or on a videoscreen. Do you still doubt my truth, Jana?" he asked without a trace of sarcasm and brusqueness.

She lifted sad eyes to his and studied the softened lines in his handsome features. He was such a mercurial creature. Why shouldn't he be kinder and calmer? He had won. She grudgingly admitted, "Your truth seems to be accurate, Commander Saar. How can I intelligently argue against such evidence?" Her hand slowly motioned to the view surrounding her, inside and outside the ship. "Yet it's so incredible and confusing," she confessed.

"The world outside your Milky Way is immense, Jana. Our two neighboring galaxies are the Androas Empire, ruled by *Kadim* Maal Triloni, who's also royalty, and the Pyropean Federation, which is controlled by Supreme Ruler Jurad Tabriz. Most of the time we live under wary truces, but frankly I don't trust either man." To her surprise, he suddenly smiled and said, "I had counted on your superior intelligence and keen perception to convince you that I spoke the truth." He tenderly and unknowingly caressed her cheek as he spoke to her.

"You win, Commander," she stated in defeat. Before she

90

could speak the question still foremost in her mind, his words and actions had beguiled her.

"I never doubted that victory for a single minute, Jana," he remarked confidently in an almost seductive tone. His deep blue eyes seemed to mesmerize her. His lack of harshness and conceit prevented any surly retort. "Let's go. I have another problem to check on in security control." He grasped her hand and guided her off the bridge of his ship, still unaware of the officer who was spying on them for Varian's worst enemy.

As they entered a room filled with small monitors, Jana immediately realized the purpose of this room. Her wide eyes glanced across multiple screens as softly muted feminine voices reached her ears. She viewed many rooms with numerous females—all being observed and held captive. Her head jerked around as the young officer on duty began to speak with Varian. In a way she was glad to have faces finally attached to voices. For the moment, Jana was too dazed by the heavy influx of facts to think clearly. Her concept of reality was being challenged and defeated, by a masterful creature who seemingly controlled her life.

Unaware of her presence, Kyle Dykstra launched into an explanation of the problem at hand. He pointed to one screen in particular as he talked. Jana's eyes followed his line of direction as she listened. "It's Sylva Omanli, sir. She's demolishing her quarters again. This time she attacked her roommates. They've screamed for help. I've tried to reason with her, but she refuses to obey. Do you want me to send her below to security?"

Varian stared at the screen. Martella had warned him that some women might never surrender to this new fate. She had told him that sometimes harsh punishments were mandatory. A rebellious *charl*'s attention must be secured before she would settle down. Varian hated being forced to punish any captive, but this one's conduct was wearing thin, and this was one *charl* mission which could not allow problems to breed! A muscle twitched in his right cheek. He leaned forward, his full attention claimed by Sylva. His blue eyes narrowed and hardened as he watched the temper tantrum the dark-haired, ivory-skinned Uranian was throwing.

Jana also focused on the same screen. She observed the

91

wildness of the female in question. Three others were huddled in a corner. As Varian turned on the audio control switch, Jana could not believe the obscenities and vulgar speech coming from that lovely woman, nor her volatile temper. She appeared uncontrollable!

Sylva had yanked covers from all the beds and shredded them. There were books and food tossed around, objects broken, furniture overthrown, and clothing scattered about the room. The quarters were devastated.

Varian issued a frigid command to Sylva, who chose to ignore it and his ominous tone. He threatened her with several terrible and wicked punishments. She still refused to halt her destruction or verbal torrent of abusive, crude language. When the others shrieked for rescue, Sylva attacked them like a crazed Amazon warrior.

"You are no longer a princess, my dear Sylva. Your world of Uranus is far behind you. You are under my control! You will halt this destructive behavior at once! If you disobey, you will pay greatly. Cease this stupidity instantly!"

Jana's mind reeled at those stunning clues. Wasn't this an expensive way to obtain servants? Her gaze scanned the monitors. No man needed this many female slaves! Did he intend to sell most to pay for his trip? Jana observed the handsome man in a new light: arrogant slaver.

Varian furiously snapped off the audio control. "Tell Ferris to confine Sylva to the brig. Send Tris to care for the others. Our rebellious and crude little Sylva is in for an unexpected awakening! Come on, Jana," Varian commanded, annoyed with all females at that point, as he was unaccustomed to defiance or dealing with slavery.

Kyle whirled and grinned at Jana. His emerald eyes sparkled and his brown hair lay in unruly curls. The line of his almost square face was broken by a cleft in his chin. Thick, long lashes and a winsome smile completed a look of youthfulness.

"I'm glad to see you're all right. I was worried about you." Kyle failed to note the black scowl and knitted brow of his commander.

Kyle's friendliness took Jana by surprise. Perhaps she could enlist another valuable ally. "So, we meet at last, *mon spectre*. I see you are quite human after all." Her eyes were enlivened with wit and animation.

92

Jana caught Varian's displeasure with his officer's amicable behavior toward her. She had seen too many people and too much evidence to deny her plight. She wanted to study the quicksilver nature and power of her captor. And, she had an overwhelming urge to pique Varian in some innocent way. To her great satisfaction, it seemed to work.

"I said let's go, Jana. I think you have more important matters to concern yourself with, Lieutenant Dykstra," Varian commanded sternly.

"Yes, Commander. I'll see to Sylva right now, sir," Kyle replied.

Jana thanked Kyle for his concern, then walked out the door. Kyle suppressed the smile from his lips, but not from his eyes.

Varian caught her elbow and firmly guided her along the passageway. They took the elevator to deck one, then went down another passageway. Jana didn't have time to notice her surroundings in the rush. He halted and pressed a button and the door to the gold room swished open.

Varian gallantly stepped aside and waved her in. Jana sighed in relief as she heard the door close. She was startled as Varian's voice severed the silence. "Kyle, turn off this monitor until further notice, except for instructions or messages." Varian breathed deeply and loudly.

"Yes, Commander," came Kyle's apprehensive reply.

Jana anxiously watched the red light on the monitoring camera as it went black. She slowly turned to face Varian. She had not expected him to remain with her. Her eyes leveled on his steady and unreadable gaze. Ten- thirty in the morning was too early for a confrontation, especially on an empty stomach, before a cup of coffee! She waited tensely.

Jana decided to display intelligent respect. After a long and unnerving silence, she ventured a tense "Yes, Commander Saar?"

He stared at her in moody observation. "First of all, Jana, don't try to inspire trouble or resentment aboard my ship. I should warn you of the danger to any man should you successfully turn his sights from duty and loyalty to me, as well as the great danger to yourself. You will wisely restrain yourself from deceiving my crew with false behavior."

Jana flushed with embarrassment and anger beneath his partially astute accusation. "I didn't realize it was dangerous to

93

be polite. Is that all, sir?'' she inquired courteously to calm her agitation.

Varian chuckled skeptically. ''Since your accident prevented you from attending the general assembly yesterday, we have a few matters to settle. You do recall my promise to answer your questions?'' he hinted. ''Hopefully you've learned by now that I'm a man of my word.'' He caught her relief on hearing the purpose for his visit.

''I also hope you'll decide to accept your fate and obey my staff's orders so I won't have to intervene on your behalf again.'' He indicated for her to sit beside him on the sofa. She ignored his directive and sat on the bed across from him. He chuckled mockingly. He noted the way she blushed and shifted uneasily beneath his intense scrutiny. Like a Southern summer night, his voice was lazy and mellow when he spoke. ''I've taken about four hundred women from your planet and around one hundred from the planet Uranus, as Earth was more populated and civilized,'' he asserted. ''The disruptive wench you just observed is Sylva Omanli from Uranus.''

Jana did not intend to question him now about Uranus, for she was more interested in his plans for her. Yet her shock at the large number of captive females was impossible to conceal.

''On this return voyage, all captives will be instructed on the politics, social customs, geography, and history of my world. I hope these lessons will enable each of you to adjust quickly and comfortably to your fates.'' Thinking it better for her to hear his news in a strong and angry mood, he chuckled impiously as he added, ''It will most assuredly increase your value.'' During the last hour, he had realized how gentle she was and he knew he must toughen her for all of their sakes; yet he dreaded doing so.

She stared in bewilderment. ''Our value? I don't follow you. Why educate prisoners? What are your plans for so many women?''

Holding his own disgust in check, Varian quickly outlined the *charl* system as sanctioned by the Supreme Council. Jana's eyes widened as he was speaking. He didn't have simple slavery in mind! Knowing she did not want to hear his answer, she still had to ask, ''Surely you don't intend to sell us and breed us like animals?''

''Children are vital for race survival, Jana. Besides, mates provide our citizens with joy and families. As soon as we reach my galaxy, I'll hold an auction on each of the thirteen planets which I mentioned to you earlier. You'll be sold last on Rigel, our capital planet.''

Her mouth dropped open as she inhaled sharply. "You actually kidnapped us to sell as . . . slave-mates? How can you be so evil?''

"We need women," he stated. "Cooperate, and it will work out.''

Jana stared at him in resentment. Now she understood Sylva's fury. After months of captivity, Sylva knew the truth and still fought its acceptance. They could call it anything they liked, but it was selective breeding. . . . She shuddered. "You can't do this. It's evil and wrong!''

He shook his sable head, wishing she knew the truth about the real reasons behind her capture, and wishing he didn't have to hurt her and use her. "This practice is legal in my galaxy, Jana, and for years was essential to its survival. It was my government, the Supreme Council and Alliance Assembly, who established the *charl* practice. They sent me on this mission. I'm a commander for the Maffei Interplanetary Alliance Star Fleet—our highest form of law enforcement. I am also a member of the Star Fleet Elite Squad, which reports only to the Supreme Council," Varian proudly informed her, wanting to impress her with his great power and status.

This fact settled in quickly. "I should have guessed you are a man of power from your arrogance. But what gives your people the right to enslave others? Or you the right to abduct them?''

"We grant ourselves that right," he responded quietly. "We have the power, skill, and knowledge to do as we wish. When we're threatened by enemies, we conquer them. When we discover a need for survival, we fill it. Soon, we hope there will be no reason to continue this practice," he admitted.

Jana shuddered to think of herself in a satanic alien's clutches.

"You should feel honored, Jana. You're the gem of my collection. You're the most beautiful and tempting creature I have encountered anywhere," he rashly confessed. His smoldering gaze engulfed her beauty and her startled expression.

"Me?" She questioned his incredible statement. "But you claim to have five hundred women on board.''

He laughed as he nodded yes, revealing a beguiling gaze which caused her to flush with warmth. "Does it make you nervous to be ranked as the prize trophy of my assignment?" he teased her.

She was to be sold and used by a stranger! Jana raged at his callous attitude toward her dark future. "You bastard! You sorry excuse for a—"

He frowned as he scolded almost tenderly, "Careful, moon-beam. Your naughty words change nothing." He didn't like the fear and aversion in her eyes. His darkened scowl suddenly dissolved into a compelling smile.

Jana struggled to quell the fury which was raging a battle with desire within her. She had foolishly allowed his good looks and charm to befuddle her. He was a tyrant first, an enchanting man second; she must not confuse their order again. Jana's gaze helplessly traveled his face and body, clad in a snug uniform whose shade intensified the color of his eyes. Nothing could be as dangerous as becoming fascinated with him as a man. Yet how she wished he were like her dream lover . . .

Jana aimlessly paced to dispel her unruly thoughts. It hadn't been wise to sit facing him! He stirred so many strange emotions within her: hatred, terror, rage, desire, and another intense one she could not yet name. She felt at odds with herself trying to comprehend and control all these feelings. Hot tears coursed down her warm cheeks as she berated herself for cowardice and fear. She felt helpless. Jana called, "I'll be back in a minute," then hurried into the bathroom for privacy to vent her torment.

Varian let her go, knowing the brunt of his news had ripped into her heart. But why was he so moved by her anguish? Why didn't he reveal her fate and leave her alone? Why hadn't he sent Martella to carry out this unpleasant task? He leaned back to await her return. If anyone needed him, Kyle knew where he could be found.

Jana sank to the cool tile floor in despair. She lay her head on her folded arms upon the vanity chair. She was doomed. Tears and pain came to her as she thought about her shattered life and lost friends. *But why me? One look at him and his crew and thousands of women would have volunteered to go home with them! Never go home.* She moaned as if in physical pain. She wept for the loss of her home, friends, and world. She cried for the loss of her identity and freedom, elements which slavery would surely deny. She wept for the torment she would endure, for she knew accepting this new existence would be difficult, if not impossible.

"Jana, do you want to finish our talk later?" he asked, unsettled to see how deeply she was suffering.

His intrusion on her grief stopped her tears. She requested a moment to freshen up. She wished he had not seen her in such a weakened state. She must repair her appearance and let him finish his say. To battle him would provoke a long and more painful meeting.

"I'll be waiting," he stated in a pleasant tone.

Within minutes Jana returned. Before she could pass by him, Varian grasped her hand and seated her reluctantly beside him on the sofa. She sat rigid, facing straight ahead. Her aquamarine eyes revealed her inner sadness, her rosy cheeks displayed the strength of her emotions.

His next statement shocked her out of her pensive mood. "It would prove pleasant and beneficial if we were friends instead of foes, Jana. We will be working and living very closely for many weeks. Perhaps a truce?"

Jana jerked her head in his direction and glared at him in disbelief. "Friends? Us?" she taunted sarcastically. "It's utterly impossible!"

"What do you have to gain by being hostile?" he reasoned gently. "I don't want this change to be any harder on you than necessary. I want you to be happy. There's no reason to quarrel or battle all the way home."

"It is *your* home, not mine, Commander Saar. Become friends with the ruthless tyrant who kidnapped and enslaved me? It's totally absurd and insane!" Her eyes glittered with contempt when he chuckled at her words.

Hoping to clarify his character in her mind, she said, "I offered you millions of dollars for my release. Surely you cannot hope to receive more than that for my sale? Why did you refuse?" Jana quivered with alarm as she wondered whose slave she would become. Why sell the "most beautiful and tempting" female he had "ever encountered, anywhere" to another man? She eyed him critically.

"Use that superior brain of yours, Jana," he softly admonished her, guessing her line of thought from her revealing gaze. "What value does your paper money have to me? Besides, I couldn't leave you behind, now could I? To have ignored such rare beauty would surely have been more criminal than my wicked actions," he purred in a lazy, sexy drawl. His sapphire eyes glimmered with an unreadable, disquieting light.

She ignored his last two statements without realizing he had spoken the truth. Her eyes flickered with enlightenment at his first words. "That's why you easily refused so much money. I thought it was because you—"

"You thought what?" he prompted, his curiosity piqued.

"You were super rich."

"I am." He hid his disappointment when she did not say, Because you wanted me. *Kahala* help him because he did! His ruse to feign an attraction to her to entice Ryker's attention had a peril which he had overlooked: she was nearly irresistible. He had assumed he could use her in his scheme without creating a romantic bond between them. Now, he wanted her, and it appeared she wanted him. He had told Martella he would behave badly to prevent Jana from falling in love with him, but did he want to carry out that promise? If he allowed this attraction to strengthen, eventually she would be hurt. Besides, these interrelated missions were hazardous enough without complicating them with a real obsession for her!

She focused curious eyes on him. "Then why all this?"

"I'm a Star Fleet officer, Jana. I have a duty to my Alliance Force and Supreme Council. The plague," he gently reminded her. Their eyes met. He laid his arm across the top of the sofa and watched her intently.

An idea came to Jana's mind. "Is there any way I can earn my freedom since my money has no value to you?" She missed the astonished look which lit his eyes when he misconstrued her question and meaning.

"Are you so desperate to avoid the pampered life of an elite *charl* that you would offer yourself to your captor?" he asked in astonishment. Would the Council chastise him for taking this woman as a temporary mistress, if he dared to lie and claim it was part of this trap for Ryker? He instantly scolded himself. He could not do that to himself, his government, or to Jana! Far worse was the suspicion that he would be unable to part with her afterward, and if he didn't defeat Ryker, Jana would be in mortal danger from that evil bastard.

She gasped, "You thought I— Never! I was referring to work, not whoredom!" she finished in heated anger.

He chuckled to hide his feelings. "A natural mistake. After all, what else could you do aboard a ship of mostly men to earn such a large amount of money?" As he spoke, he twirled a lock of her silky hair around his finger.

She pulled it from his feather-light grasp and snapped, "I could work as Tristan's assistant," she informed him. "He said he needed help."

"You could what?" he asked, wondering what those two had connived during their brief contact in sick bay.

"I can learn everything about your world. Tristan believes I have the skill and competence. Ask him!" she boldly challenged.

At a loss for an appropriate answer, he taunted, "So now it's Tristan, is it? First Kyle, now Tristan. You do work fast, don't you? Who's next?"

She rose in anger. "You don't believe I can do it, do you?"

"I'm well aware of your great capabilities, Jana. I probably know you better than you know yourself."

"Then why do you continue to harass me?" she asked.

"Perhaps because I love to see flames dance and sparkle in those *caritrary* eyes when you're very angry," he murmured huskily.

"*Caritrary*?" she questioned, enchanted by his magical gaze.

"It's a precious gem found on the planet Caguas. It's a fusion of green, blue, and lavender. It changes color according to heat and light. It's rare and valuable, like you. I've never seen anyone with eyes this color." He caressed the area just below her left eye as he mentally sank into those colorful pools.

"I'm rare and valuable?" she inquired, unable to quell her feminine curiosity and vanity. She was lost in the depths of his bewitching eyes.

He smiled, then shook his head to regain control of his wits. "Take my word for it. I'm considered a connoisseur, as you will no doubt learn."

She unthinkingly concurred, "I'm quite certain you are."

They stared into each other's eyes for a long time. "I take it you aren't married?"

His hand reached out again to caress her cheek. For a heart-stopping moment, she thought he was going to kiss her. She secretly and unexplainably wished he would. But he did not, nor did he answer her last question.

Jana shook her head to clear her crazy thoughts. He was most disarming. "Do you ever take men as slaves?"

"When we first allowed alien societies to enter our world, it nearly proved fatal to some of our outlying planets when a dissident male scientist created the virus which devastated my world by killing off so many women. He did it intentionally: no women equal no offspring and eventual death to an entire race. Thankfully he failed. Never again will we be so foolish, trusting, or kindhearted. Tris should have known better than to suggest you could work with him; the Council would never allow it."

She listened, trying to puzzle out this strange and complex man. His moods were hard to fathom. If the situation were different, she would think him overwhelmingly appealing. He put every man she had ever met to shame. "So that's why you're afraid to let me work in Dr. Zarcoff's lab. If you know me as well as you claim, surely you realize I would never do such an evil thing, in spite of your abduction of me."

Varian observed the way her gaze roved his features and frame. Her darkened eyes and parted lips left no doubts as to her train of thought. He dismissed the temptation to point this out to her or to take advantage of it. She was most assuredly unaware of her own thoughts and actions. "Do I look like a man who fears anyone or anything?" he probed, and she shook her head.

Varian had leaned toward her and was smiling. His fingertip playfully traveled down the bridge of her nose and teased around and then over her satiny lips as he said, "Don't worry about being bored, Dr. Greyson. You'll have plenty of studies to occupy your time and energies. You're already two days behind your group." He lifted a curl and tickled her nose and chin with it. "Perhaps you prefer my private tutoring?"

Spellbound, Jana smiled and she could not resist lifting her hand to caress his compelling face. The contact between them was intoxicating, as was his intense gaze. Her fingers roamed his striking features, but it was his mouth which enthralled her. Unable to stop herself as in her two dreams, her hand slipped around his neck and drew his head downward. The moment their mouths met they embraced and kissed feverishly. What little control she had retained during the last few minutes was lost. Several long kisses ensued. When his lips trailed to her ear, she murmured dreamily, "I knew you couldn't be evil. I knew you couldn't sell me."

Varian realized his error and stiffened. At last he spoke to dispel the heated aura surrounding them, an aura of intense passion which was rapidly becoming very uncomfortable and alarming to him. "Perhaps I had better set the record straight, Jana. All *charls* are off limits. No one has permission to touch you in any way. To do so is a violation of my strictest orders. Be careful how you behave around my men. I wouldn't want you tempting them like you just did me. From your surveillance tapes before your capture, I hadn't noticed you were a seductress. I won't make that mistake again. Do you understand me?"

Recovering her wits and poise, Jana's face flushed red. "Pardon me if I misunderstood your provocative behavior, Commander Saar. It seemed as if you were the one enticing me. You, sir, are most contradictory."

He cautioned, "Watch yourself, Jana. My crew members are normally loyal and wise, but you are a very tempting female. Women often do vengeful things without ever stopping to think of their tragic consequences." His tone was almost accusatory and most insulting.

"I don't care to be a temptation to any of your men," she retaliated, then added, "Nor to you, sir." He chuckled humorously, his blue eyes taunting her. "Tyrants, roguish criminals, and evil kidnappers have never held any interest for me, so you need not fear my temptation or advances!" she vowed, her own eyes filled with fiery, dancing lights.

His chest rumbled with amused laughter. "You don't say? Tell me, Jana, you honestly don't find me the least bit tempting and attractive, not even when you kissed me moments ago or when you flirted with me while you were dazed in sick bay?"

She shielded her guilty gaze with lowered lashes. "Those were mistakes. How could I possibly find a man like you the least bit tempting or alluring?"

"You forgot attractive and charming, didn't you? Tyrant and rogue, am I?" he jested. He shoved the straying lock of hair from his forehead.

"I find gentlemen with manners more appealing than barbaric rogues!"

"Like your Alex?" Varian taunted mischievously. "I know everything about you. Forget him, my love. It's unwise and futile to pine for a lost lover, especially one as unreachable and unworthy as your Alex McKenzie."

"He isn't my Alex, and I am not your love!" she snapped sharply, oblivious to the cause of her sudden fury: that potently enticing aura of his.

"And that distresses you, little moonbeam? Is that why you asked if I was married? Is that why you were trying to bewitch me?"

"You egotistical, asinine rogue! You must think every woman you meet will be struck dumb and speechless by your fantastic looks and abundant charms! Don't hold your breath where I'm concerned, Commander! I find you totally disgusting and repulsive! I pray you won't be tempted to keep your *gem*, your *prized trophy*! I would just as soon be enslaved to some vile demon as to a bastard like you."

Varian captured her face between his hands and forced her to look at him while he responded deceitfully. "There are those who vow I pass for a devil. An experiment can be arranged to test the validity of your claim. I know several men who can truly qualify as the vile demons. Would you care to discover if you prefer their company over mine, little moonbeam?"

It was foolish of her to taunt him with her very existence. He was not a man to challenge or call a bluff of this magnitude. She promptly backed down. "I'm sorry. I spoke rashly and stupidly. Please don't—" Tears filled her terrified eyes. Had she pushed him too far?

Varian was flooded with unexpected pangs of tenderness and remorse toward her. He gazed into her frightened eyes and said, "I was only teasing, Jana. I'm sorry; that wasn't kind or fair. I have no intentions of destroying a lovely flower in such a brutal and unforgivable manner, not even to prove to you I have the power to do so. However, I might be tempted to do so if you pull another stunt like you did yesterday," he warned in a light tone as he held up his bruised hand. "Try not to brand me again."

She pinkened, but vowed softly, "I promise . . ."

"Then we understand each other?" he inquired. She nodded yes with doubtful eyes. "Any questions or comments?" he probed.

"None that would change anything," she murmured.

"There will be another conference at five o'clock, in two hours."

"Is friendship among the captives off limits too?"

"Not if it doesn't interfere with your training. You might be helpful with some of the others," he remarked mysteriously, then threw her a husky "See you later" and a devastating half smile. He grinned as he left, having noticed the way she had flushed red.

Jana glanced at the camera; no red light or response to her call. She checked the servo for a meal. Perhaps her guard would return soon. Minutes later Jana was almost dozing in a bubble bath when the door swished open and Varian entered. Jana squealed and sank to her chin in the concealing water. She stared furiously at him.

Varian set a tray by the tub, hunkered down, and grinned roguishly. "I recalled you hadn't eaten and didn't have your monitor on. See you later."

Jana watched him depart without a backward glance. Would that man never cease to amaze and confound her! As she ate, Jana bathed, then dressed in a pink silk dirndl whose soft hue complemented her tanned complexion and sunny hair. After she had completed her makeup and fixed her hair, she turned from side to side to view herself. The midcalf-length dress revealed slender and shapely ankles. She quickly finished her grooming by dabbing on a hint of subtle fragrance here and there.

Her captor's handsome image stayed in her mind as she recalled his many compliments. If she had to become a *charl*, why not Varian Saar's! There were similarities in their backgrounds and stations. If she must live and mate with an alien male and bear his children, who better than that virile and intoxicating man! Jana finished dressing just in time. The signal was given. Another moment of truth had finally arrived.

Chapter Six

Jana's door opened. Voices reached her alert ears. She peeked into the passageway, where eight officers were talking and waiting for the women's arrivals. She studied the varying colors and markings of their uniforms.

Tristan caught sight of Jana and motioned her to join him. "The conference will be held in this room, Jana. Let's go inside and find you a seat before the others in your training group arrive. They've been quartered on lower decks."

The officers entered and claimed seats at the head table. Jana was placed in the front row of five lines of chairs. The room filled with females, each wearing buff-colored tunics and pants. There wasn't time to speak to them. The female officer in blue immediately began the business at hand. Martella smiled and remarked, "I'm glad to see most of you have decided to cooperate. As you'll recall, I'm Lieutenant Martella Karsh. I'm responsible for your conduct and training. To refresh memories and to enlighten the newest member of our group, I'll review your instructions and introduce the crew members who will assist this group." Jana flushed as all eyes seemed to focus on her when Martella said, "This is Jana Greyson of West Columbia, Texas. An accident prevented her attendance yesterday."

Martella addressed Jana directly. "Jana, this is Kathy Anderson from California; Stephanie Rojohn from New York; Heather Langdon from Utah; and Susan Robinson from Massachusetts." Martella began with her row and continued down all five until the females had been introduced to each other. When she finished, Martella said, "Please take the same seat each time you're here. It will help all of us with names and faces."

Jana observed the first four females who were introduced. Kathy appeared shy and modest; Stephanie, hostile and scornful; Heather, simple and childlike; and Susan, sexy and vain.

Kathy and Heather readily accepted Jana's late arrival and presence, but Stephanie and Susan coldly scrutinized her as if they challenged her right to sit in the same room.

The crew members patiently awaited their introductions. Each one rose as Martella called a name, rank, and task; then sat down. Jana's acquaintance with Tristan and Kyle was revealed by smiles. Even Ferris flashed her a blithe grin, though it seemed to her as if Kathy claimed his eye.

"I will give each of you a schedule," Martella said. "The wall clocks have been marked for your assistance. You will report to this area for all conferences and accompany the crew member listed on your schedule. You will avoid any area not marked on your sheet. Unless you have a class, remain in your room or the closest rec room. You must study and learn the materials supplied in your language. I will caution you to get along with your roommates and to be considerate of their schedules and feelings."

Martella's eyes slipped over her attentive group. "Beginning tomorrow, a group of five will have dinner here each night with one or more officers. The front row will be first, then continue backward with each line. We'll also provide other social occasions to give you an opportunity to practice etiquette and social graces. I will caution you once more—no enmity will be tolerated among you. You will conduct yourselves accordingly. Any troublemaker will be severely punished."

Before Martella could resume her instructions, the corridor door swished open to reveal the towering, agile physique of a man. He was dressed in a dove gray uniform with three gold stripes between two stars near each wrist and an emblem of a golden sunburst over his left chest muscle.

Although he was wearing a concealing vizard over his face, Jana knew from his self-assured stride who had just entered the room. She pondered the reactions of her fellow captives if he should remove that visor. Could it be possible that only she knew what fatal magic was hidden there? This honor was perplexing.

That undeniable aura of great power and command filled the large room. Jana's heart gave a flutter at his dynamic presence. She hastily attributed her strange reaction to tension, fear, and her secret insight.

A hushed silence had settled around them at his arrival.

"Please continue, Lieutenant Karsh," he ordered. His rich voice was enough to spark images of intense masculinity and virile prowess in the minds of the women. He casually leaned against the wall.

Susan leaned forward and rested her elbows on her thighs, then propped her chin on interlocking fingers. Jana witnessed the spark which flamed in the blue gaze of Susan Robinson as it lustfully devoured the virile physique before her, causing a light flushing of desire to splash across Susan's cheeks. She suggestively passed her moist pink tongue over her lips in a provocative manner, issuing an invitation a near-blind man could read!

The eyes of the other girls kept straying to Jana or the man beyond her. She tried to focus on Martella's words and face, but the knowledge of Varian's proximity kept interfering with her concentration.

"The man at the door is Varian Saar, commander of the *Wanderlust*."

When Varian stepped forward and rested his hand on Jana's left shoulder, it caused her to start. His visor earned its two-fold purpose—his emotions and observations could be kept a secret while his appearance could have no distracting effect on the women. That is, no effect on anyone except Jana, who was well aware of the perfection which was hidden there.

Jana tried to shift unnoticeably from under his gentle grasp, but this only served to bring on a more embarrassing and soul-tingling action. As she twisted sideways to force his hand to fall away, he surprised her by sliding his hand beneath her long tawny hair and fondling her slender neck. She flushed a bright, warm pink as he continued to caress her soft flesh and silky hair as if this act were unconscious, which she surmised it was not. Jana tried to quell the trembling in her body at his touch. Damn him! Why was he doing this to her? Hadn't he recently scolded her for playing a tempting seductress? What did he call his own actions?

Varian briefly addressed the captives. "I will not tolerate defiance or disruption. Peace between you women and the crew will depend solely on your own behavior. I advise against any perilous course of action and demand your full cooperation. Martella, the ladies are all yours."

The remainder of the meeting passed swiftly. They were

dismissed to return to their quarters, their classes to begin in the morning. As Susan passed Jana, blue eyes coldly scanned her, and she murmured, "I wonder how a slave earns pretty clothes and the attention of her master. You seem to have made a rapid and curious impression on these men."

Back in her quarters, Jana futilely searched for a similar beige uniform to prevent further ill feeling. While she ate, she pondered her privileged position: private quarters, lovely clothes, and Varian's attention. This special treatment mystified her. After dinner, still searching for an explanation, Jana glanced through her booklets until her eyes grew heavy and sleep claimed her.

The next morning, Jana arrived for her lessons dressed in a sapphire jumpsuit, which stood out among the tan uniforms. Jana concentrated on her instructor. She found the lesson exhilarating yet frightening as she heard a brief history of their new galaxy. There would be more detailed lessons on a rotating schedule in the days to come. She would be well acquainted with their culture before she arrived in their world. Her other morning class was on psychology and sociology. She was amazed by the differences and similarities between the two alien races. This class would definitely prove informative and important to her future.

Later Jana sat in a light daze on her own sofa to assimilate the facts she had acquired in class today. There had been no time for getting acquainted with the other women. She checked her schedule for the location of their coming meal: the meeting room. With surprise, she noticed "Recreation and Relaxation" listed afterward. She smiled humorously, as it would not be all work and no play. But perhaps she'd get a chance to exchange some private words with the other captives.

Possibly this recreation was ordered to teach the dances, games, and social activities Martella had mentioned. The commander was certainly carrying out his statement about training them to fit into his society. She couldn't help wondering if Varian would grace them with his presence at dinner. She instantly banished the excitement such forbidden thoughts inspired, and when the signal was given for dinner, she made a poised entrance. She was wearing a pale aqua Grecian-styled gown. She chided herself for the great pains she had taken with her grooming for tonight.

Her honey-colored hair captured reflections of light and brought the natural platinum streaks to life. It swayed provocatively as she moved. The aqua coloring of her gown intensified the golden glow of her skin and hair. It blended harmoniously with her aquamarine eyes, which sparkled with pleasure at the sight of Tristan coming forward to greet her.

Tristan made a deep bow as he asked, "Would you be so kind as to be my dinner companion this evening?"

Jana smiled and nodded her head in assent. "You don't know how glad I am to find you here tonight," she confessed, then changed the subject. "Tell me, how is our furry patient doing? Did he survive my surgery?"

A sarcastic voice inquired, "Am I interrupting a private tête-à-tête?"

"Please feel free to join us," Jana politely answered, assuming Susan Robinson would do so even without her invitation. No doubt the vixen was fuming because of the difference in their wardrobes again!

"What kind of accident caused your late arrival? And how do you rate a gorgeous aqua gown when the rest of us have to wear the same style and color—this drab peach?" Her baneful tone stunned Jana into momentary silence.

Tristan gallantly filled in while Jana recovered. "Jana had a fall. She was confined to sick bay for two days."

Susan scornfully ignored the middle-aged doctor as she said, "I see you've suffered no ill effects from your accident. In fact, from the attention you're receiving, I would venture you've made a head start on *friendship* with several of the crew members."

"Tris, I've not had the pleasure of meeting Dr. Greyson," a masculine voice cunningly injected just in time to curb Susan's scornful retort.

"Dr. Jana Greyson, Lieutenant Commander Nigel Sanger."

"Delighted to finally meet you, Jana," he informed her. Jana nodded and responded courteously. His amicable smile revealed two compelling dimples. "At socials, we go by first names. Call me Nigel."

Both men caught the countless daggers Susan sent in Jana's direction at Nigel's attention toward Jana instead of her. It took great self-control for the two men to keep from chuckling aloud.

Just then the call for dinner was given. Tristan took Jana's arm to lead her to the table. Before he could follow, Nigel's arm was captured possessively by Susan. He had no polite choice but to lead her to the table and seat her. Susan was visibly annoyed when he did not take the chair next to her.

Martella was seated at one end of the oblong table. She called out the names and ranks of the strangers present and the first names of those persons they had met previously. While she began the introductions to her right, Jana heard the door behind her open, then close. Another grand entrance for our dauntless commander no doubt, she mused in secret humor. Susan's sharp intake of air caught everyone's attention. Susan was staring at the latecomer. A sultry smile played provocatively across the redhead's features. Her blue eyes sparkled with lust and warmth. Jana half turned in her seat. Yes, she had accurately guessed the reason for the furor.

Jana's eyes were drawn to Varian in his rich wine uniform trimmed in gold. The snug suit molded his enviable frame, revealing its perfect contours. His physique was sleek and hard, with well-toned muscles and appealing angles. His eyes were as blue and sparkly as tropical waters; his teeth were as white as clouds. Polished jet was no darker or shinier than his wavy hair. His skin was the color of golden sherry. The chest hair exposed by his V-neck suit was as dark and silky as his ebony head. So much character and personality were displayed in his bearing and confident expression. Clearly he possessed great force. This was a man who knew he was invincible and savored it. No doubt he could make the heavens tremble with the sheer force of his iron will. Yes, Varian Saar embodied power and passion. Jana pulled her gaze from the intoxicating image as those strange emotions broke free and ran wild inside her.

"Good evening," Varian cheerfully greeted them as he came forward in his confident stride, a devastating smile upon his parted lips.

Martella Karsh jovially quipped, "I'm sure you're all acquainted with Commander Saar. If not by sight, then definitely by sound."

What a magnetic sight he presented, Jana admitted. The captives' reactions told Jana this was the first time they had viewed his magnificent features. It was easy to judge his effect on Susan Robinson; Jana fumed irrationally at the way that vixen's eyes never left his face or frame.

Varian seated himself at the end of the table, next to Jana. He began to his left as he spoke to each person, leaving Jana until last. He made light, genial conversation with his crew and polite comments to the young women.

Kathy Anderson was too absorbed with the officer beside her to find a petrifying force like Varian Saar enchanting. The bewitched Ferris Laus was as nervous and timid as he was delighted, just as Kathy was.

Susan was a different story. She did not try to hide or control the desire in her eyes and voice. Her bold look and sultry body language spoke of her skills and knowledge in the arts of seduction. Varian seemed to enjoy Susan's interest.

Stephanie Rojohn viewed Varian's charm with contempt. Before her sat the epitome of woman's downfall, a man who possessed the skill to make a woman his willing slave, then callously spurn her for that weakness. She had seen and despised his type many times before, but never in such a formidable opponent. For this, she hated him all the more.

Jana forced her attention on Tristan, trying to drown out the disturbing situation. She could not rationalize her own emotions. Why should she even care how they acted? Jana suppressed the irritating and bewildering feelings deep within her mind. She sipped on the wine they had been served, allowing its strength to relax her inner tensions and soothe her frayed nerves.

When Varian came to Heather Langdon, the young girl from Utah, she giggled and squirmed like a teenager on her first date. Her soft voice stuttered as she nervously replied to his light banter. Her doe eyes glowed under his warm gaze and attention.

Jana observed her for a while. Heather was like a pixie, she decided with a smile. She watched Heather sigh and melt under Varian's charm. Jana's smile faded as she pictured this gentle child as *charl* to some alien male. Such a travesty was unforgivable. Anger filled Jana's eyes as she pondered their fates. She had noticed Tesla Rilke's close scrutiny and genial manner toward Heather. Jana wondered why he had been telling the impressionable girl so much about his brother Spala. If *charls* were "off limits," why did it seem to her as if Ferris Laus was staking his claim on Kathy, and Tesla Rilke was doing the same with Heather for his brother!

110

Jana glanced at Varian as she tried to comprehend why he had kidnapped such a childlike female. Varian had spoken with Tristan while she had been lost in her own thoughts. Now she found his Prussian blue eyes and full attention on her as she looked his way. She flushed uncontrollably and lowered her lashes as she pretended to retrieve her wine glass with trembling fingers.

Damn, how she wished she could overcome this humiliating, aggravating habit of blushing. If only she could learn how to control it or stop it. She felt like a fool, a silly, green girl. Blushing before Varian vexed her. It seemed to give him some private insight into her thoughts. But one could not stifle an automatic, instinctive process of the human body. Why did Varian smell so good! Why did he have to sit beside her?

"No warm greeting for me, Jana?" he coaxed just above a whisper.

She bravely met his mocking gaze. "Good evening, Commander."

"Is that the best you can do, Jana? I thought you were accustomed to social dinners and light repartee," Varian reproved her with a beguiling grin.

"It should be apparent to someone of your great insight that I've never found myself in a similar predicament. In my sheltered life, I have not been asked to entertain enemies. Surely your excellent breeding will allow me time to adjust to this change in my lifestyle?"

Kahala, if she wasn't a vital force—amusing, exhilarating, and intoxicating! What a fascinating mistress she would make. "And what if I'm totally lacking in good breeding?"

"And what if the sun turns blue tomorrow?" she saucily parried, then perceptively added, "Perhaps that quirk of nature exists in your world."

He chuckled. "I'm not certain, but I think you just complimented me."

She smiled innocently. "Really? Why would I do such a ridiculous thing? Perhaps you're having trouble with English or a bad audiotranslator."

"I know we got off on the wrong foot, but do you find honesty so difficult?" Varian inquired with a rakish gleam in his sapphire eyes.

"Honesty, no. Silly small talk, yes."

111

He understood the point she was subtly making. "Everyone has their place in the scheme of things, Jana. Each woman, despite her flaws, is desired by a man of similar character. Myself, I prefer a woman who is . . ."

Jana was suddenly alert. He noted her interest and quickly dashed her hopes. "But of course you couldn't be interested in my preferences."

"I think I have an idea of how your taste in women runs." She gave herself away when she unconsciously glanced in Susan's direction.

Varian chuckled and shook his head. "You would have found my answer surprising. You underestimate my tastes. Right, Kara?"

Second Lieutenant Kara Curri, the ship's recreational and physical training officer, was a bright and witty Maffeian who possessed good looks, money, the man she loved, a pleasant and important job, and a good reputation. Kara laughed and responded, "Very choosy, just like my beloved Dario."

The two officers grinned in mutual admiration. Jana secretly delighted in viewing this easygoing side of Varian Saar. She wanted it to continue a while longer so she could study him. "And who is this lucky young man, Kara?" Jana asked to encourage the gay chatter which seemed to lessen her tension.

"Dario Rhur, whom Varian left behind during this assignment," Kara said with a pretty pout. "He doesn't want to lose two good officers to marriage so he's trying to keep us separated as much as possible," she jested.

"How cruel and heartless, Commander," Jana softly rebuked him as if it were the most natural thing in the world to do.

Varian grinned at her relaxed manner. "I see. You two conspiring against me, are you? Shall I charge you both with mutiny?" He chuckled and added, "No need to fret or fuss. Dario will join us soon. We'll be picking up the rest of our crew along the way home."

Kara recognized the reasons for Jana's high praise from Tristan and Martella. She grimaced as she thought of this enchanting creature as a *charl*. Jana should choose her own mate, as she had done. Only the survival of Kara's world could justify such an action.

Jana found it natural and easy to like Kara Curri on the spot.

The Maffeian woman reminded her of Andrea. Andrea McKay . . . With this remembrance came a surge of despondency and homesickness. What was her friend thinking and doing? Jana lowered her head as she struggled to conceal her torment. She brushed at the unbidden moisture which threatened to break loose from the corners of her eyes at any time.

Kara secretly nudged Varian, her eyes darting toward Jana. Something had suddenly dampened her spirits and brought sadness to her eyes. Varian leaned toward Jana and whispered to her. Under the protection of their close contact, he softly murmured, "Dry your eyes, Jana love. Emotions of such depth are private. I don't think you wish to share your innermost feelings with the others. Is something wrong?"

Jana lifted grateful eyes to his gentle ones. "You're right. It's just that Kara reminds me of Andrea, my best friend. When I think—" Her lips and chin quivered and more tears threatened to come forth.

Susan spoke up at that precise moment. "It's very rude to dominate the commander's full attention, Jana dear. Please don't bore him."

A protective urge gripped him. "Jana has something in her eye." He smiled as he pulled her to her feet and toward a lamp across the room. He lifted her trembling chin with his left hand. His right hand tenderly pushed her hair aside. He stared intently into her misty gaze.

"She certainly does, a starship commander," Susan said with a sneer. Kyle flashed Susan a withering look. "Sorry. I forgot she has *friends* in high places," she continued hatefully.

"That would be wise to remember," Kyle snapped in an ominous tone.

The other officers present observed this curious drama with great interest, particularly one of the lieutenants. He lifted his right hand and pretended to be mopping away perspiration above his upper lip. His thumb pressed the tiny button on the inside of his ring several times as he prayed the miniature camera inside of it was getting clear pictures of Jana and Varian. These pictures would be priceless weapons he could use to appease Ryker's and Canissia's blackmail threats. He despised being forced to betray his commander, but he had no other choice. But he had no doubt Ryker would soon slay Canissia, just as he had no doubt Varian could slay his satanic half

113

brother in their next fight. Surely when news of the real love affair between Varian and Jana provoked that devil to challenge Varian, Ryker's defeat would free him of this treacherous episode.

Varian used his napkin to dry Jana's tears as their eyes held each other captive. This tenderness increased her forbidden feelings. At this moment, he seemed like the most sensitive and compassionate man alive.

The verbal attack from Susan had instilled new determination. Jana smiled in gratitude. "I'm fine now, Varian. Thank you."

The way she had spoken his name was like a soft, loving caress. He smiled. "My pleasure, little moonbeam," he murmured huskily. If not for his audience, he would have pulled her into his arms and kissed her soundly.

Still dazed, she returned to the table where she conversed with Tristan on research and medicine over dinner. It was a constant struggle to ignore Varian and his increasing effect on her.

Later Martella said Kara would be in charge of the rest of the evening and Jana was mildly surprised to find herself alone with Tesla Rilke and Nigel Sanger. She shifted nervously as she glanced at the two strangers in the empty room. Nigel returned from a side cabinet with an oblong brown box.

Tesla called her to a side table and told her to be seated. He opened the box. "It's called *Laius*. You have a similar game called chess."

A half smile appeared across her lips as she gazed at the board and figures, relieved to learn what sport this evening would entail. She could only pray Varian had spoken the truth about no intimate contact between her and the crew. She knew all too well that she was totally at the mercy of these men and their complex leader.

On seeing her grin, Tesla commented, "I would venture you're going to challenge me, Jana. If you beat me, you can play Nigel. But I will warn you in advance, he is the best on board." He and Nigel exchanged genial grins.

Jana nodded respectfully in Nigel's direction. "What is Tesla's rating?"

"About number three, I would say."

"Who is number two?" she asked curiously.

114

"Commander Saar," came the reply she wanted.

Jana brightened. If she could learn to beat Nigel, she could probably beat Varian. First, she had to beat Tesla. She knew she was good at chess, but was she skilled enough to take him in *Laius*? Time would tell.

As he set the pieces in their appointed squares on the board, Jana recalled her father teaching her chess when she was nine. Until his death, they had kept a running competition, managing to swap victories evenly. Jana shook her head as if to clear the painful reminders of the past away. She would not share her grief or personal life with these two strangers.

She directed her full attention to the board in front of her while Tesla Rilke explained the game to her. He was very skilled and the game progressed slowly for a long time. But Jana caught on very quickly. They had been playing for about fifty minutes when Tesla made an error in judgment. He thought to lure Jana into a trap. Instead, she cunningly captured a vital piece he had failed to protect. With it out of circulation, the game was over rapidly. The navigational officer looked at Jana with new respect. "Careful, Nigel, this woman is a crafty opponent."

Jana took a short break while Nigel set up the board for their match. Jana's confidence had been boosted by her victory. When she rejoined them, Tesla handed her a glass of wine. She grinned and accused in a witty tone, "Trying to dull my wits, Tesla? How very unsportsmanlike," she teased as the friendly rapport grew among the three of them.

They all laughed as Tesla retorted, "Nigel needs all the help he can get to beat you. Give her the blue men, Nigel. Perhaps red is her lucky color. It would not do for you to knock over our ship's champion."

She glanced up at Tesla to see how he meant that last statement. His grinning face told her the remark was innocently given. "Running scared?" She impishly mocked his genial warning to Nigel. Tesla nodded and grinned.

"How would it look if you whipped the *Wanderlust*'s first officer?"

Jana smiled at Nigel. "The same way it looks for the first officer to whip the ship's commander."

The game began with vigilance on both sides. For an hour the game proceeded evenly, then Stephanie Rojohn returned.

Her skin was glistening with beads of perspiration from her game of *forsha*, the Maffei version of tennis.

Jana glanced up into her sullen face. Stephanie glared at the man across the table from Jana, then at the other one standing close by. Her features were an ugly mask of inner rage. "Is something wrong, Stephanie?" Jana asked.

Stephanie curled her lips into a snarl. "What could possibly be wrong? We're sweetly playing games and politely dining with the bastards abducting us! We're stupid, cowardly fools! Why allow them to intimidate, humiliate, and enslave us this way?" she shouted in rising fury. "This ship is full of women, free and captive. We could kill these sons of bitches and escape!"

"Stephanie!" Jana shrieked in alarm, suddenly afraid for the distraught woman.

The door opened. Stephanie was seized by two security guards in crimson uniforms. She fought like a demon-possessed maniac. She kicked, slapped, and clawed as she alternately screamed and cursed them. The two guards struggled with the enormous strength of the enraged captive.

Jana watched in wide-eyed alarm when Tristan rushed in and sedated the thrashing woman. The men lifted her limp body and carried her away. "What happened, Tris?" Jana inquired as if she had the right to ask and be answered.

"Seems Stephanie is very competitive and hostile to males who beat her in sports. You should have seen her light into Baruch! She was ordered to her quarters. The guards were to make certain she obeyed." Tristan knew what this second rebellion would inspire: intimidation by *scarfelli* . . .

"All that fighting over a lost game?" Jana inquired skeptically. "Surely there must be more to it. Will she be punished?"

"I imagine so. The others said she just seemed to go berserk when he won. Could be a case of nerves from tension and fear. Relax, Jana, it cannot be helped. She was warned plenty of times. It won't be a good example for the others if she gets away with something like this. She scratched Baruch pretty badly. I have to go tend him now. See you later."

"How would you men feel in her place—kidnapped, intimidated, enslaved? Taken from your home? She deserves understanding and leniency." Jana pushed her chair away from the table and stood on trembling legs. "I'm sorry, Nigel. May I be excused now? I'm really very tired," she said quietly.

116

Nigel scanned her tense features. She seemed overly anxious to be alone. "I'll see you tomorrow. I believe I have you for a science lesson."

"Fine," she answered absently. "See you tomorrow." She fled to her room and as quickly as possible was in her bed. After the lights had been lowered, she relived the entire terrifying episode.

The path and choice were clear: either they could be submissive or be punished. But even enduring punishment would not alter their fate. It could make their final fate worse; Varian could sell any of them to horrible men, as he had jokingly threatened with her. Wasn't his goodwill more important at this time than foolish, misplaced pride? Dangerous pride which they could not afford?

The haunting question was, had she been too friendly and submissive, as Stephanie had implied? But there was no turning back now. It was accept and endure, or . . . What were their alternatives, if any? Tears ran freely from her eyes as she cried herself to sleep.

The morning signal was given. Jana gradually sat up and stretched. How she dearly missed the bright, warm sunlight streaming through her bedroom windows; the birds cheerfully singing and twittering to herald the new day; the crisp, fragrant breeze which caused her wind chimes to tinkle; the vast periwinkle spread which covered the Texas skies this time of year; and her morning rides on Apache.

Apache . . . what would happen to her stallion? What would they do with him? With her home? Her personal things? They had no right to abduct her and take her away from her home and friends.

Jana angrily threw the covers aside and headed for the bathroom. Fury was curbed only by the instinctive caution which invaded her. She bathed, dressed, and quickly ate, then paced nervously until her door was opened. She joined Kathy, Susan, and Heather in the scheduled meeting room. She glanced toward Stephanie's empty chair.

Susan stated flatly, "She's confined to her room," then immediately pursued another topic. "What was your assignment last night, Jana?"

117

Jana knew Susan was not truly interested, but she politely answered, "I played *Laius* with Tesla and Nigel. It's kind of like chess."

"Chess," Susan cooed. "One of those brainy games. Kathy gave a ballet recital while Heather tried to win a gold medal in swimming."

"And what did you do, Susan?" Kathy asked the question Susan wanted.

"I played strip poker with Varian," Susan purred. The other women exchanged doubtful looks. Susan asked, "You all know he was not with any of you last night. Just where do you think he was?"

"Flying the ship!" Heather challenged her.

"Flying this ship when he has numerous beautiful captives on board, women at his very beck and call?" Susan said sarcastically, sneering.

"And so willing and eager, I'm sure," Heather retorted.

Susan observed how three of them had attracted the attention of the crew. "But why set your eyes and goals on the crew when their leader is more virile and handsome? It would be wiser to have him as your *friend*."

"I doubt if 'friend' is what you have in mind," Heather angrily snapped.

Susan smiled. "If one of us is to warm his bed, why not me? He might prove most generous to his personal slave. He might even decide to keep her around if she proves . . . entertaining and pleasing, shall we say? You are as dumb and naïve as you look, Heather."

Kathy glared at Susan. "Such a chore should prove easy for you. No doubt your vast experience will prove valuable to both of you. As for myself, I'll never behave like some cheap whore!"

"I saw you melt over that security man, giving him the hots for you." Susan's eyes boldly challenged Jana to deny or admit her rivalry for Varian.

When Susan refused to back off, Jana spoke up, "Don't look at me, Susan. You're welcome to the commander. I fully agree with Kathy. I prefer to be his reluctant prisoner, not his temporary whore."

"How do you know which you would prefer? Have you

already sampled both possibilities? What caused your little 'accident' and tardy appearance? Perhaps a case of rape or willing seduction?'' Susan taunted acidly.

Jana rose angrily, knocking over her chair. "You foul-mouthed witch! Keep your crude thoughts to yourself!''

"Petty squabbles so early in the morning, ladies?'' Varian's lazy drawl inquired from the doorway. "What seems to be the problem?'' Varian glanced from one woman to the other as he waited for their answers. From Jana's expression and shocking words, Susan must have said something which upset her greatly. When no reply came, he asked in a stern tone, "I asked what the problem was.'' His tone was edged with steel.

Susan lied smoothly. "Jana was upset over your treatment of Stephanie. I was only trying to convince her that Stephanie brought it on herself. Jana disagreed with me, that's all.''

Varian noted the incredulous looks on the faces of the other women which belied Susan's explanation. Kathy's mouth flew open to set the record straight, to defend the silent Jana. But Jana caught her eye and signaled no. Kathy reluctantly kept silent. Varian realized she fervently wanted to come to Jana's defense, but Jana did not want the truth revealed. Evidently it had something to do with him. . . . He would uncover the truth later.

Varian asked, "Jana, do you have anything to say for yourself?''

She gritted her teeth determinedly and met his piercing gaze. "No, Commander, I do not.''

"I see. I suggest you two call a truce and behave yourselves in the future. I do not permit spiteful, childish squabbles among my passengers. There are more important matters to take up your time and energy. Do I make myself perfectly clear?''

Susan purred silkily, "Yes, Commander. I'll do whatever you wish.'' Her double entendre was clear, as well as her triumphant sneer at Jana.

Varian ignored her. "Jana?'' he prompted and she nodded. "See that you both obey. Punishments for insolence can be very painful and humiliating, as you will all soon discover. . . .''

Jana jerked her head in his direction as Stephanie's name escaped her lips. "Sylva,'' his icy voice corrected before he turned and left.

Susan guessed from Jana's expression she knew who Sylva was. Intrigued, she questioned Jana. Jana told them what she had witnessed earlier.

"A princess from Uranus? What will they do to her?" Kathy asked.

"I don't know, Kathy. But from the look I saw in the commander's eyes, I wouldn't want to be in Sylva's place right now, or Stephanie's."

Susan's eyes widened in astonishment. "You saw him before last night? From the way he fondled you yesterday, I doubt you'll ever find yourself in her predicament," she said jealously.

"That's quite enough, Susan," Jana said threateningly.

Heather came to Jana's aid. "Leave Jana alone, Susan. You're just jealous of her."

"Jealous? After a night like we shared? Ridiculous! I have nothing to fear from our prim and modest Jana. She would never have the courage or daring to reach out and take what she desires. But I do."

"With or without last night, you have nothing to fear from me, Susan. But if we can't be friends, then I suggest we call a truce, as ordered. If it's a war you want, tell me here and now," Jana said.

Before Susan could reply, Martella entered the room and called the women to follow her. They walked to the elevator and went to the deck below. They were ushered into a glass-in observation booth which looked out onto an arenalike area. A guard positioned himself just outside the door.

As the captives looked around, they became aware of the tremendous size of the ship. To carry so many people, it must be immense. There were numerous booths filled with other captives. The apprehensive women stared at each other when they realized that the other cubicles were soundproof.

"What now?" Susan boldly questioned Martella.

"You'll see," Martella answered.

Stephanie was brought to their booth. She was hand-bound and escorted by a security guard. Sylva was marched into the center of the glass-enclosed arena by two guards. They bound her hands and hobbled her feet. The gag in her mouth prevented the fury her eyes revealed from spilling forth.

Varian entered the arena. An audio unit was switched on.

120

"This is Princess Sylva Omanli from the planet Uranus. She has defied all orders and brought total disruption to her entire unit. She leaves me with no choice but to remove her. The rest of you are here to witness a vow of obedience or a final punishment. Rest assured that you will join Sylva if you do not profit from her example. To prove my fairness, I will grant Sylva a last chance to reconsider her fate."

Varian then addressed her directly. "Sylva, will you stop your rebellion and violence? Once you demand a final battle, there will be no retreat, no truce. Your screams and pleas will be ignored. Which is it to be, cooperation or punishment? Do you challenge my *scarfelli*?"

The gag was removed for her answer. Sylva glowered in virulent hostility at Varian. She sent forth a string of vulgar invectives which could have singed the ears of the Devil himself. The gag was hastily put back in place.

Varian shook is head in disgust. "We understand your answer clearly, Sylva. Carry on, Lieutenant," he commanded and walked away. He entered a booth across from Jana and sat down between Tristan and Nigel. His eyes were glued to Sylva's belligerent face.

The security men departed. Sylva remained alone in the center of the large and silent room. A loud click was heard and a door at the far end of the arena gradually opened. For a moment only stygian blackness was visible.

Jana glanced surreptitiously at Varian to find him speaking with Nigel. A piercing scream brought Jana's gaze to Heather's wide, terror-filled eyes and ashen face. Heather's behavior warned Jana of something she was positive she did not want to view. Jana's head slowly turned. She blanched white with shock at the horrifying sight. This could not be real!

Chapter Seven

Paralyzing fear and disbelief attacked Jana's senses. Forceful pressure seemed to squeeze her chest, making it difficult to breathe. She felt as if her blood had frozen, chilling and stiffening her body. Her eyes refused to blink or close while her brain pleaded for blankness. As if she were an exquisite statuette, Jana couldn't move or speak as she watched countless fuzzy spiders tumble into the open arena. They began to scurry about with erratic movements. They were as large as grown cats, as intimidating as lions! Jana had never seen anything like them; they were hideous and heart-stopping. Where had he gotten such creatures?

Jana watched in horrified fascination as the spiders seemed to work together to stalk their prey. As the spiders advanced on her, Sylva vainly tried to hop backward. She only succeeded in falling down, the noise and vibrations attracting the attention of her predators. The wild frenzy began.

Their spinnerets worked quickly as a viscid fluid oozed out. As the liquid instantly hardened into silken thread, skillful appendages seized it and began to spin an envelope around Sylva. It was like being buried alive in a silky white tomb.

The creatures maneuvered Sylva over and over as they continued their task. Soon, only an oblong white wrapper and brown spiders filled the arena. They seized the cocoon and begin to retreat into the stygian shadows from which they had come. Jana realized in rising alarm that they were capturing Sylva.

Kathy's limp body sagged against Jana. Somewhere along this trial of horror she had fainted. Heather was sobbing and babbling hysterically to herself. Susan sat white-faced watching Sylva's retreating cocoon. Stephanie glared in hatred and renewed fury toward Varian's booth.

As Jana's eyes scanned the other booths, she saw the panic this barbaric scene had wrought. Varian had selected his tormentor perfectly. What other dramatic episode could inflict such anguish on them? She had not believed him capable of such inhuman savageness. Her heart filled with agony at this discovery.

Jana studied his powerfully attractive features. He looked unmoved, untouched by what he had ordered and witnessed. His men did not show even a faint hint of remorse or sympathy. Torment knifed her heart. How could she have been so wrong about him, so beguiled?

Varian glanced over to find Jana's piercing eyes on his face, staring at him as if she were seeing him for the very first time and in a most destructive light. The expression in her eyes alarmed him. The muscles in his stomach knotted as he wished he could have spared her this deception. But his expression never altered to hint of this inner turmoil. With her scientific mind and background, she would erroneously surmise Sylva's fate.

Varian read the raw emotions revealed in her bluish-green eyes. Her gentle spirit and sense of humanity would refuse to accept such violence for any reason. He felt a pang of regret. He wanted to explain this deceitful matter to her, to hold her in his arms and comfort her, to ask her understanding of this necessary ruse. . . .

The women were left alone to adjust to what they had witnessed. Jana's stormy eyes left Varian's profile. He secretly pressed a button.

"How could a man like that be so cruel?" Susan asked.

Jana's frayed nerves and guilty conscience caused her to lose all control. "What's the matter, Susan?" she sarcastically taunted. "Has Varian Saar lost all his charm and fascination? Don't fret. By our next dinner, you'll forget his ferocity in the fallout from all that charisma. No doubt you'll soon be playing strip poker with him again."

Jana struck out to punish her own traitorous heart. She desperately needed to eviscerate those forbidden feelings for Varian. She had also allowed herself the folly of viewing his charming image and forgetting the man behind the image he had revealed to her earlier. She must never do so again.

"And just how do you plan to treat him, Miss High and Mighty?" Susan snapped back in her own defense.

"I'll do as ordered, for now. I don't intend to become roommates with Sylva, but I won't pretend to accept this barbaric situation. We must be cautious. Susan, you of all people know women can be artful pretenders. We simply playact our assigned parts until this nightmare ends. He demands obedience. He orders us to study and learn. I shall grant him that much, nothing more." Jana didn't suspect that Varian was listening to this conversation in his booth.

"What about the respect he also mentioned?" Susan mocked Jana's reasoning. "He said disrespect and defiance were punishable."

"Respect for his power and authority, yes; but for him as a

man, no. If you still want him, Susan, take him," Jana brazenly challenged. "I would rather die than have that alien warlock touch me!"

The discussion ceased as the guard entered to lead away a moody Stephanie. Martella noticed the curious light in Stephanie's eyes as she stared at Jana, an expression of victory on her lips. Martella wondered why, but allowed it to pass for now. Martella called the women to follow her.

Ferris Laus aided a trembling, ashen-faced Kathy down the corridor. Ever since Kathy's arrival, Ferris had been drawn to her. At this moment, he resolved to buy her as his mate. He would clear it with Varian, then send Kathy to his parents on the planet Auriga for safekeeping.

Susan left with Martella. Jana slipped her arm around Heather's shoulder and tried to calm her down. "You have nothing to fear, Heather. Just do as he commands and you won't be harmed," Jana advised her.

"It was so horrible, Jana. How could he do such a wicked thing?" she cried, his golden image tarnished for her.

"I told you what Sylva did and you saw how she behaved. Then that trouble with Stephanie. He must have thought it was necessary to keep from losing control over more women. Just be quiet and follow orders. Everything will be all right. It has to," Jana encouraged Heather. Jana dared not look at Varian again. Yet her peripheral vision told her he had not departed. His gaze made her uneasy, for she could sense its presence.

"Nothing will ever be all right again, Jana. These are evil people. They pretended to be nice, to be our friends. I hate it here! I hate all of them! I hate Commander Saar!" Heather burst into a fresh wave of tears.

Martella came back to see why Jana and Heather had not followed. She halted in the doorway to view a touching scene. Jana was acting like the wiser sister as she tried to ease the fears of a younger sibling. Martella did not interfere. The older woman was pleased to learn her assessment of Jana was more than accurate. Martella glanced over their bowed heads at Varian's moody expression. Suddenly she realized Varian was eavesdropping on this particular talk.

"Listen to me, Heather. You are not a disrupter like Sylva or Stephanie. You're sweet, kind, and well behaved. The commander likes you. You have nothing to fear from him or the others. Get hold of yourself. I'll be close by if you need any help.''

"But they're bad people. I'm afraid of them. They can't be trusted."

"That's not true, Heather. Some of them are very kind. They're just different from us. Be yourself. Make them see you as their friend. Will you try that for me?" she gently coaxed.

"I'm not sure I can, Jana," she answered carefully.

"Yes, you can. Chin up. Relax." Jana smiled and hugged her.

Jana looked up to find Martella patiently waiting for them. There was a curious gleam of admiration in Martella's eyes as she smiled warmly at Jana. Jana rose and masked her irritation at being overheard saying such lies to calm the other woman.

They joined Martella and departed. Martella jovially chatted with Heather, who began to relax. Jana watched her and smiled. For Heather and most of the others, it was over. As a gradually diminishing nightmare, Sylva's fate would drift into the realm of illusion. But the seed would remain buried deep within each captive as a warning.

Later, Jana collapsed on her bed and threw her arms across her eyes. Why couldn't she convince herself of those same lies she had told Heather? She had no one to comfort or encourage her, no one to give her a much needed pep talk. She had never felt so alone and afraid. Jana decided Varian Saar could make a powerful enemy or a powerful ally. She was thankful her dinner rotation wouldn't come again for another five days. She prayed she wouldn't see Varian till then.

As the days passed, Jana got her wish. It was Kara Curri's wit and vivacity which lightened the tense situation. Jana was glad she met with this genial officer for an hour each day. Jana was scheduled for two hours with Martella, lunch, and two hours with Nigel. There was a rest break, then recreation or exercise of some type with Kara. Once these classes ended, her group would be transferred to the next two instructors and subjects. The speed and manner of the classes prevented much socializing among the women, perhaps for the best under the circumstances.

125

Today, Jana had been a captive for ten days. She eyed her daily schedule, which listed her second group dinner, along with dance lessons in the Stardust Room, whatever that was. Jana tensed at the thought of such close contact with the male crew members.

Midmorning, Martella led Jana to the library on a lower deck. She wondered why she was the only captive present. She listened attentively as an instructor expounded on their government. Martella interspliced facts about their geography. Jana was shown graphs, slides, and pictures to aid her understanding. At noon, the man left the women alone.

As they discussed history, Jana decided to press Martella who, she realized, sympathized with the captives' plight. "What about the women who are sold to men who will abuse them?" Jana asked. "Have they no rights to happiness and safety, to honor and pride? What about their resale? Doesn't this passing around of a mate lessen her value in the eyes of your people and in her own eyes? No matter how good or pampered these lives are, it's still evil and wrong. You speak as an observer only, Martella. I wonder how different your opinion would be if you were in my place and I in yours."

"You are very intelligent, Jana, and I agree with you, but it changes nothing," she admitted. "I'm trying to encourage the Supreme Council to make needed changes in our *charl* laws. In fact, I hope to persuade them to abolish this practice. But such grave matters take time. I would like you to know it will be intelligent, superior *charls* like you, Jana, who will influence those decisions. Prove you are worthy to become a citizen, to marry your owner. Show your courage, wits, and strength. Don't let your actions shout bitterness, hatred, disrespect. Don't appear a threat or an enemy, Jana; appear a friend and evoke the promise of a better future for all. I will be honest with you; others don't agree with me yet, and get angry when it's discussed."

Jana knew it was foolish to provoke brutal punishment or torture or death. For the moment, it was best to use her "courage, wits, and strength" to stay alive until she decided how to end this slavery. There must be a path to freedom, and she would find it! She would not allow herself to be a victim or coward, at least no longer than necessary to weather this current storm! Whatever happened, she must endure with dignity. People often faced crises beyond their control; she must not allow this one to destroy her!

After lunch, the remainder of their time together was spent informing Jana of the various laws and rules of conduct which she would be expected to practice. She was given a short break and told to wait for an escort to Nigel's science laboratory on another deck of the ship.

After Martella left, Jana wandered around the large room. Despite technological and scientific advances, this location proved that man still loved to read books. Jana fingered several volumes, suddenly eager to begin her lessons in their language, which oddly was not listed as a requirement. Jana surmised it was because of the audiotranslators which interpreted any language it received.

A door had swished open. Jana assumed it was Nigel or her escort. Before she could step into view, Varian's voice prevented it. Jana didn't want to see him in private; he was too beguiling. She anxiously waited for him to leave and prayed he wouldn't discover her presence.

"Since when did you develop an interest in medical science?" Tristan teased the scowling man at his side. He retrieved a book at the far end of the library and handed it to Varian. "This should answer all of your questions."

"Wipe that grin off your face, Tris, or I'll demote you for disrespect," Varian jested. "You know what I'm seeking, so change the subject."

Tristan changed the topic to another disturbing one. "Why don't you tell Jana the truth about Sylva and the *scarfelli?* With her scientific brain, you know what she's thinking. Have you seen her since then?"

Varian frowned, then shook his head. "You expect me to tell her it was only a simulation? That sweet Sylva is actually confined to solitary in the security brig? No way. That little ruse worked perfectly. I have those women right where I need them—full of respect and minus defiance."

Tristan argued. "But it isn't necessary to make Jana despise you and fear you. Tell her the truth; it'll help her," he urged compassionately.

"Thanks to you and Martella, she's receiving plenty of special treatment. I would lose all power and control if these captives learned the truth, and don't think kind-hearted Jana

127

wouldn't delight in telling them. You didn't see the way she was looking at me after that spectacle. I'd never convince her Sylva is just fine unless I take her to the brig. You know what Jana and everyone else will think if I keep showing her favoritism. They'll get the wrong idea, Tris, especially Jana. She's already shown too much attraction to me. An infatuation for me could spoil her new life.''

"You're wrong, Varian," Tristan protested softly. "She can be trusted.''

"Am I? You, Martella, and Nigel all think she's superior and unique. I've done as you three asked, I've allowed her extra attention and privileges. If I'm any more lenient, she won't respect my authority at all. Don't you dare tell her the truth about *scarfelli*, or Sylva.''

Tristan was concerned over Varian's obstinate attitude. "If she could read our language or if she asked any of our people about those large spiders, she'd learn they don't kill or eat people. She'd learn those *scarfelli* were trained for alien terror tactics. Why are you so worried? Have you ever known me to disobey orders?''

"Of course not. But there's something about Jana Greyson which affects my crew strangely. Not a single one of you dislikes her. It wouldn't surprise me to discover she's an alien witch! Maybe you'd better examine her again," Varian hinted roguishly, then winked.

"If you stop being mean, she'll settle down," Tristan suggested merrily.

"No, it's best for both of us if Jana paints me an evil black," Varian said, chuckling wickedly.

Tristan grasped his underlying meaning. "Has that black image of yours ever discouraged any woman?" Tristan challenged, winking at his friend. "Surely you're not missing Canissia Garthon? She's worse than her father, Supreme Councilman Segall. I surely do wish those seats weren't for life.''

"I'll handle Cass when I get home. As for Jana Greyson, the kindest thing I can do for her is to prevent any affection or delusions about me.''

"And what makes you think she has either?" Tristan quipped.

"Let's just say I'm generously preventing a new problem from being born," he remarked, his voice suddenly cold and harsh. "Let's go. I have work to do." The door swished twice as they departed.

When Nigel arrived, he apologized for his tardiness. Pushing aside the puzzling conversation she had overheard between Tristan and Varian, Jana followed him down a long corridor in the gigantic ship. She sat down across from Nigel to begin her science lesson. His words confounded her. In comparison to hers, his race was so advanced that it staggered the human mind. Enthralled by his fascinating talk, she didn't notice how swiftly the time passed. Jana listened, questioned, and reasoned. She revealed none of the lack of understanding that many of the other women had displayed.

Caught up in Nigel's lesson, Jana temporarily forgot her dire circumstances. She laughed easily and relaxed completely with him. "I feel as if I've mysteriously stepped into a realm of magic and fantasy. I suppose that sounds silly, doesn't it?" She laughed in merriment.

"Where would man be without dreams and visions to encourage him, or his science fiction to disprove or discover? To cease to learn is to cease being interesting, alive, and vital. Avoid that pitfall, Jana. You're much too rare and special to—" He halted at the astonished expression on her face. "Tell me, Jana," he asked, to change the topic. "When are we going to finish that *Laius* match? You've sparked my interest in whether or not you can beat me." His hazel eyes twinkled.

"Worried about your position as champion?" she teased.

"Something tells me I should be," he answered.

"I'll make you a deal. Teach me all your tricks and I'll teach you mine."

He chuckled. "Agreed. No competition yet, just training." His eyes sparkled with intrigue. What a choice mate for some lucky male!

Jana suggested, "We'll play our real match the day before I leave. That way, if I do win, you will remain the best on your ship."

"You wily female. How very considerate. You think of every angle."

"I wouldn't wish to offend my partner and teacher, now would I?"

"Beating me would certainly do that," Nigel jested with a heavy sigh.

"Answer a question for me, Nigel. Just how big is this starship?"

"Come in here and I'll show you." He walked into an adjoining office and over to the side wall. He pulled down a diagram of the *Wanderlust*.

"The ship is constructed in a U-shape with three decks. In this left wing, deck three contains the crew's quarters, rec rooms, and mess halls; the second deck where we are now contains some of the lower officers' quarters, sick bay, and the science labs; the first deck above us contains the conference room, the commander's quarters, the upper officers' quarters, and our rec rooms and mess hall. The gold room, which is for a high-ranking guest, is here." He pointed to a suite not far from Varian's!

"If it's for guests, why does it have a camera and no locks?" she probed.

Nigel didn't tell her there was a control button beneath the lower edge of the painting over her sofa which caused the picture to move aside to reveal a layout which contained video-audio communications, a viewer screen comparable to television, a door release switch, and a button to open a side-wall panel to display a large window. It wouldn't do for Jana to discover that arrangement. He told her what truths he could. "Doors work by voice communication or an electrocard. The camera was installed for this voyage. When we return to base, things will return to normal."

"I see, the room was converted to an elegant prison for this special trek?"

Nigel smiled grimly and went back to his explanation. He pointed to each section as he spoke to her. "The circular foresection contains the bridge, navigations, and communications on deck one. On deck two we have the transporter, security control, and weaponry arsenal. On the lower deck we have the psychology-sociology lab, the history lab, data centers, and the engineering section. We have six docking bays, one located at the far end of each deck. On the first level, there is an emergency jettison pod on each side. On level two, we have a shuttlecraft in each bay. Deck three has takeoff and landing pads for spacers." He smiled and clarified, "Spacers are swift, agile fighters. Tesla Rilke's an expert pilot."

He inhaled, then went on. "There's a planetarium bubble above the apex of the bridge for observation and enjoyment. I'll show it to you. It's exhilarating to go up there. You feel as if you're suspended in time and space, like standing in the door to the Universe. You're a part of the heavens. Sometimes that feeling is awesome."

"I'm glad to hear it affects someone else that way," she remarked.

Nigel chuckled. "The other wing contains the environmental and life-support units, the brig and security holding rooms, the computer and data-processing departments, and geological and meteorological units on deck three. On deck two we have the library, crew's quarters, and conference rooms. On deck one we have the monitor control room, conference and activity rooms, the botanical conservatory, and the Stardust Room."

"It's so huge. What are the conservatory and the Stardust Room?"

"The conservatory is a semiglass-enclosed room where we grow and store plants from all over the galaxy. It's very beautiful and fragrant in there. The Stardust Room is for dining and dancing. Only the officers and invited guests can enter. The food and view are excellent. You'll see for yourself."

She smiled and nodded agreement. "What's on the agenda for—" she began, but was interrupted by a call over the telecom.

"Lieutenant Sanger, is Miss Greyson with you?"

"Yes, Kyle. She's right here. Do you need her for something?"

"Sir, she needs to dress for dinner. It's late. Is there a problem?"

"Just bad timing, Kyle. We got caught up in our lesson. I lost track of the time. Thanks."

"Yes, sir," the security chief replied and signed off.

"Seems we'll have to finish this discussion tomorrow. I had better get you back to your room before they sound a red alert for you."

"A red alert?" she echoed as they headed out the door.

Nigel playfully winked at her. "You know—the sound of stomping boots and clinking weapons as security men hunt you down," he jested.

"But I'm with you," Jana argued lightly.

"I have to follow the rules and regulations too. I'm only second in command," Nigel remarked flippantly as he escorted her to her quarters.

"You would make a good commander," she told him. He was so likable. They had much in common. Despite her rank, he showed respect for her. Evidently she had Nigel, Martella, and Tristan to thank for her reception and treatment. How could she regard Nigel Sanger as an enemy?

"Thanks for the vote of confidence," Nigel said.

Jana hurried to bathe and dress. Recalling Nigel's brief description of the Stardust Room, she selected a cream-colored gown dotted with lavender flowers and trimmed with lavender lace and silk ribbons. She secured an amethyst rosette at the hollow of her throat. Jana gathered up her hair and arranged it in leaf-curls, leaving short wispy ringlets to dangle down the nape of her neck. Lovelocks fell softly near her ears.

As she worked, Jana pondered the mystery and allure of Varian Saar. She couldn't forget his stirring words and contact at the last dinner, nor the contradiction between the Sylva episode and the library talk. It thrilled her to know that he had not killed or injured Sylva. Varian had mentioned Alex twice and warned her to avoid his men. Was Varian married or attached to "Cass?" Was he rankled by an unbidden attraction to her? Why did Varian want her to believe he was an evil monster? There must be an illuminating clue to this dark mystery which she couldn't yet perceive.

The signal for dinner was issued before she finished. When Kyle asked if there was a problem delaying her exit, Jana replied, "Just running late, Kyle. I'll be ready in a flash. Just keep my door open."

"Agreed, if you'll save me a dance after I finish my watch," he hinted.

"Sounds perfect to me. See you later," she responded merrily. After all, Varian had declared that everyone on board liked and respected her!

* * *

Varian wondered if Jana was stalling their next meeting. He had avoided her for days, hoping to give her time to settle down. Maybe he should clear up her misconceptions about Susan. After the Sylva incident, he wondered how Jana would behave tonight. He concluded that a mixture of silk and sword might be best. Her corridor door opened and they nearly collided. Varian teased, "Surely it doesn't take this long to enhance your looks. Get moving, woman. Your dance instructors are restless."

Jana mischievously responded to his mellow mood. She snapped to attention, saluting Varian as she clicked her heels together as if she were a member of *Kadim* Maal Triloni's Androas Empire troops. "Yes, sir, slave driver. I'm ready now. I was la—"

His deep blue eyes narrowed as he heard her seeming mockery. Why did she have to rebel against him? Weren't this grisly mission and Ryker's treachery enough trouble without being forced to whip this temptress into line? He would curse *Kahala* if he did not survive this ravishing creature!

Irritated, Varian snapped, "Why must you always seek to incur my wrath? Must I crush you into submission? Make an example of you as with Sylva?" His eyes engulfed her face and body. He felt perilous stirrings of desire at the mere sight of her enchanting beauty.

Jana was confused by his quicksilver mood and sudden show of temper: the dark spirits which plagued him. "I'm hurrying, Commander. Nigel and I lost track of time," she nervously explained.

"I was referring to your blatant defiance of orders. You're too bright and clever to pull a rash stunt like this," he chided her.

She inquired in sincere confusion, "What have I done wrong, sir?"

"The dress, Jana," he informed her, tugging on the ribbons.

Jana glanced at her gown and anxiously questioned, "Is it inappropriate? They said dancing in the Stardust Room. I assumed I was to—"

"Inappropriate? Surely you have enough sense to realize you're supposed to choose one of those laid out for you. Why do you defy me?"

"Laid out?" Jana echoed as her gaze went past him to three

elegant gowns which she had failed to notice. "I ran straight to the bathroom to bathe and dress, sir. I didn't see them. Do you wish me to change?" she inquired, hoping to appease his black temper.

"As quickly as possible," he replied. As he stepped aside, he berated himself for his too hasty and turbulent reaction. Yet, teasings of suspicion entered his mind. Had she planned to make a grand entrance at dinner, clothed in defiance? Her words in the booth echoed in his mind: "Artful pretenders, playact our assigned roles . . ."

Jana went to the bed. Her eyes scanned the three gowns which were so different in color and style from the rest of her wardrobe. One gown was a slinky cranberry-colored silk, another was an emerald-green satin, and the last was an enticing peacock-blue silk. "Which one?" she asked.

"Hold up each one," he ordered, determined to test her "I'll do as ordered" claim or to expose the extent of her reckless bravery. Jana did as he commanded. His gaze swept over her as she held up each gown in turn. "The blue, and hurry. You're late for dinner and dancing class." He could imagine the impression they would make entering late and together.

Jana snatched up the blue gown and rushed into the bathroom to change. The way the gown was designed, she could not fasten it. She had no choice but to ask for assistance. Varian sealed the opening after she had the gown in place. He pulled her taut body around to face him. The gown scintillated with sparks of deep blue and jade green. His gaze passed over her from tawny head to foot. The gown dipped to a low V-shape in the front, gathered snuggly at the waist, then fell softly to the floor. There was an arabesque at the abdomen in lighter, contrasting shades of blue and green.

"I can't get this necklace off," she added nervously. Jana's trembly fingers struggled with the stubborn clasp, as she fretted at its refusal to cooperate.

He turned her and removed it, tossing it on the bedside table. He pulled her around and eyed her up and down. She flushed a deep rose under his scrutiny. His body unexpectedly burst into flame. There was a fine line to be walked with this enchantress; first, he needed to find it! "You'll pass." He intentionally bedeviled her, attempting to hide his inner turmoil.

Jana frowned at him. Her reckless spirit was piqued beyond

control. "I honestly didn't see the gowns, Commander Saar, so your anger is quite unnecessary," she rashly admonished. "I'm not some insensate piece of property to be decorated and displayed for you and your men. I have pride and feelings. What difference does it make which gown I wear tonight?" Her multi-hued eyes flashed in rising anger.

"Careful, little moonbeam," he warned. Damn, what an enchanting picture she made: a blend of fire and ice. She was provocative, elegant, and radiant; she was refined purity. Varian smiled satanically. "You are what I say you are," he softly declared in a husky voice. His hand possessively stroked her warm, satiny cheek and his finger caught the lovelock near her ear. He flashed a devastatingly breathtaking smile.

Jana's heart fluttered wildly. She trembled. She lowered her lids to conceal his strange and maddening effect and the wanton feelings which coursed through her. To alter the smoldering mood his overpowering presence ignited, she asked, "And what am I, Commander?"

He laughed with a rakish air. "Fishing for compliments, Jana?"

"You missed my point, sir." *Damn you!* she fumed in exasperation. He had such a disarming way of unnerving her with his enchanting smile and magnetism. A capricious mood captured her. She smiled up at him with glowing eyes. Her fingertips brazenly traced the proud line of his jaw and strong chin. She lightly ran her forefinger over his sensual lower lip with provocative slowness, then lowered her hand to rest casually upon his muscular chest, to study his heart rate. She murmured in a silky tone, "Compliments aren't necessary, Varian. The fact that I'm your elite prisoner is proof of your high opinion of me. Is that not so?" she challenged.

Her tone was seductive. Her eyes held a hint of mystery and promise. Jana felt his heartbeat quicken beneath her hand as he responded to her actions. She caught the sudden tautness of rigid control that held his towering frame. His eyes began to glow and darken with a smoldering light. "You don't have to be so mean to prove your power over me. I am at your mercy."

Varian warmed noticeably as he questioned her motives. Flirtation or retaliation? Probing her status? Testing his self-control or attraction to her? His lips curled up at one corner in an enticing grin. His appreciative gaze swept over her. He warned huskily, "Careful, little moonbeam, you're way out of your sector playing the bewitching temptress with me."

"Am I?" Jana boldly discounted his taunt. "You don't find me the least bit tempting or attractive?" Her sparkling eyes dared him to respond, to deny the truth.

Varian replied, "I'm a hot-blooded man, Jana. I suggest you back off before you start something I'll be only too happy to finish." His sapphire eyes flamed like twin blue fires.

Jana mistakenly assumed he was teasing her. He had already made his position on mingling with *charls* very clear, in public and in private. She smiled up at him and sighed heavily. As she dropped her hand away, she murmured, "Too bad . . . I wanted to test that irresistible magic your reputation boasts of so highly. Are you really that devastating to women? I suppose a lowly *charl* is beneath your touch or attention. Would you still spurn me if I were a free woman? Who and what are you, Varian Saar? Besides a magical creature who drives a woman wild with uncontrollable desire."

Without warning, Varian seized Jana in his powerful arms and covered her mouth with his. His lips were warm and persistent. Caught totally unprepared, she helplessly melted into his embrace and surrendered her eager mouth to his demanding one. At her response, his arms tightened around her and his mouth seared across hers in a sudden blaze of unrestrained passion. His tongue tasted and stimulated her. Varian kissed until she was weak and breathless, as was he.

A fiery, unknown hunger raced unbridled within her veins, for she was still a stranger to sex. Jana pressed closer to Varian. Her arms voluntarily encircled his narrow waist and she clung to him in fierce longing. He besieged all of her senses at once, totally intoxicating her. She tasted him; she heard his erratic respiration and the husky murmuring of her name. His manly fragrance assailed her nostrils. Her hands explored the muscles on his back. Her senses fused to form one indelible image.

Suddenly nothing else mattered to Jana. Logic and discretion were tossed aside as she experienced emotions which were rampant, emotions as wild and fiery as the solar winds. Varian had been transformed from her alien captor and tormentor into a man—a man she desperately wanted, a man who stirred her very soul to sing with joy and elation, a man who told her there was so much more to love and passion than she had ever

136

dreamed possible. At last, she was ready and eager to explore ecstasy, with this man as her guide.

To him, Jana had ceased to be his prized trophy with a purity and reputation to be protected. His plot to ensnare Ryker was forgotten. He felt an intense need for her which was obsessive and irrational. He was a master artist falling for his creation. No, he was a Star Fleet Commander, a special agent on a secret mission! He was supposed to fake a relationship, not entangle their emotions! As reality called out to him, Varian forcefully quelled the fires which had threatened to engulf him. Now, he had to do the same with Jana. "Does my irresistible magic pass your strict tests, Jana love? Am I as beguiling as you were told? Does my prowess have the same effect on alien women? Is your test over, or shall I fan those probing flames a little higher?" he challenged, his words drawing emotional blood.

Varian felt her stiffen in his arms as his words registered. Jana looked up at him, her face flushed with warring emotions. She was still clasped against him, as if too numb to move and too dazed to think. He felt her tremble as her gaze roamed his mocking expression. He wished she would look away before that mask slipped off! The shame and hurt in her eyes tore at him. He tried to push these unfamiliar and annoying feelings aside, but failed. Perhaps . . . No, it was deadly to even consider taking Jana as his mistress, more so to do it.

"I don't understand you or your cruel games. Why must you be so vicious to me? Do I bring out some evil streak in you?"

"Listen to me closely and carefully, Jana. Don't be misled by your status on my cargo list or your special classes. I'm having you groomed as a superior mate for a prestigious Maffeian leader. I am not in the market for a *charl*, and I never will be. Nor do I need or want an alien mistress. Save your fantasies to share with your mate. Please don't provoke me to hurt you." He added, "I'll be your protector, teacher, and friend . . . until your auction on Rigel. Then and there, we part forever. Do you understand me?"

In a quiet voice Jana stated, "If you're quite finished with your little joke, Commander, I believe the others are waiting for us." Tears sparkled on her lashes and her poise was strained, but pride tinged her voice.

Varian could not send Jana out like this. To alter her anguish to spirited resentment, he pressed, "You did not answer my question, Jana. Did I pass your tests? Is your feminine curiosity sated, or do you require a further investigation? You scientists do have this thing about experiments and indisputable data, don't you? Always wanting to examine or dissect or analyze everything, even emotions."

Her answer stunned and pleased him. "If anything, Commander Saar, you are far more disarming than I was told." But her next statement cut sharply. "If you can extract such an uncontrollable response from a woman who loathes you as I do, a woman who truly found you desirable would stand the same chance of survival as a fly caught in a spider's web." She glared at him with frosty eyes as she went on, "As you well know, most women are petrified of spiders, especially a large and predacious species such as yourself or your *scarfelli*. Tell me, sir, do you spike my food with some powerful aphrodisiac just to supply you with amusement? Is it through magic potions or mind-controlling drugs that we *charls* will be mastered? Do us both a favor and stay the hell away from me! If your malicious sport is over, shall we go?" Her eyes sparkled with antagonism as she steeled herself against him.

"You took me by surprise, Jana, but I was wrong to accept your challenge and tempt you. I'm unaccustomed to dealing with such an innocent. Please don't come on to me again. I can't promise to resist you, but I can promise we'll part soon."

His words were painful and embarrassing to her. She ignored his apology. "My curiosity about your prowess has been permanently satisfied. In the future, make sure your generous lessons are verbal."

Varian escorted a distant Jana to the Stardust Room. At the entrance, he remarked devilishly, "Chin up, moonbeam. It could have been worse. If I were truly the heartless beast you think I am, I would have finished what you unwisely began in there. My self-control amazes even me. You are a beautiful and tempting creature, Jana Greyson. In the future, I'll have to be more cautious."

Her eyes glared at him with open skepticism. "Depreciate the value of your investment?" she scoffed. "Not in a million years, Commander. I assumed you had spoken the truth about no mingling with your cargo. I should never have called your bluff, even if you did make me angry. Sometimes you provoke me beyond control! I suggest we both forget the entire episode.

Mark it up to your expertise and my inexperience. Or it could be the strain of this contemptible situation. As you said, there are more important things to claim my attention. However, I do appreciate the value you place on my chastity. I only pray you continue to protect it so valiantly and unselfishly.''

"Rest assured I plan to do just that, little moonbeam.'' Varian realized how wrong Jana was. She didn't know how close she had come to his seducing her, and damn the consequences! If she knew her life would be in mortal danger from a devil who was kin to him, she would praise his rejection.

Jana's gaze roamed around the room, taking in its elegance. Its decor was intended to give one the feeling of dining on an open terrace beneath the stars and moonlight. There were scenic outdoor murals on two of the side walls, while the remaining two walls were of a transparent glass. The ceiling was a retractable panel which could be moved aside to reveal the heavens. Small pinlike bulbs were mounted in such a fashion as to blend unnoticeably with the twinkling stars overhead. The remaining fixtures, furniture, and decorations were a careful harmonizing of amber, sky-blue, and forest-green. Nigel had been correct; it was indeed a romantic and tranquil setting. Soft music seemed to come from every direction at the same time. Muted laughter and quiet chatter filtered between the dreamy strains of music. The room was filled with an aura of peace and gaiety, neither of which she could feel at that moment.

"Well?" Varian prompted at her silence. "What do you think of it?'' His hand made a sweeping wave over the view before her.

"Not that my opinion matters, but it's beautiful. Are we going to sit down somewhere? I feel on display already.'' The reason was simple: her blue gown and the other captives' yellow ones. He led her to a table near the juncture of the two glassed walls and seated her.

Jana was relieved to discover the captives had been seated one to a table with several members of his crew. Besides Varian and herself, there were four others at their table—Nigel, Kara, Tristan, and Martella.

The others were perplexed by Jana's silence. Each one wondered what had brought on this change in her, though Varian appeared to be his usual charming and entertaining self. He seemed oblivious to any problem or change in Jana. Or was it that he knew the reason behind her mood and simply chose to ignore it? Better still, was he the cause of it? Perhaps it was the same reason they were late in arriving.

Dinner was finally over. Martella asked Varian to dance, to see if the others could draw Jana out of her solemn mood. He readily accepted, eager to put some distance between him and Jana. He had pushed himself to appear calm and collected for about as long as he could stand it.

Nigel and Tristan observed the frigid glare in Jana's eyes which glittered like chips of colored ice as she watched Varian's retreating back.

Tristan remarked, "Jana, you look a little pale and tense."

"I'm just tired and homesick," she said to stifle their curiosity. "If you gentlemen will excuse me, I'll freshen up."

As time passed as slowly as the summer sun around Rigel, the *Wanderlust*'s home base, Varian began to shift restlessly. His worried gaze kept returning to Jana's empty chair between Nigel and Tristan. He had danced with Martella, Susan, Heather, and Kathy. But what he truly wanted was the feel of Jana Greyson in his arms. . . .

Varian felt at odds with himself. The frivolous chatter and amorous attentions of the other women were annoying and meaningless to him. He wished he could escape this dutiful game he was playing and merely enjoy that bewitching female for a few hours. He knew he could not, for many reasons. He must continue to play his satanic role—a part which he found most despicable at this moment. Too much was at stake, including her life.

Varian's thoughts and emotions were plagued by memories of her feverish response. He could envisage her enchanting smile and sparkling eyes. Her fragrant lure had invaded his senses and recklessly he had sampled the heady promise of intoxicating passion she had offered to him. She had been within his grasp and he had chosen to repel her. But why did his rejection bring him such—such what? he wondered, unable or unwilling to explore his tumultuous dilemma.

Nigel was leaning against the transparent wall speaking to Kyle, who had just arrived. Nigel had been watching the storm clouds building in Varian's eyes and wondered at their cause.

"Where's Jana? I don't see her around," Kyle asked.

Nigel shrugged. "She went out. I hope she didn't return to her quarters without permission. I would hate to see her get into trouble again."

The concern in his tone alerted the sensitive Kyle. "What happened?"

"You tell me, Kyle," Nigel parried. He could read the mild distress in Kyle's face. "Do you know why she's upset?" he probed.

"All I know is Varian was upset with her earlier tonight. Something to do with her dress. After he arrived in her quarters, I thought I should turn off her monitor. I've never seen Varian like this. I'm worried, Nigel."

Varian walked toward them. "Nigel, I think it's about time I go and check on our wayward Earthling. You had better come along," he added mysteriously, as if afraid to trust himself alone with Jana.

To glean a clue to this mystery Nigel teased Varian, "Need a referee?"

"We might," Varian replied seriously as his blue eyes frosted. "Kyle, you take over for me. Use that charm of yours to camouflage my absence."

"Yes, sir," came Kyle's reply and affectionate grin.

Varian realized that Kyle must have observed what had taken place in Jana's room. "I don't have to remind you there are good reasons behind my actions toward Jana."

"I know," Kyle replied, then warned, "But you should be more careful, Varian. Others won't understand this unusual behavior. Perhaps you should disconnect her monitor to avoid anyone else witnessing a similar scene."

Nigel followed Varian out into the corridor. To their surprise, they saw Jana and Kara slowly approaching them laughing and talking like two old friends who had not seen each other in years. The men patiently waited.

"I was worried about you, Jana," Varian said as the women drew near. "You've been missing for quite some time. Are you all right?"

Jana smiled sweetly and replied, "I'm sorry, sir. Kara and I started talking in the ladies' room, and I lost track of time. That seems to be a bad habit of mine today." She turned to Nigel. "I'll forgive you for making me late tonight if you'll be so kind as to instruct me in dancing."

Nigel chuckled. "I must apologize for my part in your tardiness. Next time don't be such an excellent student. At your service, my lady," he remarked as he made a gallant bow, then offered her his arm.

Jana took it and was escorted inside. Varian turned to Kara. "I don't know what you said or did, but thanks. It seems I was a little rough on her earlier this evening. Does she seem all right to you?" he asked.

Kara sent him a bewildered look. "Jana was upset and tense when you two arrived for dinner. It looked to me as if she only needed a little privacy and compassion. Did she do something wrong?"

"A slight misunderstanding. I hope you and Jana can become friends. Just remember to keep everyone's private life private," he advised.

Kara wondered if she was mistaken about the contrite tone in his voice. His eyes had glittered with jealousy and envy at Jana's easy rapport with the first officer and her selection of Nigel as her dance partner. Perhaps Jana was getting to Varian after all. . . .

It did not take long for Nigel to teach Jana several of his native dances. Tristan, Kyle, Nigel, and numerous other men gave her ample opportunities for practicing her new skills. With carefree abandon, she danced; she conversed; she laughed. Despite his earlier warnings, she subtly flirted. It was exhilarating and wonderful. She graciously yet gingerly accepted the much needed attention she was receiving from his crew. She hungered to feel and to display her worth as a woman and her esteem as a person. Knowing his rules for their conduct, she did not feel threatened.

As Jana concealed her gaze beneath thick lashes or behind fallen curls, she observed her effect on the starship commander. She might be green, but she could recognize bold interest! Like it or not, she did appeal to him! Perhaps he wasn't as unreachable as he and others believed! Was he afraid a mate would demand changes in him and his carefree lifestyle? How could she learn more about his existence and his feelings? Whatever, she knew she wanted Varian Saar! She wouldn't give up quickly or easily. . . .

Varian had about reached his limits of patience. She was the center of attention for his men. Her silvery laughter rankled his taut nerves. Evidently she was trying to make him jealous, or perhaps gain his attention with her antics. Trouble was, she was doing a damn good job of it! Before Varian could ponder these theories further, he finished his dance with Susan. He had tuned out the redhead's silly chatter and brazen overtures. He felt a light tap on his shoulder. He turned to find Jana next to him.

"Care to test my new skills, Commander Saar? I hear you're a matchless dancer. Why not give me the opportunity to satisfy my curiosity about that claim?" Jana's colorful eyes sparkled with the challenge.

At a table nearby, a traitorous officer was keenly observing Jana and Varian, surreptitiously taking more pictures. But he was beginning to worry about this repulsive and perilous betrayal, for those two looked as if they were actually falling in love! But he was trapped! The lieutenant had to save his career, his reputation, his family, and his own life. He didn't care about Ryker Triloni's promises of glory and riches! He didn't want to touch that wicked bitch Canissia again! If the people blackmailing and threatening him weren't Ryker Triloni and Canissia Garthon, he would betray them to the authorities! But what sane man would challenge the devil himself and his wicked handmaiden? As agreed, he would do this one last job for them. He just wanted out of this quicksand.

Chapter Eight

Varian flashed a knowing grin, which she promptly returned. "Of course if you're tired or you're claimed, I'll understand." Jana smiled provocatively and turned to leave, but Varian reached out and seized her hand in his. Wanton or not, her time was limited on his starship!

"I believe it's your turn to show me up," Varian jested, his words carrying a deceptive calm. He drew her into his possessive embrace.

They left Susan standing in the middle of the dance floor,

fuming at Jana's intrusive conduct. She made her way back to her own table and sat down, determined to have revenge on Jana.

"Why the sudden change in mood?" Varian questioned. "I was beginning to think I had destroyed any chance of earning your cooperation."

"I must apologize for my conduct and my part in our misunderstanding. But you are a most charming man, and you did bait me." Laughing softly as he grinned, she added, "I'll try to behave myself. It seems you have my best interests at heart, and I do appreciate it." She reminded herself to speak demurely.

Her expression and tone waxed serious. "To answer your question, I've given my situation a great deal of thought. It's ridiculous not to take advantage of my training period. Everyone keeps telling me this impending destiny won't be anything to fear. I would prefer to have you as an ally, protector, and teacher. If that's still agreeable to you."

"I see. Anything else?" he inquired in undisguised pleasure.

Jana watched him closely with fathomless eyes. She had piqued his curiosity. If she couldn't have him, damn him for abducting her and selling her! Damn him for opening her to pervasive longings! "Inexperience certainly has its pitfalls. It seems I have much to learn and time is short. I'm rather naïve for a doctor and a scientist," she jested. "Perhaps I was too busy working in a laboratory to learn about men. Maybe you were right when you accused me of experimenting with emotions. I suppose my scientific training does sneak out on unexpected occasions. I'm sorry I behaved so shamelessly."

Varian played right into her hands when he asked, "What did you learn tonight, Jana? I'm greatly intrigued by this change of heart."

"If sex is like its preceding passion, it must be fantastic. Considering the reason for my capture, I find that reality encouraging." She daringly continued, "It's actually possible to desire a man for his masculine appeal, even a fearsome stranger one might dislike or mistrust. Is there any chance you have a twin who's single and needs a mate, one who doesn't share your bias against *charls*? At least tell me you aren't one of a kind," she coaxed mirthfully. She felt the tensing of his hard

144

body. She read the brief glint of anger in his sapphire eyes before he could conceal them.

"I'm the sole survivor of the Saar name," he responded icily. "As to my uniqueness, such conclusions are in the eyes and mind of the beholder."

"Could I ask . . . Never mind." She quickly rejected a probing path.

"Don't stop in the middle of a sentence, Jana," he chided her.

She eyed him intently, then asked, "Have I misread your signals about me? When you say certain words, you have a cold expression and tone of voice. Do you have an aversion to alien women, to *charls*? I guess I'm asking if you find me repulsive. Did I offend you with . . . my touch?" She watched Varian watch her, but he didn't answer. "If you feel repulsed, do the other men in your world concur with you? Or is yours some personal prejudice against me?" His penetrating gaze drilled into her murky one.

After a lengthy silence, Jana ventured, "Am I not making sense, or being too inquisitive? I need to know what to expect from this man who will purchase me and carry me home." She moved the back of her hand over his cheek as she dreamily asked, "Is this only a masterly disguise? Or do Maffeians resemble Earthlings this closely? Is this slave raid a deception, or a real attempt at race survival? Will I be accepted and cherished as you all claim? Or will the man who buys me treat me like you do? Please tell me the truth, Varian. Don't let me create false dreams."

"It wouldn't profit you to hear my feelings on this matter. I offered you friendship, Jana; that should tell you all you need to know. We have explained *charl* practice honestly. You're very beautiful and desirable; if you don't realize your immense value, you sorely lack a vital education."

"Then provide it, Professor Saar."

As another dance began, Varian chuckled. "I think such a class can be arranged for you. It's hard to imagine a doctor needing sex education."

"Tristan?" said Jana sweetly to obliterate his smug look. It did.

"Why Tristan?" His eyes revealed his disappointment.

"The best person would be an expert in that particular field, Jana. Tristan is not."

"Who, if not a doctor?" Jana appeared to mentally go over his crew members. Her eyes brightened. She looked up at him and questioned, "You?"

"Can you name anyone on board better qualified?" he smugly challenged.

Jana grinned impishly and parried, "There's Susan. We're both women."

Varian frowned, then arched one brow rakishly. "You wouldn't profit from her lessons. You're soft and warm and natural. Your air of innocence is a potent attraction. We don't want to tamper with it, and surely not tarnish it. You have a new illusion; sex is not purely physical."

She acted and responded as if his last statement was the only one spoken. "But it appears that way with you, sir, and you are the expert."

Varian smiled. "There are emotions other than love involved, Jana. A mutual desire is one."

"Mutual desire," she echoed, then lapsed into thoughtful silence.

Their bodies moved in fluid unison to the soft music. Varian unconsciously drew in their extended arms and locked her right arm to his left side. His cheek rested against her fragrant hair. He drew her closer to his fiery body. He closed his eyes and allowed the music and Jana to fill his senses. No male would dare to claim Jana from his arms!

Jana artfully swayed against his firm body. She closed her eyes and flowed with him and the music, gradually climbing a blissfully tortuous spiral. It seemed as if her entire body was responding to his erotic messages. As she hazily floated between reality and fantasy, she sighed dreamily and nestled closer.

Jana's nearness, touch, and essence called forth the emotions Varian had been trying to suppress all evening. His body naturally responded to her enticing signals. Susan's grating laughter nearby shattered the dangerous spell over him. Varian's lips moved close to Jana's ear. He tenderly whispered, "The dance is almost over, Jana. Compose yourself. This isn't the time or place to study emotions, and such lessons won't go past the verbal stage. As you can see, a mutual attraction can be untimely and annoying.'' The dance ended. Varian almost reluctantly released her from the warm confines of his arms. He wanted nothing more than to sweep her into his arms and carry her to his quarters where he could make passionate love to her for hours. The expression which greeted him was far removed from what he had expected to see, had hoped to see.

Thanks to his warning, her wits cleared and her passions cooled. ''You are a superb dancer, Commander Saar. That was very nice.''

Varian stared at her in disbelief. Desire danced in his sapphire eyes. While he had been squirming in the flames of passion, their contact had not had the slightest effect on her! He grimaced in irritation. So much for her false innocence. She could be a real teaser.

''After much thought, it doesn't appear a good idea for you to tutor me, Varian. It wouldn't be wise to fan those flames which sparked between us earlier. Maybe that task belongs to my future mate. But thank you for the dance and enlightenment.''

Slightly perturbed by her lack of response, he muttered, ''My pleasure.'' It rankled him to view her perky, quicksilver mood at his expense.

Jana sighed wearily. ''Commander, it's rather late and I'm very tired tonight. Is it permissible for me to return to my quarters?''

Varian's emotions were in a turmoil and his body enflamed with desire. How dare a *charl* sneak into his life and wreak such havoc on his emotions! Who did Jana think she was, anyway? Teasing him, deceiving him, tempting him! His gaze drifted to Susan as the lusty vixen issued a sultry invitation in his direction. That was another problem which needed handling, and he was in the right mood to do so! He summoned Nigel. ''Give Jana a last dance, then escort her to her quarters. Good night,'' he murmured absently, then headed in Susan's direction.

His intention seemed clear to Jana. How could a man allow one female to feed the hungers created by another woman? So much for his deceitful claim that sexual coupling wasn't a physical release!

Jana danced with Nigel as she tried to keep her gaze and mind off Varian and Susan. She despised the way they were

147

cozying up, the way they were whispering and laughing. Susan was all over the submissive beast! She would never forgive Varian if he carried out this vindictive sport!

Nigel's gaze shifted back and forth between the woman in his arms and the scene in the corner. He was baffled by his friend's behavior toward both females. Had Varian lost his wits completely? Nigel wanted to spare Jana further embarrassment and anguish. He smiled and suggested, "It's late, and we had a busy day. You ready to go?"

Jana lifted softened eyes to his compassionate gaze. She astutely grasped his intention. She smiled appreciatively and nodded. And she thought Varian Saar was a special man! How blind and stupid could a woman be! Jana and Nigel departed before the music ended.

When Varian sneaked a glance in their direction to see how his conduct was affecting Jana, he was rankled to find them gone. So much for Jana tonight. He concentrated his attention on Susan.

Nigel led Jana across the corridor and into the botanical garden. He plucked a lacy tropical flower and handed it to her. She examined it, then inhaled its fragrance. "That should add color and perfume to your quarters. Perhaps coax a smile to that lovely face."

"You are a most exceptional man. I won't forget you and your help, Lieutenant Nigel Sanger. What's it called?" she inquired, teasing her nose with the blue and green blossom with its bold splotches of crimson and yellow.

"*Tarkitilae Moosi*, the eyes of Kimon, our goddess of love and beauty. It's Varian's favorite to—" He halted at his foolish slip.

As if she had missed it, she squealed, "Look, Nigel! A shooting star. Hurry, make a wish," she declared in childlike wonder.

"I wish you a long and happy life, Little Earthling," he remarked amiably, just as he was summoned on the intercom. He shrugged and grinned as he stepped to the nearest unit and replied, "Lieutenant Sanger here."

"Sir, I need you on the bridge. Commander Saar doesn't want to be disturbed unless it's an emergency." The voice assailed Jana's frayed nerves.

Nigel grimaced. "I'm on my way, Baruch." He turned to-

148

ward Jana. "I'll see you home first," he teased lightly, pointedly.

Jana smiled. "Surely I can be trusted to cover such a short distance. I promise, straight to my room. No detours or mischief. I'll see you in the morning. You can explain shooting stars." She waved good night and turned away.

Nigel entered the elevator and snapped, "Bridge!"

About to round the corner, laughter and voices halted Jana. She peered around the edge. She clenched her fists and teeth as Varian and Susan, arm in arm, strolled down the hall and entered his quarters. The door swished shut behind them. Silence filled the long passageway. Jana stared at the sealed door, and damned Varian's soul to the flames of hell. As if agony were tearing her body to small pieces, she painfully made her way to her suite. She pressed the button, then entered her golden prison only moments before her poise vanished. She headed for the servo, rashly ordering one drink after another. She gulped one down swiftly, then seized another and repeated the reckless urge to numb her shattering torment.

Jana hadn't consumed the deadening limit before Varian's score-settling sport with Susan was complete and a security man was escorting the enraged and flustered captive to her quarters. Varian had spurned Susan and she was furious at the slight.

The next morning, Jana and Susan collided on the way to their separate classes. Susan sneered at her and said, "You look awful. What did you do, cry all night because I was screwing your dreamboat? This is one time all your beauty, charm, and money can't get you the one prize you want more than anything. Don't fret, Jana dear. You'll soon have a new master to practice your angelic charms on. Perhaps he won't be as choosy as Varian, nor as talented between the sheets. I pity you that first night with him. He'll probably strip you and rape you within one hour after your purchase. I can just hear you now, crying and pleading. He'll probably tie you to the bed and take you over and over. Do you know how it feels to have sex with a despicable creep? Too bad you can't convince our handsome captor to train you how to please and enjoy a real man.

"If Varian sells you to the man he described last night, you need not worry about your pride and safety. You won't last that long. If you survive his savage attacks and sadistic fantasies, you'll plead for sweet mercy. The devil he has in mind for you will make Varian Saar look like an angel. No doubt that's the purpose behind his selection. My, my, Jana," she clucked mockingly. "Whatever did you do or say to Varian to inspire such fury and spite. If I were you, I would try to dispel his hunger for revenge before this trip ends." Susan laughed maliciously as she sauntered down the hall, hoping this vengeful sport was worth any punishment!

Jana back raced to her suite door, slapping her sweaty palm against the button. She ran into the bathroom, feeling nauseated. Her head was pounding and she splashed cold water on her face and took several swallows. She stared at her reflection. Susan was right; she looked terrible. Her eyes were puffy and bloodshot; her face was almost sallow. Tears rushed down her cheeks in a torrent of dejection. Jana sat in the vanity chair and covered her face with her hands.

Neither woman had noticed the first officer poised in his doorway. Nigel had been about to leave his quarters to fetch Jana for their class. Susan's vicious tirade had inspired him to halt and listen. He was infuriated by her malicious attack on Jana, but had not stopped it as there were clues he wanted to glean. Varian would never say such vile things. Nigel's shrewd mind added, *unless there was a good reason!* Something powerful and volatile was going on between Jana and Varian. Varian had not been himself since she had come aboard. Nigel was in a quandary; should he get involved in such a personal affair?

Nigel entered Jana's suite. He ordered her to lie on the bed and rest. He got a cold, wet cloth and covered her forehead. To conceal his concern, he teased her about sampling too much party wine and staying up so late. "You've been studying long hours, Jana. Don't push yourself so hard. I'll get Tris to bring you something for that headache. Just lie there and relax. I'll check on you later."

So that he would not have to alert Jana to the communications panel in her room, Nigel left for his own quarters to summon Tristan. Evidently Varian had ordered her monitor off except for brief contacts. Before Nigel reached his door, Varian's opened. Their gazes met. Nigel waited for his friend's approach.

"I thought you had Jana for class this morning," Varian remarked.

"I was just about to call Tris to examine her. She's sick. I think she needs a day off. She's pale and shaky. She has a slight fever and severe headache. I think she feels as bad as she looks."

"I should check on her," Varian stated reluctantly. Hearing she was ill, his worry overshadowed his illogical lesson in jealousy.

"After that little display with Susan last night, I doubt your visit would be appreciated. Friend to friend, I think you should leave Jana alone for a while." Nigel related the bridge call in Jana's presence, then allowed Varian to draw his own speculations about its effect.

Varian pondered Nigel's words and mood. "I suppose you're right. Take care of her," he ordered hoarsely, then headed for the bridge.

Jana was permitted two uninterrupted days of rest. Over and over, she analyzed certain conversations and events. She eventually decided there was no understanding Commander Varian Saar.

The ensuing week passed swiftly for Jana, since her schedule remained full. Jana tried to keep her mind off the subjects which could upset her delicate balance of confidence and tranquility. She threw herself into her task of learning everything these aliens could teach her. Whoever was to be her fate, she would prepare herself as best she could to confront him on equal ground. During this exacting period, Jana's days and nights passed in a sort of emotional limbo. Whenever Varian's image appeared to plague her, she tried to dispel it with rigid concentration on her work. But each time she saw or confronted Varian, her heart betrayed her vow to despise him. His attraction steadily became more compelling. Worse, it seemed as if her captor was annoyed by her lack of attention. This conclusion terrified her, for she feared it would be a challenge to him.

Varian was well aware of Jana's retreat from him. He berated his inane, conflicting behavior. No wonder she was so edgy and wary. Varian admitted his conduct and strategy befuddled even him. He had started off wanting to prevent her appeal to his crew, then failed by parading her before them. The dinners and dances had been a mistake. He should have kept everything on a level of business or simple kindness. Somewhere his plans had gone awry.

He couldn't have Jana Greyson; it would mean certain death for her at Ryker's hands. But hadn't he known that from the night of her capture when she had gazed up into his face? Or later when she had brought his body to life while she lay asleep? Or those verbal sparrings which he had enjoyed so immensely?

But Varian was fooled by Jana's deceptive front. He believed she had resigned herself to her impending fate with another mate, that she was looking forward to her new life, to their separation. Despite his plans and resolve, as the many days and nights rushed toward a final separation, Varian fumed as he saw his power over her decreasing while hers over him was increasing.

Varian decided it was time to put his wily plot back into motion, to show his hunger while preventing hers. After all, this new talent would take time and effort to create and perfect. His pride was stung. His desire was aroused. His ego was challenged. His mind was baffled. His duty called out to him. Each day Varian casually caressed a kiss to her forehead, the tip of her pert nose, or cheek. He enjoyed this little sport of provoking her. It became a sort of irrational punishment for being out of his reach.

Once Jana was sitting at a conference table in Nigel's office. Varian slipped up behind her and kissed her on the back of her neck, then sensuously ravished her earlobe. Jana whirled with wide eyes to see if Nigel had lost his mind by daring to make a pass at her, even in jest. She was about to admonish him, but found her parted lips claimed by Varian's insistent mouth. He pulled her to her feet and captured her squirming body in his strong grip.

Seeing she was powerless to stop him or free herself, Jana melted into his arms and returned his feverish kiss. Why not? She could always excuse her weakness as submission to his brute strength and compelling authority. Besides, his kiss sent thrills to her very core and his power over her was irresistible. As their lips parted, Jana tried to hide the enormous hunger she was feeling for him. She was only partially successful. Her quivering body and flushed cheeks told him he had gotten to her.

Yet she scolded him, "You've previously satisfied my feminine curiosity, Commander. It requires no further testing or exploration. I'm busy."

"I was satisfying my own curiosity," Varian huskily informed her.

"How so?" Jana inquired of this man she presumed knew everything.

He grinned mysteriously. "I think you already know."

"I don't have the vaguest idea what you're talking about."

"Don't you now?" Varian taunted her. He grinned satanically and strolled out, leaving a flustered Jana gaping after him. If he kept up this sport a few weeks, he would have no trouble displaying an obsession for her while she exposed anger at his torment. His conduct should bait Ryker; her conduct should defend her from Ryker!

That same day, Varian altered her schedule, to include every other evening meal in the Stardust Room, at his table. To keep her on her toes, he missed the first two meals, then suddenly appeared for the next one. He praised his wits, for he was beginning to enjoy himself again.

One night, Varian tantalized her with unnerving nibbles on her ear during a dance. He whispered flowery compliments about her progress and ravishing appearance. He told her how lucky her owner would be to purchase such fire and innocence, as his warm breath and touch nearly devastated her warring senses. Jana scolded him for his lecherous behavior. "I might be your prisoner, but damn you, leave me alone. I'm off limits, remember? Don't fondle me in public or in private. I can't stand your touch."

"Because you think I've shared it with Susan?" he hinted. "I can promise you, Jana, I haven't touched a single alien on this ship except you." At her look of doubt, he related the facts of the night in question. "You see, I was only teaching Susan a much-needed lesson. Everything she's told you about me or the two of us is lies. I swear."

"Even if I believed you," Jana said, "I could care less what you do with Susan or any other female who catches your eye, as long as it isn't me!"

153

"That's the problem; you're the only one who does appeal to me. I'm having a terrible time deciding how to handle such an impossible predicament. Am I a fool to sell an untested product?" He caressed her flaming cheek. "Especially such a tempting treat who does her damnedest to tantalize me."

"I'm not enticing or tantalizing you! I'm spurning you!" she insisted.

Jana fled his tormenting embrace as gracefully as possible when the dance ended. She sought the solitude and serenity of the botanical garden. She feared to expose the fires he had ignited in her with his bold advances. She walked to the large transascreen and gazed outside. Her hand covered her mouth as if that action could still her rapid respiration and trembling.

Without her knowledge, Varian followed her. He softly accused from the shadows behind her, "I thought you had become immune to me. Was my touch so disturbing you had to flee to safety?"

Jana whirled and told him angrily, "You're spiteful! You're making respect and friendship impossible." Varian strolled forward and reached out for her. Jana could only retreat a few more steps. "I hate you, you deceitful son of a bitch! Stay away from me!"

Varian pinned her against the clear wall with his brawny body. His heated gaze lazily traveled her features, then came to rest on her terrified eyes. "Do you really loathe me, Jana?" Varian challenged. "Why do you keep tempting me if you want to be left alone?" His hands captured her face between them. His head lowered and he kissed her thoroughly. His tongue parted her resisting lips and invaded her mouth. Before he initiated his final strategy he needed to savor her sweetness one last time.

The kiss was tender and enticing. Jana struggled to stifle the flames which he sparked. She could not. Why fight a losing battle? His magic was too great for her. Her arms encircled his back. She pressed her slender body close to his powerful frame, surrendering her lips and her will to him.

Varian retained his rigid self-control with great difficulty as he hungrily claimed her eager mouth time after time. His hands wandered over her lithe body, caressing and exploring fiery curves. His lips left hers to plant light kisses over her face and throat. The urge to take her was almost too painful to bear.

Damnation! A real affair between them now was too dangerous. It was too late to halt the scheme he had put in motion. His coded messages had been sent; her publicity was circulating. The last thing he needed to battle was her offer of love, which would surely defeat him. This little moonbeam must not be allowed to shine on him. It was too late. . . .

Jana lay her face against his shoulder. Without the torment of his lips on hers, she suddenly comprehended what was taking place. She sensed his gradual withdrawal. "I thought you were immune to me. Your pounding heart and unbridled passion claim you aren't, my dashing space pirate. Why fight such powerful desires? Can you deny you want to hold me in your arms and kiss me? Perhaps you crave to seduce me? Do I drive you as wild with hunger as you do me?" she inquired, sensuously passing her tongue over her lips as she provocatively rubbed her body against his.

Jana's hands boldly roved his chest and arms, then slid down his waist and brazenly wandered over the proof of his arousal. She murmured, "Despite your aversion to me and your resolve to sell me, you cannot ignore me or resist me, can you? If you do not find me irresistible, why do you pursue me and force your attentions on me? Why do you torture yourself by enflaming your desires, then cruelly deny them?" Her palm slipped over the hard declaration of his passion.

When he stiffened and groaned, she smiled triumphantly and demanded, "Will you pine over my loss while another man sates his desires with the body you captured and crave? Or will you forget your stupid pride and make me your *charl*? Claim me tonight, or don't come near me again. I warn you, if you do not take me while you can, I will haunt you forever."

Varian glared at her with piercing eyes. The truth in her words rankled him beyond control. "I suggest you return to your quarters immediately and think over your precarious position and treacherous tongue. I will not tolerate such wanton behavior or immodest speech ever again."

"If we can't yield to this attraction between us, then keep your word, Commander, and leave me alone," Jana replied.

After her departure, Varian slammed his fist against the wall so violently that it rumbled in protest and his hand smarted. He swore angrily as he rubbed it. He raged at the fates and demanded they coerce Ryker into answering his challenge.

155

Once and for all, this lethal and bitter rivalry must end, end before this radiant moonbeam was lost to him forever!

Varian was testy in private. He paced restlessly and aimlessly to relieve the tautness and fury he did not as yet understand. The closer they got to the Milky Way barrier and Jana's auction, the blacker his mood.

Kara and Martella watched helplessly. The strain was obvious to Tristan and Nigel too. They fearfully waited for the tempest they knew was soon to come. It was a struggle for them to keep silent, with their friend and with the vulnerable Earthling. Another person was also watching this tormenting drama unfold. The traitorous lieutenant wondered if everyone but Jana and Varian were aware of the depth of their feelings. . . .

One afternoon, Tristan had been with Jana in the library on the second deck, explaining several advanced techniques in research. He still hoped to gain her help as his temporary assistant until they orbited Rigel. Wanting to discuss a new experiment with her, he left to get a book he needed from his laboratory. But it took much longer than expected.

Jana was standing beside one of the bookshelves. She was completely engrossed in a fascinating illustrated collection of legends and myths. She did not hear the door open and close behind her.

Varian halted as he recognized the woman with her back to him. He glared at the book in his tight grip: *Alien Biology: Mating, Reproduction, and Birth Control* by Cassin Tern. Varian did not stop to think Jana couldn't read his language. Fury attacked him at being caught with this particular book, by this particular woman, especially after having spent the last few hours responding to calls about her from prospective buyers. He lay the book facedown in a chair. The spring snapped swiftly and violently. . . .

"Attention!" the flinty voice thundered into the tranquil silence.

Jana jumped and whirled around, dropping her book to the floor.

"I think it's time we straighten out your insolent and rebellious conduct, my smug little Earthling," Varian gritted out between clenched teeth.

A tic in his jawline warned her of enormous anger, which was directed at her for some curious reason. "Commander, I—" she hesitantly began.

"Silence!" he shouted before she could continue. He cursed himself for dangling this woman before the rapacious appetites of all the men in his galaxy. How could he possibly refuse to sell her without revealing himself? His friends had warned him to beware of his scheme against Ryker. He wanted Jana fiercely; that alone prevented him from being able to have her.

"But I want—" She tried to argue, to explain.

Varian roughly pulled her to within inches of his taut body. "Silence!"

Her terrified eyes widened. Jana clamped her lips together and tried to still her trembling. Tears of pain and alarm glistened in her sea-water eyes as she awaited his next action or word. She was at a total loss to understand his attack. He was never like this with the others!

He knew what he was about to say and do was brutal, but he had no choice. He must turn Jana against him. "I am weary of your flirtatious, arrogant manner, Jana. You have pushed me too hard. I made a grave mistake in telling you how valuable you are. You forget yourself and place, alien *charl*! I'm the master here. You've done your damnedest to embarrass me before my crew and the other captives. Cease your defiance or I'll punish you as severely as Sylva," he rashly threatened in the heat of his anger.

Tears escaped her eyes and eased down her flushed cheeks. Could this be the same man who had held her in his arms and kissed her so passionately, who had made her very soul sing with joy and desire! How had she so misjudged him? Just above a hoarse whisper she solemnly asked, "How can you accuse me of such lies? Why do you hate me, Varian?"

He stared down into her face with its brave, resigned expression. He hastily released her as if her flesh had liquefied into acid and was eating into his hand. Jana lowered her head and wept. Varian tensed. Did she actually believe he— *My stars!* he fumed. *What am I doing to her?* Varian was a man who normally had himself and every situation under rigid control. He was known for his cool head and steel nerves. He had unknowingly allowed this fragile creature to eat away that cool exterior and the rigid control. He had struck out blindly in his frustration.

"Freshen your hair and face, then return to your quarters, Jana," he said in a softened, controlled tone. "We'll discuss this matter later."

Jana pulled a towel from a holder and wet it. She wiped her face and eyes as she brought her tears under control. She took several deep breaths and drank water to remove the painful lump in her throat and chest. She instinctively knew this man was deeply troubled, and she had something to do with it.

The door swished open as a cheerful Tristan strolled in, apologizing for his delay in returning. He fell into anxious silence as the black aura in the room touched him. He caught the look of surprise in Varian's eyes at his unexpected appearance. Varian's guilty gaze went to Jana. Discontent showed in his eyes.

Jana came forward. "We'll discuss it another time, Dr. Zarcoff. It's very late, and I've obviously committed some intolerable error." She stared oddly at Varian. "I'm tired of you harassing and tempting me all the time, Commander Saar. I'm doing my best to adjust to your people and this situation. Evidently you lied when you said you would be my friend. If you continue to treat me like some savage sport, be prepared to carry out your threat, because Sylva will appear a docile cat when compared to me." She exited gracefully and proudly.

Tristan was first to recover his wits. "Great stars, Varian! Why?"

"I'll be damned if I even know myself, Tris. This situation provokes the very devil in me. Half the time I don't know what I'm saying or doing when she's around," he admitted peevishly.

"I see," Tristan muttered in obvious irritation.

"Do you? Then how about enlightening me?"

"Don't you have any idea why you feel so angry and resentful toward her? Don't you know why you pick on her?"

"What do you mean, Tris?" he inquired.

Tristan chuckled. "You said it yourself. You've never known a woman like Jana before. Could it be thoughts of her coming fate bother you more than you'd like to admit? Could it be resentment at being unable to start something which has

158

no future? Could it be you regret dangling her under Ryker's nose? Could it be the light of love and jealousy I see burning in those stormy eyes of yours?''

Varian silenced him with a scowl. ''That would be pure insanity.''

''If you say so,'' Tristan skeptically quipped.

''I do say so! Forget such absurd ideas,'' he ordered as those forbidden thoughts lingered to trouble his mind.

''You should know your feelings better than anyone,'' Tristan replied with a mocking smile and light chuckle. ''Jana's smart and brave, Varian. Why don't you seek her help in defeating Ryker? Wouldn't it be easier and nicer to work with her, than to work against her?''

Varian laughed. ''Are you serious, or as crazy as I'm getting? If she knew the truth about me or Ryker, she might blow this case for revenge. Have you forgotten we abducted her and she's ignorant of her world's fate?''

''Why not offer her freedom for her assistance? Wouldn't it be wonderful to spend the rest of the voyage getting to know her and enjoying her?''

''If Jana helped me entrap Ryker or revealed her feelings for me, she wouldn't be alive ten minutes after we left orbit. If it wasn't Ryker after her, it would be another Saar adversary. You know I can't take on the responsibility of a mate. A Star Fleet officer can't keep a woman on his ship and I don't have the authority to free her. If it wasn't for those *charl* laws. . . . Dammit, too many people know about her; everybody knows about her! *Kahala*, this timing with Jana couldn't be worse!''

''And that, Rogue Saar, explains your behavior. But don't you think it's time to stop punishing Jana for matters beyond either your or her control?'' Tristan said, holding up the book and nodding to it. ''As Jana's captor and seller, you're placing the blame for her unfortunate destiny on the wrong shoulders.''

Varian grimaced at the challenging grin on Tristan's face and stalked out. In his quarters, Varian threw his body on his wide bed. What did it matter how he felt? He was cognizant of too many detrimental facts. He could enjoy and protect Jana only if she was with him; and he couldn't keep a mistress aboard a starship, especially such a distracting one! Neither could he leave her at his home or in a private location to visit as frequently as time and duty allowed; discovery and danger from an enemy were too great. A man in his position couldn't afford to reveal any kind of weakness which could be exploited. Besides Ryker Triloni, *Kadim* Maal Triloni, Supreme Ruler Jurad Tabriz and his son Prince Taemin, many other rivals lengthened his threat list.

Varian knew he could have Jana only if he resigned his command, defeated all of his enemies, and remained close at hand, which he could not. Nor could he hold her captive or stall her auction for years. He could be slain in the line of duty; then what would happen to her when his estate went to the only surviving Saar blood heir: Ryker? Unaccustomed to defeat or helplessness, he was stormed by frustration and fury. Worse, Jana was making it harder on him with her offers of surrender. Her spells were just as irresistible as Shara's had been for his father, without using secret herbs and hypnotic potions from the "black arts!" Someone would pay for his misery and sacrifices: Ryker Triloni!

In the Maffei Galaxy, Canissia Garthon stared at the publicity pictures of Jana Greyson. The other captives did not interest her. Her body trembled with jealousy. Her hands grasped the pictures and crumpled them, one by one. Promotion about this exquisite Earthling captive was widely circulated; gossip about the alien creature filled her ears at every stop she made. Jokes blossomed like wildflowers about Varian's good fortune in spending weeks with this beauty before her sale to another man, which all doubted would take place!

Never had an alien captive received so much publicity and public attention. Men talked as if this Jana Greyson were a real goddess. It seemed that they all planned to attend the auctions just for a peek at her. Many of them had already decided to bid on her. Millions of *katoogas* were being discussed as the opening bid. In the next breath, those men declared Varian Saar would never allow them to outbid him. Canissia raged over this rival. She needed to find a way to get rid of Jana as quickly as possible.

She was anxiously awaiting the *Wanderlust*'s arrival at the planet Auriga, the third planet on Varian's preannounced schedule. On the first two stops, Varian and his security team would be on full alert for his foes. Canissia decided it was best if she did not expose her surveillance to her former lover. On Auriga, her spy would have a full report on this alien enchantress. If Jana had captured Varian's eye, she would be sorry in many ways. Surely Varian Saar would never buy a mate, no matter how beautiful and intelligent? If he did, it would become a race to see who would slay his heart's desire first! The choices were many: herself, Ryker, Jurad, Maal, and others.

A wicked grin distorted Canissia's face as a malicious idea came to mind. Getting rid of this golden temptress might be simple, if she showed this publicity to Supreme Ruler Jurad and his son Prince Taemin. Why shouldn't they be tempted to take possession of Varian's enchantress? After all, Galen Saar—Varian and Ryker Triloni's father—had taken possession of Jurad's enchantress. No matter if the handsome and virile Galen was innocent of treachery and enticement, Princess Shara had surrendered herself totally to him, including her sanity and life. Galen's son's golden-haired, green-eyed enchantress would be the perfect replacement for the deceased Shara, Canissia decided.

First, she had to figure a way for Jurad or Taemin to bid on Jana, as they were not Maffeian citizens. The Pyropean capital planet of Cenza was far away; it was the perfect place for Jana to live, or exist, as the case might be if the evil prince purchased her. Of course, the sadistic redhead speculated, she could send her ship's captain and current lover Zan Rima to relate this suggestion to the neighboring rulers. Jurad or Taemin could then provide Zan with the appropriate funds to buy Jana. Once the ravishing Earthling vanished, who would be the wiser to her location and fate?

As for Ryker, he probably knew about Varian's trek by now. Perhaps she should have told him about it. Ryker Triloni was evil and unpredictable; there was no telling how this information would affect the vengeful prince on Darkar.

Zan was even now away on an errand for his beloved enchantress. Thoughts of Varian and Ryker enflamed her passions, while memories of their stinging rejections provoked her evil urges. She summoned two members of her all-male crew, a blond and an ebony-haired male who were both muscular and very tall, one to fill in for each Saar. What Zan didn't know couldn't cause trouble. If he did, she would rid herself of him. She pretended to discuss their next voyage while she served them a special wine, a drink laced with the potion provided by Ryker: the blend of a strong hypnotic drug and a powerful aphrodisiac. She waited suspensefully for the chemicals, whose spells would not be remembered, to take effect.

When Canissia knew the two entranced men were under her control, she ordered them to strip and lie upon her bed. She eyed the proof of their immense hunger for sex which would take hours to appease. She eagerly ripped off her garments and joined them.

On Darkar in the secret complex of Trilabs, Ryker was speaking with Moloch Shira, a man from the planet Thule in the Maffei Galaxy who bore a bitter grudge against Ryker's half brother. "Varian will be on alert at his first stop, Moloch. Be careful. When you retrieve the report from my agent aboard his ship, I'll be nearby. After you deliver it and I see what's really going on aboard his ship with that alien bitch, I'll give you a report to pass to my agent when they stop on Thule. Since that's your home, it won't look suspicious for you to be seen there. I might need you to do another favor for me after I read that report. . . ."

"Anything, Ryker, just help me destroy that bastard who ruined my career in the Star Fleet," Moloch said, forgetting it was his own drunkenness which caused a tragic space accident, resulting in his banishment from the Alliance Force. "I swear, no one will know there's a connection between me and you. And remember you promised to hand Canissia Garthon over to me as a reward. By the time this matter is settled, I'll have that secret room all ready for her."

"When the time comes, Moloch, I'll make sure you have Canissia all to yourself for as long as you wish. In fact, I would appreciate it if she doesn't ever see the light of day again. I can provide certain drugs to end your fun cleanly and painlessly, and a few to make your amusement more enjoyable."

"I don't want her end to be painless or quick. I want her at my mercy."

Ryker smiled in agreement. "Then I have several drugs which will interest you. I'll deliver them when I deliver that treacherous bitch to you."

When Moloch left and Ryker's mistress joined him, she

questioned his laughter. "Such gullibility and ignorance, Precious. He'll never see death coming, nor will Canissia." Ryker reached for his mistress and deftly removed her lab coat and other garments. He began to lavish attention on her supple breasts as his hand worked below.

She moaned and swayed as she watched him pleasure her, but asked, "What do you think of that female on Varian's ship? I was spying on you two."

Ryker watched her. "What do you mean?" He pressed her to the floor and trailed kisses over the length of her fiery body.

"She's beautiful, and you know who she favors! Do you plan to get your hands on her? Then what will you do with her?" she demanded, as if he had answered her previous question affirmatively.

Ryker fondled her breasts, almost painfully nibbling on her peaks. He teased, "I bet Varian is squirming day and night with Princess Shara's image aboard his ship. I wonder if Jana has the same effect on him as my mother, a ravishing Androas princess, had on his father?"

Jana leisurely bathed and selected her garment for dinner. She laid the red silk jumpsuit on her bed. Clad in a satin wrapper and panties, she stood before the mirror, brushing her long hair.

The door swished open to her bathroom and Varian mounted the steps. Their gazes met and locked in the mirror. Neither spoke nor moved for a time. Finally, Jana turned and looked up into his bronzed face. "I don't know what I did this afternoon, but I'm sorry for provoking you. For some curious reason, I always seem to rub you the wrong way. I never know how to behave correctly around you. If you'll just explain the rules to me, I'll try my best not to antagonize you again." Her eyes watered and she lowered her head as she continued, "I suppose this crazy situation would be easier to deal with if I didn't find you so damn irresistible . . . and so damn unattainable! Maybe I have been playing the wanton. No matter, I think it's time I stop behaving like an ass or a child, because you can't stand me, and I can't seem to ignore you. Why did you have to be the captain of this starship?"

Jana looked up at him and moved her finger over his lips.

"I wish I didn't know . . . I wish there hadn't been any contact between us. You'll be an impossible act to follow. Tell me, Varian, how do I end this painful hostility and trouble between us?"

This was not the scene he had envisioned before his arrival. He had come to apologize and make a truce. Those plans vanished. Varian's fingers grasped her chin and his thumb caressed her lower lip. "It's really very simple, little moonbeam," he whispered in an emotion-laced voice. "Just prevent me from wanting you beyond control and reason. There are things you don't know and can't understand, Jana, things which cannot be changed. I do find you perilously desirable. But I must not take you as a mistress and I cannot take you as a mate. I get angry because your potent allure makes it harder on me. You're so beautiful that I keep forgetting how innocent you are. I forget you aren't a free woman and I'm not a free man; you don't have the right to surrender to me, and I don't have the right to seduce you."

Varian gazed deeply into her troubled eyes as one tear rolled down her cheek. "For both our sakes, Jana, never yield to me, never. If you do, I swear I'll place you at the top of my list of adversaries." He snapped a gold bracelet on her wrist. "It's two days late, but happy birthday, moonbeam. I'm truly sorry that friendship has been so difficult between us. From now on, I'll try my damnedest to control my temper. Beware of me, Jana; I can hurt you deeply without meaning to do so." He kissed her hungrily, then departed as she sagged weakly against the vanity.

PART II
Stardust and Shadows

As the playful Gods gather to watch mortals below,
The helpless Fates warn sadly for only they know:
Casting out "Stardust" demands love and life;
Fleeing its "Shadows" creates bitter strife . . .

Chapter Nine

Jana felt dizzy. Her veins coursed with fiery desire while tremors swept over her flushed body. She ached to embrace him, to kiss him greedily, to make love to him without shame or inhibition. His eyes and voice had exposed remorse, anger, frustration, and passion. If he was so wealthy and powerful and found her so desirable, what terrible obstacle stood between them? What awesome demand had fate placed on his shoulders? What haunting burden did this man carry?

She knew now that she would freely and eagerly surrender her body and soul to Varian's loving assault, even if she could have him for only a short time. For once they were parted, there would be no second chance to weigh their feelings.

Varian Saar stood at the transascreen in his quarters staring out into space without absorbing the immense view. The fated day would strike when they eased into parking orbit at Zamarra. The *charl*'s training period was complete; the climax to his cover mission was about to begin with the first auction tomorrow. During the night, his ship would reach the Maffei Galaxy. The flood of relief which he had expected to engulf him did not take place. The info tapes were locked in Varian's safe, one which would self-destruct if anyone tampered with it.

On Zamarra, Varian would set his primary assignment into motion, secretly passing a top-secret tape to the first of thirteen *avatars*, the tapes that would inform them that the Milky Way Galaxy was in danger. Any attempt to destroy or divert the enormous meteor must be kept from their enemies—Ryker and *Kadim* Maal and Supreme Ruler Jurad—at all costs. Those leaders would be tempted to enslave and kill countless Earthlings and Uranians, and more likely attack the Maffei Alliance while its best starships were away on a mission to save Earth. And once he displayed Jana to whet appetites, and to cover the reason for his meetings with Planetary rulers, her new course would be under way. Once she was traveling it, there would be no turning back for him or her.

Varian was tense and jittery. He wished he could meet with Supreme Councilman Draco Procyon and Supreme Council leader *Kadim* Tirol Trygue to analyze this conflicting drama, as he was certain his good friend and grandfather could provide crucial advice. But he couldn't alter his mission course; dates and schedules had been made, and Jana's publicity material was widely spread. In addition, it was too risky to send coded messages to Draco and his grandfather this close to home. This was a time when Varian knew he must use his own judgment.

To think of Jana's loss fired him with blazing jealousy and regret. Jana was the cause or answer to so many of his problems. Or was he merely getting too emotionally involved in this mission and his covert scheme? He should never have gotten close to her!

Varian decided he would attend the last dinner dance in the Stardust Room where his officers would be celebrating their successful voyage. Some would be anticipating a short leave with family or friends; a few would be reassigned to other missions or ships. He told staff coordinator Martella Karsh to include Kathy and Heather and to seat them at the table with Ferris Laus and Tesla Rilke, as he would financially make certain that Ferris obtained Kathy as a mate and Rilke's brother Spala obtained Heather as his mate. He then ordered Martella to seat the ten elite Uranians at an oblong table in the center of the room to enjoy the merriment, as promised as a reward for their cooperation and successful training. Robots were to be activated to assume the duties of certain crew members until the festivities ended. Varian said he would skip the social hour and dance; he would appear only for dinner.

His final order for Martella was to seat Jana at a table with Tristan, herself, Nigel, Kara, and Kyle; that news seemed to sadden the female officer. Martella lowered her somber gaze and inhaled deeply before speaking, as she could not keep her opinions to herself.

"Varian, we're too close to the first auction for me to hold silent while you initiate this destructive farce. If this was strictly a personal matter, I would not question it or your commands. But this is part of a Star Fleet and Elite Squad mission, and I'm a member of both units. I must protest this dangerous manipulation of Jana Greyson. I had hoped that after spending weeks with her, you would change your plans. You must not use a fake enchantment for Jana to provoke Ryker. I think you're making two grave mistakes where she's concerned: one by making her your Ryker-decoy and two by selling her."

Martella leaned forward on his desk as she reasoned urgently, "Do you really think you can ever find another woman like Jana, one so well suited to you and your life? Do you honestly think you'll be able to forget her? To bear seeing her with another man? Once she's sold, it's forever."

"I can't change our destinies. Isn't it better for her to become another man's mate than to die for becoming mine? I've been trying to get rid of my enemies for years. Until I do, I can't become involved with Jana. I would rather lose her than see her tortured and killed."

"Varian, Varian," Martella chided, "she's already involved. Are you blind, my friend? She's in love with you. Rejecting her and selling her will destroy her more quickly and be crueler than Ryker or Jurad ever could. If you don't find a way to control who buys her, she could get a terrible owner. Whoever gets her will make it hard on her, for she won't yield to him while loving you. Think about your feelings and actions. Think about faking a sale to Draco Procyon; let him guard her for you until you can openly claim her."

The party began with frivolous chatter and unlimited drinks to soothe nerves. Music drifted around the women to dispel their fears and distract their minds. Tonight, the women were attired in gowns in a variety of styles and colors, so that Jana was not the customary standout. Varian did not arrive until dinner was served; then he seemed to almost sneak into the room.

Varian seated himself with his back to Jana. The food was superb. The atmosphere was curiously gay. The women seemed elated and charmed. Dinner ended, and champagne flowed freely. When the dancing began, Varian realized that Jana's seat was empty. Not wishing to depart before her return, he allowed half an hour to pass before questioning her absence.

When no one knew of her whereabouts or motive for a lengthy absence, Varian left to look for her. Jana couldn't be found anywhere. Varian recalled one last location to check before involving security in a search of the ship. When he entered the observation bubble, Varian saw her. Jana was standing with her back to the door, her forehead resting on the clear wall. It looked as if she were asleep her feet. The music which filled the area was louder than normal, preventing her from hearing his entrance. It seemed as if she were using the mellow sounds to block out reality. She was mentally very far away.

Varian pressed the privacy lock, then observed her. He realized he was losing Jana right before his eyes, just as if her auction had already taken place. Obviously she had stolen away to force reality into her heart and mind, to resign herself to face tomorrow and the next two weeks. Soon, this stunning creature would belong to another man. Soon, Jana would be out of his life forever. Soon, Jana would be possessed, enjoyed, cherished by a stranger. And there would be only bittersweet memories left between them. . . . After lowering the music volume, Varian slowly approached her. He leaned his left side against the transascreen and focused that piercing blue stare on her. He was close enough to touch her, but he didn't. Nor did he speak to her.

Until Jana inhaled deeply and swallowed, she did not look at him. She ceased toying with the gold bracelet which had held her attention. When she did half turn and glance up into his stoic face, she smiled faintly. She tried to joke lightly. "I suppose I've been gone too long. Perhaps the party is too dull without my provoking personality?

When Varian didn't react or respond, Jana said, "The bracelet is lovely, Varian. It was kind and thoughtful of you to remember my birthday. I hope I haven't annoyed you again tonight. It's so beautiful and peaceful here that I lost track of time." Her gaze shifted to the scenery outside the massive ship. She watched clouds drift in the indigo vastness before them. She observed two small moons shining in the distance as they orbited a large and dark planet. "Is that Zamarra?" she inquired in a muffled tone, pointing at the body in their flight path.

Varian perceived a strain and withdrawal in her. Her smiles no longer reached and brightened her eyes. Her silvery laughter and cultured voice were hoarse and tight. She was trembling.

"What were you thinking about when I arrived?"

"How scared I am about tomorrow and the coming weeks," Jana replied honestly. She shuddered. "I was wondering what your world holds in store for me. I would prefer to be arriving under different circumstances, but that can't be helped. I suppose I'll adjust to this new existence; at least you all keep telling me I will," she stated wistfully. "It won't be easy, will it? I don't think I've ever been this terrified, not even when you abducted me or continually harassed me. I wonder what's truly out there waiting for me," she murmured in overwhelming dread.

"Your new existence can be whatever you make of it, Jana. Be strong, and brave, and patient. Be tolerant and understanding. Be gentle and loving, and obedient and respectful. Do these things, moonbeam, and you'll find safety and happiness. Be proud and happy, Jana Greyson."

Jana turned and looked up at him. A tear rolled down her left cheek. "What about your future, Varian? What would happen to you if all of your money and fame disappeared? What if some accident disabled or disfigured you? Who would be there to help you? To love you and comfort you? To share your life? I would guess enemies, male and female, are countless. Who would be there for you if you could no longer take what you desire with your wealth, strength, and power? Who are you, Varian? What do you want from life?"

Varian winced. "What you're really asking is who do I want and need. If you're leading this conversation in the direction I think you are, don't do it."

Jana did not avert her gaze. "You're too cynical about women and love. One day, you'll meet a special woman who will make your downfall painless and rewarding. Do not fear, the woman who is fortunate enough to win your heart and attention will not demand your soul. She won't ask or expect you to change yourself or your existence for her. She'll only want your love and passion, nothing more."

"No commitment? No chains? No demands of any kind?" he hinted.

"If she truly loves you and wants you, she will settle for

whatever part of you she can have. How could she make demands which might drive you away? She's there somewhere," Jana remarked, waving her hand over the span of space before them.

"And what would Varian Saar do with a special woman? He's a starship commander. What female would make such a sacrifice worthwhile?" he inquired tenderly as he tried to discourage this painful talk.

Jana laughed, a real laugh. "When you meet such a woman, my pompous and stubborn commander, you'll know. Her pull will be so strong that nothing and no one else will matter. You'll see," she playfully warned.

"For the present, I'm doomed to ignorance and loneliness," he retorted. "I'm free, and I need to remain that way for a while longer."

"Are you truly free? Are you happy?" she asked quietly, pointedly.

Her question pierced his heart. He asked, "What difference does that make to you, my lovely and nosy Earthling? Do you think you can make me happy? Can you bewitch me? Hold my undivided attention? Fill my heart with love, my body with passion, and my mind with commitment?" Dreading to deal with her allure, Varian prayed she would respond as she did.

"I harbor no illusions about you or us, Commander Saar. I would not be so foolish or vain as to think I possessed such awesome powers of enchantment. You're right; I was being too nosy. I guess I'm in a forgetful, crazy mood. Would you like to share a farewell dance in the Stardust Room? We could toast your successful voyage and my new destiny." When he frowned at her last sentence, she pleaded softly, "Don't become angry with me again. Let our truce last another two weeks," she coaxed earnestly. "I promise, no more questions or vexing comments. I'll be polite and genial."

"Tomorrow's a busy day, Jana. I think I'll turn in. Would you like to return to the Stardust Room, or would you like me to escort you to your quarters? You'll be accompanying me in the morning. I promised to show you off at every port. Martella will supply you with the proper wardrobe."

His news was spirit-crushing. She should have kept silent, for he always wanted to hurt her when they got too cozy. "If I'm to be displayed like a work of art, I should look my very best. A good night's sleep sounds perfect, Commander Saar. What time should I be ready to leave?"

"Ten o'clock. We'll have an exhibition, then lunch, then the auction. Your clothes should be laid out on the sofa in your quarters."

"I'll make certain I don't overlook them this time. Shall we go, sir?"

No word was spoken between them on the way to her quarters. Jana bid him a hasty good night. Varian's frame prevented the door from closing. He caught her wrist and drew her toward him. His cobalt gaze seared into her limpid one. "I don't need to warn you to be on your very best behavior tomorrow; we don't want any problems this close to home, and I don't want you to begin this new life badly," he cautioned, then hastily kissed her on the forehead before leaving.

Jana glared at the closed door. "Don't worry, my dashing commander. You'll be proud of your highly trained *femme fatale*. And hopefully you'll be squirming in your seat while I wantonly entice every man in the room!" she said, and ripped off the bracelet and flung it across the room.

The next morning Varian arrived to escort Jana to the waiting shuttle. As she was not quite ready, he sat down to wait for her. A sparkle caught his eye. He retrieved her discarded birthday gift from the floor near the sofa table. He knew it hadn't been dropped. Yet, when she joined him, he stated, "You must have dropped this." *Kahala,* did she have to look so sexy and magnetic in everything she donned, even a simple purple jumpsuit!

"Would a penniless captive wear an expensive bracelet to a flesh sale? Won't it look odd or bold for me to display a gift from another man?"

"You can do as I say, and I say you can wear the gift, if you wish."

Jana caught a hidden clue to his words: a test of some sort. She hurriedly pondered his meaning and her response. She took the bracelet, and snapped it on her wrist. "I hope it has your name and address inscribed on it in case I get lost. I'm ready to go," she informed him.

They went to the docking bay and boarded a shuttlecraft. As

they headed for the planet surface, Jana's eyes were clued to the scene below them. "I don't see anything but water," she commented in confusion.

"Zamarra is an undersea world, little moonbeam. Don't be afraid. You'll be safe with me." He warmed as Jana kept snuggling closer and closer to him as the watery surface drew closer to the spacecraft. "Relax, love. We won't sink. There's a landing pad nearby. We'll be picked up there."

Jana's worried gaze met his amused one. "I hope you don't find me a buyer here. I can't swim," she teased. "I would be petrified living beneath all that water. Are there cities? Or are these people half fish?"

Varian chuckled. "You'll see. Relax, Zamarra isn't for you."

Seated behind them, Martella, Tristan, and Nigel exchanged glances, pleased at Varian's kind treatment of Jana.

The shuttlecraft landed on a clear surface above the turquoise water. Suddenly another craft surfaced and docked at the edge of the landing pad. Varian took Jana's hand and escorted her into the seacraft. When they were seated, Jana asked where the captives were. Varian informed her they would follow later. Jana sighed and relaxed against his reassuring body.

Jana was amazed by the setting as the craft sank into the watery domain. She saw unusual plants and aquatic animals. Her head and eyes jerked this way and that as she tried to take in so much at once. Suddenly, a massive city enclosed in various sized bubble domes appeared below the craft. Jana watched in wonder as the craft skimmed along the outer surface of the largest clear dome. Finally it entered a docking area where the seacraft's door was attached to a portal which opened to allow their entrance to the undersea city. Jana stared at the greenish-blue water above and around them. If those walls should give way under the tremendous force of so much water. . .

"Come along, little moonbeam. You can worry about learning to swim later." He took her hand and guided her into an area where they boarded a tram which would take them into the center of this strange world.

The city was a world of white and green. Walkways and buildings were constructed of ivory stone. Sweeping green plants decorated the landscape. Each time she glanced skyward, Jana was reminded of the ocean above them. She learned that smaller cities or private dwellings were connected to the main complex via tunnels. She was astounded to hear the entire planet was underwater! There were two thousand large cities like this one, and over four hundred thousand smaller complexes! She guessed why Varian had chosen Zamarra for the sale of the Uranians; the lack of sunlight had created an extremely pale- complexioned race, much like them.

Jana, Varian, Nigel, Martella, and Tristan saw many sights, then stopped for lunch. The unfamiliar selections of food were both aromatic and delectable. She was given samples from everyone's plates. She tried all of the dishes, afraid to ask what she was eating. To any observant eye, it would appear as if five close friends were having a good time.

The others chuckled as they watched her. Their group seemed relaxed and cheerful during this sunny interlude. They laughed, joked, ate, and talked without making reference to the day's business. They took turns filling Jana's head with stories of their past adventures and the exotic places they had visited and would visit again.

As they made their way to the auction hall, Jana didn't let herself think about where they were going or why. Her eyes darted from side to side as she took in the sights. They entered a courtyard surrounded by arcades on three sides, with a fourth wall displaying numerous balconies jutting out from a large building. In the center of the yard sat a raised platform about ten by sixteen feet. Jana's eyes darted from the balconies to the platform, then back again. She immediately discerned the purpose of this evil place: a slave market.

Jana watched as the balconies began to fill with many men and a few women. Their manner suggested a sporting event rather than the stark reality of human bondage. Anger mounted inside her and glinted in her eyes. These people dared to call themselves superior to her race; yet they still practiced this barbaric behavior!

Jana's resentful gaze scanned the growing crowd, which was inspecting her from head to foot as a shrewd Texan would examine a bull or cattle before a costly purchase. Aversion and bitterness welled up in her throat as she looked around for a familiar face. Tristan was signing several papers not far away; he shook his head at some error and departed to correct it. Nigel, who was giving instructions to security men, left the enclosed area to position the five guards. Near the platform,

Martella was explaining how the auctioning procedure was carried out and was comforting the frightened Uranians. Varian was not to be seen. Jana shuddered. She feared she was going to be ill on the spot.

Jana felt piercing eyes on her, a stare which was potent and evil. The eerie sensation became so intense that goosebumps and shivers raced over her body. She glanced around to discover the cause of her sudden unease. Her eyes locked with those of an insidious man with an ashen complexion and harsh features. His voracious gaze was degrading, as if he were ripping off her garment and devouring the exposed flesh. Over and over he suggestively licked his full lips. His heavy jowls told her he was a greedy, overindulgent man. He clasped his hands and twisted them while Jana paled. She felt as if she were chained nude before his lewd gaze, as if his fat tongue and rough hands were working ravenously and salaciously upon her helpless frame!

The man's eyes traveled over her frozen features. He grinned at her response. His ebony gaze seemed drawn to her tawny hair and colorful eyes. Many rings encircled his stubby fingers, and numerous gold chains and medallions hung around his bullish neck. He was wearing a flowing blue-black caftan and around his head of grimy black hair, he had secured a black band shot with golden threads. Despite her glare of contempt, he continued his bold and unnerving scrutiny. He held an instrument or a small camera to one eye. He appeared to be viewing her with a miniature field glass. She felt like a creature under a microscope.

Forcing her gaze away from him, Jana realized many of the other men were ogling her in a similar manner. She didn't like this place or these people! Hostility and alarm filled her. She wanted out of here!

Jana turned her back to the crowd. Her searching gaze located Varian leaning against an arch not far away; he was not alone. Jana eyed the porcelain-skinned, jet-eyed, raven-haired beauty who was laughing and conversing intimately with him. The smile on the Zamarrian's ruby lips was seductively inviting. The female caressed Varian's chest and shoulders with a familiarity and hunger which enraged the tormented Jana. She despised the way that femme fatale was pressing her luscious body against her love's.

176

Jana looked around for one of her friends. When she glanced in Varian's direction, he was departing with that brazen vixen, who was clinging tightly to his arm. Jana was alone and afraid beneath the pressing gazes of too many lecherous strangers. Without stopping to think, she began to walk swiftly and blindly toward the entrance to this horrid place. All she could think about was escaping these lustful men and this grim location.

"Jana!" Varian called out to stop her frantic exit. When she kept moving, Varian pursued her and seized her wrist. "Where do you think you're going?" he asked as he whirled her around to face him. He saw her whitened face, frightened gaze, and trembling body. "What's wrong, moonbeam?" he inquired with a sudden tenderness which irrationally provoked her.

Jana focused glittery eyes on his concerned expression. "You left me all alone! Those awful men kept gaping at me as if I were naked! I hate this place! I hate these barbarians! I want to return to your ship!"

Varian glanced over Jana's head to comprehend the reasons for her panicky flight. He smiled encouragingly. "I'm sorry, moonbeam. Stay close to me. No one will dare bother you at my side. You can't blame them for craving such a rare treat," he teased, cuffing her chin affectionately.

Jana lowered her head, so that she would not burst into tears and fling herself into his arms. "God, I wish this filthy, degrading business were over."

Varian's hand stroked her silky hair, then raised her chin. "You have nothing to fear, moonbeam. Those men know you're not for sale. There isn't a man here who can afford to enter the doors to your auction. I would protect you with my life, if necessary. They're only envious of me for capturing and enjoying the most ravishing mistress in the Universe."

She shrieked in astonishment. "They think I . . . belong to you?"

"That's right," he calmly confessed. "It seemed best to mislead these lusty Zamarrians to prevent any nasty problems."

"What about your *friend* over there? Did you also mislead her? Or doesn't she mind sharing you with an alien mistress?" she said, sneering frostily.

Varian chuckled, warming at her display of jealousy. "Don't fret, moonbeam; I've never sampled her charms or shared her bed. Rayna's what you Earthlings call a high-class prostitute. She uses that little act you just witnessed to pass information about enemies of the Alliance Force to me. You'd be surprised what slips past a man's lips in the throes of passion," he jested mirthfully. "Rayna knows me too well to believe the rumors about us."

Jana ignored Varian's indiscreet words. What did she care if this sensual Rayna was a secret agent? Rayna wanted to share her information with Varian in bed, not on the street! Clever Rayna might make that demand before passing along her stolen clues! No doubt Varian would do anything necessary to comply with his loyalty to the Alliance! "I see," Jana purred cattily. "Won't these patrons think it strange that you openly play around with a whore in front of your mistress? If you must seek additional attention elsewhere, just how special and fulfilling can I be? How safe will I be then?"

Varian considered his behavior. "A point well made, little moonbeam. I should definitely postpone my visit to her dwelling until I have you safely on board my ship." He goaded Jana in order to extract the desired response for his enemies he knew were in the area: Varian's bewitchment and Jana's resistance.

Jana puffed up with rising fury. "Why trouble yourself on my behalf? Surely these customers have thoroughly examined me by now. After all, you did say none of them could afford my asking price. Why not return me to the ship and get on with your clandestine meeting?" she suggested sullenly.

Varian seized her arm and warned between clenched teeth, "Obey me, Jana. I don't want any trouble today. Rest assured no man will approach you, or I'll slay him on the spot. Now smile and behave yourself."

Varian pulled her around just as she narrowed her eyes and spat at him through clenched teeth. "Then I shan't be afraid anymore. What man in his right mind would challenge the intrepid Varian Saar?"

Varian grinned. Jana's reaction couldn't have been more perfect. "Stick close, little moonbeam," he advised as he walked away. Confident his scheme of deception was in motion, he relaxed.

Jana glared at his retreating back. He could be so insufferable, so mean, so arrogant! When Varian realized that Jana hadn't followed him, he turned, came back, and reached out to take her hand. Jana tried to yank it out of his grasp. He scowled and squeezed it until she winced and relented. As if he were issuing orders for her conduct, he whispered, "I'm being an ass again. Sorry, Jana. Let's get this nasty affair over quickly."

Jana looked up into his roguish face and frowned in confusion. "You are one exasperating, bewildering man, Varian Saar."

"It runs in the blood," he mirthfully replied. "You're stuck with me."

"Fat chance," she scoffed distractedly, bringing hearty laughter from the man at her side.

A distinguished man of around sixty approached them. There was a genteel aura about him. The smile he sent to Jana was warm, but the one for Varian exhibited deep respect and admiration. He was introduced as *Avatar* Suran, the ruler of the planet. The impressive man held up his hand in greeting, palm facing Jana. She nervously lifted her hand and pressed her palm against his as she had been taught aboard Varian's ship.

"It's a pleasure, Dr. Greyson," the ivory-faced man told her.

"It's an honor to meet you, sir," she replied courteously, wondering why Varian had given her medical status along with her full name.

The man looked at Varian and smiled. "Her publicity speaks truthfully. Some man will be extremely lucky to acquire such a superior mate." He dropped the small box in his hand, spilling its contents. While he chatted with Jana, Varian hunkered down and politely retrieved the box and items, slipping a miniature tape into the box. "If I were younger and single, I would be compelled to spend my entire fortune on a jewel like you. Thank you, Varian," the man said cheerfully as he accepted the box and held it tightly. His dark eyes briefly fused with fathomless blue ones. "I'd best get along home. I have some vital business to handle. You take care of this little gem. If I were the *Wanderlust* captain, she wouldn't be for sale," Suran declared boldly, to Varian's vexation. Suran chuckled, then strolled away.

To dispel Varian's sudden dark mood, Jana impishly sing-songed, "If I were the *Wanderlust* captain, I wouldn't be a prisoner; you would be mine and I won't reveal what I would do with you. He was very nice," she added seriously, as if the previous remarks were forgotten.

Fortunately the auction went off without any unpleasantness or trouble, to Jana's astonishment. After each successful bidding, the woman was taken away gently and respectfully. Nothing in the buyers' expressions or moods suggested that these *charls* were anything less than priceless treasures or cherished mates.

Varian left during the final sale. Jana returned to the ship with Nigel, Tristan, Martella, Vaiden, Daxley, and Baruch. Later, she dined with them in the Stardust Room, acutely aware of Varian's absence and painfully suspecting the reason behind it: Rayna. After a game of *Laius* with Nigel as the winner, Jana returned to her quarters for a restless night's sleep.

Zan's space cruiser was swiftly heading for his rendezvous with Canissia Garthon's ship. The pictures of Jana and Varian at the auction on Zamarra would be delivered by Canissia to Prince Taemin and his father, Jurad. . . .

Moloch Shira, too, had been surreptitiously observing the couple all day, frequently changing disguises to avoid being noticed as he took notes and pictures for Ryker Triloni. As prearranged, he had retrieved the report packet from the traitorous officer on Varian's ship. Added to his investigation of Jana and Varian today, Ryker Triloni should be able to obtain a good, close look at the relationship between his half brother and the alien enchantress.

Chapter Ten

Jana was awakened by gentle nudgings. "Your monitor isn't on, Jana. You must rise and hurry. We leave for Thule in less than an hour."

"What?" Jana mumbled drowsily. She yawned and

stretched, trying to come to full awareness as she looked into Martella's anxious face.

"Didn't Commander Saar tell you, you're to attend the auction on each planet? We reached Thule early this morning. You bathe and dress, and I'll order your breakfast. It'll be in the servo when you finish. Your clothes are on the sofa. Hurry along, or we'll keep everyone waiting."

As Tristan, Martella, and Jana were transported to Thule a short time later, she wondered if there was a special reason why Varian had left before them. If it was to meet another woman, why had he taken Nigel along?

Jana watched the planet surface grow larger and clearer. As with Zamarra, the cities and private dwellings of Thule were covered with massive clear domes. This time, according to Tristan's explanation, the inverted beehives were constructed to protect the inhabitants from excessively hot rays from their two moons, which were more like reflective suns. She searched the horizon in every direction. She could make out at least three enormous domes which were like the hubs of wagon wheels, with clear tunnels radiating like spokes in all directions to smaller domes, which in turn radiated in a half-moon design to five even smaller domes. She was told that each community was self-contained, but was connected to all others by an underground tram system.

Jana observed her surroundings as they hurried to the building where the *charl* exhibition and sale would take place. Most of the dwellings were flat-roofed and square. There was a wide range of exterior paint colors on the stuccolike surfaces, but all were in soft hues. Most windows and doors were in arch designs. The structure where the auction was to be held seemed to be a dinner theater from its interior design.

Jana was seated near an open arch. Martella and Tristan left her to carry out their assigned duties but it wasn't long before Nigel came to join her. Pleased with his arrival, Jana relaxed as much as this repulsive occasion would permit. The auction began without Varian.

"This is so humiliating, Nigel. And it's so hard to be displayed and be forced to watch others being sold, including Susan," she remarked hotly, gesturing at the stage where her former rival stood in a beguiling pose next to Stephanie.

"I'm sorry if it offends you, Jana." Nigel saw the fires of

rebellion dancing within her eyes. He knew Varian would be forced to react harshly if she relented to those emotions. Nothing and no one must interfere with their mission. When it looked as if she were about to loudly protest this practice, he warned, "Don't interfere, Jana. You wouldn't want to join them today." He nodded toward the stage. "If you publicly embarrass Varian, he will be forced to punish you harshly. Such actions would have a detrimental effect on your impending fate. Please, stay calm and quiet," he entreated her. "Don't forget you're a captive, and he's a Star Fleet commander."

Jana almost bit her tongue to curb her surly response. She trembled from the effort required to keep her body in the chair. She vainly tried to shut out the bargaining sounds which reached her ears. Even if none of the patrons were crude or impolite, this procedure distressed her greatly.

A staggering realization had touched Jana this morning; she would soon find herself on a similar platform enduring this procedure. Nigel's words vanquished her courage. She, also, was a defenseless captive, soon to be sold to the highest bidder. She had to get away from here. When it came time for Susan's sale, Jana experienced no relief and delight. She was the first captive to be sold whom Jana had known closely.

"The ladies' room is just outside the doorway, Nigel. May I be excused for a few minutes? I promise to return shortly." She smiled genially to deceive him. She would allow enough time for this detestable business to be completed without her presence. Surely it couldn't last much longer.

Nigel nodded permission. He knew that Varian was meeting with Thule's planetary ruler, *Avatar* Feaji, at this very moment to pass along the secret mission tape. Still, Nigel wished Varian would arrive soon.

Jana hurried down the hallway, oblivious to a man who was observing her carefully. As she passed through an arch, she was intercepted and halted. "If you'll excuse me, sir," she hinted politely and tried to pass him.

The man seized her right arm in an uncomfortable grip. He realized that Jana did not remember seeing him yesterday on Zamarra when her contemptuous gaze swept over him. His leering half-smile infuriated her. She yanked on her arm and demanded, "Release me this instant. How dare you touch me!"

182

"Shut up, alien whore. I want to check out the merchandise. You are the widely acclaimed jewel of Saar's collection?" He sneered at her. "Are you really worth so much money, Jana Greyson? From what I hear, Saar has already sampled this delectable product and everyone knows a used product sells for less. What kind of bargain is he offering for an ex-mistress these days? Usually they're not worth much when he finishes with them." Moloch used his crude insults and frightening implications to draw more facts from Jana for Ryker. He had already passed Ryker's latest message to the spy aboard the *Wanderlust*: orders to supply Canissia with duplicates of the exact information and pictures which the spy had already passed to Ryker via Moloch yesterday.

Jana stiffened as his eyes insultingly drifted over her. "I must admit, Saar does have excellent taste, as usual. At least you should be well trained to service your new owner. Is that so?" he asked.

Jana jerked her arm free and landed a stunning slap across the man's face. "You bastard! How dare you touch me or insult me! Get out of my way!"

"In case you've been denied the facts, my lovely and fiery Earthling, captives go to the highest bidder. You've nothing to say about your sale or new owner, nor does your captor. Since I'm an extremely wealthy man who intends to place a bid on you, I suggest you be nicer. You could regret this foolish conduct when you find yourself my mate in fifteen days."

Despite her rising panic and fear, Jana bravely shouted, "Let me go!"

"Oh, yes," he murmured ominously, "I'm going to enjoy taming you, my little wildcat. My name is Moloch Shira. I'm from this planet of Thule, and no doubt your imminent mate. I should warn you, Jana, I can be extremely gentle and pleasant or I can be extremely tough and harsh." His smile and gaze were as hard as stone. "If you show me you can be agreeable and you still have something left over after Varian's voracious feeding, I might offer you a lengthier relationship than he gave you. Our colorings would blend perfectly in our offspring."

"I would rather die than have you touch me."

"Die? Not hardly. Rumor accurately has it you'll demand the highest price ever paid for any alien mate. Men all over this galaxy are plotting for your bid. I can make you beg for death every night, if you want it that way. For you see, Jana Greyson, I can easily afford your price. So I would soften that tongue if I were you, little ice-maiden. I would be willing to bet a small fortune you're worth every *katooga* Saar is asking, just as I'm willing to bet an equal fortune you're not Saar's mistress. The truth will come out at your auction on Rigel; Saar must declare your sexual status. Unless he's been careless and allowed one of his officers to taste your sweet charms,'' he murmured huskily as his fingers drifted down her left arm, "you'll be sold as a virgin. Isn't that right, Jana? Saar has seduced countless women in his day and will lay countless more, but he would never make love to an alien breeder. No, Varian Saar would never reveal such a humiliating weakness.''

Moloch noted her hesitation to deny his words. He observed her acute fear. Jana was a surprise to him. He had expected matchless beauty and charm and intelligence, but not such magnetic vulnerability and softness. Moloch's hand slid up her arm and captured a breast.

Jana reacted immediately. She balled her fist and hit him with all her strength. The man grabbed her wrists and warned, "You'll pay for that, alien witch! You will pay dearly every time I take you. If I have to spend every *katooga* I have to purchase you, I will. After I've sated myself, I'll sell you to the meanest bastard I can locate.'' His green eyes glittered with vengeful fires.

"Varian will kill you for this. Let go of me!'' Jana shrieked at him.

Jana fell backward against the wall as Moloch was forcefully seized and thrown to the hard floor. Moloch glared up into the blue eyes of Varian Saar as they blazed with fury. Varian's expression was like a mask of pure rage which instilled caution in Moloch. Jana was too shaky to fling herself into Varian's arms; it wasn't necessary.

Varian stepped over to her, his strong arms encompassed her and held her tightly against his taut frame. He lifted her chin and gazed into her petrified eyes. "You all right, moonbeam?'' he questioned tenderly.

Jana's wide gaze shifted to the man who was brushing off his garments. She buried her face against Varian's chest. She didn't see the murderous look in Varian's eyes as he comforted her in a deceptively calm tone.

"You're safe, Jana. This reckless fool won't come near you again." Varian wanted nothing more than to tear Moloch limb from limb. He suspected Moloch was currently employed by Ryker. He brought his intense rage under control. Moloch's day would come, just like Ryker's. . . .

Moloch had gleaned the clues Ryker needed. Varian's look, voice, and possessive embrace had told him plenty. Still, he couldn't resist goading him. If Ryker didn't want Jana, then he certainly did! "A misunderstanding. Your little alien just changed her mind about trying to bribe me into buying her. Confronted with all that beauty and charm, I lost my head. You are still planning to sell her in two weeks?"

Jana's head jerked around in disbelief. "That's a lie! I never—"

Varian's finger on her lips shushed her. "Never mind, moonbeam. The truth is obvious. Moloch and I have our differences, but we know each other well. He thinks he has a grievance against me, but he's wrong."

Moloch grinned malevolently and said, "I will make certain I'm on Rigel for this special auction. She's one gem I'm determined to have, Saar, at any price. I'll be seeing you both soon."

Varian felt Jana sway weakly against him. His embrace involuntarily tightened around her shoulders. "There will be no samples today or any other day. If you dare come near Jana again before the auction, I'll make you regret ever seeing me. Do we understand each other?" he snarled, teeth bared like a wild animal about to attack his prey.

"Perfectly. Be sure you protect her from your black moods and your lust. Most buyers don't like tarnished treasures, even exquisite ones."

As Varian struggled to retain his precarious grip on his temper, Jana watched the noxious creature swagger away. Hurt and resentment filled her. She pushed herself out of his arms. "Thanks for the rescue," she murmured.

"I should have guarded you better, moonbeam. You would tempt even the gods to seize you. A mortal man is powerless to resist you, if he finds you alone and defenseless. I'll make certain this never happens again. I could have beaten Moloch senseless, but it isn't wise for a starship commander to kill such a rich and powerful man for offending a . . . you." Varian

185

wanted to bite off his tongue for his stupid choice of words. He had best settle down.

So, chivalry was wasted on a mere *charl*, a slave. Jana felt as if Varian had punched her forcefully in the abdomen. Apparently he had lied to her. So much for defending her. Had he been misleading her all along, perhaps to make her docile and pliant?

As if reading her thoughts, Varian promised, "I'll kill any man, including Moloch, if he ever harms you. You have my word, Jana."

She looked up at him. His voice had been cold and credible. His eyes looked honest. "You can't make such a promise, Commander Saar. Once I'm sold, your power over me will end, as will your protection. If I understand this procedure correctly, you'll have nothing to say about my sale or my owner. Don't try to control me with such harmful lies. I can't afford to offend prospective buyers, like I did Moloch. You know what can happen if a beast like that purchases me. Are you sure these displays are necessary? We're talking about my safety and survival," she reminded him.

"No matter who buys you, Jana, he will never harm you. If he tries, I'll find a way to stop him. If necessary, I'll provoke him into a lethal fight. I swear to you, I'll never allow any man to hurt you."

"Why can't you keep me, Varian?" Jana bravely queried. "I promise I'll do anything you ask. I won't interfere in your private life. Can't you buy me or arrange to keep me? Even if you don't want me as your mate, you could find something useful for me to do. I swear, no questions or pressure."

Varian was caught off guard by her plea. "Don't do this, Jana. You ask for the impossible. There is no place in my life for a woman, especially no time soon. I could make your life as miserable as Moloch could," he reasoned firmly. He waited for her denial or protest to come, which it did not.

"Is the money so important? If you can't keep me, then why can't you sell me or give me to someone like Nigel. He needs a mate, doesn't he? He's kind and gentle, and he likes me for myself. If not Nigel, then someone like him. Surely you have some kind friends who are single. You captured me; don't you have a right to dispose of me as you see fit?"

Varian needed to halt this conversation quickly. There was

only one way. "I don't own you, Jana; the Supreme Council does. I can't select your buyer, and Nigel can't afford your opening bid. Nor can he or any starship officer keep a mistress or mate on board. And what intelligent man could leave a tempting mate like you behind? He'd never keep his mind on his duty. I'm sorry, Jana, but I have no control over this matter."

"You captured me, Varian, doesn't that give you some responsibility where my life is concerned? Do my existence and happiness mean nothing to you?"

"I promised you safety, Jana, that's the best I can offer," he replied, knowing full well he could and was going to do more. . . .

"There will be times when you aren't around, Commander. How can you promise to prevent any abuse of me from across the span of a galaxy or two? Suppose my buyer is just as rich and powerful as you are? How do you propose to interfere in the treatment of his legal mate? Surely you can see why I doubt your claim of protection after my auction?"

There was only one way he could keep her, and it must remain a secret even from her. "I'm a very intimidating person, Jana. I'll make sure your owner gets my message about keeping you safe. No man would dare to challenge my black temper and high rank."

"Moloch did minutes ago, and you were only a few feet away. I cannot help but doubt the power of threats at a time when a whole galaxy separates us. Even if you recall my existence after the first month, you'll be too busy to check up on me. I will accept and expect your protection until my auction. After that," she said as she lowered her gaze to the floor, "either I adapt and survive with my own wits, or I don't. It's really very simple. After all, Commander, what does a captor owe his victim?"

"Jana, it isn't like that, and you know it," he scolded her.

"You're wrong, Commander. I can't depend on your empty promises. I can't expect you to drop everything and rush to my aid, and you wouldn't. If you think for one moment that you would place yourself between a *charl* and her owner, you're fooling yourself. I'm not that gullible or stupid. Please don't try to pacify or delude me; I'm not a child."

Her words stung him deeply. But what could he say or do,

particularly tonight? "Come along, moonbeam, and stick close to me."

"I haven't made it to the ladies' room yet. Your adversary stopped me. If any new troubles arise, I'll handle them. I was simply caught by surprise this time. You won't have to bloody your hands tor me, Commander. Any bastard who dares to attack me will find himself in the fight of his life. It is permissible for a slave to defend her life and honor, isn't it?" she scoffed acidly.

Varian thought it best to let her words slide. "I'll wait here."

Jana shrugged. "Suit yourself. You always do. I'll return shortly."

After Jana left, Nigel came looking for her. Varian explained her delay. "Moloch threatened her. Make sure he's watched. If he isn't working for Ryker, I'll take him down hard next time he comes near her!"

"She could be facing worse foes in the next two weeks. I tried to warn you this scheme had dangerous flaws in it." To change the subject, Nigel told him, "I gave Daxley and Vaiden permission to visit their families. I sent Braq, Tesla, and Baruch to the Merrick Company. They're demonstrating new high-tech equipment. I'll join them when we're done here."

"You sure the ship can run with six of her lieutenants missing?" Varian jested to lighten his gloom, unaware that he faced another problem. One of those officers was a traitor.

The next morning Jana had no appetite. She was ready to leave by ten o'clock, but her schedule called for a three-o'clock departure. Never had the gold room seemed more like a prison than it did this morning. She stretched out on the bed, stomach down. She seemed to lack all spirit today.

Varian had slept little. Even a long, hot shower did little to improve his frame of mind. He had no desire to travel to the planet surface any sooner than necessary. He was tense and moody this morning, feelings which were becoming too familiar to please him. Maybe he should check on Jana. Perhaps they could spend some time together.

Varian entered her quarters. He noticed her lying on the bed, her face turned to the wall. He wondered if she was asleep. He walked to the head of the bed and bent forward to discover her eyes were open. Yet she didn't make any attempt to acknowledge his arrival. "Good morning, Jana."

"Good morning, Commander Saar," she responded tonelessly.

"It looks and sounds as if you had a night just like mine, miserable. How about a walk or a game of *Laius* while we wait for the shuttle?"

"If you wish," she replied listlessly.

He reached for her hand and pulled her to her feet. Varian led her to his quarters and seated her at a small gaming table. The room was charged with warring emotions. After the game began, their knees often touched before Jana shifted to halt this disturbing sensation. Her calm appearance concealed the turmoil raging within her. Just as Varian's stoic expression denied the turbulent winds which were storming his mind and body. The chemistry between them heightened with each passing minute.

Soon, Jana became edgy. She wanted and needed to be away from him and this disquieting atmosphere. Her inability to concentrate and her urgency to be gone as quickly as possible caused her to purposely lose the game. Eager to be dismissed, she sighed wearily and started to rise.

Even though this game was the furthest thing from his mind with her so close and enchanting, he was determined to begin another round. He wanted and needed to talk with her, to savor her company. He wanted to draw her out and destroy the wall she had erected between them last night. He wanted her to forget the frightening episodes which she had endured recently. He wanted her to smile and be happy.

Varian cleverly teased, "You gave that game away, Jana. I think your mind is elsewhere. Or do I offer too much distraction?" His blue eyes twinkled with mischief as he said, "If you win the next game, you can select a special reward . . . anything you desire, except your freedom."

Jana's astonished gaze came up to lock with his challenging one as she tried to control the sudden tremors which swept over her body. "Anything, Commander? That's a very big wager for such a meager game and simple victory," she remarked skeptically.

"Where are your sporting instincts, Jana? How can you refuse such a challenge?" He rashly encouraged her cooperation with, "Surely you would like to demand some secret desire? I'll honor your choice."

Jana's eyes glittered at that fantasy-evoking statement. Her gaze sparkled with devilment and a beguiling grin tugged at her lips. "Anything but my freedom? Didn't you overlook an important restriction? What if I demanded for you to purchase me. Careful, Rogue Saar, you're slipping." Jana eyed him intently as a playful grin crossed his features. For a heart-stopping minute, he neither accepted nor rejected that restriction. "A secret desire," she echoed seductively. "That's quite tempting. Are you serious?" she quizzed. Their eyes met and searched. Before he could respond, she inquired, "What if you win? I have nothing of value to offer you, so what reward could you claim? I'm already obedient, respectful, and well trained. The only thing I have is the bracelet you gave me."

Varian chuckled, his eyes full of mystery. "To tell you in advance would spoil the suspense. The winner will be given until midnight to decide and reveal his, or her, demand. Fair enough?"

Jana pondered his words. "It seems quite a risk for you since I have nothing to offer. On the other hand, you're in a position to be generous. How could you possibly profit from this victory?"

"I assure you, moonbeam, I can and will find a way to savor such a triumph. For example, I could demand trust in me or your full cooperation in any situation. Several very tempting ideas come to mind."

"But you already have my cooperation."

"But I foresee a few situations which you might find unpleasant where I could use your assistance, without questions or arguments."

"Can I trust you to honor your loss, if it comes to that?"

He drilled his gaze into hers. "I swear to you I'll honor your request and my promise," he vowed with his hand over his heart.

Jana couldn't detect a trace of mockery or deception in him. She quivered. "You have no heart to swear on," she taunted him. "But I'll accept your wager and your word of honor," she recklessly ventured, extending her hand. "Shall we shake on it and seal our bargain?"

Varian's hand grasped hers firmly. His merry gaze locked

with hers as he quickly sealed their fateful deal. "Agreed, moonbeam. Just don't try to back out on me. Aren't you a wee bit worried about what I'll demand?"

"Why should I be concerned? You've already rejected my only worry numerous times. Win or not, you can't get much from me."

"That remains to be seen, doesn't it?" he teased her wickedly.

Jana scoffed at his cocky attitude. She would give anything to beat him, to wipe that smug grin off his face! *You've painted yourself into a corner, mon commandant. We'll just see how you deal with my request!*

"Tell me, Commander, what will you do if my prize is too excruciatingly painful to honor? What if I have expensive tastes? Or dangerous ones? Are you certain you'll go through with this bargain?" she asked him a final time.

"I am a wealthy man, Jana. I can afford to indulge you. As to being painful, I do hope you aren't considering a brutal beating for revenge."

"That does sound tempting, Rogue Saar, but rest easy. I have no intention of marring that handsome face."

"Upon my honor, I'll pay your price, if you win," he jested. "Nothing is forbidden except your freedom and staying with me. I have no power to grant either. Do you swear to surrender whatever prize I select?"

She looked him straight in the eye and vowed unflinchingly, "I promise to yield whatever prize you demand from me. And I accept your two restrictions," she stated to aggravate him.

"Give it your best shot, Jana, for I fully intend to win and collect."

Jana laughed cheerfully. I suggest you be on the alert, Rogue Saar. I heard Nigel is the ship's champion, and I've beaten him on numerous occasions. I should also warn you, I never accept a gamble which isn't stacked in my favor. Perhaps you'd remember those facts next time," she announced confidently to unsettle him. She wanted to win this game!

Jana laughed aloud as she viewed his reaction to those statements. "Perhaps you should be worried, sir. Are you, sure you don't want to withdraw your offer before it's too late?" she teased, hoping to increase his anxiety. After all, she would need all the help she could find.

"I have the uncanny feeling that I've been set up," he accused jovially.

"Only if I have the power to control your thoughts and actions, my love. This was your idea," she boldly taunted before smiling at him.

The game was played slowly and cautiously. Time passed without notice. Jana refused his offer of a drink. She wanted to remain as alert as possible. Each one forfeited and captured several of their opponent's pieces. It appeared the game was heading for a stalemate.

Varian secretly observed Jana's fierce concentration and resolve to win. He wondered what she would demand as her prize. It looked as if he would never know, for neither of them could win this carefully played game. Piqued beyond control, Varian impulsively threw the game and allowed her to win.

At her triumphant grin, he suddenly wondered if he had acted too rashly. "Well? What shall it be, champ?" he inquired, accepting his loss.

Jana focused a smug and mysterious gaze on him. "If you'll recall, you said the winner could have all day to choose and announce his or her demand. I'll let you know by tonight. I don't want to select such a monumental gift too impetuously. I'm starved. How about lunch, Rogue Saar?"

"I have the feeling you already know what you want from me. Why stall in voicing your demand?" he questioned, his curiosity burning wildly.

Jana laughed. "I'd like to see you squirm and fidget for a change. Who knows? With all you possess, you'll probably find my request simple."

"Make your choice before midnight," he reminded her, "or you forfeit any prize." His smoldering gaze swept over her and he licked his lips.

Varian watched Jana as she gracefully rose and bid him a sunny farewell. He arched his brows suspiciously. He was unaccustomed to being teased in such a manner. After Jana left for lunch, Varian paced his quarters, scolding himself. The tension of her unknown choice gnawed at him.

Jana and Varian were greeted by *Avatar* Seid Rhoedea and his two daughters on the planet Auriga. Karita raced into the welcoming arms of Kyle Dykstra, who lifted her and swung her around before kissing her soundly and shamelessly. The two lovers were gone within minutes. Arianna patiently waited for Varian to approach her, but he didn't. He seemed content to converse with her father and his captive.

Naturally that didn't sit well with the dusky female. She joined them and edged Jana aside. Varian behaved as if he hadn't noticed the woman's conduct. Soon, he grasped Jana's hand and led her away from the grinning father and glaring daughter. Seid Rhoedea clutched the tape in his pocket.

As Varian had told Jana, Kathy Anderson was placed in Ferris Laus's parents' care, who seemed more than pleased with their son's choice. Ferris wasn't bothered by the fact that Varian Saar had insisted on supplying part of the purchase price, and had stipulated Ferris keep that fact a secret. Ferris knew the money was nothing to Varian and he knew Varian was doing this good deed for Ferris and Kathy as well as for himself and Jana.

Joy flooded Jana as she watched the Lauses and Kathy leave. She remained with Nigel during the auction, which went off without a twist, while Varian spent his time with the ruler and his daughter.

When Arianna and Varian joined Nigel and Jana at the refreshment bar, Jana had to bite her tongue when the woman kept trying to embarrass her. She couldn't allow it to show. Jana remained poised and polite, until Varian was about to leave with that clinging, cloying vine.

Out of Arianna's hearing, he ordered, "Nigel, you take Jana back to the ship. If I come back tonight, it'll be late. You're in charge of the bridge."

"No," Jana boldly protested. "We have unfinished business to settle before midnight, Commander. Our talk first, then your visit with Arianna."

Acknowledging her request, they returned to his quarters, where he stalled the inevitable by pouring two glasses of wine. "A toast to our wager. May neither of us regret that game or your reward." Jana downed the wine. "Could you make your request quickly? I did leave someone waiting for me," he reminded her, wanting this scene to end quickly.

"I decided I want a sexual education as my prize," she calmly stated.

193

He grimaced. "You can't be serious?"

"I've never been more serious, Commander Saar."

"Should I keep my word on such a self-destructive matter?"

Her eyes frosted as she awaited his refusal. "I do not request that you honor your word, Commander, I demand it. I want complete training!"

Her angry outburst incited his. "Damn you! From whom, Jana?"

"You," she stated unwaveringly. "I want you as my teacher. You've tempted and teased me for weeks. Everyone believes I'm your mistress, so why not make it true? Even if my new owner vowed I came to him as a virgin, no one would believe it. You gave your word of honor to grant me the desire of my choice. I desire two weeks as your student in bed."

"Two weeks?" he echoed in astonishment.

"Your restriction specified I couldn't remain with you, but it didn't say I couldn't . . . borrow you for two weeks. Isn't that right?"

"Do you realize what you're asking of me, Jana?"

"Two weeks of your time and attention," she replied very quietly.

"They're nothing compared to—" He fell silent, then turned to get another drink. He tossed down a stiff whiskey. "Don't do this," he almost pleaded without turning to face her. Surely it would seal their fates!

"Then it's settled. Return to Arianna. I won't keep you any longer. It was a stupid idea anyway. Good night, Commander."

"Where the hell are you going?" he stormed.

"To my quarters to ponder your worthless word of honor, you traitor."

"But you said it was settled," he fumed.

"It is settled. If you can't honor your word, I certainly wouldn't ask another officer to do so! Your refusal to grant my winning request cancels our bargain. I can't hop into bed with just any man. Mutual attraction is required, remember? Your answer is no, isn't it?" she challenged.

The buzzer sounded. Varian answered the intercom. "Sir, Arianna is calling. She wants to know how much longer you'll be delayed."

Varian glanced at Jana, who sighed heavily and turned to

194

leave. He knew with every fiber of his being that he shouldn't make this decision. Should he selfishly accept her demand? What a bittersweet trap!

"Just a moment, moonbeam," he said, then bolted forward to halt her departure. Seizing her wrist, he pulled her to his desk and spoke into the intercom, "Tell the Rhoedeas I won't be returning to Auriga. I have vital business here. Don't disturb me again tonight unless it's an emergency." The communications officer acknowledged the order and signed off.

"Damn you, Jana Greyson," he muttered in a cross between joy and torment. "As surely as my eyes are blue, we'll both live to regret this night."

At that very moment far away in the Pyropean Galaxy, Supreme Ruler Jurad and his son Prince Taemin were reviewing the information which Canissia's agent, Zan, had passed along. They began to make plans to check out this mystery for themselves. They decided to visit a friend on the planet Lynrac at the precise time of Varian's stop there. Between now and then, Canissia could keep them well informed on Varian Saar's actions.

On the planet Auriga below the starship *Wanderlust,* several of Varian's officers and crew members were enjoying the final few hours of a well-deserved one-day furlough. One officer who had met secretly with Canissia Carthon early that afternoon was under her drug-induced control. After turning over his traitorous report and pictures to her, he was undone by the glass of chemical-laced champagne he sipped to toast the termination of their association.

Canissia laughed wickedly as she stared at the man who could not resist her. "Tell me everything, my handsome slave."

Unable to disobey, Lieutenant Baruch Tirana revealed not only the truth about Jana and Varian but also his bargain with Ryker Triloni.

"That bastard! So, I can trust him no more than he can trust me. Listen to me carefully, Baruch. Whenever Ryker questions you, you will swear you believe this romance with Jana Greyson is a charade to dupe him. Tell Ryker you think Varian is using Jana to spite him in some way. Convince Ryker that Varian doesn't truly love or desire Jana. Remember this when you awaken and do not disobey my orders. Do you understand me?''

''Yes,'' came Baruch's reply.

''What did Ryker offer you as a reward for betraying me?''

Baruch repeated Ryker's offer. ''He said I could have you, but I told him I didn't want you.''

''Is that true, Baruch? You no longer desire me?'' she taunted.

The ship's system officer of the *Wanderlust* had no choice but to answer, ''I hate you and want to resist you, but I crave your body.''

''Remove your clothes,'' she commanded. When he had obeyed, she ordered, ''Remove mine.'' Again, he complied. ''Now, my traitorous lover, give me great pleasure. You will sate my desires.'' Canissia laughed wildly as the man did her bidding. Later, she would study Ryker's actions and motives.

On the planetoid Darkar, Ryker was sitting at his desk staring at Jana's pictures and reading Moloch's last report. Jana was very beautiful, but was she unique enough to captivate his brother? More than that, earn Varian's love? Perhaps Varian had selected this female for another reason. Something about this situation didn't seem right.

''What's wrong, my love?'' his mistress inquired moodily.

''He is up to something, Precious. If he really loved this alien enchantress, it would be the best-kept secret in the Universe. He isn't fooling me; the question is why.''

''What about Canissia? She's deceiving you.''

''I know, I have spies everywhere. I know about her little dealings with Jurad and Prince Taemin. I know she'll question Baruch. When she does, he'll let it slip that he is working for me. She'll know I'm on to her. That should worry her plenty.''

''What if she tries to betray you?''

''Aren't you forgetting I'm the only source for her little excesses? Little Canissia thinks she's so clever. She has few secrets. Right about now, she should be working Baruch over. I plan to have Varian and this Jana watched closely. Unless something changes, he won't incite any public interest in her.

As a matter of fact, I plan to look around and discover why he wants me off Darkar.''

"You think it's all a charade? You think there's nothing between them?''

"Knowing my half brother, I would be shocked if it was true.''

Chapter Eleven

As she tried to jerk free, Jana scoffed, "Please don't degrade yourself to placate a lowly captive. You're right, Commander, this is sheer madness.''

To avoid a struggle, Varian released her and yelled, "Door, secure lock!'' The voice-operated mechanism responded instantly. There was no need to deny themselves this time together, for he would possess her. Martella's suggestion about a fake sale to Draco was brilliant. He would remove the fears which Moloch had instilled in her about sex. He could no longer resist Jana. Surely they were matched by fate, so why fight their destinies?

After pressing the release switch several times, Jana turned and shouted at him, "Open this door, Varian Saar! The wager's off!''

He refused. "Sorry, moonbeam, but it's too late. I've ached for you since before your capture. After I seized you, every time we touched or kissed, the aching increased. I would enjoy nothing more than making love to you. Believe it or not, I denied myself to protect you. However, I will not agree to one night's training; it's two weeks or nothing.''

"No other women during my time period?'' She added the stipulation.

"None, moonbeam. We can't expect to keep our affair a secret from my crew or the public. People gossip. Do you understand and agree?''

"Yes,'' she asserted bravely, then moistened her dry lips.

Varian realized she wanted him as much as he wanted her.

"Then we'll just have to face any consequences and rumors as they come up."

"I expect you to make it worth my while."

"Then so be it. Go inside and relax." Varian tenderly caressed her rosy cheek. "I'll come to you in fifteen minutes. Be clothed and ready to flee, or undressed and waiting in my bed. This is your last chance to escape, Jana."

"I want this time with you, Varian Saar, no matter what." She entered his bedroom and closed the door.

Varian issued an order to prevent any interruptions. He pressed the intercom button to alert security control. "Ferris, log in Jana Greyson's location as my quarters for the next two weeks. I'll see to her schedule from now on."

"Yes, sir," Ferris responded happily. He couldn't wait to tell Kathy this good news. He would always be grateful to Varian for Kathy.

Ferris beamed with joy and excitement. If Varian Saar fell in love with Jana, surely he would want to marry her. In that case, his commander would throw all of his energy, power, and wealth behind the fight to abolish the practice which separated Varian from Jana just as it separated him from Kathy. Ferris chuckled and remarked to the man who had brought him a snack, "How about that, Baruch? From where I stand, Varian and Jana are perfect together. I know that will rub Ryker Triloni the wrong way, but Varian can protect her."

Baruch Tirana sighed heavily. He was worried and afraid; he could remember nothing after that glass of champagne with Canissia. *Kahala,* help them all.

Jana showered, then slipped into Varian's bed. She pulled the silky sheet to her neck, shivering in apprehension and suspense. How she wished she weren't so naïve and scared! She feared Varian would be disappointed with her. Jana waited, and waited, and waited. Surely an hour had passed. . . .

Varian stared out the transascreen in his office area. If only he was sure this was the right thing. He wanted her and needed her, but this was so dangerous, more so than his ruse of bewitchment by her.

Varian knew what must be done to protect her. He had to deny her importance to him before enemies, coldly and cruelly pretend he had seduced her, and now that he was sated, was casting her aside. Until it was safe to expose his feelings and claim on her. . . . He grimaced, then shuddered with foreboding. Was history repeating itself? An alien enchantress was lying in his bed waiting for him. He was entrapping himself. He thought of his father and Shara on another ship, in another time. . . .

Jana slipped out of the bed and stood in the doorway, clad in Varian's maroon wrapper. She observed him, as he wrestled with dark ghosts from his past. Who and what had hurt him so deeply, made him so mistrusting and cynical? He looked plagued by anguish, confusion, and bitterness. Why was he so afraid of her, of possessing her, of surrendering to her? She dared not pry, but she knew some awesome battle was being waged inside his heart and head. Had he changed his mind? Should she allow him to escape?

Jana approached him and slipped between his towering frame and the transascreen. She placed her hands on his chest. "Please don't refuse me now. I need you, Varian. I want you. I swear, no strings or battles or demands before or after my auction. I swear, I'll let you go when the time comes."

Varian's troubled gaze lowered to meet her entreating one. She untied the sash and allowed the robe to flutter to the floor. Jana went up on her tiptoes and kissed him hungrily. She clasped her arms around his neck and clung fiercely to him. Intense longing glittered in her eyes as she huskily coaxed, "Love me, Varian. Please, if only once."

That was Varian's undoing. He groaned with rising desire. He seized her tawny head between his large hands and feverishly pressed his lips to hers. Varian gathered her naked body in his arms and carried her to his bed. He gazed down at the scene which had haunted his mind: Jana lying naked and willing in his bed. He stepped to his control panel and pressed several buttons. Dreamy music and very soft lighting came on. A heady fragrance which reminded her of countless tropical flowers filled the air. Varian stripped off his clothes and stood naked before her, a work of desire and power. He was about to join her, when her voice halted him.

"Wait a moment," she requested softly as her gaze boldly roamed his body. Jana began at his sable head, then moved her eyes over his face very slowly. He was so handsome. His features implied the same strengths his body did. His arms bulged with muscles, firm and smooth ones. His chest and back rippled with his movements. His chest was covered with a wispy black mat which narrowed like his waist to drift past a flat stomach and into a dense mat which surrounded his manhood, an area which her gaze hurriedly skipped over for now. His thighs and calves were supple and sleek. Not an ounce of extra fat could be seen. His flesh was bronzed, slick and firm to the touch. He was breathtaking. When she found the courage to focus on his loins, she noticed the manly shaft was growing larger. It stood away from his body.

Varian laughed when Jana blushed and jerked her eyes from the intimidating sight. "I want you, Jana Greyson, and I need you. This moment should have come weeks ago," he admitted.

Varian eased into bed. He read her panic and tension. She was gripping the edge of the sheet so tightly that her knuckles blanched white. He gently pushed aside a straying lock of golden hair. He softly caressed her rosy cheek, then grasped her icy hands with his warm ones. She trembled and stiffened. He caught her chin and lifted it until their eyes met.

"Don't be afraid, moonbeam. I won't hurt you more than necessary. You've got to relax, Jana. I'm not an evil monster come to devour you," he teased, eliciting a tiny smile.

"I feel so insecure, Varian. I don't know much about . . . this kind of thing. What am I supposed to do?" she asked seriously, timidly.

He placed her arms on the pillow to halo her head. He smiled tenderly and responded, "Tonight, nothing but experience and enjoy. Close those beautiful eyes and lie still. Just relax and let me love you, Jana."

Varian smiled before his mouth claimed hers very gently. Jana obeyed, closing her eyes and opening her senses. As much as she wanted to embrace him, she remained as he had placed her. He worked carefully and leisurely to arouse her, to dispel her anxieties. His tongue darted in and out of her mouth and across her lips. He playfully and stirringly teased both earlobes, his hot breath enlivening her senses. His mouth slipped down her throat, halting at her throbbing pulse. His lips brushed over her collarbone, then moved down her cleft to encircle the base of each firm mound. With tantalizing slowness, he traveled up one breast to moisten and arouse the brown peak, then shifted to the other point before darting from one taut nipple to the other. When his mouth relinquished, his forefinger and thumb would deftly caress the protruding tip and refuse to allow it any release from its blissful attack. One hand worked its way down her stomach, gently fondling every inch along the way.

His fingertips stroked up and down her inner thighs, moving closer to her womanhood. Jana quivered with suspense, anticipation, and pleasure. His ardent mouth left her breasts to capture her lips and to savor her tasty nectar as his hand made its final trip to her thigh. This time his hand covered the furry area and heightened its warmth with his palm. With calculated speed and pressure, his fingers began the next steps along the path toward rapture. He skillfully intoxicated her until she moaned and writhed in need. His mouth and hands continued their heady and patient assault. At last, he eased on top of her and settled his fiery shaft against the last barrier of his possession of her innocence.

"Look at me, Jana," his rich and husky voice softly commanded.

When her gaze locked on the intense blue of his, she prayed he wouldn't withdraw, not now. His eyes were glazing with passion and hunger. Jana's fingertips grazed over his sensual lips. When he offered her one last chance to change her mind, she whispered raggedly, "Please don't stop now. I want you and I need you, Varian."

He smiled and sighed heavily in relief. His mouth claimed hers again. When she trembled, he knew it wasn't from fear, but tension and yearning. "You shall have me, moonbeam," he murmured in her ear.

Jana was ecstatically tormented with fiery desire. For the first time, he would not pull away from her and leave her hanging in frustration. He would belong to her for thirteen nights. Her arms lifted to encircle his neck. She abandoned her mind and body to her rising passion and his blissful possession. Senses whirling madly and lost in the dreamy aura of his touch and skills, she was yanked alert by the burning pain which shot through her as his blazing torch drove into her dark recess. She hadn't meant to cry out, but she did from surprise and discomfort.

Varian captured her face between his hands and fused their gazes. He tenderly advised, "Relax, love; the pain will fade

201

quickly." As his lips covered her face with kisses, he confessed, "I've craved this moment night after night. It was so hard to deny such hungers and pleasures with you. I tried to resist this temptation, Jana. You have driven me wild and crazy with longing. You're mine now. Mine, moonbeam." Varian prayed he was telling her the truth that the pain would subside rapidly. He hoped he had been gentle and patient with his foreplay. He was distressed at hurting her. Despite his numerous sexual encounters, he had never taken a virgin before, intentionally. Jana was his now, his. . . . He dared fate to take her from him!

Jana shifted her head to seal their lips. Her arms about him tightened. Her hands started to explore his back and to draw him closer. She surrendered to the pleasures which surely awaited her. As Varian began to move gingerly inside her, she sighed and smiled. The searing pain had vanished. The stimulating sensations were wonderful, overpowering. All tautness and hesitation left her. Her body began to respond to his instinctively and voluntarily. Engulfed by fiery passion, her mouth almost savagely meshed against his; her tongue flittered a provocative dance with his. Her body arched upward and seductively wriggled against his smoldering frame, as if urging his manhood deeper into her snug and moist casing.

Wanting him even closer to her, Jana bent her knees and draped her supple legs over his firm ones, then clutched him possessively. No matter her innocence, Jana's inflamed body artfully and naturally matched Varian's rhythm. Her hunger was tremendous and fierce. Her body, words, and movements begged for release from this all- consuming furnace of passion.

Varian perceived her high level of arousal. He slightly increased his pace and force. He expertly guided her up passion's spiral until the summit was attained. He was gentle and patient; he was passionate and tender; he was taking and giving; he was pushing his control to the limits.

Jana briefly fluttered on the verge of conquest, her liquid green eyes opened and melted into his limpid blue ones. His lips rested on hers and their noses touched lightly. As they seemingly shared respiration, their igneous gazes remained locked. Varian masterfully drove in and out of her receptive body until her expression and reaction exposed her release.

Jana caught her breath sharply and blinked her eyes; her

202

stomach and groin tightened momentarily, then ravenously endured the quivers of sheer bliss which raced along the sensitive nerves he was stroking. He rotated his hips side to side and painlessly ground his groin against hers as if to make certain he left no spot unsated. Jana's mind was spinning; yet she kept her gaze fused with his. Her cheeks were flushed brightly and her eyes were darkened by raging desire. Simultaneously her senses were bombarded. She was aware of the contact between their damp bodies. Several odors teased her nose: his sweat and after-shave, her perspiration and perfume, and the musky scent of lovemaking. Her tongue teased over his lips as she shamelessly watched him. She wanted to observe his pleasure and hunger, to witness the moment of his conquest which came before her climactic spasms ceased.

The instant Jana began her downward spiral, Varian dashed aside his control and swiftly pursued her toward a valley of blissful satisfaction. "You're mine now," he vowed once more, then seized her lips as he rode out the turbulent waves of passion.

When his needs were sated for a time, he was breathing heavily. Moisture glistened over his face and torso. He didn't want to break their intimate contact, but he didn't want to relax his exhausted body on hers. He clasped her securely against him and rolled onto his back, carrying her along without slipping from within her. With fingers buried in her thick hair, he continued to savor her kisses and touch. Gradually his respiration and pounding heart slowed to normal.

Jana didn't mind the dampness on his chest as she laid her face and hair against it. She cuddled peacefully into his lingering embrace. At last, she knew who and what she had waited for. She understood love and passion, for she had experienced both. She realized what she had sensed that first time she had gazed up into his sapphire eyes, or when she heard his voice and confronted his awesome presence: this was the man who held her fate within his grasp and could hold her heart if she weakened for an instant. She had weakened. She loved this man and wanted him for a lifetime. She would never regret this decision or forget this night. After knowing him fully, whatever happened now, it would be worth any price she must pay.

Jana closed her eyes as tears slipped from them to mingle with his sweat. So many emotions assailed her. Joy and resignation flooded her. The next two weeks must create enough memories to last her a lifetime. But she would trade nothing to have her innocence returned. Some bittersweet madness had engulfed her, for she fiercely loved and desired her captor.

Varian felt the hot tears slip to his chest and run off his shoulder. Dread and panic chewed at him. "I'm sorry, Jana. I honestly tried not to hurt you more than necessary. Is there anything I can do?"

Jana lifted her head and looked down at him. She smiled. "You were extremely gentle, Varian. Like you said, the pain lasted only an instant."

He was confused. "Why are you crying? Are you sorry for yielding?"

As one hand toyed with his hair and the other teased over his lips, she asserted candidly, "I have no regrets. It was the most exciting and pleasing experience I've ever known. I suppose crying at a time like this is normal; it's a special moment for me, an emotional moment. You know, conquering the unknown? Becoming a full-fledged woman? Your prowess isn't overrated. No wonder Maffeian women cast aside all shame and pride to chase you." After Jana's teeth playfully tugged on his upper lip and then the lower one, she hinted seductively, "Something lost for something gained?"

"Was it worth the swap?" he probed inquisitively, loving her mood.

Without shame, she looked him in the eye and declared, "Most definitely. I couldn't have chosen a better prize than you as my tutor, Rogue Saar. If you have any champagne, we should toast this rare moment." Jana flipped to her back and didn't bother to cover her naked body. "Isn't it wonderful? No quarrels. No temptations. No hostility. At long last, Jana Greyson and Varian Saar can have fun and be friends."

Varian shifted to his side and teased the tips of her breasts with a lock of her hair. "And lovers," he cheerfully added.

"And lovers," she happily echoed. "I must be a brazen huzzy at heart, for this is the best adventure a woman could have. Thank you, Rogue Saar."

Varian also ignored nudity to get one large glass of champagne. Leaning against fluffy pillows at his side, Jana toasted, "To Varian Saar, my handsome and enchanting space pirate, and to many nights of passion."

After she had sipped the pale pink liquid, he took the glass and then a deep swallow. His eyes danced wickedly as he toasted, "To Jana Greyson, who has proven her value is higher than I realized, if possible. May you always remember this night without sadness or regret or resentment." Varian took another long drink from the sparkling liquid, then passed it to Jana.

She accepted the toast. She teased, "Since I'm new at this game of love, it will be your responsibility as my instructor to make certain I leave with no regrets. Fill these next two weeks with blissful passion and countless stimulating lessons." She drained the glass, then smiled over its rim.

"Don't tell me I've created an insatiable creature who plans to feed on me day and night?" he teased.

Jana laughed. "Do you doubt Rogue Saar can tame what he rashly created? Tell me, Sir Pirate, am I too much of a challenge for the legendary playboy of the Universe?"

He chuckled and warmed beneath her glowing gaze. "I promise to do my best to appease that fiery temper of yours."

"I must need lessons in alien anatomy; I didn't think my temper was what needed appeasement."

Varian couldn't conceal his pleasure. "Shall we learn together then?"

Varian took Jana with a renewed hunger and eagerness which surprised him when he realized her ardor matched his own. He instructed and guided her along the path to discovering how to give and receive the most pleasure possible. Later, he would teach her the many facets to lovemaking. For tonight, she needed only to experience a gentle awakening to passion and knowledge.

Afterward, she found that sleep came quickly. Varian gazed down into her serene face and passion-swollen lips. His possessive embrace nestled her closer to him. His lips moved over the sheen of perspiration on her forehead. He brushed aside damp hair from her face while his fingertips drifted down her arm and over her back. With the fresh scent of lovemaking still hanging in the air and clinging to their bodies, he wanted her again!

How would he ever be able to stand beside an auction platform while men bid on her like an inanimate treasure, even if it were a farce? How could he let her walk away believing she was the possession of another man? Yet he must. How could he force himself to risk destroying her feelings for him? *Kahala* help him! Could he? Must he?

Varian didn't care what the Assembly and Supreme Council had to say about his taking Jana as his mistress. What could they do after the fact? Get rid of their best Star Fleet commander and matchless Elite Squad agent? Still, no matter how vital and valuable he was to the Alliance Force and Supreme Council, they would not permit any officer to keep a mistress on his ship. This love and desire for Jana Greyson could be costly. He was too young and restless to resign his command. Even if he quit the Force, he couldn't keep Jana glued to him every moment. The instant he left her side . . . If only there was a safe place where he could leave her while he carried out his mission. It was too perilous to expose his love. One of his enemies would find a way to get to her, either to slay her for revenge or to use her against him. Even the most heavily guarded or allegedly impenetrable locations could be breached by a clever man; he had proven that many times!

Jana was in his blood now and he wanted her desperately. He raged against the forces which could destroy his dreams and his love. Varian clutched her to his tormented body. Against her hair, he murmured hoarsely, "Forgive me, my love, for the anguish and shame you will endure because of me. And from me . . ." As he inhaled the fragrance of her silky hair, he whispered, "I need you, moonbeam, tonight and forever. Forgive me for risking our lives to capture this time of magical madness."

His caresses and movements aroused Jana. She snuggled against him as his name dreamily escaped her lips. His smoldering blood flamed to life instantly. He began to tease her lips with stirring kisses and her body with enticing caresses. When she moaned softly, he pressed his advantage by sensuously assailing her breasts. Even before she was fully awakened, she was responding to him and he was moving blissfully within her body.

As their passions peaked and ebbed, she relaxed in his strong arms. She teased, "You failed to inform me of your voracious appetite. Will I be denied sufficient sleep every night?"

"Sleep while I'm on duty. All of my free time is assigned to your education."

"Perhaps the muse took pity on us. She knows I need every lesson you can teach. Shall I return to my quarters to allow you to get some sleep?"

"If you dare to leave my arms, I'll be forced to tie you to my bed and wreak havoc on your lovely body."

Jana giggled. "I must confess, Rogue Saar, I love your method of wreaking havoc. I only wish I had challenged you to a game of *Laius* sooner."

"Careful, moonbeam," he huskily warned. "You wouldn't want to fall for a heartless rogue like me."

"Why not?" she retorted insouciantly. "Don't all women fall in love with you?" Jana pouted prettily and drew swirly designs on his chest with her nails. "I might devour you if my appetite runs wild."

"Like this?" he hinted, then feasted on her breasts. After they tussled for a time, she cuddled against his side and both slept peacefully.

The fourth auction on the planet Lhasa went smoothly. As Varian had promised, Heather Langdon was sold to the younger brother of Tesla Rilke. After a brief display, Jana was allowed to skip the auction to stroll around with Nigel and Kara before they enjoyed a fabulous lunch. Soon, it was time to return to the ship. Jana dared not question Varian's whereabouts.

Nigel accompanied Jana to the gold room. He halted at the door and spoke into the audiocontrolled door panel, "Computer, code 231. Make next voice print of Jana Greyson as a controller for this suite."

He instructed Jana to speak certain words into the panel. Afterward, the door responded to her voice. "We believe you've earned our trust."

Jana beamed with pleasure. She decided to visit Tristan. She was sitting on a laboratory stool listening to the doctor explain his current experiment when she was grabbed from behind, pulled backward, and kissed soundly! When she was placed upright again, she stared at Varian.

Varian grinned. "Did you miss me today?" he asked. He wiggled between her thighs. He slipped his arms around her waist and interlocked his fingers. A compelling smile teased at his full lips and sapphire eyes.

Jana merely gaped at him. He was wearing what the U.S. Army would call a camouflage suit, and looked stunning.

"Don't let me hinder you two," Tristan stated, then chuckled.

Varian allowed his glowing eyes to linger warmly over Jana's pink face and wide eyes. "I don't intend to, Tris," he quipped just before his mouth claimed Jana's in a long and fiery kiss which stole her breath and sapped her strength. When he released her shaky body, he grinned raffishly and told her, "I'll see you in my quarters later. Don't let Tris keep you too long." He walked out, leaving Jana stunned and staring after him.

When she regained her wits and tongue, she murmured mostly to herself, "Whatever was that all about?"

Tristan laughed. "I wouldn't have the vaguest idea. But it appears that our commander is bewitched by a certain girl."

Jana glanced at his twinkling eyes. "Don't be silly, Tris," she chided, then laughed nervously. To change the topic, Jana questioned his research.

Hours passed as they chatted about a mutually loved topic. Jana observed Tristan as he set up his next experiment. No one would have guessed Jana was a prisoner. When Tristan glanced over her shoulder and asked, "What brings you here again, Varian?" Jana turned and met her love's gaze.

"A tardy woman and a severe case of loneliness. Come along, Jana."

Tristan apologized for keeping her so late. "We got engrossed in our talk. Can Jana join me for dinner?" Tristan inquired craftily.

"Jana has previous plans with me, Tris." Jana blushed at his insinuation. "Sorry, but time is too short as it is," he hinted.

"Varian!" Jana shrieked in modesty and dismay. "Please—"

"No need to beg. I'm your adoring slave for two weeks. What is your command, Princess Moonbeam?" he inquired playfully.

"Let's get out of here before you embarrass me further," she replied. In the passageway, she said, "If you carry on like a moonstruck romantic, people will think you've gone mad," she continued.

"Why are you so concerned? Wouldn't you enjoy being the first to bewitch Varian Saar? People will think you possess awesome powers."

"Please don't behave so foolishly."

"You think it would embarrass me to show affection for you?" he questioned oddly. "On the contrary, moonbeam, it would look crazy if I appeared unaffected by you. Besides, I do have an ulterior motive," he hinted. "It's in your best interest to be a victim to my lusty appetite. It will only heighten your appeal. When we're in public, you must look and act as if I've wronged you, as though I forced you into my bed and arms."

Jana halted in midstep and stared at him. "What are you saying?"

Varian grasped her hand and led her into his lounging area where a table and dinner were awaiting them. He seated her. "Listen to me, Jana Greyson! Your reputation and safety must be guarded! Your future happiness depends on us convincing everyone of this. You can win the hearts of most men and women if you play the delicate creature who was forced to endure the depravities of Varian Saar! Dammit, woman! You will obey me in this vital matter!"

"Do you honestly think any man would want to follow you in a woman's life?"

"The kind of man who feels that way isn't worth walking in your shadow, much less worthy of buying you! Men such as Moloch will feel that way. He went after you on Thule because he knew you were still an innocent, despite my pretense. With your glow of purity, I was a fool to think anyone would believe there was something between us. I should have slain Moloch for even touching you!"

"Careful, Commander; such concern and kindness might serve to polish your tarnished image," she jested. She was warmed and touched by his motives. "Do you mind if we don't use my study time to discuss imminent men in my life?"

Varian checked his playful retort when he saw her expression. "You're right, moonbeam. Business shouldn't infringe on our private time." When Jana said she was finished with her meal and rose to leave, he asked, "Where are you going? You hardly touched your food."

"We ate a late lunch on Lhasa, a big one. I'm going to my quarters to bathe and change," she explained truthfully.

"No need, moonbeam. You share my quarters now. I've had all of your things moved in here," he casually announced, then continued eating.

"Are you sure about sharing quarters? Don't you need some privacy?"

"I'll have plenty in two weeks. For now, I want to enjoy your company.

Jana entered his bathroom and bathed. When she went to join him attired in an azure satin gown and robe, he was sitting on the sofa in his study area, deep in thought. "Varian?" she called to him.

"Go on to bed, Jana, I have some work to do." He didn't look up at her.

Jana questioned this sudden change in mood. Why was he so mercurial? She jested, "Not on my wager time, Rogue Saar. My clock's running out."

Varian was only too aware of that fact. "So is mine," he snapped.

Jana headed for the corridor door after snapping, "I'll see you tomorrow! I can tell you're in no mood for me tonight. I'll sleep elsewhere." Varian bolted to his feet, letting papers flutter to the floor. He seized her wrists while she struggled against him. "Let go of me, you beast!" They tumbled to the floor. He pinned her beneath his powerful frame. He tried to calm her anger and subdue her. "Get off me! I'm not sleeping here tonight."

"We'll just see about that." He jumped up and seized her. He tossed her over his shoulder and headed for his bedroom. He imprisoned her kicking legs. He chuckled when she pounded him on the back with her fists and cursed him.

Varian's chest rumbled with laughter. "Such filthy language from such a pretty mouth. You might as well cease your fighting and cursing, woman. This is my ship and you're my captive. You promised me two wild and wonderful weeks, and I'll have them one way or another." He threw her on his bed and fell atop her, pinning her beneath him again.

"You devil. Hell will freeze over before I surrender to you again."

"Will it now?" he taunted. His mouth closed over hers, silencing her next remark. He seared kisses over her face and throat. His hands smoothly and deftly undressed her. His lips traveled down her breasts and teased their taut nipples without mercy. One hand moved lower to titillate her past anger and

210

resistance. "It was only a practice session for tomorrow. You know, my order to fake the helpless and angry victim? I'm sorry."

Jana swatted at him, then scolded his deceit. She moaned and submitted to him completely. She loosened his shirt closure and pulled it off his shoulders. She showered kisses on his face as he removed his pants and boots.

They came together with a fierce intensity which staggered the senses. Each took and gave freely and eagerly. They made love slowly, then once again swiftly and with new urgency. Passions soared wildly and freely.

Varian encouraged her to touch and take him as she desired and dared. Never had a woman given him such incomparable pleasures. It was the loving way in which she came to him and gave to him which made the difference. It was her mood during this sharing experience. It was the tone of her voice, the look in her eyes, the way she touched him, the depth of her kisses, and the total bliss afterward which set their lovemaking apart from all other unions he had known. In the height of passion, he vowed,"You are mine, Jana; never forget that, no matter what happens."

They scaled the loftiest pinnacle of passion and shared a bliss which few lovers found during a lifetime together, then shared serene slumber.

The next day, Jana spent her free time with Tristan or with Nigel and language studies. She knew time was running out in that area too. Jana thought it was best not to crowd Varian, for he was used to freedom. Another night of passionate lovemaking was shared before they reached the fifth planet, Zandia, a world covered by jungles and rain forests where every thousand miles a large area had been cleared for a city. Except for the honor of meeting *Avatar* Kael, nothing unusual or exciting took place.

On the planet Balfae, Jana met Salazar, ruler of a world which was a startling contrast of deserts and lush islands, whose cities reminded her of ancient ones in the Far East. On their seventh stop, at Kudora, Jana learned that most of the planet surface was covered with snow or ice! Frigid waters existed where the ivory blanket didn't lie and a lack of brisk winds and a curious atmosphere pleasingly masked the glacial weather. Sylva Omanli appeared and was sold. When Jana stared inquisitively at him, Varian shrugged and grinned. Jana smiled to conceal her prior knowledge about Sylva's survival.

In eight days, Jana had attended seven auctions on seven different worlds. She had shared six nights in Varian's quarters. On the morning of the eighth auction, on the planet Therraccus, a stunning world of metal and glass, Varian informed her she would not be attending this particular sale. He advised her to rest until his return tonight. Wanting to spend every available minute with him, Jana tried to alter his decision. Varian wouldn't discuss it; he seemed preoccupied. It didn't take a genius to realize there was a special reason why Varian didn't want her along today. Jana wisely acquiesced, and Varian departed without her.

To avoid suspicion, Varian chatted with two friends while Nigel secretly passed the info tape to *Avatar* Chukar Dimi. During the latter half of the auction, Varian was leaning against a steel post when suddenly a mocking voice sliced off the remainder of his daydreams about Jana.

"Were's your alien today? I was hoping to examine her. I find myself intrigued by any woman who can catch a Saar's eye. Is it true you can't resist her? Or do you merely seek to enjoy her for a spell?"

The reason Varian had prevented Jana from visiting Therraccus stood before him. Sighing a prayer of thanks for *Avatar* Dimi's timely warning about Ryker Triloni's presence, Varian looked him in the eye. The handsome man before him was only one inch shorter than he was, and four months younger, which made Varian their father's heir instead of his half brother. Varian noticed the lingering scar from his knife wound across Ryker's right jawline.

Chilling laughter came forth as the Androas prince observed Varian's line of vision. "I left it as a reminder of our unfinished war, brother dear. Either I'll take it to my grave, or I'll have it removed the day you enter yours." Emerald eyes were alert and piercing. "It's been a long time, Varian. Rumors tell that you've been enjoying yourself."

Varian chuckled mockingly. He couldn't decide if he was pleased or worried that his clever strategy had worked.

"No offer of truce, brother? Isn't this private war becoming

212

dull? You can never defeat me, Ryker. Why do you keep deluding yourself?'' Blue eyes narrowed. ''As for rumors, we both know they can't be trusted.''

Ryker Triloni nonchalantly responded, ''Consider this the lull before the storm. Just giving you time to grow cocky. My victory cannot be denied. Rumor also says this alien is forced to sleep in your quarters and obey your every whim.'' Ryker laughed as he observed his foe. ''I find it hard to believe a second illustrious Commander Saar would tempt fate so.''

Ryker continued, ''I was shocked to hear you had surrendered to her charms while she resisted yours. Her absence today piques my curiosity even more, intentionally, I'm sure. Why do you really want to keep us apart? If it isn't a trick, her pictures show a remarkable resemblance to Princess Shara Triloni; and we know your father couldn't resist my mother. How many bastards do you plan to sire with this ravishing *charl?* I hope none, brother dear, as I detest slaying children.''

A tic quivered in Varian's jawline. He struggled to retain control of his temper. He no longer wanted to encourage Ryker to fall for his ruse. He would find another way to defeat his self-appointed rival.

Varian taunted, ''If anyone knows about unfortunate bastards, it's you, Ryker.''

Ryker glared at Varian, briefly losing his self-control. ''Shara was one of the most beautiful and coveted treasures in the Universe,'' he stated angrily. ''Nothing less than your blood and life will appease me and Grandfather. On second thought, perhaps your little captive's life will settle part of our score,'' he hinted, watching the effect of his threatening words on Varian.

Varian deceptively grinned and remarked, ''That's a perfect compromise. Why don't you put your wits and fame and wealth to better use? Why don't you attend the auction on Rigel and bid on Jana? You need heirs, and she would make you a challenging mate. You know, you two have plenty in common. I'll make her a gift from brother to brother, a peace token.''

Ryker laughed coldly. ''You don't fool me, Varian. You're up to something. Either you're trying to discourage me or entice me with your tarnished goods. Which is it?''

''Jana is very special, she might be the magic to cure you. Much as I hate to admit it, she is the perfect match for you.

213

She's a doctor, a chemist. A matchless beauty who's charming, and entertaining. If I bought her, I'm afraid I would find her resistance embarrassing," Varian asserted coldly when Ryker smiled triumphantly.

Varian glared back. "When I find the woman I'll want to marry, I won't be intimidated by you. Who knows, maybe I have a sadistic streak like yours, and I intend to substitute her for Shara; play out the Galen/Shara drama again, this time with a different climax!"

"Like Mother, she could become pregnant; and we don't want that, do we?" Ryker scoffed, "Now, now, big brother, we both know how hard Father tried to spare me the life and shame of illegitimacy. I was luckier than most; luckier than your child would be if I get Jana and she's already pregnant with your child."

"Don't be so bitter," Varian taunted. "If Tristan had recognized Shara's actions and motives sooner, this rivalry between us wouldn't exist. Why don't you place the blame where it belongs, Ryker, with Shara and Maal? We both know Shara was planning to beguile Jurad and seize his empire. When Jurad finally admits the truth, he'll turn on you and your grandfather. Too bad you carry too much of the Triloni blood and influence. My father and mother pleaded with Shara and Maal to send you to live with us; if . . ."

"Careful, Commander Saar, one shouldn't make such defaming accusations. You know Supreme Ruler Jurad and his son trust me. Besides, what would I want with their Pyropean Federation?"

"For one thing, to keep Jurad from learning the truth. You may be rich and powerful, Ryker, but you'll never conquer the Maffei Alliance. You'll never get my inheritance." Varian drilled his gaze into Ryker's. "If I could find proof of Shara's deceptions during her time with our father, you'd lose everything."

Ryker murmured provokingly, "One day I just might let you read in Shara's diary about Commander Galen Saar, mighty Star Fleet warrior, falling prey to a tragic destiny. Galen and Shara's behavior might shock you. What makes these alien enchantresses so irresistible, so hazardous to Saars?" Ryker warned, "Be very careful, this is one time *Kadim* Tirol can't help you. In fact, he'll probably reprimand you publicly for your wicked conduct with Jana. With luck, she'll complete the circle of vengeance which Shara began. Perhaps even slay the last Saar for me.''

"No way, Ryker. It sticks in your craw that Shara didn't slay me and Grandfather seven years ago before her suicide. I'd bet Maal sent her to the planet Eire to kill all of us.''

"At least then I would have what's coming to me. While I'm on Cenza, I'll be sure and tell Jurad and Taemin all about your Jana. I'm sure they'll find this new Saar mistress intriguing. If I'm not too busy, I'll be on Rigel for the auction. It will prove most interesting.''

Ryker withdrew three pictures from his ebony shirt. He studied them intently before handing them to Varian. He grinned sardonically. "Interesting, are they not? One might think you were actually in love with her, if one didn't know you better . . .''

Varian watched Ryker's departure, then looked down at the color photos. His heart skipped a beat. The images were not what he had expected. Two of the pictures had been taken aboard his starship! Varian glared at the one taken in the Stardust Room and the other one in the botanical garden. Who on board the *Wanderlust* was the traitorous spy?

Chapter Twelve

Varian entered his quarters in a dangerous mood. He dropped into his desk chair and fell into deep thought. He couldn't believe there was a traitor on aboard his ship! Worse, as only officers and their guests were allowed in the Stardust Room, the treacherous villain had to be one of his own lieutenants!

Varian wondered if the guilty party knew that Ryker would show those pictures to him, and at this stop. If so, the culprit would now be nervous.

What did Ryker think about the emotions revealed in these shots? What other private or public moments had been captured on film or audiotaped? Each of these pictures portrayed Varian's original scheme perfectly: his hunger and selfish demands on a resistant and helpless victim. Did Ryker also have facts or pictures which exposed his true feelings? Did Ryker know about this past glorious week which had been shared with Jana?

With a disloyal officer on board, should he halt his affair with Jana? Would that influence Ryker's conclusions and actions? He had expected gossip about him and Jana, but not treachery! Except for his quarters, no area was safe from prying eyes. If Ryker was still not aware of Varian's secret plan to use Jana to entrap his half brother, he would be soon if Varian was careless, or if the spy was one of the other four people who knew. Varian instinctively knew it could not be Nigel, Tristan, Kyle, or Martella.

It galled Varian to know he would be forced to watch and control his words and conduct on his own ship! It was now clearer than ever that Jana's feelings and behavior could be used against her. That conclusion removed any remaining doubts about forcing Jana to display contempt for his use of her as a temporary mistress.

It was late, and Varian presumed Jana was in bed asleep. Drumming inside his head was the thought of only one more week, one more week with Jana. Even if it were one hundred years, that still wouldn't be enough. If he abruptly severed their relationship, it would look suspicious; and it would cut her deeply. If he asked her to play the victim here on his ship as on the planets, that would require explanations which he couldn't give. Suppose Ryker already knew the truth! He berated himself for digging this lethal pit, then falling into it. For now, he had to convince all foes she was nothing special to him. *Kahala,* help him, for she must unsuspectingly aid that painful ruse!

Jana stood in the doorway to Varian's darkened bedroom. She watched the range of emotions which came and went on his handsome face. For a man with so much power, he exposed a helplessness and frustration which baffled her. Something had happened which angered him. She watched him flex his body as if it were sore and stiff.

A prickling sensation touched Varian's mind, that sixth sense which alerted a warrior or hunter to watchful eyes or warned him of approaching dangers. Yet, the stare was soft and warm. He glanced over at Jana's figure clad in a sensual teal-blue

216

gown. Jana was eyeing him intensely, the way an artist did when he wanted to commit to memory every line, feature, and detail of an object of interest which must be recorded on canvas at a later date. When she noticed his gaze on her, it didn't seem to halt her scrutiny.

Varian removed his shirt and tossed it aside. He placed his interlocked fingers behind his head. He smiled and relaxed as a calming glow suffused his body and mind. Silent, as if enthralled by a magical spell which words would shatter, he derived pleasure from the way her eyes softened as she visually invaded his body.

There was something different about the way Jana was looking at him; Jana's gaze was gratifying, and inflaming. But did she love him? In view of his past deeds, was it too much to expect?

Jana smiled, then went to his servo for two glasses of wine. She placed his on the desk, but gradually finished hers. Standing behind him, she began to massage his neck, kneading the tension out of his shoulders. He moaned and shifted under the delightful touches. After a while, her fingernails playfully traveled down his chest like tiny and tickly bugs, to wander around in the curly mat on his bronze chest. Her palms flattened against his torso, tracing the ripples of hard and smooth muscles. Varian squirmed and chuckled, then pulled her onto his lap.

He didn't speak. Jana didn't stop. She very slowly and provocatively ran a fingertip across his finely chiseled jawline and strong chin. She stroked his hair. Tonight it reminded her of the windblown head of a sailor fresh from the sea. As she caressed his cheek with the back of her hand, she realized the noticeable effect her touch and gaze were having.

Varian's breathing was quickening. His body alternately tightened and relaxed. Flames smoldered in his blood and loins, and became fierce hunger. Forgotten were thoughts of dismissing her.

In a silky tone, she murmured, "Adonis would envy the way you look now. It should be a crime for any man to have such awesome powers of enchantment." Her gaze met his. Without warning, the spell was broken. She blushed instantly. She shook her head. "How did it go today? Would you like another drink?" she asked.

Varian grasped her around the waist and held her captive in his lap. "Not so fast, moonbeam. You can't tease a man and then try to douse his passions by changing the subject."

She stared at him. "I wasn't teasing you. I only tried to relax you."

"With you, a look is all it takes. Never look at another man like that, at least during the week. Such a bold and fiery gaze is an open invitation to seize you and make love to you."

"Why didn't you stop me?" she asked.

"Because a caress is only a taste of what is to come. You must yield what you just promised." He nuzzled her neck.

"You are insatiable. I was not playing temptress. I was merely admiring you. Is that why you didn't let me tag along today, afraid I would be tempting in the wrong place at the wrong time?" she jested mirthfully as he grew serious.

"Actually, I was warned that a lecherous fiend would be there today; I didn't want to subject you to him," he stated.

Jana played along with what she took as a joke to keep from answering her. "I'm deeply grateful, kind sir," she stated in a heavy Southern drawl.

Varian scooped her up in his arms and carried her to his bed where he made passionate and urgent love to her. Later, wrapped in each other's arms, they fell asleep.

The next morning passed strangely as the ship reached their ninth stop at Caguas. Varian kept Jana in his quarters as he rehearsed her for the assigned role as "victim." Varian insisted she play this part everywhere except in his quarters. Naturally she protested the deceitful charade. When he explained that even loyal crew members could speak too freely or mistakenly under certain conditions, Jana still rebelled. Varian grew angry and stern with her, and Jana realized he was quite serious; she knew there must be a critical motive behind his order.

Jana accompanied Varian to the rocky and desolate surface of Caguas, a planet of countless mines which possessed a vast wealth of ores and gems. As far as she could see in any direction, there were mountains and towering rock formations and sandy stretches of nothingness. To escape the harsh climate and arduous terrain, dwellings had been gouged from the sides of cliffs and mounds, then connected by an above-ground tunnel system. There were large cavelike areas used for social functions and businesses. It was a rough and gloomy place, one which Jana was glad to leave after doing her acting task and meeting *Avatar* Faeroe. It was on to Lynrac.

Canissia Garthon had ceased her surveillance of Varian Saar after his stop on Therraccus, before she could be sighted and connected to Ryker Triloni or his many spies. She had expected Ryker to appear on Caguas, the planet which his planetoid orbited. She was delighted the devil had fooled her and Varian, for it had allowed her to meet with Baruch Tirana before and after the spy's talk with Ryker. Now, she was positive the traitor had supplied that beast with false information about Varian and Jana.

Canissia felt she had the facts and means needed to sever the relationship between Jana and Varian. She would hold her distance from the primary object of her desires until he reached the planet Eire, where his grandfather *Kadim* Tirol Trygue lived and awaited his heir's arrival.

Canissia reflected on the two secret meetings with Lieutenant Baruch Tirana after which she had vowed never to approach or blackmail him again. The evil daughter of Supreme Council member Segall Garthon laughed satanically as she congratulated herself on her cunning. Just as she had plotted, Ryker was fooled completely about Varian's interest in Jana. She thanked her lucky star she had reached Baruch before he had met with Ryker. Using hypnotic drugs, she had made certain the spy would not reveal the love affair between Varian Saar and his beautiful captive. Eventually Ryker would discover it, but not in time to thwart her plans to have Supreme Ruler Jurad win the alien beauty at auction and take her far away from Canissia's territory and desires. Whether or not Varian loved Jana, his ego would compel him to defend her against Ryker's threats. Canissia could not permit Varian and Ryker to battle over another woman!

By now, she believed the ignorant Ryker was on his way to meet with Jurad and Taemin to discuss a deal to undermine Varian Saar and subsequent conquest of the Maffei Galaxy.

Canissia laughed coldly, for she knew that meanwhile, Jurad and his son were on their way to the planet Lynrac to inspect Jana and to observe Varian's feelings for themselves. Once Pyropean men declared their interest in Jana, Ryker would have no choice but to back off and allow them to obtain her. Since Jurad's possession of Jana would tear her from Varian's side, Ryker wouldn't need to personally involve himself in Jana's destruction and Varian's torment.

Canissia slipped into the bubble bath which had been prepared by her lover and ship captain. "Poor Ryker," she murmured sarcastically, "he doesn't know I've duped him again. He believes Varian is simply faking an enchantment for Jana to gain his attention. Ryker will go mad trying to unmask Varian's motive for luring him toward Jana. Ryker was easy to convince that his rival was too proud to fall in love with a *charl*, especially to marry a woman Varian had to purchase like an animal. Also Ryker has never known love or any emotions other than hatred or revenge. It's logical for him to assume treachery rather than real attraction."

As Zan bathed his cherished mistress, Canissia laughed and remarked, "Yes, my dear Zan, your love is smarter than the Saar brothers combined. Varian is entangled by his lust for an alien temptress, and Baruch has convinced Ryker it's only a trick. Jana no longer intrigues Ryker. He thinks the little Earthling merely a pawn. Is Ryker blind, my adoring Zan? Look at those pictures taken by Baruch, love is written all over them. Too bad I'll have to rip them apart. You do understand I have to marry either Varian or another Supreme Council member?" she asked seductively.

Before he could reply, Canissia continued, "It must be done, my love. Nothing will change between us. I need rank, power, and riches."

Zan brought wine from the bottle on her desk. As her lover was drinking his glass of wine, Canissia entreated him to scrub her back. While he obeyed, she discreetly poured her glass of white wine into the water. She turned and smiled at her enthralled captain, then told him to strip and sit on the edge of the large tub with his feet in the water. Even without the mind-controlling chemicals added to the wine, Zan would have done Canissia's bidding.

Her eyes roamed his virile body. "Soon, my tasty treat, I shall be forced to replace you. You are too possessive and know far too much. As soon as I'm rid of Jana Greyson, you

220

must be eliminated. There will be no evidence of your existence or murder.''

Canissia knelt before the entranced man and fondled his sleek and muscular frame. ''When you are gone, I can use those two crewmen to play the roles of Varian and Ryker again. That afternoon was so exciting. You are in love with me, Zan, and that makes you dangerous.''

On the *Wanderlust*, Jana was having a curious day after sleeping late. While Varian was meeting secretly with Kyle Dykstra in the security chief's quarters, Jana tried to return to his suite from her visit with Tristan, but the control panel would not respond. When Varian didn't answer her summons, Jana wondered why he had altered the entrance code. As they were en route to the next planet, he had to be on the ship. Nigel, Tristan, Martella, and Kara were in a staff meeting, so she couldn't visit with any of her friends. She went to the gold room to await Varian's return and explanation. It didn't seem wise to go searching for him, not after his instructions about her ''role.'' Several hours passed.

An unfamiliar voice on the monitor startled Jana as it informed her, ''Commander Saar said to return to his quarters immediately.''

Jana hurried down the passageway in confusion. She paused before his door, wishing it were the only barrier separating them. *Please, God, let me reach him before it's too late.* She took several deep breaths. The door swished open before her hand made contact with the call button. Varian seized her arm and nearly yanked her inside. She asked hastily, ''Is something wrong, Varian? I couldn't get in. Who was that on the security monitor?''

Before responding to her questions, his mouth covered hers in a feverish kiss and his arms hugged her so tightly she could hardly breathe. When their lips parted, he replied sternly, ''I told you not to leave my quarters without my permission. Did you talk to anyone besides Tris?''

At his contact and behavior, Jana's head was spinning. She murmured, ''No one. I had a headache, so I went to see Tris for medication. I promise I didn't say or do anything wrong. When I returned, your door wouldn't open.''

221

"Security control was testing it. I had no idea you were locked out until my return. I had to track you. The voice on the monitor was a new lieutenant we picked up on Therraccus. She was on leave during my voyage to your world. I don't want you returning to the gold room, for any reason. I told you, Jana, unless you have my permission to leave this suite, remain here at all times. That includes no visits to Tristan or Kara or anyone unless I clear them. Do you understand me this time?"

"Am I being punished for an offense, or is there another reason?"

He hesitated, then answered tenderly, "Just do as you're told, Jana. I'm picking up the rest of my crew as we head for base on Rigel, and they don't know you. It's a precaution against any nasty problems. Despite our relationship, you are one of my captives, and it does look strange for you to have free run of my ship. I would like to prevent any jokes or gossip about us. Please, don't question or defy me; just do as I ask."

Jana realized something was troubling him, so she smiled and nodded. "I'm sorry about disobeying, Varian. It won't happen again. I do forget my place at times."

Hours later, they shared a cozy dinner. While Jana bathed, Varian completed a report on his security breach and how he planned to handle it. When he entered his bedroom, Jana was leaving the bathroom to get into bed. Varian gently grasped her arm as she was passing him. He smiled as he lifted her gown over her head and let it drop to the floor. "You won't need that tonight, moonbeam. I've been on a slow burn for you all day."

A pink glow of passion brightened Jana's face and upper chest. Boldly she removed his shirt, then nestled against his chest. "I seem to stay on a burn for you, Rogue Saar. I'm going to miss you terribly," she vowed softly, then surged upward to fasten her lips to his as she tried to mask her show of emotion.

Neither spoke again as they sank to his bed. They stimulated their desires until they came together in a union of smoldering bliss. When Jana lay on her back calming her breath, Varian rested on his side and left elbow with his right leg over her thigh; his knee was insinuated intimately between her legs and his fingertips brushed over her naked flesh. His gaze was locked on Jana's face. He looked as if he wanted to say something, but couldn't. Finally, he bent forward and kissed her with a tenderness and longing which surprised her. Slumber was ignored for another hour as he made sweet love to her.

After meeting *Avatar* Barasha Vaux, ruler of the ultramodern planet of Lynrac, Jana was escorted to a private salon. She was relieved to be out of the limelight. She had been embarrassed by the sensuous black silk jumpsuit which she was wearing. The waist was sashed snugly. Dramatic dolman sleeves accented the sultry top with its V-neck bodice. The black displayed a larger and more dramatic ''V'' which bared most of her shoulders and back, with an exquisite and sturdy spider's web of lace holding the two sides in place. She felt like a provocative black widow! Jana stood by the glass window gazing out at the imposing city before her. The blend of glass and metal inspired a feeling of loneliness. Her troubled mind began to drift over the last ten days and so many planets. Only two more stops and four days until her auction on Rigel. . . .

''You must be Jana Greyson,'' a thickly accented voice hinted from behind her. When she jumped and whirled, the elegantly attired man clasped her hand in greeting and apologized for startling her. ''Forgive the intrusion. I was told to wait here for *Avatar* Vaux. I am Jurad Tabriz, and this is my son Taemin. We have heard much about a goddess from Earth; we are honored and delighted to meet you. I fear the accounts of your beauty did not do you justice. Is that not true, my son?''

The twenty-five-year-old Taemin smiled appreciatively and agreed. ''You are right, Father. Never have I seen a more exquisite female. She is one to inspire lovely dreams,'' he stated in a rich and caressing voice.

Jana didn't know what to say or how to respond to such compliments. From her studies, she recognized the names of the rulers of the Pyropean Federation. Jana was charmed by their polite and genial manners. She smiled and replied graciously, ''It is I who am honored and delighted to meet you, Supreme Ruler Jurad and Prince Taemin. I have been studying

223

the histories and customs of these new worlds, but there is still much to learn. I ask your pardon if I have not properly greeted men of your station.''

Jurad appeared charmed by her manner, and invited her to sit with them. The older man, about fifty, displayed immense prowess and confidence. His aura alleged he was a man who made a loyal friend or a fierce enemy. Despite his amiable expression and cordial behavior, Jana sensed he was a man who masked his thoughts from others. The ruler was tall with a physique of oak-like hardness and strength. His gray eyes were penetrating, but impervious. His shoulder-grazing hair was as blond as the Sahara sands and his flesh was as golden as honey. He had a rugged, attractive mien which strangely called to mind an ancient Viking lord.

The same was true of his son, except for an added dash of virility and looks. Taemin's eyes were a deeper, more intense gray. His hair was a darker blond and his flesh was a coppery hue. His garments were made of a material which resembled khaki and were heavily trimmed with leather. Strapped to his narrow waist was a holster with a laser gun and a jewel-encrusted dagger. His demeanor bespoke courage, daring, and danger; the average male who dared to challenge such a power was a fool. This forceful man was no ordinary member of royalty; he was capable of defending not only himself but his entire planet. Jana couldn't help but be impressed by him.

''How can your captor sell such a rare beauty? What madness controls him? I must check on the legality of attending a Maffei auction and placing a bid for you. In our world, we do not practice such barbaric customs of capturing, selling, and enslaving our mates. If it is possible to obtain you as Taemin's mate, would this be agreeable to you? I do not wish to offend you by purchasing you as I do other treasures, but it must be done this way. If the transaction occurs, you will become his bride. Once you have accepted your role at his side and proven your royalty to us, you will be allowed the freedom to come and go as you wish, in our world and with your security guards. Do you concur, my son?''

The prince's gaze slowly traveled over Jana. Despite the desire which danced in his charcoal-gray eyes, his visual inspection was not lecherous or offensive, for Taemin knew how to control his expressions. A winning smile teased at his lips

224

as he replied, "I have met no woman who is more worthy to become my wife than this woman who has both beauty and intelligence, a woman of superb breeding and great courage. I would like nothing more than to have her at my side as soon as possible, as I have yearned for her since her pictures crossed my hands. Even so, I had not believed she could be real until this moment. I shall be very gentle and patient, my ray of sunlight. I know you have endured many changes and terrors in your life since your capture. If the Maffei Council allows me to purchase you, I will carry you home with me to Cenza. There, you will be granted a month to acquaint yourself with my people and our customs, then we will marry. Do you object to me or such plans?" he inquired.

Jana's cheeks burned beneath the fires in his gaze and voice. They were actually consulting her about her feelings and fate? Her astonishment was evident. "Become your wife? How is that possible? You're a prince, and I'm a—a slave, a prisoner."

Jurad smiled and said, "Only in the eyes and laws of the Maffeians. Were there another way to win you for my son, we would do so. You are far too special for them. You were destined to love and rule at Prince Taemin's side. Surely the fates guided us to this meeting, for our ship lost power for an entire night; if not, we would be on our way home and our paths would never have crossed," the older man lied convincingly. At last, revenge was at hand. Jana would be payment for his past loss of Princess Shara for his son could claim a bride who would bring anguish to a bitter adversary. From Canissia's reports, Varian loved and desired this ravishing creature. If they could persuade the Supreme Council of this galaxy to make truce through the gift or sale of Jana to Taemin, Galen Saar's firstborn son would be in torment and his grandfather Tirol would share that anguish. Perfect retribution!

Jana blushed and lowered her lashes. She stammered, "I don't—don't know what to—to say. This is so—so unexpected and . . . baffling."

The prince quickly said, "Then say what is in your heart, my radiant gem." Taemin's strong hand caressed her flaming cheek with surprising gentleness. What intelligent creature trapped by cruel fate would refuse marriage to a handsome and wealthy ruler?

The door opened and Varian entered with Nigel. He halted

225

and glared at the scene. He stepped forward, seized Jana's wrist, and yanked her away from the prince. "How dare you touch my property," he snarled. Varian's gaze swept over the prince, then his father. "What are you two doing here?" Varian demanded harshly.

Jana perceived dangerous emotional currents. It was clear these three men were bitter enemies. She shuddered apprehensively. Jana couldn't believe Varian's rudeness to such illustrious rulers, unless somehow they were fakes. She listened for clues to her lover's incredible behavior.

Supreme Ruler Jurad Tabriz stated, "The rulers of our world do not find it necessary to explain our comings and goings to even a high-ranking officer of the Maffei Alliance Force. Do you forget there is a lady present?"

At Jurad's criticism, Varian tensed. He dared not show any sign of weakness. "You forget yourself, Jurad. Today, you are in my domain and under my jurisdiction. I asked what brings you here?"

The ruler laughed. "You are mistaken. I travel with the permission and protection of your Supreme Council. There is a truce between our galaxies, remember? I came here on business which does not concern you." He glanced at Jana and smiled. "Or didn't until moments ago. Are your auctions open to any man with the proper finances to back his bid? I am greatly impressed with this creature, and I wish to purchase her. Name your price, any amount."

Varian was staggered by Jurad's offer. "Forget it. I wouldn't sell Jana to you if you crawled on your hands and knees and begged me. Leave my captive out of our private war."

Jurad replied in a scolding tone, "I do not view such a matchless gem as a prize of war. She would not settle our conflict. Once I was denied the woman of my heart and humiliated before the eyes of all who shared our Universe, but this radiant creature would not endure punishment as retribution for Saarian crimes against me. Nor would she serve as a replacement for my lost love. I seek Jana's hand to join it with Taemin's in marriage. She must not be caught in this battle between us as Shara was."

"Do you offer me a challenge or a compromise, Jurad? One day your misguided faith in Ryker may defeat you." Varian asked.

Taemin spoke up. "If you seek a challenge, seller of female flesh, then look to me, not my father. I am the one who desires Jana as my wife, future queen of Cenza and supreme ruleress of the Pyropean Federation. I demand to acquire her. Our federation will look kindly upon your favorable response." Blazing gray eyes challenged fiery blue ones.

"You demand?" Varian scoffed, then laughed. "You're wasting your time; the Maffeian law states that the buyer must be Maffeian, single, and financially secure."

"Wouldn't the Council make a concession in this particular case?" Jurad injected. "Surely you and *Kadim* Tirol owe us this much?"

"One day, you'll thank *Kahala* Shara never shared your bed and life. Forget your interest in Jana."

Jurad inquired to shame Varian, "I cannot fathom your cruelty in placing such a jewel on an auction block. Why do you punish her this way? It is common knowledge you will not keep her, though you have selfishly used her. What has she done to earn your spite?"

"Your ownership would be far more degrading to her than an auction. I would slay her before allowing either of you to have her," Varian taunted. Why hadn't he been warned of their presence? These men might torture Jana for vengeance against him. Why was Jurad so damn blind and stubborn where the Trilonis were concerned? Varian hungered to locate the evidence to end their bitter conflict, that diary which Ryker had mentioned at their recent meeting. Did Ryker have the diary, or had Shara destroyed it before her death?

How could Varian speak so horribly? A defensive stance was one thing; this vicious attack was another. "Please, Commander," Jana said, hoping to soothe him.

"Silence, Earthling!" he thundered, determined to conceal his love for her before these two foes. "Nigel, escort her to my quarters. If she shows any defiance, lock her in the arena until my return."

"Yes, Commander," Nigel responded, then took Jana's arm.

Jana was shocked by his hatefulness to the Pyropean leaders. When she tried to say good-bye politely, Varian jerked her to his chest. "You endanger yourself, alien. Speak only with permission."

227

Bravely she replied, "As you wish, sir."

Jurad shouted, "Cease this brutality at once, Commander Saar. If my offer for her is so antagonizing, then I withdraw it. Do not punish an innocent woman for your hatred of me."

"I do as I please, Jurad. Do not interfere in my affairs." Varian shoved Jana away from him. "Get her out of here, Nigel."

Nigel took Jana to the ship. He refused to talk until they were alone. "Listen to me very carefully, Jana Greyson. There are critical matters here which you do not understand and I cannot explain. Jurad's offer for you was part of a deception to get at Varian; they've been fierce opponents for years. Don't be fooled by his charming words. Please forget what just happened."

"Who are Shara and Ryker? What happened between Varian and Jurad?"

"Don't ever mention those names to Varian! I'm warning you as a friend, Jana, let this matter slide. It has to do with things from the past, dark and deadly affairs. If you press Varian, I'd hate to guess his reaction. This conflict brings out the worst in Varian. If you care about Varian and staying with him, forget it."

"Was Jurad lying about marriage with Taemin? Do Maffei owners ever marry the mates they purchase?" Jana insisted on one particular answer.

Jana saw Nigel stiffen at her loaded questions. "Our law does not permit such a marriage," came his crushing reply. "Listen to me, Jana, Jurad and Taemin were deceiving you. The prince wouldn't marry you. They would torture you, slay you, then return your body to Varian."

"Is it possible for an alien to marry a Pyropean?" she pressed.

Nigel sighed loudly, knowing his answer would mislead her. "Yes, Jana. They do not practice the capture of *charls*. Taemin could marry you."

"Then how do you know he was lying?" she challenged.

"I can't explain," he said, refusing to end her confusion.

"Can a Maffeian captive earn freedom?" she demanded.

"It's practically unheard of, but possible under certain conditions. As far as I know, there have been only three cases in my lifetime. Unique service or exceptional courage supplied all three occasions.''

Jana asked one last question, ''Is there any way I can earn my freedom?''

''Not before we reach Star Fleet base and hold our final auction on Rigel,'' Nigel answered reluctantly. ''Someday we hope these *charl* laws will change, but change requires time. It will come too late for you. I'm sorry, but you wanted the truth.''

Jana felt anguish knife her chest. She stood up, hesitated, then turned and queried, ''Varian *is* going to auction me on Rigel, isn't he?''

Nigel lowered his head. As far as he knew, Varian's hands were bound by duty and the past. When he finally looked up, he said, ''I'm sorry, Jana. He has no choice.''

''You're wrong, Nigel, he does have a choice, and he's made it.''

Chapter Thirteen

When Varian returned after midnight, he stretched out on his office sofa and dozed fitfully until nine o'clock. Without moving from his cramped position, he detected from the feel of his ship that she was orbiting the planet Mailiorca. Damn the secrets of this mission which denied him from being able to explain his past and present actions as far as his love was concerned! Jana had been through too much. He would be damn lucky if he didn't destroy her tender feelings before they reached his base. There, he doubtlessly would devastate her when he carried out an auction which must look real. *Kahala* help him, for Jana had to believe and unsuspectingly aid this mandatory mock sale. But if something went wrong, she could be lost to him forever.

He didn't want to take her below today, not to confront Canissia Garthon. But he had no choice; Canissia's father,

Supreme Councilman Segall Garthon wanted to meet Jana, as did several prospective bidders. He couldn't refuse such orders, as Jana was owned by the Supreme Council. No doubt he would receive a verbal reprimand for taking advantage of his vulnerable captive.

He was deeply worried. He had decided Martella's scheme could work, but what if his secret bid on her to be made by his friend Draco Procyon wasn't the highest one? What if Draco wouldn't take part in this wild and desperate plan of his? As for Varian Saar, he dared not attempt a purchase which would reveal his love to everyone. With Jurad and Taemin Tabriz and other extremely wealthy men making known their interest in Jana, Varian was scared for the first time in his life. No matter how much wealth and power a man possessed, another always came along with more. At least it didn't seem as if Ryker or *Kadim* Maal Triloni were intrigued by Jana. If reports were accurate, Ryker had left the Maffei Galaxy for the Pyropean Federation. Suddenly a cold sweat attacked Varian. If Ryker was in league with Jurad and his son as Varian believed, Ryker would have known the two rulers were in the Maffei Galaxy awaiting Jana's arrival. Ryker had lied about heading for Jurad's palace. Was he still secretly on Darkar waiting for Varian to make a move?

Varian brooded. He raged at his helplessness; for the safest path for Jana seemed to be a total separation from him, a seemingly brutal and heartless rejection. Her auction would be the highest form of betrayal to her. But how could he give up the woman he loved?

Hours later on the planet Mailiorca, Varian met with a surprise; yesterday Supreme Council member Segall Garthon had left suddenly for Eire, native planet of *Kadim* Tirol Trygue and Varian's last stop before Rigel. Varian surreptitiously made contact with *Avatar* Kwan while his beloved Jana was being displayed.

Varian couldn't relax during his conversations with friends. He knew Canissia was around somewhere today. He hated the thought of Jana being subjected to that vicious female. He hoped to get Jana away from the auction hall before Canissia revealed herself. Varian concluded that something devious was afoot, for Cass's absence was very unusual.

Years ago the redhead had been exciting and daring to Varian. She had learned the skills of seduction at a very young age. As the daughter of a Supreme Council member and he the grandson of the *Kadim,* as well as the son of the supreme commander of all Maffei Alliance forces, they had spent time together during their teenage years. Cass had been ravishing. Her looks, status, wealth, and sexual talents had made her a desirable companion.

She now owned her own luxury starcruiser with a crew of ten. She roamed the galaxy, seeking pleasures and wild adventures, or sometimes seeking Varian. Over the years, she had become more and more selfish, daring, and spiteful.

Canissia Garthon was not a creature for the average man to reject or defy, or for an inexperienced woman to challenge. For years it had been widely known that Varian Saar was her only weakness. And it had become apparent that Varian held no affection and little respect for the vixen though her aging father continued to encourage a marriage between them. He wondered if the vain Canissia was becoming concerned over losing her beauty and status; she was thirty years old and her father could die or be compelled to resign his Council seat, which would take away her high status and much of her power and wealth.

Canissia was fearless. She had visited places some men feared to go. But Varian suspected Canissia had fingers in places they didn't belong; dangerous, illegal places. He knew she had become acquainted with Ryker, Jurad, and Taemin during the last few years. Since those enemies were interested in Jana, he cautioned himself to be alert and polite around Canissia. If he was very nice to her, perhaps she would drop clues to his rivals' plans.

Jana was delighted that her performance on this planet was nearing an end. As she chatted with *Avatar* Kwan and Nigel, she noticed that a beautiful woman had joined Varian in the corner of the room. Jana could feel the withering heat from that redhead's blazing eyes each time the woman looked at her.

231

Jana tried to concentrate on the conversation with Kwan and Nigel, but her attention kept straying to Varian and his ravishing companion. As if dancing, the woman swayed seductively against Varian's body as the two chatted, seemingly as if old and good friends. No, as if they were or had been closer than friends!

When Canissia noticed Varian's eyes frequently straying to Jana, she fumed. Despite Baruch Tirana's claims of an emotional and sexual bond between the alien temptress and Varian, she had secretly hoped those facts were untrue. Outraged, she taunted Varian, "Careful, love, you are far too fascinated and charmed by your captive. She'll never forgive you for selling her. Are you sure you're ready to part with Jana?" she murmured.

"If I were you, Cass, I'd be glad she's a captive. Otherwise, she would give you plenty of competition," he teased.

"What's so special about her?" Canissia asked, sneering.

"Besides being exceedingly beautiful, highly intelligent, well bred, utterly charming, and totally satisfying— she's obedient. Like it or not, Jana does what I say and when I say and where I say. Plus, Jana is marvelous company out of bed." Varian flashed her a mischievous grin and chuckled wickedly as he baited her.

The cunning Canissia altered her tactics. She licked her lips and shrugged. "Which reminds me, you and I have some catching up to do, my love. I don't mind if you keep Jana around a while longer. You might enjoy having two different mistresses. You would be surprised how exciting it is to have two lovers who work together," she hinted crudely. She wondered why Varian was not defending Jana against her insulting suggestions. Varian, she realized, was being too nice.

"Never fear, Cass, Jana will soon be gone. Her auction is in two days."

"If you don't change your mind and keep her a while longer," the redhead stated skeptically. She hoped the tiny recorder in her necklace was working. She might make use of this conversation one day. . . .

Varian winked at Canissia and teased, "If I win Jana at her auction in two days, I'll sell her and marry you."

Canissia eyed Varian intently. Her expression altered to as-

232

tonishment. "You're serious about selling Jana. I must confess I thought you cared for her."

"Come now, Cass," he chided her playfully, "You never believed that. Varian Saar wouldn't buy a mate he can't marry."

"Why don't you join me tonight?" she invited.

Varian smiled and shook his head. "Like you said, I plan to sate myself with that alien treat before her auction. Time is running out."

Canissia shrugged and kissed Varian's cheek. Varian glanced across the room to find Jana's somber eyes on him. He held that probing gaze until he was standing before her. He whispered in her ear, "I'll explain that scene later."

Jana had not questioned his absence from their bed last night or his behavior toward the Pyropean rulers yesterday. She smiled guardedly and followed his lead. Was she being a fool? Jana realized how very little she knew about him. She could easily hate him for taking her so cruelly from Earth. She also realized only the planet Eire remained between this one and Rigel. The trap seemed to be closing around her like a spider's web.

Jana realized Varian was reserved and edgy, When they left the room, he silently escorted Jana to an awaiting shuttle and had the pilot take them miles from the city. The pilot landed, dropped them off, then left.

Jana glanced around at the lovely setting, wondering why he had brought her here. So many warring emotions filled her soul. She didn't know what he expected, wanted, or needed. She was careful to avoid eye contact. She was suspicious of this outing and this man, Their time together was almost over. Would he slay her here? Her fate didn't matter, if he didn't care for her, and if he did, how could he bear to sell her to another?

Varian chuckled and jested, "Relax, moonbeam. I don't bite, at least not as hard as you do."

Jana didn't smile. "Why are we here?" she asked bluntly.

Varian didn't reply. He led her to a nearby stream which was fed by a thundering waterfall. He strolled toward it with Jana in tow. He halted to watch its endless movement and intrinsic beauty. The silvery-green water was the clearest she had ever seen. The surrounding grass was lush and strange with its purplish-blue curly blades. A gentle breeze ruffled their hair and clothing. He guided her to the steep embankment near the cascading falls. Large rocks, clumps of needlelike grass, and mauve-colored flowers decorated the untamed hideaway. A heady fragrance drifted into her nose and brought a smile.

Varian plucked one of the flowers and handed it to her. It resembled an English primrose. As she teased it under her nose, Varian told her, "It's called a *Talias*. It's very rare and exotic. It's a crime to pull them."

Jana looked his way to discover he was telling the truth. "Then why did you? A man of the law should obey the laws," she admonished.

"Sometimes laws must be broken or ignored," he moodily replied as he stared across the meadow beyond the stream. "Sometimes they're wrong or old."

"Why, Commander Saar of the Alliance Force, whatever the law, patriotic citizens must obey it," she responded, to elicit further conversation on this curious topic.

Varian walked to the edge of the stream near the base of the falls and sat down. He crossed his legs and picked a blade of grass. He finally replied, "I've always fulfilled my duty, no matter the cost."

Jana walked downstream, then halted to stare at the beauty and tranquility which surrounded her, wishing it would share some of its serenity with her. A long silence followed, a silence which grew heavy. When Varian stepped up behind her and encircled her slim waist with his strong arms, she feared he would detect the fierce pounding of her heart. When he pulled her close to him and nestled the side of his face against her silky hair, Jana fought to master her wild emotions. Desperate longing and sadness filled her. She needed and wanted this man; she loved him.

Jana abruptly pulled away from him. "I'm starving. It's past lunchtime. When did you tell the shuttle pilot to come after us?" she asked.

Varian pretended to be unaware of her fears and emotions as he struggled to control his own. He wanted nothing more at that precise moment than to make tender and consuming love to her on the grassy bank, to remain there with her in his arms, to hide from the world with all of its duties and responsibilities.

Varian pulled out his communicator and called his ship. He

issued several orders and asked a few questions. He patiently waited for them to be obeyed. "The advantages of superior technology," he hinted as he gestured toward a suddenly materializing picnic basket, which appeared as if by magic. "Energy and mass displacement can be rewarding at times."

Varian picked up the basket and opened it. He removed fruits, cheeses, crackers, wine, and two glasses and spread them on the grass. "You may be seated, moonbeam. What's your pleasure?" Varian served Jana, then himself. He tried to lighten her gray mood with jokes and smiles.

A stabbing thought pierced her mind: if her owner lived in a remote or private area of this alien world, she might never see this man again. She cautioned herself not to spoil this day. "I had forgotten your superiority. You are amazing, Rogue Saar." Jana sipped a heady wine.

Varian finished eating and stretched out on his back. He observed her for a time, then teased, "Do you always eat so slowly?"

"Must you always eat so swiftly? Slow down and enjoy your food and companion."

Varian drew her down beside him. "I had another way in mind to enjoy my companion," he quipped. "Notice, no dessert was ordered? I seem to recall missing my treat yesterday, in fact for two days this week."

"Did you expect a treat each day, you glutton?" she teased.

"Naturally. I'm always starving. My appetite for you increases with each passing day. You sorely deny my needs."

"You can't blame me for your weakness. Perhaps I should lock you in your quarters and seduce you every four hours," she suggested with glimmering eyes.

"How about every hour?" he playfully retorted.

"I doubt even my lusty Rogue Saar has that much hunger and stamina."

"Shall we put him to the test and see?" he ventured as he propped himself up on his elbow and gazed down into her face.

"I suppose part-time is better than nothing. My education is still sadly lacking, and class is nearly over. Why not?" she responded.

He leaned forward and brushed his lips over hers. He whispered hoarsely, "Don't, Jana. For today, forget about Eire and Rigel. Just be with me."

"These next few days and stops are easier for you to ignore than for me. Sometimes this episode is more like a dream than harsh reality. I can't decide if I wish the auction were postponed or pushed forward. The closer we get to Rigel, the greater my fears. I—"

Varian pressed his fingertips against her lips. "Don't say any more, Jana."

Jana pushed away his hand, then sat up. In a ragged voice she told him, "Sorry, I forgot you don't want to hear about my insignificant feelings. We'd better get back to your ship; it's getting late, very late. . . ."

Varian had come to his knees. He seized her forearms and drew Jana against his chest. In a strained tone, he asked, "What are you so afraid of, Jana? Do I make you upset today?"

Jana looked up into his impenetrable gaze. She searched for a sign of something she needed to read there. Her eyes shone brightly with a threat of tears which didn't come. She lowered her gaze. "First, you tell me to hush; then, you ask me to explain my feelings. I don't understand you at all, Varian. What go you want from me? I'm trying my damnedest to get through this affair with a little pride and dignity. Don't try to strip off my thin mask."

Varian abruptly seized her and seared a passionate kiss over her mouth. He forced her lips apart to accept his fiery assault. When Jana tried to twist free, his hands imprisoned her head between them. His kiss became rougher and hotter.

Jana's senses reeled and swayed traitorously. She helplessly yielded to his embrace. Her hands encircled his waist and she pressed against him.

Varian lifted her and carried her to the grassy bank near the stream, then lay down beside her. And as Jana's mind spun wildly and madly, his tall, lithe frame covered her burning flesh. Just when he had her trembling with intense need, his communicator buzzed loudly and persistently.

"What is it?" he snapped into the instrument.

"Varian, I think you'd better return now. Something's come up which concerns you," Nigel said, radioing from the ship.

"What happened, Nigel?" he questioned, not ready to leave this spot.

"Are you sure you want this over the communicator?" Nigel hinted.

236

"Evidently it's private and important, so I'll take a stroll." Jana stood up and walked to the rushing waterfall, which would block out their voices.

Varian glanced at her slender back and grimaced. "Go ahead."

"The *Galactic Gem* discovered your agent's body on the beach at Eire."

It was ironic, Varian thought grimly, that his father's old ship was involved, the same ship which had witnessed the treachery of Princess Shara thirty-two years ago. "Any sign of his partner?" he inquired, fearing for the life of the second agent whom he had sent to Darkar to unmask Ryker. Surely there was no hope for the agent's survival. Did this also mean that there was no hope of Ryker not guessing his ruse? It could even get worse if Ryker believed Jana was Varian's willing accomplice.

"None yet. Ryker knows about your scheme, Varian."

This news was staggering. "Yes, but how much? We'll come on board immediately, Nigel. Give orders to get us to Eire as fast as possible. I'll meet you in your quarters; we've got some plans to make."

In fifteen minutes, Jana was soaking in a bubble bath. She knew something awful was happening. Nigel's message had upset Varian. She had never seen, or ever expected to see, him so deeply worried.

Varian asked Nigel, "Was there anything on Vejar's body?"

"Nothing but an empty satchel chained to his wrist."

"How was he slain?" Varian had to know.

"Both jugular veins were slit from jaw to collarbone. Wait a minute," the first officer told him, "another coded message is coming through now."

Varian awaited the news which he was sure to come, and did. "Dohler's body was just found on Rigel. That's a body at each of our remaining stops. I think Ryker's message is loud and clear. I have Star Fleet base checking on the air traffic around both planets for the past two days, but I'm sure it's a waste of time. Ryker is too clever for such a simple slip-up."

Varian inhaled wearily. It had taken him two weeks before his trek to the Milky Way Galaxy to persuade the leader of

237

the Star Fleet, Supreme Commander Sard, and his grandfather *Kadim* Tirol to try to ensnare Ryker. He had convinced them Ryker might drop his rigid guard while Varian was away so long. Then, in case the two agents had not found a way into Ryker's secret complex, he had rashly used Jana as a decoy to lure Ryker off Darkar. Perhaps that was the folly that had piqued Ryker's curiosity and alerted him to Varian's treachery. Now both of the men secretly assigned to Trilabs were dead. That meant no evidence to unmask or arrest that deadly enemy anytime soon. Both officers' faces had been surgically altered and their false backgrounds had been prepared by experts; so how had Ryker discovered their identities or suspected their mission? Varian had lured Ryker off Darkar for several days, but had Ryker covertly returned home, after claiming to be heading for Cenza, to find the two Elite Squad agents sifting through his files? Or had someone betrayed Dohler and Vejar to Ryker? Canissia was many vile things, but could she be a traitor? The timing of the two murders and the placement of the bodies were what alarmed Varian, as they had Nigel Sanger.

Varian didn't forget there was a spy on his ship who was keeping Ryker better informed on Varian than Varian was informed about Ryker. But the spy aboard his ship *could not* have known about his secret agents.

The telecom signaled again. "What is it, Kyle?" Varian asked, having placed the security control chief in charge of all coded messages as a precaution.

"Jurad Tabriz and his son have arrived on Eire to confer with *Kadim* Tirol, Draco Procyon, and Segall Garthon. They've asked to purchase Jana as Taemin's bride before the public auction. If not, they've requested permission to attend Jana's auction and to make an offer for her. Jurad is hinting at a new peace treaty if the Council complies with his demand."

Exasperated, Varian said, "Can it get any worse!"

"I'm afraid so, Varian. Moloch just docked his shuttle on Rigel. He's deposited quite a large sum in the bank, then rented a security box. It seems he wants to make sure we don't learn how much he's bringing to the auction. Ryker's ship is orbiting the planet Karlim in Jurad's territory, but I would bet my stripes he isn't on it. I don't have to tell you, security on Darkar has been stepped up. We are in a crisis situation."

* * *

When Jana hadn't seen or heard from Varian by early afternoon of the next day, she wondered if she should stay put as
ordered. Who could she call for news or instructions? How?
What was going on? The entry buzzer sounded. She answered
it, to find Martella standing there.

"Jana, you need to be ready to leave at three for a meeting
on Eire with the Supreme Council. This conference is important
to Commander Saar; please behave. I need not warn you that
first impressions can be critical. As you've learned, the Supreme Council makes new laws or changes old ones," she
hinted.

Jana seized her hands and smiled. "You've been a good
friend and teacher, Martella. I can't thank you enough for all
you've done for me and the others. Is Varian around? I would
like to speak with him before this meeting."

"He's been on Eire since our arrival at dawn. He won't be
returning to the *Wanderlust*. You're on your own."

In twenty minutes, Jana was mounting the steps leading to
the palatial home of the most powerful leader of this galaxy,
Kadim Tirol Trygue. Positioned on a high cliff overlooking the
ocean, the white mansion was stunningly beautiful. Lieutenant
Commander Nigel Sanger, who was attired in a dashing dress
uniform, was her escort. Jana smiled and nervously remarked,
"Does it show that I'm scared stiff?"

"Relax, you look perfect, Dr. Greyson."

"Do I use the helpless-victim charade?" Jana probed.

"Yes," he replied, then smiled encouragingly.

Jana prayed that her courage would not fail her. Her behavior
during this meeting might be her last chance to forestall her
auction and show Varian she could fit into his life.

There was a great marble-floored entrance hall inside which
led to three sets of stairs: the one to her right led to a balustraded
balcony which encircled the enormous room to return via the
staircase to her left. The balcony overlooked the huge room,
and countless doors led from it into numerous rooms. The third
flight of steps led down to a large room where a group of men
were conferring.

Jana's gaze hurriedly passed over the men in the room and
picked out the three who were strangers to her. At Nigel's side,

239

she gracefully descended the central stairway and crossed the highly polished floor. She was keenly aware that all eyes were on her, and all conversations had ceased. No one could have guessed the turmoil which filled the beautiful and elegant Earthling. During the distraction of her entrance, *Kadim* Tirol Tyrgue, Councilman Draco Procyon, and Varian Saar unobtrusively passed messages. . . .

Jana's assessing gaze roamed over the powerful ruler and then scanned the two Council members, Draco Procyon and Segall Garthon, but she avoided even a brief glance at her grinning captor. When the head of the Council smiled in amusement, Jana didn't react. Clearly the handsome gray-haired *Kadim* Tirol Trygue was perceptive, intelligent, and good-humored.

"She is far more beautiful than her pictures. Welcome to my home, Jana Greyson of Earth. I have been eager to meet the female who captured Commander Saar's eyes and blinded them to his duty. Now I see why he was so bewitched." Tirol looked fondly at Varian. "How can I possibly reprimand you for taking an action which even I would have found irresistible. May I have the honor of sharing private words with you?" he asked Jana.

Jana politely replied, "I am honored to meet the prestigious and powerful ruler of the Maffei Galaxy. As I am the prisoner of your illustrious starship commander, perhaps your request should be directed to him."

Varian chuckled and remarked, "I told you she had plenty of spunk. Permission granted."

Jana still didn't look at Varian as she placed her hand in Tirol's outstretched one. He led her to a lovely solarium and seated her. For a few moments nothing was said between them. Jana wondered why this male looked vaguely familiar, for she had not viewed any pictures of him. His hair was sandy with streaks of gray; his eyes were as pale and shiny as rare blue diamonds. Just reaching six feet, he was sturdy for an older man.

"I feel I should apologize for Commander Saar's outrageous behavior, even though it is most abnormal conduct for him. I must confess I was distressed when I heard the news. Now that I've had the opportunity to study your files and to meet you, his impulsive action is understandable. Still, I fear it has given you a bitter introduction to our world."

Jana opened her mouth to speak, but didn't. Warring emotions flooded her eyes. *Kadim* Tirol comprehended her dilemma: she wanted to defend Varian, but she was trying to obey Varian's commands to play the vulnerable, misused captive. Clearly it dismayed her to have Varian's image tarnished in his ruler's eyes. Tirol was impressed by her gentility, her honesty. He advised, "There is no need to worry, my dear. Given time, I hope you find my world and people acceptable."

Jana said, "Despite my abduction, I have not been abused by Commander Saar or his staff. They went to great trouble to train us to fit into your world." Correctly reading his empathy for her, she decided to speak freely. "But isn't it time to cease this cruel process? Surely your men can choose mates in a better way? You appear far too gentle to continue such a barbarous practice."

"This is our law, Jana. But I am a perceptive man. Despite your bitter words, you and Varian are wise to keep your true relationship a secret. He is a man with many enemies. He is carefree and adventurous, little Earthling. For your sake, I pray you never forget that."

Jana berated the crimson flush which splashed across her cheeks, but found the wisdom to avoid protesting further. "Thank you for your honesty, sir. Was this your idea or Commander Saar's?"

Kadim Tirol replied, "Mine alone. Varian is like a son to me, Jana; he has been since his father's death. Although he finds your auction disagreeable, he will proceed with it. Afterward, he will be away for many months. While he's gone, he hopes you will find peace. It would be best for all concerned if you could find the courage to accept your new destiny. A distracted mind can get a man killed, Jana. If you love him, let him go."

"I don't intend to make Varian suffer because of the laws of his world. I realize only too well all connections between us will end with my auction, but I would appreciate your keeping this talk private between us. I don't need his pity. I just want a few more days with him. Do you understand?"

"Yes, I do. You are very brave. Go, meet the other guests.

For both your sakes, try to embrace your destiny. I will make certain your owner learns of my respect for you."

Masking her deep disappointment, Jana was introduced to Councilman Draco Procyon. To her surprise she found him utterly charming and fascinating. He owned a private planetoid named Karnak which orbited the capital planet, Rigel. The amber-eyed widower of thirty-eight was involved in many businesses, all lucrative ones. His hair was such a dark blond that it almost looked light brown at a quick glance. His features were as symmetrical as those on ancient Greek statues. He wasn't handsome like Varian, but he was very appealing. He had a warm and enchanting smile. A decidedly likable person who invited admiration, he made her want to study him closer. Draco exuded a quiet strength, a keen intelligence, and a strong sense of justice. Draco had only one disadvantage as her possible owner: he and Varian were very good friends, and friends shared visits.

Time passed slowly. She tried not to think about Tirol's words or Varian's behavior. Since her arrival, he hadn't approached her. She sighed wearily from the strain of this demandingly long performance. Draco smiled and excused himself when Councilman Segall Garthon came forward to meet her. Jana sipped a glass of wine as she gingerly conversed with the man who was the father of the ravishing redhead who had visually seared her with her flaming eyes at their last stop, the woman she had discovered was the "Cass" whom Varian and Tristan had mentioned in the library that day while she was hiding. She wished she had been introduced to the beautiful Maffeian female, but either Varian or Canissia had prevented it. Perhaps Canissia had felt Jana was beneath her.

Jana found little of interest about Segall Garthon. Besides being plain in appearance, he was boring. She wondered how this male had won a seat on the all-powerful three-man Supreme Council. Evidently he was not the same man he had been years ago! Noticeably, he held great love and pride for his only daughter, for he talked about Canissia incessantly. Jana wouldn't have minded if Segall hadn't made it sound as if Canissia and Varian had been sweethearts since the age of ten! Worse, he had made it sound as if those two were fated to marry one day soon. Jana quivered inside. Was the supreme councilman's daughter the real barrier between them?

At last, Draco Procyon came to rescue Jana. The two rulers chatted briefly. Draco smiled and suggested that Jana go freshen up, as the hour was nearing for her departure. Jana sensed the kind man was helping her escape from Segall's depressing attention. She smiled and left. When she returned, only two people remained: Varian and Tirol. It was obvious the two men were talking privately, so Jana sat down and waited across the room. Suddenly she felt nervous around her lover and the powerful ruler!

Before meeting Jana, Varian had not realized how lonely he was. A man in his position was viewed differently than the average man. Responsibilities had prevented him from expressing his emotions. Since his parents' deaths, he had been wary and cynical. Jana had taught him to feel again. Once this mission was over, and the fate of Earth was resolved and matters were settled, if necessary he would beg his grandfather to do everything in his great power to change the *charl* laws so he could marry Jana Greyson!

Varian talked gravely with Tirol. "I'm in a terrible trap, Grandfather. She's the only woman I've ever loved, the first one I've wanted to share my life with. It's ripping me up inside to know I can't have her, that I have to be the one to sell her to another man. She'll never understand or forgive me. Why should she? This practice is cruel."

When Tirol asked if Varian wanted to purchase Jana, Varian lowered his head and inhaled wearily. He hadn't planned to unload such burdens on his grandfather tonight. It was in fact illegal to have Draco purchase Jana only to hold her for him. Obviously, Varian didn't want to involve his grandfather. After things were settled, he would confess the truth.

When Varian responded, his voice was filled with the turmoil which ate at him. "You know why I can't publicly claim her, Grandfather. A real man doesn't destroy something or someone he loves and wants more than his own life." Glancing at Jana's back from across the immense room, he motioned to the space between them as he vowed sadly, "As long as my half brother craves my life and name, there will be a distance separating us larger than this one. Please, help me do whatever is necessary to protect her, even if it means losing her," he beseeched gravely. "I can exist without Jana in my arms easier than I can survive with her lifeblood on my hands."

Tirol grasped Varian by the shoulders and stared deeply into his sapphire eyes. What Tirol read there distressed him greatly, for he empathized with his grandson. "You love her this much, Varian?" the *Kadim* asked softly.

"Yes, Grandfather, I do. Yet, with all my power and wealth, I can't have her because I might be unable to protect her," he replied honestly. "There is no place where I could leave her during my assignments which wouldn't endanger her and those keeping her. I have no choice but to pretend she was merely a conquest whose sale means little to me."

"I assigned Martella Karsh to handle the *charl* process during your mission because I knew how difficult you would find it even though it was a necessary cover tactic. She sent me several messages during your return voyage which I've already taken actions on."

Shocked, Varian listened closely to Tirol's words. When he finished his revelations, Varian inquired, "Why did you ask Martella to spy on me? What was the point of sending pictures of me and Jana to Ryker?"

"You confuse me, son. Clarify yourself."

Varian related his meeting with Ryker and his discovery of the spy. Tirol appeared alarmed by that news. When he told Varian that was not part of Martella's assignment, the two men deliberated on the identity of the traitor.

"How do you plan to check out those officers without arousing their suspicions?" Tirol inquired after they had hit on three possibilities.

Varian revealed his cunning strategy. "I plan to share a different secret with each one, let him have a one-day shore leave on Rigel, then see which of the three lies is acted upon by Ryker. But are you sure you want to know about this matter with Draco? I didn't know Martella would relate that idea to you too."

Tirol embraced his grandson and heir. "Surely you don't begrudge an old man a little share of the excitement and romance? I'm glad you found a woman like Jana Greyson, and you should keep her. You do me proud, son. Now take your moonbeam to your ship while I do some serious planning. We have to make certain Draco's bid is the highest."

When Varian ended the conversation with Tirol and headed her way, Jana hurriedly composed herself. During all her travels and stops in his world, no one had mentioned the relationship between Varian Saar and Tirol Trygue. They were obviously old friends, she decided.

"Ready to go, moonbeam? I'm sure you're exhausted from your conquests tonight. The next time you get me so riled up watching you entice bachelors, I just might grab your hand, take you into the nearest room, and who knows what will happen," he threatened, a grin on his lips.

"I was only being polite, and Nigel is our friend. Surely you're not jealous?" she teased boldly.

"Presently, you're private property, and everyone keeps forgetting and ignoring that fact, including you."

Jana shrugged nonchalantly. Varian backed her against a pillar and pinned her body to it with his. He grasped her wrists and imprisoned her hands over her head with one of his, then tickled her wildly with the free one. Jana squirmed and giggled. "Stop, Varian," she squealed. "This isn't fair; you're stronger than I am. Have mercy," she cried out between peals of laughter.

He replied huskily, "I shall show none."

"Varian!" she shrieked as he tickled her again. "Uncle! Uncle!"

Chuckling uncontrollably, he questioned, "What kind of language is that?"

"Earth slang. It means 'I yield; I give up,'" she said, panting.

Varian's hands released her to capture her upturned face between them. Lowering his face very close to hers, he demanded, "Do you yield all, woman?"

Jana scowled as she accused, "Rogue! Tyrant!"

"Then I shall take my prize of war home with me this very moment. Come along, moonbeam; I wish to examine my trophy inch by inch." Varian took her hand and guided her up the stairs and out the door to his waiting shuttle.

Tirol leaned against the wall in the alcove and smiled. How like Galen and Amaya they were. He was pleased for them.

When Varian and Jana reached his quarters in the *Wanderlust,* Jana was out of her clothes and into bed before Varian completed his routine checks with his officers before turning in for the night. When he entered his bedroom, Jana pretended to be asleep just to tease him.

245

Varian had keen senses, and he knew the creature beside his naked body wasn't asleep. He stretched out on his back and closed his eyes, without drawing up the cover. He patiently awaited Jana's reaction.

Jana slightly parted her eyelids and observed the situation. So he wanted to play games tonight, did he? Jana rolled to her side and began to nibble at Varian's left ear as her fingertips softly grazed his torso. When Varian feigned deep sleep, nothing could have pleased Jana more. Her hand daringly headed down his chest to halt temptingly at his flat and taut belly. As her nails gently teased circles around it, Jana's lips worked their way down his throat. She murmured as if to herself, "Sleep on, space demon, for I shall pleasure myself tonight since your veins course with ice water and mine throb with molten lava."

Her tongue danced over and around the tips on his hard chest. He twitched. Her hand provocatively slipped down his body and carefully grasped his manhood. With leisurely strokes, she tantalized him until his manhood was thick and firm. "Sleep while I play, space demon, but I shall instill respect and passion in you before I sate my hungers." Jana shifted her body as her lips seductively and stirringly followed the same path which her hand had just traveled.

When Varian realized he couldn't master his emotions very much longer, he seized Jana and rolled her onto her back. He drove his fiery shaft into her eager body. He held out as long as possible, then poured his love and sated passion into her.

When he could speak, Varian gazed down at her and apologized. "I'm sorry, love, but I couldn't hold out a moment longer. You nearly drove me wild. I wasn't prepared to use so much self-control tonight. Sorry to leave you hanging."

Jana grinned and quipped, "But you didn't, love. Molten blood, remember?"

Varian was stunned by her reply. He had been so engrossed and enslaved by her uninhibited behavior that he had not realized she was so close to ecstasy. He grinned sheepishly, perplexed by his total loss of control. He inhaled erratically "I skipped that particular lesson, but I see now you didn't require it. I hadn't realized you were ready for such . . . intimacy, such total sharing of passions."

"Only with you," she responded candidly. "Did I— Was

it— Oh, hell, do I need more practice or instructions on this lesson?'' she stammered.

Laughter filled her ears. "Are you jesting, moonbeam! No one has ever learned that lesson better," he answered honestly. He looked as if he were about to add something else, but mastered the impulse. Instead, he pulled Jana into his arms and sighed peacefully. "Sleep well."

Jana nestled against him and murmured, "Now I can."

Chapter Fourteen

Jana was awakened early the next morning by a tickling sensation. When masculine laughter filled the air, she suspiciously opened one eye and peered at the man reclining near her. He held one of her long curls in his grip. She flashed him an admonishing glare.

"Do you plan to lie in bed all day while I work so hard?" he asked as he nonchalantly flicked the curl over one taut nipple and then the other.

"I plan to spend this day collecting on my wager. Doesn't my wager include daylight hours as well as nighttime ones?"

"You greedy vixen. I have work to do," he replied.

"You most assuredly do, you have a captive student who needs more lessons."

His body flamed. "What if my time is limited?"

Jana laughed in his face. Her hand slid down his abdomen and gently captured him. His stomach muscles tightened and he inhaled sharply at her fiery touch. His manly shaft instantly responded to her feather caresses. "Then I shall change the order of today's priorities." She leaned forward and nibbled at his lips. "You have created a fierce hunger in me. It demands regular feedings. Everything else must wait."

"Yes," he agreed, closing his quivering fingers around hers as they drifted up and down his pulsing manhood.

Jana rolled off the bed. "Right after my bath."

"Come back here, woman," he ordered.

"Restrain yourself. We had a late night. I'm not fully awake, yet." She raced into the bathroom, sat down in the oval tub, and allowed the warm water to surround her. She added a floral fragrance, then leaned back and relaxed.

Varian entered the room, devilment sparkling in his sapphire eyes. "Your lessons are far from over, witch." He joined her.

She shrieked in surprise. "What do you think you're doing!"

"Didn't you know, masters often bathe with their captives?"

"Does this mean you've never tried it?"

He grinned. "Me? I'm far too modest."

She eyed him with open doubt. "Since you're here, you can scrub my back. I've yet to experience that pampered, lavish existence you allotted for us *charls*."

Varian smiled and relaxed. "Is it proper for a master to wait upon his slave?"

Jana knelt between his legs and soaped his hairy chest and powerful shoulders as if it were an everyday ritual between them. "If I help you bathe, then you'll help me? Isn't half the fun of educating a student sharing in her lessons?"

Varian nodded. He leaned back and accepted her loving caresses. She massaged his muscles with creamy suds. Before she could protest his actions, she found herself seated across his lap with his manhood touching her in a most intimate and enticing way. As she washed his shoulders, he eased within her. A sensual smile teased his lips as he witnessed the effect of his erotic movements on her.

Varian's deft hands lathered her breasts and leisurely tantalized them. As their eyes met and shared the fires of desire, she whispered seductively, "I see what you meant about the pleasures of sharing a bath. Lesson number eight?"

Varian laughed and pulled her face to his to kiss her. Soon, their play became feverish. He lifted her out of the tub and laid her on the cool tiles, then urgently possessed her. Afterward, he leaned back and stared contentedly down into her face. He cupped her chin and kissed her mouth very slowly. He looked as if he were about to say something, but couldn't. He shrugged oddly, then eased back into the tub. "Coming?" he invited.

Jana shamelessly reclined on her side watching him. Her eyes held a look of tenderness and promise which distracted and thrilled him, one which sent quivers of alarm racing through his body. To end it at this untimely moment, he jested, "Get that took out of your eye. I have work waiting for me."

Jana laughed softly and sank down into the water as he stepped out of the tub. "I suppose I can be put off until tonight . . . if that's all the stamina you can muster in the morning. I had believed you had more in you."

Varian pretended to dress quickly in self-defense. While Jana soaked in the fragrant water, she mused on her lover. He was such a multifaceted, complex, wonderful creature. Sometimes he seemed so content and happy around her. Why couldn't he love her?

When Jana finished her bath, Varian wasn't in his quarters, nor was her breakfast. After a while, she went to see if Tristan knew of his location, or the schedule for Rigel. She had been told last night that the ship would be orbiting the capital by one o'clock today. So little time left to spend with Varian.

Jana approached the entry to the officers' rec room, then halted as she heard her name mentioned twice by two female flight officers who were discussing her.

"Why haven't you done anything, Nuala? She's keeping Varian from you."

"Varian gave strict orders that no one is to trouble his temporary mistress. He'd better be glad he's keeping the alien bitch confined to his quarters. Else I might go wild and slit her golden throat! She'll be gone soon, but I'll still be here. He's even smelling like her! Did you get a whiff of him in the mess hall? I would think Shara taught him to never trust alien beauties after what she did to Amaya and Galen. I bet he scrubs and scrubs every time he finishes with her. Oh well . . . poor thing, he really has her fooled. But that's the only way she will do anything and everything he wants." A burst of malicious laughter followed.

"All of the men say Jana is an alien enchantress. I wouldn't be surprised if that's why he's deluding her. I've heard that nothing tastes sweeter than vengeance. If he can't get to the alien bitch who fucked up his life six or seven years ago, what better sensation than using someone who favors her? They have the same color hair and nearly the same color eyes. Varian will never forget what Shara did to Amaya and Galen. Poor Galen, everyone knows Shara went to *Kadim* Tirol's home to slay

Amaya and Varian. That should have taught our lusty commander to be careful when choosing a mistress, especially taking one by force. I wonder what he has in store for Jana at her auction. She must be awfully good in bed.''

Jana couldn't listen anymore. She fled back toward Varian's quarters. What a fool she was! She rushed into Varian's quarters where she paced angrily. She had gotten herself into this tormenting mess. But what choice did she have except to endure it.

Lieutenant Nuala Matoo scoffed to her friend Ensign Tarina Sloyan, ''I can't believe Varian would drop into the same trap his father did—falling for an alien enchantress . . .''

Varian entered the rec room and looked at the two women sitting at the table. He watched Nuala rise and approach him. She sniffed several times, then covered her mouth to suppress her giggles. He stared at her as if she had lost her mind, then glanced inquisitively at the other woman.

''I don't want to sound brash, sir, but you smell like flowers,'' Nuala hinted.

Tarina lowered her head and tried to restrain her giggles as Nuala added, ''I think you should take another bath, alone.''

Just then Varian scowled. ''I'll make certain I leave out the fragrance next time. As for you, Lieutenant Matoo, and you, Ensign Sloyan, I believe you two should be on duty right now.''

Nuala instantly grew serious. ''I'm sorry, sir. I only intended to warn you of a matter which could cause you many annoying jests today.''

Tarina also apologized. But Varian would not be appeased.

''I want both of you to go to Alliance Headquarters and pick up your transfer papers. They will be ready. There's plenty of time for you two to clear out of your quarters before you leave today. That way, you won't have to return to my ship. Perhaps your new commander won't mind your nasty tongues as I do.'' When Nuala started to protest, Varian said, ''Count yourself lucky I don't demote you or have you dismissed from service. If you ever mention me or Jana Greyson in such a degrading manner again, I'll make certain you're out of the Alliance Force for good.''

Nuala went white, then flushed a deep red. ''You heard us?''

''Be gone as soon as we're in parking orbit,'' he told them.

250

He had told Kyle to run monitor checks on each location every hour or so. Varian had been hoping to pick up a clue about his ship's spy, not this irritating conversation.

Varian stormed into his office and dropped into his chair. If it wasn't one thing these days, it was another! He looked up to find Jana poised in the doorway to his bedroom, her expression one of anger and mistrust. He arched one brow quizzically. "You mad at me for some reason, moonbeam?"

Jana eyed him up and down, then inquired sarcastically, "You're back awfully soon. I thought you had lots of work to do."

"I do. First, I need another bath," he stated brusquely, his anger lingering.

Before he explained his problem, Jana remarked sarcastically, "Contrary to popular belief, I don't have any contagious alien germs, so you don't have to *scrub and scrub* several times a day."

Varian stared at her as the reason for her mood struck him. She, too, had overheard the malicious conversation. "Don't I get a chance to exonerate myself, or am I judged guilty of crimes I didn't commit?" And he quickly explained how he had dealt with the insubordinate officers.

Jana was eyeing him skeptically. He continued sullenly, "I need another bath because I'm being teased for smelling like a woman. Next time, add the perfume bubbles after I get out."

"Next time, don't interrupt a lady's bath, unless invited."

"Listen to me, Jana," he entreated earnestly. "I'm not anxious to get rid of you. From the beginning, I've tried to be honest with you, about your fate and about our relationship. As to the words of my crew members, I warned you of possible resentments by those who were left behind and didn't have the chance to get to know you. I was hoping there wouldn't be any scenes like you evidently witnessed, but that was why I asked you to remain in my quarters for the rest of our voyage. I swear, most of my crew adores you. Don't let this episode spoil our last few days."

"Who is Shara?" she asked.

Varian didn't try to conceal his anger. Visibly he was deliberating what to tell her, if anything. It couldn't be the truth about Shara and Ryker, or she might guess why he was *selling* her. "Confessions about my private feelings or my past were not part of our two-week deal, Jana. But I will tell this much; you are not a substitute for any woman for any reason."

"Is she beautiful?" she challenged.

Varian grimaced. His body tensed; his eyes narrowed and frosted; he gritted his teeth. "She was my enemy, but she has been dead for seven years. To answer your next two questions: no, I was never in love with her; and no, you aren't a substitute for appeasing old wounds which she inflicted. I'll also answer a question you might be afraid to ask: if she were standing here instead of you, I would choke her to death with my bare hands." When Jana went pale at his honest show of fierce hatred, he asserted, "Rest assured, Jana Greyson; I do not see Shara when I look at you. If I did, you wouldn't be in my quarters and surely not in my bed. From now on, this topic is as dead as she is; do you understand?"

Jana recalled when and where she had heard Shara's name, from the lips of Pyropean Supreme Ruler Jurad. She remembered Varian calling it "our private war"; but Jurad had said, "Once I was denied the woman of my heart and humiliated . . . as retribution for Saarian crimes against me. Nor would she serve as a replacement for my lost love . . . caught in this battle between us as *Shara* was." Then Varian had shouted, "One day you'll thank *Kahala* Shara never shared your bed and life."

Did Varian choose Jurad's intended wife as a mistress years ago. Or did she bewitch and seduce Varian? Did Shara then pick Varian Saar over Ruler Jurad Tabriz, creating a bitter "conflict" between the two powerful men? Did Varian make it worse by refusing her hand? How did she die? Who was Amaya? What did Shara do to her and this Galen? How could Varian hate so deeply and intensely? Worse, did she resemble Shara?

"Do you understand me, Jana?" he persisted at her silence.

"Would you answer one last question?" she entreated.

Varian frowned and replied, "Ask, and then I'll see."

"Is my wager the only reason I'm confined to your quarters for two weeks?"

Varian knew she wasn't referring to amorous feelings as the motive. "No, Jana, it isn't." He saw her pang of anguish. "You're here because I'm a selfish man who used it to appease my guilt over taking you into my bed. I warned you from the

252

beginning that you were dangerously tempting, Jana Greyson. If I wanted or needed a mate, I can think of no woman better suited to me than you,'' he vowed.

With only one and a half days left before her auction, this was the time to relate some tormenting things to Jana: some true, some false, and some a blend of both. "I've never been a man who was satisfied with being confined to just one woman. At this crucial point in my life, what woman could tempt me to give up my career to settle down to a boring life at home? I'll admit I'm selfish and spoiled; maybe I'm even cruel at times. But I'm not stupid. I would love to keep you with me longer, but I can't. Besides duty and regulations, it wouldn't be good for you or me. I hope I'm not being too blunt and insensitive, but I think you need to hear such things. Right?''

Jana's heart was crushed by his words, words which she believed. She couldn't force him to love her. And he was trying to let her down gently. She couldn't alter the situation, so why fight a long battle? She had fallen in love with him as he was; so why try to change him?

"I care about you, Jana. I want you happy and safe. That's why I ordered our little charade. Forgive me for hurting you and embarrassing you?''

At last, she spoke. "There's nothing to forgive, Varian. Knowing what I do, I would make the same choices. You're a very exceptional man. I'll miss you, and you'll hold a very special place in my heart. I wish we did have more time together, but we made a bargain, and you've kept your end of it. Whatever happens, I'll never forget you and these two weeks.''

When Varian started toward her, Jana's words stopped him. "Don't, Varian, not right now. I need a little time alone.'' She entered his bedroom and pressed the switch to close the door.

Varian wanted to go after her, but it was wrong to increase her anguish. He prayed he could settle this mission and his turbulent past before she learned to live without him, before she learned to hate him.

He sat down at his desk. She wasn't the only one hurting. He couldn't decide if he was tormented by the absence of one particular confession or not: she hadn't admitted love for him. She hadn't attempted to persuade him to keep her. She hadn't raged at him for hurting her, for shaming her, for using her. She hadn't cried or pleaded. She hadn't called him names.

When Varian couldn't concentrate on his papers, he went to check on Jana. He found her sitting cross-legged on his bed, calmly looking at a book! She was wearing a yellow caftan which was hiked above her knees and wadded between her thighs. She glanced up at him, then returned her impervious gaze to the book. "Have you eaten anything today?" he inquired solicitously.

"Now that you mention it, no; and I'm starved," she responded.

Varian stepped to the communication panel and ordered two lunches. Jana freshened up while she waited for the meal. After they ate, Varian asked if she would sit in his office and look at the book. He explained, "I have a lot on my mind. Your sunny smile lightens the gloom of my work. Please," he coaxed.

"All right," she replied. She sat sideways on the divan and curled her legs backward. She presented a most distracting picture as she snuggled against a plump pillow, engrossed in a pictorial history book. Time passed slowly.

Varian was affected by the intimate setting. He leaned back in his chair and watched her. She had so much to give a man, and he wanted it all. It was strange to feel so content just being in her presence. They had fun together. She was intellectually stimulating and their passions were equally matched. Stars above, he loved her and needed her!

Varian crossed the room and looked down at her. She met his gaze, but did nothing more to encourage him. He ran one finger over her slightly parted lips, across her chin, down her throat, and began to make tiny traces on her chest. His eyes observed his actions.

"Decorating me with flowers or staking a claim, Rogue Saar?"

He halted his stimulating action. He smiled and murmured against her lips, "I already have a claim on you for a while longer, moonbeam."

In a blaze of unrestrained passion, he captured and savored her mouth. They quickly undressed and he took her almost frantically. At the instant before their mutual release, he inquired raggedly, "Do you want me as much as I want you, Jana?"

A stinging barb refused to form in her mouth which would

shatter this rapturous moment. In a passion-muffled voice, she replied, "More so . . ."

Varian carried them over the crest of sheer bliss. He didn't realize Jana had comprehended the bittersweet messages which he had been absently drawing on her chest. Varian had been writing his name, time and time again! Jana had been studying his language for eight weeks, and had a good grasp of it. The invisible tracings intrigued and pained her deeply. Not his name, but the swirling letters which said, "I love you, moonbeam."

As Jana lay curled in his embrace, she wondered if she had misread the swirls or if he had been playing some mental game. It couldn't be true. If so, he would never sell her. The words tormented her.

Varian tightened his hold on her, then released it. She was as elusive, as magical, and as fleeting and evanescent as his pet name for her. He retrieved a box from his desk. "I'm going to miss you, Jana. I have a gift for you," he stated and opened the box and withdrew a floral necklace. He fastened the gold chain around her neck, then kissed her. "This is for you, moonbeam."

Jana lifted the exquisite cluster of tiny flowers and studied the intricate workmanship. The swaying stems formed the Maffeian letters "V" and "S." "When did you buy it? Where?"

"On Caguas. Some of those miners are superb artists. I designed it myself. Just to avoid any surprise jests, these are my initials," he told her, tracing them with his forefinger.

"Advertising your prior ownership?" Jana sweetly admonished him.

"I wouldn't want you to forget me. Besides my craftily concealed initials, it carries a hidden secret: souvenirs of our good times." He lifted the flowers one by one to reveal five miniature pictures of the two of them.

Each picture called to mind the moment it captured. She looked up into his eyes. "I shall treasure it always." She kissed him lightly.

"Is that a proper kiss of gratitude?" he teased.

"A proper one would one make us very late. I fear that your touch added to such kindness might inflame me beyond caution and I would demand to be satisfied."

He was overjoyed by her response and failed to notice that

unshed tears brightened her eyes. "Do I really have such an overwhelming effect on you?"

"That's a question best left to your imagination," she retorted. "I wish I had something special to give you," she stated.

"You did give me something special, two of the best weeks of my life. Now get dressed so I can show you around. No exhibitions, just funtime."

"You're not kidding?" she hinted. "Playtime, no work?"

In less than an hour, Jana found herself strolling down a lovely byway on Eire. They halted under a fragrant trellis to savor its beauty. "I wish I could show you other areas of the planets which we've visited so briefly. All you've seen are busy ports and cities. The things I could show you, moonbeam," he murmured wistfully. As they walked on, he told her many things about his world.

When they returned to the ship, they dined and danced in the Stardust Room for hours. She was perplexed by his mellow mood. After they arrived in his quarters, he made love to her twice: once in an urgent rush and once in a leisurely manner. Jana fell asleep wondering at this new side of him.

Varian awakened the next morning to the full awareness of the end of this monumental journey. He cautiously arose so as not to disturb Jana from her peaceful slumber. He watched her snuggle into the warmth left by his body. She smiled as she clutched his pillow and drifted deeper into sleep. He stood there for a few moments, moments which seemed to be rushing by too swiftly. Her auction was tomorrow; his departure for her world was the next morning. Why had he become so attached to her, knowing this time would arrive?

Varian dressed then headed for the bridge to check on matters there and to leave orders for the officers' furloughs. He filed his reports and gathered the tapes for his meeting with the Supreme Council, Alliance Assembly, and Supreme Commander Brec Sard. This was going to be one long and bitter conference.

Varian, Tristan, Martella, Nigel, and Kyle left the ship to head for Alliance Headquarters. The *Wanderlust*'s report and suggestions concerning the grim situation in the Milky Way Galaxy had been supplied on the tapes which he had passed out along his journey home, tapes which had been studied for the discussion which would be held today by the thirteen *avatars* and three supreme councilmen who comprised the sixteen-member Alliance Assembly. His mission had been praised as a success, if one could say the confirming of a calamity which was threatening to devastate Earth and the enslaving of five hundred women were triumphs.

The conference was lengthy and exhausting. Science Officer Nigel Sanger did most of the explaining of data and of possible actions or precautions. He went over the theory of diverting or destroying the meteor with the combined powers of many starships and chemical lasers. He related the perils involved in each of his suggestions. To Earth, the largest hazard was the meteor's impact on nuclear weapon installations. If the massive meteor struck the planet surface, Earth could be doomed. The Maffeians were not sure if they could deflect and shatter it. Their greatest concern was leaving the Maffei Galaxy open to enemy attack while their starships were away taking that gamble. The danger of obtaining the chemicals needed for that assignment was discussed, for most feared that Ryker Triloni would expose these facts to his grandfather *Kadim* Maal Triloni. Naturally, Varian and Tirol felt that way.

Although Ryker Triloni had been accepted as a Maffei citizen and had lived in their galaxy for seven years, most feared and mistrusted him. His parentage and tragic history were not secrets to these rulers, nor was the fierce conflict between the two sons of Galen Saar, a man whose loss had been felt deeply in both private and military circles. Yet these rulers wisely respected the awesome powers which Ryker Triloni and Trilabs possessed: in their hands the power to preserve their world or in the hands of their enemies the power to destroy it. To date, Ryker had been their ally. But most were intimidated by the dark rivalry with Varian, which might set Ryker off.

Tirol concluded aloud, ''We have a while longer to consider this grave matter. We can't do anything until all of our starships have returned from their current assignments. We can meet again then to decide if it's wise to send six ships to attack the meteor. Regardless of our final decision, many Earthlings may have been rescued. And if we vote against sending out six ships simultaneously, we can still rotate one or two to rescue more Earthlings until time runs out for them.'' *Kadim* Tirol went on to relate his previous actions on the matter at hand: the sending out of rescue ships. The Assembly of thirteen *avatars* agreed with the *Kadim*'s prior decision, as Brec Sard had agreed.

The week after the *Wanderlust* had left Earth, Tirol had ordered Brec to select five of his most trusted commanders and efficient starships. At the last moment, each commander had been ordered to furlough all nonessential crew members, then carry out the sealed orders. Each assignment involved a secret voyage to Earth to abduct six hundred men and women in their twenties and to deliver them to the outermost planetoid Anais in the Maffei Galaxy, which, mostly uninhabited, was comparable to Earth. Two ships at a time performed this assignment during a two-week interval, one going to and one coming from Earth; that way, only two starships would be out of the Maffei Galaxy at a time, hopefully without anyone's knowledge.

Tirol went on to say the first starship had completed her journey at starlight speed, before the *Wanderlust* held its auction on their third stop. The second starship should return to base in a couple of days. The third starship would return to base in a few weeks. The fourth starship would leave Earth with her precious cargo the day before Varian's arrival there. After Varian collected another six hundred aliens of both sexes, he was to deliver his human cargo to Anais, then return to base for the Alliance Assembly's final decision on how to deal with either the meteor or the crisis it presented. Using Earth's time, today was August 13; the rescue missions would be completed by August 30, and Varian should be orbiting Rigel again by mid-September. That would leave just enough time for dealing with the meteor or making one last rescue run.

Tirol went on to explain that the fifth starship was traveling between Rigel and Anais during this same time period. That starship was only responsible for delivering food, seeds, tools, supplies, medicines, equipment, temporary shelters, and clothing for the three thousand Earthlings who would be relocated. On the final trip to Anais, the starship would leave the Earthlings weapons for self-defense. The other commanders had been instructed to make certain they captured citizens in vital roles. Varian would make certain Jana's best friend, Andrea McKay, was one of those females rescued.

Tirol said he would be contemplating ways to acquire the chemical lasers and gases needed from Trilabs. If he could not create a perfect excuse to explain such an enormous purchase, he would forget that perilous course of action. He could not risk endangering and destroying their world by trying to save Earth. He didn't tell the Council or Assembly that Ryker was already questioning the amount of decontamination chemicals which the Alliance had been purchasing during the last few months. Without those decontamination chemicals, the Earthlings could infect the rescuing Maffeians with deadly germs.

The powerful head of the Council and Assembly announced his final decision on another matter. If the meteor crashed into Earth and set off nuclear explosions, all rescues must cease immediately and the Earthlings should be kept from suffering. Varian loathed the idea of being personally responsible for *Stardust* seedings of Earth's atmosphere but the "dusting" chemical would insure a peaceful demise for countless Earthlings who could not be rescued before the disaster and agony struck. He cringed. If Jana had any inkling of her world's peril, she would be crushed.

The Supreme Council's word was law, and Tirol issued it. Now to prevent the Pyropeans or Androsians from preying on the ill-fated or relocated Earthlings, he cautioned everyone involved in this affair to keep it secret. Yet, Tirol feared someone would drop a clue; too many were involved to prevent it, and certainly too many Alliance crewmen were on leaves for it not to arouse suspicions. All he could ask for was time, as much as possible for the mission to end.

Kadim Tirol dismissed everyone except Varian and the other two Council members. As preplanned, Tirol and Varian began to set their traps for exposing the incompetence of Segall and the traitorous actions of Canissia. To keep Canissia ignorant of their actions, Segall Garthon had been the last member to receive the taped report of Varian's mission; and Segall had not been informed of the starships which had been performing rescue missions on Earth for weeks. Tirol had alerted Draco, then swore his friend to secrecy. Too many Supreme Council secrets were being leaked; Tirol, Draco, Brec Sard, and Varian suspected it was occurring through Segall and Canissia Garthon. If that could be proven true, it was the perfect way to force Segall from the Council, even if they were certain his slips were unintentional.

Tirol commented gravely to ensnare Segall, "It's a good thing I didn't tell the Assembly I actually have eight starships pulling rescue duty rather than five. I'm sure those rulers would panic with so many ships assigned elsewhere."

Segall stared at the leader and protested, "You endanger us all to aid one alien planet? You must recall all but one or two instantly."

Tirol replied, "Soon, Segall. Have no fear. Even if one of the assemblymen drops a clue, our foes will think only one or two ships are gone. If our enemies learn nothing of the eight, we will remain safe." Now, all he had to do was listen for this lie to appear in the wrong quarters. He glanced at Varian and inquired, "How soon can you leave for Earth?"

Varian was prepared to give his answer. "I'm holding the final auction tomorrow afternoon. My ship is being resupplied and checked over thoroughly today and tomorrow. I've been giving the officers who just returned with me a few days' furlough. I'll leave orbit on the second dawn from today."

Segall inquired, "Is this last girl special to you, Commander Saar? Are you planning to bid on her?" His daughter suspected Varian loved Jana. Segall thought he knew why Canissia was urging her father to purchase Jana. No doubt his daughter wanted to make certain the alien beauty was out of Varian's reach. He couldn't blame Canissia; she wanted Varian, and Varian was the perfect husband for his only child. Besides, Jana was a tempting creature. Perhaps he should consider acquiring such a delightful mate.

Varian knew Segall was testing him on behalf of his daughter. He nonchalantly replied, "Jana is unique and satisfying, sir, but she would crimp my lifestyle. If I may be so forward, sir, I would caution you against buying her and putting Jana and Cass in the same home and social circle."

Tirol and Draco watched Segall. "I see your point," he asserted. "Cass and I hope you will become a frequent guest of ours again. She loves you."

Draco Procyon sighed loudly and dramatically. "Thank heavens, you don't plan to bid on her because I'm eager to have Jana. I've had my bankers and accountants going over my assets for days to come up with the highest bid I can place. That's the trouble with these private auctions, one sealed bid and that's it. Win or lose, no second chances. Who came up with this rule?"

Tirol laughed and said, "I did. It isn't good for friends or

260

rivals to engage in bidding wars. One secret offer makes it appear a stroke of luck or fate to be the winner. Besides, it earns us more money; men who truly want a certain treasure will bid outrageously to make sure they get it."

Draco teased, "Now I see why you're the *Kadim*."

"I shall be glad to see you obtain her, Draco. She'll be an asset to you."

Segall cleverly suggested, "Since you appear so fond of Jana and she of you, Commander Saar, the Council should vote to present her to you as a gift, a reward. After all, you two are . . . very close. On numerous occasions, you've displayed enormous courage and loyalty to the Alliance Force and Council. I'm sure Tirol and Draco would agree to this payment of Jana."

Varian shook his head. "That's very generous of you, Segall. Jana is a valuable jewel, but I couldn't accept her. I'm happy being a carefree bachelor. When I get ready to settle down, I'll choose a wife, not a captive mate. Besides, too many people are teasing me about her favoring Shara Triloni. Of course nothing matches except their coloring, but I don't like being the butt of gossip. Jana is a very special creature, but she's not for me. It would be selfish to keep her as a mistress and perhaps provoke one of my foes to slay her because he thinks she's won my heart. There are too many females available to fulfill desires to endanger an innocent's life for a little pleasure. Thank you, but I will proceed with her auction as scheduled."

The conversation ended, and Segall Garthon departed. The three remaining men gazed at each other. "Well, it's done," Varian stated. "Let's see how Cass takes all of this news and what she does with it. At least Jana will be safe."

"You two have everything set for the auction?" Tirol queried.

Draco inhaled deeply. "If all goes as planned, I'll obtain Jana and hold her for Varian. I hate keeping her in the dark, but it can't be helped."

Tirol grimaced and replied, "We'd best all pray your bid is the highest. . . ."

When Varian returned to his ship he learned that a letter had been delivered by mail shuttle during his absence. He went to his quarters and found Jana soaking in a hot tub of bubbles. "I see that you made certain I wouldn't be tempted to join you," he jested, dripping fragrant water over her nose. "If you can be dressed in one hour, I might be tempted to show you more sights this afternoon."

Jana's eyes beamed with pleasure. "You're being far too sweet and unselfish these last few days. I might get the wrong idea," she warned as he left the bathroom.

Varian sat down at his desk. He opened the letter and frowned as he read the unsigned taunt which began with a famous poem:

Don't show me *Kahala*, a forbidden domain;
Don't offer me moondust instead of great fame.
Don't yield to my kisses with poisonous lips;
Don't offer me love with false swaying hips.
Don't come to my bed, then leave before dawn;
Don't pry me with passion, then treat me so wrong.
Don't offer me a life with cruel, choking ties;
Don't fill my ears with softly spoken lies.

Varian clenched his jaw until it ached. Jana's name had been written over "*Kahala*" and "moondust." "To Varian" had been inserted before line three and "Jana" had been signed beneath the last one. "What the hell!"

"What, my love?" Jana asked as she entered the room.

Varian glanced up at her. He tossed the letter on his desk and stood up to flex taut muscles. "Talking to myself, moonbeam. Just a stupid joke. I'll be ready to leave as soon as I see Nigel and leave orders for my crew."

After his departure, Jana hurried to his desk and read the letter which had vexed him. She grimaced. Why couldn't people leave them alone?

"If this ruse works," Varian told Nigel, "we'll have Cass trapped and our leak plugged. You've got security men watching Daxley, Vaiden, and Baruch?"

"As soon as we reached base, I assigned the best surveillance agents available. They will be invisible to our suspects."

"And I told each a lie. Now, all we have to do is see which lie gets to Ryker and spurs him into action. I sent out orders

262

this morning to have Moloch watched so he won't interfere with my ploy."

In less than an hour, Jana felt like it was hunting season in the Texas high country with her as the fleeing puma and Varian as the cattle baron determined to have her golden hide! They had eaten a light lunch and danced twice in a secluded room in the Elysian Restaurant. "Are you trying to seduce me?" she teased as Varian drew her closer to his chest and nibbled on her ear. She trembled. Every time she eased away from him to retain control of her poise, he came after her! Was it "open season" on her? He was being awfully possessive and romantic. Why were they in a private dining room of the restaurant?

When he guided her to the table, he poured two glasses of champagne and toasted, "To our last day and night of ecstasy." Varian clicked his glass to hers, then downed the bubbly liquid. He set down his glass, then looked at her untouched one. He observed her troubled gaze.

Jana lifted the glass and responded, "May this day and night be the best we've shared." She drained the glass without her eyes leaving his.

As Jana turned to set her glass on the table, Varian smacked her on the rump and stated jovially, "Let's go, woman; we have things to do and see."

"Have you been drinking too much?" she inquired suspiciously.

"No! I think you might find our zoo and museum very interesting." Now that he had his grandfather's and Draco's help with keeping Jana safe, he could relax slightly.

At the zoo, Varian related the names, origins, and habits of the unusual creatures. He told her many fascinating tales about their captures, as if he had taken a personal hand in such activities.

Later at the museum, they toured its many rooms while Varian explained the artwork and displays. Jana was captivated by the talent exhibited before her. She was delighted when Varian purchased her a lovely souvenir, a tiny painting of a *Talias* flower in full bloom, just like the ones which they had seen near the waterfall and he had picked illegally.

Jana was bewildered when Varian escorted her into a towering structure, spoke with a man, then led her to an elevator which whisked them skyward at a breathtaking speed. They left it to walk a short distance. Varian slipped a card into a narrow slit and the door swished open wide, as did Jana's gaze. Varian chuckled. "I believe Earthlings call it a hotel, a love nest," he jested.

"Hotel?" she echoed, her eyes scanning the luxurious suite. Two walls appeared to be solid one-way glass. All furnishings and fabrics were soothing shades of blue, green, mauve, and cream. Every piece of furniture looked plush and comfortable. Shimmering blades of a soft metal partially concealed two areas of the large room: to her right, a sunken tub; to her left, a round bed. "Are we staying here tonight? We didn't bring any clothes."

"Only for a few hours, moonbeam," Varian calmly announced, then headed toward the tub, discarding clothes along the way.

"Varian! What are you doing?" she shrieked in utter bewilderment.

He stopped and turned. He took an arrogant stance: legs spread apart, hands on hips, chest expanded, a bold expression on his face. His eyes smoldered and his sensual lips curled up at one corner. His voice caressed her. "One final charade you said. I decided to play a lecherous demon come to Rigel to capture the most beautiful and coveted female in the Universe. After searching the restaurant, the zoo, and the museum, I found her and locked her inside a room, quivering at my mercy. I must try to beguile her into becoming my willing slave. Then I shall seduce her without restraint. First, I must conquer her body, heart, and soul. Her body," he stated in a husky whisper, "I can take by force or bewitchment, but her heart and soul must be granted willingly. If I succeed, I will return from where I came with her as a cherished *charl*. We shall rule the dark regions together, with her as my sunlight, never to be parted. Well?"

"Then take me, Sir Demon, for I willingly agree to your terms."

Their lips met and melded into a fiery kiss. Garments were seized and tossed aside as they sank to the thickly carpeted floor to make wonderful, wild love. The moment their passions melted into one with a rapturous release, his communicator signaled an emergency. It continued to buzz frantically until he left her side, grabbed his belt, and answered, "What is it!"

"Sorry, sir," came Nigel's voice. "They need you at headquarters, now."

"The stars be damned! Why? Who?" he demanded in frustration.

"Tirol."

"Tell the *Kadim* I'll be there shortly," Varian responded moodily.

He headed for the tub and rinsed off quickly. He yanked on his pants and boots. Varian headed for the door, as if she and their blissful moment were all but forgotten. "Sir Demon?" she called out to him.

Varian whirled and . . . actually flushed. "Your shirt," she hinted, swinging it from one finger. "A bare chest like that might drive females wild with lust and men crazy with envy, not to mention me wild with anger at your desertion. Shall I wait here, or return to the ship?"

Varian walked toward her. He took his shirt and slipped it over his head. Jana adjusted his collar and cuffs, then smoothed out any creases in the material. She fluffed his sable hair with her fingers. "Splendidly handsome and terribly devastating. However have you managed to remain single for so long? Surely there must be one female alive with the magic to get this heart."

Varian caught the hand on his chest and squeezed it gently. "What heart?"

"Of course, now I understand. You have no heart to claim."

"I'm sorry about this intrusion, Jana. I won't be longer than necessary. I don't like having lesson number ten interrupted," he hinted wickedly.

Canissia was standing behind her father massaging his stiff neck. She had laced his wine with a mild tongue and mind loosener. When he was totally relaxed, she questioned him about the Assembly and Council meetings. She hadn't wanted her father to purchase Jana Greyson; she had merely wanted him to reveal an interest in the alien female to extract Varian's reaction. She was relieved to hear that Varian was not going to bid on Jana and why. Still, she was certain that Varian had deep feelings for Jana. She had to make sure Jana was unavailable if or when Varian changed his mind and tried to recover her. What man would refuse to comply with Commander Varian Saar's wishes? She listened to the other facts which Segall revealed to her.

Canissia knew she could not expose the news of the eight rescue ships to Ryker or to anyone else. She didn't have to concern herself with protecting the Earthlings, as others had access to those facts and could let a clue slip. But since only five men—Tirol, Varian, Draco, Brec, and her father—knew about the eight rescue ships, it was too risky to sell or to trade that information. Nor could she expose what Varian had told her father about Jana or her father's offer of Jana to Varian, for that information could also be traced to that private talk. She did need one more meeting with Baruch Tirana, even if she had promised to leave him alone. Zan had been trailing Baruch today, so she knew the traitorous officer was on leave and was staying at a hotel whose rooms had hidden entrances and two-way mirrors. She could slip into the hotel and into Baruch's room without anyone seeing her. She could spike his wine for one final questioning and night of erotic pleasures. With luck, perhaps Baruch could supply some little fact to sell to Ryker.

Chapter Fifteen

Jana watched the sunlight vanish as she lingered in the silky bath water. She wondered what was keeping Varian. Surely lie didn't intend to leave her alone in the hotel on their last night together. When dried and dressed, she stood near the transparent wall, gazing out at the enormous city of towering ultramodern structures. The room was dark, for she didn't know where the light controls were or how to operate them. She couldn't call room service for instructions, if this alien hotel supplied it, for she didn't know how to use the communications system. How strange that she had gotten accustomed to being taken care of so quickly and completely!

Jana pondered this curious day and her current solitude.

Was Varian trying to tell her something with actions which he couldn't or wouldn't do with words? Had she been left alone as a test, to see if she would obey orders or to see if she would try to escape her impending doom? To where? How? Did he want to learn if she despised her imminent fate so deeply that she would act impulsively? Was this a test of her emotions, her courage, her wits, her desires? Did he want her to flee her auction to another man?

"Jana Greyson," she scolded aloud, "you have the wildest imagination! One more day and this torment will be over." Before dinner tomorrow, she would discover the identity of her owner.

The door opened and Varian entered, carrying two packages. He squinted to locate her in the dim light. "Why are you standing in the dark, moonbeam?"

Jana laughed softly. "Because I'm ignorant of your controls. I was beginning to think I would spend our last night alone."

"I had to meet with the *Kadim*. I brought you something to wear tonight. See how it fits," he said, pressing the switch which filled the room with a soft glow of light He wished this party for prospective buyers wasn't necessary, but he and his grandfather needed to know who had arrived for Jana's auction. He had intended to show pictures of her and videotapes and relate the facts about her, but Tirol suggested she make an appearance to test the reactions of her impending bidders. Varian had a new worry: Moloch was making an obvious display of his intention to bid for Jana, but Ryker had not arrived or any of his men.

Jana lifted the chic knee-length white dress.

Varian noticed her lack of enthusiasm. "You don't like it?" he queried.

"What are your plans for me and it tonight?" she asked instead of answering. She looked at him as he removed formal garments for himself from the other box.

"A party at *Avatar* Lopear's. I told him we couldn't stay long. It isn't too far from here, so I thought we would walk. We'll leave as soon as you're ready."

"I don't have any cosmetics or a brush," she said anxiously.

"In the box, love. Martella helped me, so I should have everything."

Jana dressed quickly, wanting to get this final "display" behind her. She followed Varian to the door, surprised to find one of his crew members waiting to take their belongings back to the shuttle. Jana blushed at having such intimacy exposed. If Varian or the ensign noticed, neither let on.

As they walked along, Varian whispered, "This couldn't be helped, Jana. Please relax. I'll get us out of there as quickly as I can."

As they strolled toward the home of Rigel's planetary ruler, *Avatar* Lopear, Varian's expression suddenly changed. Jana's puzzled gaze followed his line of vision to land on Moloch Shira. An overpowering aura of savagery and evil permeated the air around him. Moloch shifted his satanic gaze to her and his lips curled into an insulting sneer. The man passed his razor eyes over Jana's body, visually cutting away both her garments and courage.

Moloch blocked their path. "What do we have here? The dauntless Commander Saar enjoying his last night with his alien treat? If you find her so tasty and pleasing, why are you going through with her auction? If I'm lucky, I'll be able to answer that question for myself tomorrow night."

The message written in Moloch's eyes instilled alarm in Jana. Why did this man hate Varian so intensely? What would Moloch do to her if he won the auction? Even if he didn't become her owner, some stranger would, perhaps an enemy of Varian's with an ax to grind. What would such a ruthless man do to spite Varian? Especially if he or another foe thought Varian loved her.

"If you're that lucky, you'll regret being so mean to her every time you meet her," Varian taunted to hide his consternation. "You should know by now that first impressions are hard to forget, and yours couldn't have been worse."

Moloch stiffened. But he could relax now, for his work for Ryker was over. As soon as Jana's auction ended, Ryker was to deliver Canissia to him. Still, he would try to buy Jana at auction. After using her and harassing Varian, he could easily find a buyer for her. If rumor was accurate, Prince Taemin had an itch for Jana. If so, he could easily recover two or three times his expenses for buying Jana. Plus, Ryker, too, might change his mind about needing Jana.

As if by magic, Nigel appeared. Varian glanced at his friend and ordered, "Take Jana back to the ship, Nigel. I'm late for a party and Cass is waiting for me. If Moloch wants another look at my gem, he can get it tomorrow."

Nigel took Jana's hand and led her away. She was too upset to argue or resist. Nigel explained how Varian had issued an emergency summons to get her out of a nasty situation. "I'm sorry you had to witness such a crude display, Jana. Varian didn't want you to be subjected to the likes of Moloch and his friends tonight anyway. He'll probably claim you're ill or too upset to be present. You're lucky he's sending you back to the ship tonight. Otherwise one of your biggest rivals would be at your throat all evening."

"Canissia Garthon?"

Nigel nodded and said, "Thank heavens Varian is immune to her." They chatted aimlessly until they reached the ship where they parted at the entrance to Varian's quarters.

Jana was lying in his bed when Varian returned. He walked to the bed, stripped off his clothes, lay down half atop her, and began showering her with kisses and caresses: all without a word! He called on all of his reserve energy, imagination, superior knowledge, proficiency, and experience while making love to her. He wanted her in many ways; she willingly agreed. He made love to her for hours, trying to sate his enormous appetite for her.

Jana followed each of his instructions, then called on her own instincts to please him. She did more than her part to make sure this was their best night of shared bliss. She had never been bolder or greedier. She amazed and thrilled Varian with her full cooperation and fiery responses.

Varian had not possessed a woman with such a total giving and taking of passion. He had never craved a woman as he did Jana. He had never shared himself as he did with Jana. He attained heights of pleasure and sensation which he hadn't realized existed. This rapturous contentment and total relaxation afterward were new to him. He knew why, the missing element had been love.

Later, when Varian had not mentioned the party, or buyers, Jana propped her chin on her clasped hands on his chest, and asked, "How does a private auction work?"

Varian was unprepared for her question. Not now, his glance seemed to say.

"Yes, Varian, I must know what to expect tomorrow. Who's coming?"

His spirits took a violent, spiraling plunge downward. "It's carried out by sealed bid. Each man will be given only one opportunity to select his offer, record it, seal the envelope, then hope for the best." He listed the men who had insured their attendance with the posting of an opening amount of 500,000 *katoogas*, a sum equal to half a million dollars on Earth. "When the bids are unsealed and read aloud, the largest one will automatically—" He halted as Jana flipped onto her back and closed her eyes tightly as if grimacing in agony. A tear rolled into her tousled hair.

"Jana, I wish it didn't—"

"Don't say anything more. Please," she hurriedly interrupted him. "I think I understand how it works. Good night, Varian." She turned away from him.

"I promise you'll get a good man, moonbeam. I swear it."

Jana stayed on her left side away from him. "How can you make such a promise? If you can't control the results or select the buyer, then you can't be certain Moloch Shira won't get me! Or someone as wicked!"

"Money, Jana love," he hinted. "There are several bidders far wealthier than Moloch or others like him. Good men, Jana. Have no doubts or fears."

"You're gambling with me, Varian! Who can predict the outcome of such an event? Or predict what value any of those men will place on me? Or place on vengeance toward you! Moloch is resolved to get at you through me; there must be others like him too. Why did you do this to me?"

"Trust me, Jana. He won't get you. I would kill him first."

"You liar! You won't slay him or any man over me! I'm in this mess because I . . . trusted you! I believed you would protect me! But you can't! Martella said you were leaving right after the auction. I swear to you, Varian Saar, if I go to Moloch or a man like him, I'll never forgive you for such treachery and lies! I'll hate you forever! I swear to you, I'll die before I let a man like that touch me!" she vowed, eyes blazing.

"Listen to me carefully, Jana. If the man who obtains you isn't a just and kind person, I swear I won't leave you with him. On my life and honor, I won't turn you over to Moloch or any other low-life bastard. I swear it."

Jana fused her gaze with his. Something deep within her demanded that she believe him. Her hand reached up to caress his cheek. Tears burned her eyes. How fiercely this separation pained her. She wanted to beg him to keep her. She couldn't and she mustn't. Such words and actions had to come from Varian. She licked her dry lips and murmured, "God, how I'm going to miss you. Why did I ever allow myself to succumb to your charms?"

"Would you do me one favor, moonbeam? Try not to hate me. Try to see my side in all of this mess. Try to ignore all the lies about me, about why I took advantage of you. Try to find peace in your new life."

Jana wondered if Varian was as entrapped by this detestable situation as she was, if he was hurting as badly as she was. If only he would explain himself, his emotions, his troubled past. Jana smiled faintly. Again, Varian gave her the impression that he wanted to speak plaguing thoughts. He looked so miserable. "Sleep, my love, we have a busy day ahead," she told him sensitively. She snuggled into his arms and closed her eyes.

It was almost noon when Varian awoke with a start. He sat up and rubbed his sandy eyes and stubbled face. He eased off the bed to flex his stiff body. He dared not glance at Jana. He slipped quietly into his bathroom to shave, shower, and dress. Soon, he must rouse her and set into motion a terrible day which they would both curse and remember. . . .

Varian gently shook her shoulder and called her name. "Jana, it's time to get up. You need to eat and dress. We have to leave by two-thirty."

"Is it very late?" she asked as she sat up and rubbed her sleepy eyes.

"It's one. You seemed exhausted, so I let you sleep as long as I could."

Jana placed her feet on the floor. Ignoring her naked figure, she yawned and stretched. "You're right. Do I have time for a leisurely soak?"

"How about I wait thirty minutes before sending for our lunch?"

"Sounds terrific. See you later," she muttered groggily.

When he told her time was up, she completed her bath and

271

rejoined him. Dampened wisps of tawny hair clung to the edges of her lovely face and the nape of her neck where the long curls were pinned up. Sweet fragrance invaded his senses. She hadn't bothered to don a robe; the ice-blue silk gown molded enticingly to her moist figure where she had dried hurriedly. Her golden flesh glowed with velvety softness. He wondered how she could have been so unaware of her matchless beauty. She did indeed appear the helpless angel this morning, a weary one, a subdued one. They hardly spoke during the meal. He watched her leave to dress for her auction.

Jana's gaze touched on today's outfit on his bed, as each display garment had been chosen for her. She lifted the gossamer sheath and fingered its fine texture. It was as soft as a cotton ball and as light as a butterfly's wings. Mellow hues of rose, green, and blue splashed softly across the diaphanous voile, shimmering on the translucent material like costly oils mingling on an artist's palette. She lifted the matching rose bandeau to be worn underneath, her only other garment. It was an outfit definitely selected to hint at every feminine attribute while cunningly exposing none clearly or wantonly. Rose silk slippers lay beside a small cluster of matching leaves for her hair.

Jana snatched up the colorful garb and was about to shred it with her bare hands. She forcibly quelled that impulse. Why not give in one last time and get this ordeal finished! Jana pulled on both garments and the slippers. She went into the bathroom to arrange her hair and attach the leafy adornment. Terror washed over her. How could she submit to such indignities? She was about to be exhibited and sold as a legal slave, to be taken away by a stranger, away from the only security and home and friends she had! She would be torn from the arms of the only man she had ever loved. She would be forced to mate with her owner. How could she endure such horrors? How could Varian allow them?

Varian entered the bedroom. "I was about to see what was keeping you so long, moonbeam. We have to go. It's late."

Jana winced. "It's only two-thirty. Isn't the auction at three?"

"The bids will be taken then, but you should be . . . there earlier."

"For one final exhibition? Let's not keep your clients waiting, Commander,'' she said, struggling to hold back her tears and protests.

Varian frowned. ''I have a farewell gift for you, Jana. Hopefully it will remind you of the good times we've shared and of our close friendship.'' He pulled a gold filigree band from his pocket and slipped it on her left ring finger. Without realizing the significance of this ring style and finger placement to Jana's people, he was hurt deeply by her reaction to his gift.

Jana stared at the delicately braided circle which was imbedded with chrysoberyl gems, the exact shade of her multicolored eyes! In spite of its beauty and extravagance, she was greatly disturbed by its similarity to a wedding band. Was his action innocent or mockingly cruel? No matter, the ring could not remain on her finger or leave with her! Jana had the petrifying feeling that Varian was going through with this auction and ''farewell.''

''It's very . . . beautiful and . . . exquisite. But I can't accept it. It's far too expensive and . . . personal. I need no final reminders of our days together.'' She removed the ring and pressed it into his hand. ''I can't take it, not today.''

''Then I'll hold it until you feel you can accept it and wear it,'' he replied.

Jana forced her gaze to meet his. ''After the auction, that day will never come. You'll understand my reluctance when you understand our significance behind such a gift. I think it's best if we say our farewells here in private. When we leave this ship, I expect your protective charade to be in full force, for one final episode. Now I understand the value of your farces.''

When Jana turned to leave, Varian seized her with possessive fierceness and held her tightly. She was alarmed by his inexplicable behavior, his restrained fury. If he wanted her, why was he getting rid of her! ''You're hurting me, Varian! I can't breathe!'' Varian loosened his grip, but did not release her. ''You said we were late,'' she reminded him, hoping to spur him into frantic motion. In a way, she did.

Varian captured her face between his hands and murmured urgently, ''I want you, Jana Greyson.'' He would be gone soon. There was a chance he might never return from this perilous mission to Earth. The imminence of their brutal separation chewed viciously at him.

Her eyes blinked in confusion. He had not said need in a sexual sense, but "want" in an emotional one. "Is it too late, Jana?" he countered before he claimed her mouth in a crushing kiss which was filled with all of the hunger he was experiencing and wanted her to share.

Jana's senses began to spin wildly. She found herself beneath Varian on the bed, hungrily responding to his fiery onslaught of brief madness. Could she make him forget the time and miss the auction? Could she love him so urgently he would change his mind? Jana totally and ardently surrendered her lips, body, and will to him. The decision of control would be left in his hands! As far as she cared, only Varian Saar and their mutual passion existed.

Varian moaned in rising need as he sensed her total submission. With suddenly awkward fingers, he worked on the closing on her sheath. He had to get her garments off and feel her heart beating next to his. He needed their bodies to join in blissful rapture. He needed comfort in this time of anguish.

The communicator buzzer sounded. It persisted until he pulled away to answer it, swearing angrily as he did so. "Dammit! What is it now?" he ranted as he struggled to gain control of his wayward emotions.

"Sorry to disturb you, sir, but the shuttle is waiting. It's past time to leave," came Nigel's apologetic reminder.

Varian inhaled deeply as he made the only decision he could. To take her this close to her auction was selfishly insensitive! "We'll join you shortly, Nigel. Prepare to leave."

Jana brazenly and desperately caressed his cheek. "So much for my last lesson. I would swear the mood, time, and place could never be better. I need you, Varian Saar, and I want you," she shamelessly confessed.

Varian gazed down at her. Did he dare turn away from his duty to the Alliance Force, to his grandfather, to Jana's world, to himself? Did he dare ignore or risk all for her, including both of their lives? In six months, he could . . .

Jana perceived his hesitation and pressed him. "You could postpone the auction for an hour or so. You could claim I was ill."

"What about all those buyers who are eagerly awaiting your fate?"

"Let them wait. This is a farewell gift I won't refuse." She enticed him in another way. One last chance to influence him, to halt this madness. . . .

"Don't tempt me, woman. I might forget myself."

Varian shoved himself from the bed. "Are you positive you don't want the ring, Jana?"

"Wanting it isn't the problem, Varian. I can't accept it."

"As you wish," he murmured.

Jana's control snapped. "As you wish, as you wish, as you wish! Damn you, Varian Saar! If I had my wish, I would—"

When she halted her outburst, he rashly demanded, "You would what?"

Jana glared at him. Varian dared not dwell on the matter. He escorted her to the shuttle. When they arrived at the assigned location, Jana's gaze widened in irritation. The room was huge, as was the stage. On the platform sat an imposing podium and three stools. There were fifteen small tables and chairs positioned several feet apart. On each table, there was a pen, one piece of paper, and one envelope. The room was well illuminated with multiple recessed lights, five of which were directed at the podium on the stage.

She mentally sneered, *All the better to see you with, my dear*. . . .

Varian seated Jana on one of the platform stools. He joined Nigel at the podium and the two talked in whispers. His tension was mounting. None of his foes had been entrapped or foiled, nor had Canissia or Baruch, who, he was convinced, was the traitor on his ship! He wondered if he was making terrible mistakes in judgment. What if one of his enemies or rivals bid higher than Draco? What if this whole secret matter went awry?

The buyers began to enter the room, one or two at a time. Soft chatter and laughter reached Jana's ears. She remained poised like a statuette. Pride and contempt shone fiercely on her face for this affair, although her expression was guarded. Many of the bidders had familiar faces from her travels, some smiled and nodded politely at her.

Jana barely contained her apprehension when her gaze touched on the smirking face of Moloch Shira. Was it too late for rescue?

Varian stepped before Jana's line of vision. Her gaze sought solace from his. If only he could hold her for a moment, an instant. "You're actually going through with this sale, aren't you?" she had to ask.

Varian realized that Jana had expected him to prevent it. No wonder she had been so unconcerned; she hadn't believed the auction would take place! "I can't stop it or participate, Jana. I'm sorry if you believed otherwise."

"Look me in the eye and swear this is what you want."

For her protection from his enemies during his lengthy absence, Varian did as she asked, the hardest thing he had ever done in his life. If he lived forever, he wouldn't forget the look on her face as he stated, "I swear it, Jana Greyson."

Jana ordered herself not to behave like a deranged fool in front of the others and Varian. She merely stared at him as she allowed his words to sink in.

Nigel made the announcement: "Everyone is present now. Shall we begin?"

The ten Maffeian bidders were introduced: two *avatars*, three *zartiffs*, four private citizens, and Councilman Draco Procyon. Attending, but not bidding, were Councilman Segall Garthon, Supreme Commander Brec Sard, Rigel's *Avatar* Lopear, and Alliance Supreme Council leader *Kadim* Tirol Trygue.

Varian joined Nigel at the podium. He told the attentive audience all about Jana, then had Nigel bring her to the front of the stage. He ended his speech with: "The opening bid is five hundred thousand *katoogas*. You have ten minutes to view her, select your offer, record it, and hold it until Lieutenant Commander Sanger collects them. You may begin your deliberations now." He set the clock on the podium to ring in ten minutes.

Jana glanced at the ticking clock, at the men before her, then at Varian Saar's profile. She knew this was no joke, no trick, no illusion.

Just as the clock on the podium was ticking away on his and Jana's entwined destiny, the intergalactic clock was ticking for a monstrous catastrophe. And just as both clocks had alarms set for him, Varian knew he must deal personally with both episodes. It was strange how the imminent doom of Jana's world had brought them together and was now tearing them apart. It was strange how this alien creature had inspired a secret scheme to end two intergalactic rivalries; now both foes—the Trilonis and the Tabrizes—were seeking to use this same radiant weapon against him. How strange it was that life seemed to travel in repetitive circles.

Jana jumped when the buzzer sounded her fate. Varian ordered Nigel to collect the envelopes. Nigel glanced at Jana and sent her an encouraging smile. Jana refused to look at Varian. She bravely kept her gaze locked on Nigel and his progress. When he accepted the last envelope from Draco, she inhaled deeply to slow her racing heart. Soon, it would be over.

Varian broke the seal on the first envelope and the reading began, but Jana only heard the amounts and one name: "2,850,000; 3,275,000; 2,700,000; 3,400,000; 2,925,000; Moloch, 4,000,500 . . ." Varian glanced at the belligerent smirk on the man's face. He wanted to seize him by the throat and strangle him.

Jana's gaze flew to Moloch's sneer, and she feared she would faint or retch.

Varian unsealed the next envelope to read on. She heard only the amounts: "3,950,000; 4,000,000; 3,975,000 . . . Varian broke the seal on the last bid and stared at it. He glanced at Draco and arched a brow inquisitively. "Councilman Procyon, 8,888,888," he said.

Jana's gaze shifted instantly to Draco's smiling face. If her life had depended on it, she couldn't have prevented the beaming smile from exposing her relief.

A flurry of reactions engulfed the room: sighs of regret, offers of congratulations, merry jokes, and whispers of surprise. Moloch glared malevolently at Varian before he stormed out. Two other bidders continued to appraise Jana and to discuss her enormous beauty and value; it was easy for them to see why Varian had wanted Jana, but not why he hadn't bid on her. They, like others, assumed the Alliance officer was sated with her. Already Draco was receiving offers to purchase her, extravagant offers! He grinned and shook his head, pleased with his success.

There wasn't a man in the room who didn't question the emotions of Draco Procyon, the wicked behavior of Varian Saar, and the absence of Ryker Triloni. Slowly the room emptied of all bidders except the winner. Jana ignored Varian as she approached Draco. She impulsively hugged him and said, "Thank you, Draco."

"I am a damn lucky man," Draco admitted, pleased at Jana's reaction. "I was afraid my bid would be insultingly low. I just carried off three expensive business deals, and my cash flow wasn't at its best."

"Low? No one else came near you. You won't regret this; I promise."

Draco smiled genially and said, "Every man in this room knew you were worth much more. You see, Jana, we men have this terrible habit of trying to sneak things over on each other. Each man let it be *leaked* that he was offering one or two million, then each raised his bid. I fooled them all."

She pressed with false eagerness, "Can we leave for my new home on Karnak? I can't wait to see it; I've been told it's very beautiful and serene." Jana flashed him a smile of gratitude. She wanted to get out of this place as quickly as possible. She didn't want to see Varian or speak with him again.

"I'm afraid you can't come home till morning. I'll prepare things for your arrival. Varian will deliver you and your papers when he collects my payment."

"You can't be serious?" Jana protested frantically. "I belong to you now. Surely he can trust you to pay him tomorrow? I thought you two were friends?"

"Friendship and trust have nothing to do with a business transaction, Jana. I'm afraid I can't take control of you until payment is made. It's too dangerous to carry that much money. The law states: possession after the payment is made, and ownership papers are signed and sealed by the officer in charge. Don't worry, everything will be fine. You'll be home before lunch tomorrow."

Jana's face grew red and she trembled. What was Varian pulling? Why hadn't he revealed this stipulation to her this morning? "Surely you don't mean I have to return to his ship until morning? I can't spend the night there again." The look on her face and tone of her voice expressed her anger.

Draco was vexed by Varian's cruel demand on this gentle creature. No matter how much his friend wanted these last few hours with his secret love, it wasn't right to force a shameful situation on her. Jana did not know this auction had been fixed. She did not know that Varian had supplied the money for Draco's bid. Jana did not know she would live as his guest until Varian, her real owner, could settle his life and retrieve her. Jana Greyson thought she belonged to him, and he wished she did. . . . "I'm sorry, Jana, it has to be this way. It won't come between us," he added kindly, wondering if that was her main concern.

Jana searched his understanding gaze. How lucky she was that this man was so kind. "I can't," she murmured. "Please, isn't there something you can do to convince him to release me?"

"I'm certain he planned your auction too late for a winner to take possession of you today, just in case things didn't go to his liking," Draco hinted. "The banks are closed, so no winner could claim you until morning. That would give Varian the time to alter a bad situation," he explained.

"But you aren't a 'bad situation,' " she refuted. "You're his friend, a member of the Supreme Council. Why can't he let go peacefully?" Jana ignored Draco's speculation about Varian's concern for her safety.

Draco attempted a different tack to calm her. "Don't antagonize him, Jana. You're too close to freedom from him and a chance for happiness. Don't risk spoiling the birth of a new life. Varian can be a stubborn, volatile man."

Varian and Nigel joined them. Jana shifted closer to Draco and glared at her captor. All three men were aware of Jana's fury.

Varian remarked, "I hope you two are pleased with the auction results. You really pulled a clever and costly maneuver, old friend." He openly congratulated the man who would take her from his side and bed!

"I couldn't be more pleased, Varian," Draco commented casually.

Jana forced a smile of agreement. "I should be heading for Karnak with my owner, not back to your ship, Commander Saar. Surely you can trust your good friend not to welsh on his word? Such a requirement is degrading."

Varian comprehended Jana's point. He scanned her fiery eyes and read her emotional distress. "Sorry, moonbeam, but regulations must be followed. I can't show favoritism with my friends. Draco understands and complies."

"In his place, I wouldn't," she boldly declared. She flashed Varian a glare which said she despised him.

It was very late when Varian returned from his final meeting with Tirol, Brec, and Draco. In a few hours, he would he heading back to the Milky Way Galaxy to check on the progress of the meteor and to rescue more Earthlings. Varian was anxious to see Jana, to find some way of convincing her this sale was for the best. Yet, he still couldn't afford to drop even a tiny clue to the truth. . . .

Varian was surprised to find Jana missing from his quarters, as it was extremely late. Surely she wasn't hiding from him, mocking him? Comprehension struck him like a hard blow. He hastily made his way to the quarters where she had been originally assigned. He suppressed his humor and respect for her cunning, for this matter was grave and painful to her. He approached the quiescent figure lying in bed in the semidark room. He gazed down at her and mentally apologized. *Sorry, love, but your anger and fatigue cannot deter me tonight.*

Varian sat down on the edge of the bed and spoke her name tenderly. She was dressed scantily in a chocolate-brown nightgown of the softest satin with ivory lace trim. An intoxicating floral fragrance invaded his nostrils and stirred his imagination. Her silvery blond tresses were spread around her head. He caressed her cheek. She did not move or speak, as if asleep.

Seeing how deeply and peacefully she was slumbering, Varian was almost reluctant to disturb her. A lengthy distance and time, possibly death, would separate them at noon. "Sorry, moonbeam, but you will have ample time to catch up on your sleep and rest at Karnak after I'm gone. Tonight, I need you far too much to be chivalrous or kindhearted." He shook her gently at first and called her name, then shook her firmly. Still, no response.

Varian eyed her warily. Her respiration was slow and even. Her body was limp. Her skin temperature and color were normal. He tried harder to arouse her. When he could not succeed, alarm flooded him. She was sleeping too deeply! Surely Jana wouldn't try anything foolish. He went to the picture over the sofa and pressed the release switch. He contacted Tristan in his quarters. "Tris!" he shouted. "Tris, I need you!"

A groggy Tristan answered, "What is it, Varian?" When Varian described Jana's condition and the reason for his concern, the baffled doctor replied, "No problem. I gave Jana the sedative at ten. She'll sleep until—"

Varian sliced off the remainder of his sentence. "You did what!"

Tristan was fully alert by then. "She was nearly hysterical. You can't blame her, not after what she went through today."

"How long does this sedative last?" Varian inquired.

"Until eight or nine tomorrow. Why don't you wait until she explains?" Guilt chewed at Tristan. He couldn't bring himself to tell Varian there was a drug which could counteract the sedative. Varian would surely order its use.

"I have no choice then but to let her sleep it off. 'Nite, Tris." Varian returned to Jana's bedside and gazed down at her for a long time. He had an irrational desire to punish her for this vengeful deed. He clenched his fists and teeth over and over.

"Damn you, Jana Greyson! Don't you know I would never sell you? Don't you see this is only a trick to protect you until I return?"

He paced the room as he stormed at her and himself. She had cleverly and tormentingly outwitted him, and herself. The only reason he had been able to restrain himself this morning was in knowing he would have her tonight, all night and all morning! His mind was a maelstrom of desire and spite. Within his heart and mind, fury battled with understanding, and love battled with retribution.

Varian sat down beside her once more. He stroked her tawny hair and golden flesh. "Have I hurt you so deeply I can never reach you again? What if I don't survive this mission?" A great sense of remorse crushed his heart. He returned to his quarters and hurriedly downed many strong drinks. At last, he fell into exhausted slumber, to have his dreams mock his loss.

Despite his restless night, Varian arose early the next morning. As if a dark force had been set loose against him, the momentous day started off badly and got worse. He left for Rigel to handle a last-minute flight problem. His foul temper was evident to anyone who came into contact with him. When questioned, he shrugged and blamed a hefty bout of partying. Clearly his troubled mind was not on his task of resupplying his ship or on his coming voyage.

Tristan had miscalculated the effect of the sedative on Jana's alien system. Jana awoke early and spent hours restlessly pacing her room, awaiting Varian's appearance. How had her deceit struck him? What would he say to her? The hours had crawled by since her eyes opened on this sad day. When Varian didn't appear she began to think that perhaps her ex-lover hadn't intended to spend the night with her after all. Perhaps Draco had spoken truthfully about the reason for keeping her after the auction. Perhaps Varian hadn't returned to his ship last night to discover her missing from his quarters, or perhaps he was on board, but didn't want to see her alone again. Uncertainty created panic within Jana.

Perhaps Varian did have scruples and couldn't touch her now that she belonged to his friend Draco. She had denied and punished herself, not Varian. Even if she hadn't been drugged beyond arousal, he was too proud to force himself on her. To send for her today would only show feelings he might not want exposed, such as his enormous desire for her. Soon, she would be delivered to Draco. It was too late to reclaim what she had so spitefully forfeited forever. She wept bitterly at her careless mistake.

The door to her suite swished open. Jana shrieked, for she was wrapped only in a bath towel. Kyle sent her an embarrassed look, then said, "Commander Saar said for you to report to his quarters immediately, Jana." He smiled and lowered his gaze.

"Right now? But I'm not dressed . . ." she said, her face flushed with embarrassment. Evidently it was time for her departure.

Kyle was bewildered by Jana's return to her old quarters and Varian's dark mood all morning. "He said to come instantly, without delay."

"I see," she murmured, grabbing up a robe. "Don't worry, Kyle, orders are orders."

Kyle escorted her the few feet. He pressed the call button and Varian's door opened. "Here she is, sir. Shall I wait outside to escort her back?"

"That won't be necessary, Lieutenant Dykstra. You may return to duty."

Kyle nodded and left, sending Jana a brief smile. Varian

continued reading and making notes. He did not look up or acknowledge Jana's presence. She waited patiently as the minutes crept past. Finally she asked, "Do you want to see me or not, Commander Saar?"

Varian's sable head lifted, as did one brow. "Commander Saar, is it?" he mocked her. "Aren't we behaving too formally with such an intimate friend? We have no audience to impress or delude, love. Permission granted to call me Varian, and to relax." He returned to his work.

Piqued by his behavior, she pressed, "You did send for me, sir. Time is very short. I should be getting dressed to leave."

"In a moment," came his nonchalant reply, spoken without a glance up at her.

Jana aimlessly walked around the confines of his office, a room which reeked loudly of his masculine presence. More time passed and her apprehensions mounted. "Commander Saar, couldn't you spare a few minutes to complete our business so I can leave? I'm to be on Karnak before noon."

At last Varian looked up and scanned her lovely features. "Our *business* will require more than a *few minutes,* moonbeam. Have a glass of wine and relax. I'm almost finished here. Once we begin, I don't want to be disturbed or distracted."

Jana stalked to the bar and did as he suggested to calm her frayed nerves. She refused to offer him one. She sat on the divan slowly sipping the sherry. It was a constant battle to keep her eyes off Varian. She finished the drink and poured herself another one. To avoid facing him, she turned sideways on the divan and struggled to force her thoughts away from the magnetic creature near her. She rested her arm along the back of the sofa and placed her chin on it. She sent her mind on a dreamy journey to a beautiful waterfall.

The silence was broken only by the rustling of papers and the faint scratches of his writing instrument. Jana sighed heavily and lifted her head, glancing his way. She found him watching her, curiously and intently. Their gazes locked. "Why did you send for me? Why are you keeping me waiting like this?"

His gaze warned her of mischief. "Unfinished business, moonbeam."

"We have none. The deal has been settled, and I belong to Draco now."

He chuckled playfully, huskily. "The deal I was referring to was your wager. As I recall, it was to include two weeks in my quarters and bed. You still owe me one night, but I'll be forced to settle for a few hours.''

Jana's eyes grew wide with disbelief. Had she heard him correctly? He would make love to her all the way to Karnak! ''Surely you don't expect . . . intend for us to . . . sleep together again! You can't, Varian!''

Varian stated calmly, ''Sleep is the last thing on my mind.''

''You lecherous beast! I belong to another man! You sold me! At this very minute, you're delivering me to him! You actually think I'll— No!''

''You don't belong to him yet, Jana, not until payment is made and papers are signed. Besides, the auction doesn't change the deal we made. I warned you it was two weeks or nothing, and you agreed.''

''I am his property! How can you do this to your friend? To me? Isn't revenge and brutal force beneath the all-powerful Commander Varian Saar?'' Jana scowled at the still grinning rogue. ''I accept the responsibility for my wager. I merely assumed that you would consider it terminated by my auction to another man, as I assumed it was. I had no idea I would be returning to your ship after being sold to someone else! Do you realize what your friend Draco must be thinking? What if he asks me if we—if you—Oh, hellfire! This isn't right, Varian! Don't you have any morals or conscience?''

Instantly he replied, ''Sorry, moonbeam, but I don't have time for either. I want you.'' Sapphire eyes probed bluish-green ones. He looked determined.

''Then you shouldn't have sold me!'' she shouted at him.

''I had no choice!'' he yelled back at her. ''I told you I couldn't keep you. I warned you from the beginning this affair could go no place. And don't ask me to explain because I can't. Please don't fight me on this,'' he urged.

Jana inhaled, then sighed loudly. ''All right, Varian.'' Maybe he didn't have a choice! ''Come and take me for the last time ever. Show us an hour we shall both long remember.''

The fiery sparkle in her eyes encouraged him to respond feverishly. Fires ignited and burned within him. He was before her in a split second, pulling her into his arms and covering her mouth with his. Gone were his anger and tension. His only thought was of possessing Jana to the fullest. His lips were insistent, as were his hands.

Jana acknowledged his frantic urgency. She clung to him and forgot her own bitterness. She was in his warm arms and all else ceased to be important. For now, Varian Saar belonged only to her. For now, she was the only woman he craved. She grasped his head between her hands and gazed deeply into his sapphire eyes, eyes so full of hunger and . . . Sadness? Jana pulled his head downward until their lips met. Her arms went around his neck tightly and she clung to him as if she would never release her grip. She was mystified by his mood. If she didn't know better . . .

Varian's lips left hers to sear over her face and ears. He murmured her name over and over between kisses. "You don't know how much I need you, moonbeam, how much I want you. If only . . ." Varian embraced her so tightly and kissed her so savagely that pain shot through her lips and body.

But Jana did not cry out or pull away from him. Varian carried her to his bed. He laid her down and sent his gaze on an exploratory trek over her body. When he joined her on the bed, their mouths joined and their hands caressed. Varian kept leaning back to gaze into her face, as if to question her response, fearful it would stop abruptly.

Where was so much he wanted to confess, and there was one promise he wanted to extract from her: to love him, trust him, and wait for him. He couldn't. Instead, he allowed his behavior to speak for him, to speak a language which baffled Jana more than her sale to another man.

It was a time which inspired a total union of bodies and spirits, a sweetness of promised love, a forgetfulness of reality and fate's demands. It was a time to fill with tender memories and join forces to obtain rapture's peak. It was a time to savor each kiss, each touch, each word, each gaze. It was a time to pray this moment would never end, yet to realize it would, all too soon.

They talked about the days they had shared, the places they had visited together, and the friends she had made. Varian asked numerous questions about her childhood, home, and parents. They chatted about everything— but today.

As they rested together, relishing the tranquil aftermath of urgent lovemaking, Communications Officer Vaiden Chaz shattered their private world. "Commander Saar, we'll be orbiting Karnak in twenty minutes. Any instructions?"

Varian's eyes briefly darted to Jana's. He reached for the intercom button. "Nigel has the bridge. I'll remain in my quarters. Signal me when we're locked into orbit." After Vaiden acknowledged those directives, Varian stared at the intercom. He asked himself once again if the treacherous spy could be Vaiden Chaz, Baruch Tirana, or Daxley Prada. He hated to suspect any of his three officers, but it had to be one of them. Soon, his trap would spring on the traitor.

"Varian?" she called to him. "Is there enough time to"— she saw him stiffen in dread—"make love to me once more?" His relief at hearing the end of her question was evident in his appreciative gaze and smile.

"We'll make time," he replied tenderly, happily.

Canissia Garthon raced into Zan's arms when her beguiled captain returned from his grim task. She snuggled against her lover and pretended to quiver in fear. She hugged him possessively as she nestled her face to his hard chest. She inquired, "Did you get rid of Baruch's body, my love?"

"Don't worry, Cassie my sweet. It's done," Zan replied, holding her tightly.

"Are you certain his body can't be located and examined? Those rare drugs can be traced to Ryker Triloni and then to me. All I wanted was some information from him. How could I know his silly heart wasn't able to handle Ryker's new truth serum?" she lied. She dared not tell the possessive Zan what and how much of those rare drugs she had given to Lieutenant Baruch Tirana. After all, it had been an accident. She had wanted more clues about Varian, Jana, and the impending auction. It was too bad Baruch's heart couldn't take any more. At the very least she no longer had to fear Baruch might unmask her to the authorities, to Varian Saar, or to Ryker Triloni. She smiled wickedly. She would let Ryker wonder what had happened to his little double agent. No one knew she had slain Baruch except Zan, and she could take care of him.

Zan unsuspectingly comforted his beloved mistress. "No one will ever find him or know what happened."

"Oh, Zan," she cooed seductively, "you're so clever and strong. Whatever would I do without you to protect me and take care of me? You deserve a special treat. Name anything you desire, and I shall buy it for you."

"All I desire is you, Cassie my sweet," he murmured against her forehead.

She gazed into his eyes and deceitfully promised, "Then you can have me, my love, any way you desire and until your passions are sated."

Nigel, Tristan, Kara, Kyle, and several others had come to say good-bye. Jana was moved by their affection. She hugged each one, then questioned Tristan about Martella's absence. She learned that Martella Karsh was already assigned by the Alliance Force to another mission. After a few moments of genial talk, Jana hugged each one again, then hurried into the shuttle before she lost control of her tears.

Just a short while ago she had bathed, then searched through her clothing for a simple jumpsuit which held the least painful memory. Everything else must be left behind. Varian could give them to his next mistress or captive or discard them! When she noticed he had included the expensive jewels in her personal case, she stared in amazement. Then fury assailed her. She wasn't some high-priced whore! How dare he insult her with extravagant gems! Nor did she want the bracelet, necklace, ring, or painting which he had slipped into one case.

Jana had dressed and brushed her hair with care. She let it tumble down her back, full and free. She refused to wear any jewelry, except her own birthstone ring, a ruby which was surrounded by diamonds, the last gift from her father before his death. She resolved that as soon as Draco furnished her with another wardrobe, she would dispose of everything she was wearing!

On the way down to Karnak, Jana didn't look at Varian or speak to him. Taking her cue, Varian behaved in the same reserved manner. Draco met them at the landing area where Jana chatted genially to cover her anguish. "Your private world is beautiful, Draco. How many people live on your planetoid? Do you have *esprees*?" She inquired about their breed of horses. One question tumbled over another as she faked exuberance and curiosity.

Draco laughed merrily. "There'll be plenty of time to answer your questions and to look around later today. First, Varian and I must conclude our business so he can be on his way. We'll go into my office. I have everything ready."

Draco headed down a long corridor to his left. Varian called out before following him, "Jana, we'll need you to come along with us."

Jana was staring at the breathtaking opulence of her new surroundings. Never had she seen a more exquisitely decorated and constructed mansion. She was astonished by the splendor which flourished around her. In all of her travels on Earth and in this galaxy, she had not seen anything to compare with Draco's private world. She was utterly entranced.

"Jana! Come along," Varian called. Her gaiety rankled him!

Jana slowly followed Varian as she continued to gaze all around her. She could hardly believe her new home. This represented the wealth, status, and tastes of Draco Procyon? "It's overpowering, isn't it? So grand and flawless. So serene. I'll like it here," she remarked innocently. "You never warned me Draco was so rich. Now I see how he could afford to bid so much. Do you think he'll be pleased with me?"

Varian grabbed her hand and pulled her along at a fast pace. He caught himself before scoffing, *Just wait until you see our home on Altair!* Nor did he snap, *Draco isn't half as wealthy as I am!* Instead he snarled, "You can admire your new home later! I have a ship and crew on standby, remember?"

Jana glared at him and tartly replied, "By all means hurry back to them!" She entered the study into which Draco had vanished, then stopped inside the door.

When Varian walked over to the desk, Draco handed him a paper and said, "Here's my bank voucher. You have the purchase agreements ready to sign?"

Varian leaned over and signed two documents of ownership, then placed his official seal on them as a Star Fleet commander. Before folding it and stuffing it into his pocket, Varian didn't even glance at the bank voucher which ordered the transfer of 8,888,888 *katoogas* into the Maffei Alliance account from Draco Procyon's private account, money which had come from Varian Saar's personal account days ago. After Draco signed both pages, Varian left the copy on the desk and took the original, to be placed in the *Charl* agency files. As far as anyone could tell, Draco Procyon legally owned Jana Greyson, an Earthling who had been captured and auctioned by Varian Saar, an officer of the Elite Squad who had been acting under the authority of the Supreme Council.

Varian gazed at the paper which proclaimed his love to be the legal mate of his friend Draco. He couldn't wait for the day when Draco pretended to sell Jana back to him. There was one other advantage to this ruse of Draco's ownership; if anything happened to him on this voyage or before he could settle his war with Ryker, Jana would have a good home and owner. For all intents and purposes, she was Draco's mate until Draco legally signed the paper to release her. Varian carefully folded the document, then placed it inside another pocket.

Varian approached Jana. "This is where we part company, moonbeam. I'm going to miss you. I hope you'll be very happy here."

Jana flushed at his amorous words. When Varian gently grasped her arm to pull her to him for a farewell embrace, she thought she would break down. She jerked free and stepped out of his reach. She warned, "Get your hands off me! Nothing pleases me more than to get away from you. The charade is over!"

"Jana, you will cease this rude conduct immediately. I will not tolerate such behavior to my friend in our home," Draco stated.

Her new owner's authoritative tone silenced her instantly. She had not been prepared for Varian's words, nor for Draco's stern reaction. The man possessed a stronger character than she had realized. Draco could be just as strong as he could be gentle! But, she had alertly caught his words "our home."

Varian quickly spoke up in her defense. "It's all right, Draco. She has good reasons to despise me and to want her freedom from me."

Jana faced Draco and said, "I'm sorry, sir. My behavior was impolite, but this whole affair has been extremely difficult for me."

Draco smiled. "Perhaps you should retire to your room to rest for a while. I'll come for you later and show you around your new home." He pressed a buzzer on his desk, to which a servant responded quickly. "Show Jana to her suite and provide whatever she needs. I'll speak with you later, Jana."

"Thank you, sir. I am truly sorry." Jana headed for the door to follow the servant. She was struggling hard not to cry.

"Good-bye, Jana," came the timbre voice of the man she loved. "Be happy."

Jana halted, her posture stiff, but did not turn to look at Varian or return his farewell. She inhaled deeply, then left the room. The door closed behind her.

"I think she loathes me, old friend, and is glad to be rid of me."

Draco watched Varian intently. "I think you're right this time. Like you said, she has plenty of good reason. Not the lowest of which has to do with your tardiness today; it is four o'clock. Accept it for now, she's mine."

Varian winced. "Only on paper and in public eyes. You and Karnak will be good for Jana. Take care of her, Draco, especially if I don't return."

They shook hands before parting. Draco dropped wearily into his desk chair. He stared at the legal document in his grasp. For once, Varian Saar was a damn fool, a blind one! Didn't the illustrious commander realize this sale could drive an immovable wedge between him and Jana? By the time Varian returned, if he did, it might be too late to recover Jana. She could hate Varian, and be in love with her new owner, or the man whom she believed was her owner. Money had been paid for her in Draco Procyon's name. And Draco Procyon was the name listed as owner on the bill of sale. Yes, legally Jana Greyson belonged to him . . . Varian should be glad they were old and dear friends! Any other man might refuse to return Jana at a later date, and Varian's lips would be sealed by law and his hands bound to stay off Jana!

Varian returned to his ship alone, more alone than he had ever been in his life. He stood at his window until Karnak was lost from sight.

PART III
Moondust and Magic

As the playful Gods gather to watch mortals below,
The helpless Fates warn sadly, for only they know
Beware, ye men with foolish dreams and false prides;
Dangers abound for loves lost from your sides.
On wings of magic, passion and victory wish to ride;
But how can they conquer a Universe so wide . . .

Chapter Sixteen

Jana's life on Karnak began under difficult circumstances. She followed Draco's servant to her private suite, but found it impossible to relax as instructed, or perhaps as ordered. She could not decide if her existence was ending or beginning so great was the agony in her heart. Only her bitter resentment made it endurable.

She strolled onto a teardrop-shaped patio which was surrounded by exotic flowers in full radiance and sat on a stone bench near a small fish pond. She was reminded of midspring in the South. A light breeze which played through her hair and across her skin was warm and fresh. She inhaled deeply and lifted her face skyward while confusion flooded her. How could she feel the warmth of the sun and the coolness of the breeze when the enclosed garden was covered with a bulbous dome? Evidently nature's effects were nothing more than perfect reproductions. No sound from the outside world reached her ears. She had total privacy. For pleasure or security?

"You appear calmer, Jana," stated a gentle voice from behind her.

She turned and smiled faintly. "Your home is exceptionally lovely." She shivered with apprehension. They were alone for the first time. What did she know about this man? What would she do if he desired to bed her right now? Or tonight? It was too soon after their meeting. Too soon after Varian.

Jana's heart screamed, *Why have you done this wicked thing to me, my love?* She forced a brave smile to surface. She must act normally. What was normal behavior under these conditions? Slavery was so unreal to her; and it was as if she were a guest here. She had to depend on her wits to get her new life started on the right road. Without a doubt, there were fates worse than this man and this place.

"I am very proud of my home. However, I didn't build her or buy her. It was all inherited, even my businesses," Draco said.

"But you have the skill and knowledge to keep them and to increase your good fortune. Your reputation has preceded you, Draco. I am honored you chose to bid on me, and lucky you succeeded." My, how she and her life had changed since June 14! Today was August 15; she should be starting the first day of her new job at Johns Hopkins medical research complex, not starting a new life on a distant world with a kind stranger.

Draco warmed to her and returned her smile. "No more than I am honored to share all of it with you. We're both very lucky people, Jana Greyson of Earth."

Jana flushed. "You are far too generous. Thank you."

"Varian told me you left your belongings on his ship. I can understand your reluctance to wear them again." He observed her reaction.

"I hope it wasn't presumptuous of me, but I didn't feel they were mine to keep. They also carried memories of days I would like to forget. I doubt they would be appropriate garments for the . . . your *charl*. Do you object?"

"Not in the least. In fact, there is a complete wardrobe awaiting you here, one which, I suspect, better suits your personality and new position. At your leisure, you may examine it. Feel free to ask for anything else you need. You will have an ample allowance to spend as you wish." Jana was speechless at his generosity.

Draco added, "I hope you will view my house as your home and me as your family. You may come and go as you please here on Karnak, but trips to Rigel are not allowed unless you are accompanied by me or my guards. I'm a wealthy and powerful man, so I do have rivals and a few enemies. Besides the inducements of kidnapping you for money or favors or revenge, you are an exceedingly beautiful woman. You must be careful even when you travel with me.

"You may take, or use, or do as you wish within taste and reason. If I have not misjudged you, you're trustworthy, responsible, intelligent, and well bred. I want you to be happy and safe here." Draco understood his responsibility to Jana, and he did what was necessary to carry it out. After all, if anything happened to Varian, he could keep Jana and truly make her his mate. His tone altered as he continued, "Your duty lies with me. My wife was killed years ago, and I have no mistress. I expect you to conduct yourself as the lady of this house. You will attend all functions with me. When the occasion arises, you will serve as hostess here. I shall be proud to have you at my side and in my home. Your position here is an honorable one, a coveted one. Never allow anyone to treat you otherwise. Be yourself, Jana Greyson. Let no one and nothing humiliate or harm you," he stressed. "Do you understand my expectations?" he inquired.

Jana nodded yes, but she was puzzled. This wasn't the kind of existence she had imagined! Her life here sounded more like a job than the role of purchased mate. He had not mentioned their intimate relationship, but it wasn't necessary. "I don't know what to say, Draco. I hadn't expected . . ."

Draco grinned and finished her sentence, "A home and a family? Partial freedom? Pride? Respect? Total acceptance? You'll have them all here, Jana."

When tears filled her eyes and escaped down her cheeks, Draco comforted her. "Be at peace, Jana," he said. "I'll leave you alone to sort out your feelings. I'll see you at dinner shortly. If you need anything, call one of the servants. Oh, yes," he added. "You aren't a servant here, Jana, you're the mistress."

Jana watched him depart. Her thoughts were a whirlwind of confusion. Later, as if perceiving her fatigue, Draco made sure dinner passed swiftly. Afterward she had been astounded to learn they would not be sharing the same bedroom. She had her own suite: a luxurious bedroom, a splendid bathroom, a lovely dressing room, a tranquil garden, and several enormous closets. Her clothes and accessories were beautiful. There were jewels in every color, and style. There was nothing more she could want or need. Clearly Draco had provided a wardrobe for the mate of one of the galaxy's richest, most prominent, and renowned men. But how had he obtained these items so swiftly? It looked as if he had never once doubted his victory at her auction and had prepared for it!

Jana examined her plush surroundings. She was back in the familiar world of wealth, respect, and eminence. She must never behave as a pathetic, helpless slave! When she realized what she could be facing this very moment, Jana admitted she was fortunate beyond her wildest dreams. She could not alter this new destiny, so she ordered herself to deal with it. She must not allow anything to cause her to disappoint Draco.

Varian had used her, then jettisoned her. He had tantalized her for weeks, until she was tricked into urging his possession of her! Varian Saar was unreachable, immovable. Guilt filled her, for those accusations were untrue, except for the last one. He had warned her from the beginning that their affair was fleeting. She had foolishly believed he would change his mind and keep her. Yet, unlike a regular love affair when a man severs a relationship, he had literally sold her into bondage to another man. Could she forgive him? Never.

Draco was different. He was sensitive and understanding. She must make certain he never regretted her purchase. Draco must become her sole concern.

A week passed on Karnak as Jana adjusted to a tranquil existence. Each day Draco and Jana ate together; they talked for hours, and they toured the grounds or rode together. They laughed and joked; they enjoyed sports or games. She warmed to Draco's easygoing and charming manner. She savored the respect of his servants and friends and she resolved to find happiness once more. Perhaps in time she would forget Varian, who hovered over her like an oppressive shadow of Evil.

Varian wasn't faring as well as his lost love. After his departure from Karnak, he had secluded himself in his quarters in the starship *Wanderlust*. The full brunt of his betrayal of Jana had struck home. He had been so busy seeking a clever ruse to protect her while he carried out his duties that he really hadn't stopped to analyze their situation. Knowing her sale was a farce, he had ignored the fact that it was a real sale and a terrible ordeal for Jana. Until those last minutes on Draco's private world, the reality of this *charl* matter and her anguish had eluded him. As a Star Fleet officer assigned to a grave mission, he had been forced to continue the charade. He had placed Nigel in charge of the bridge, as he needed time alone.

The *Wanderlust* was on course to the edge of their galaxy to check on the meteor's course and speed, then it was on to Earth for their rescue mission. This time, his abductions would be different. His last voyage to Earth had been to abduct females to be sold as *charls,* captives who had been used as a cover for his real mission. This voyage, both males and females would be abducted. This time no one would be enslaved or sold. It was a pure and simple rescue mission. The Earthlings would live free and happy on Anais.

Excitement ran heavy among the crew. But as they carried on the normal procedures for a new mission, many minds lingered on the alien girl left behind on Karnak, the one who made their commander so moody. She had wormed her way into their hearts, lives, and minds too. Many missed Jana, and comprehended the effect of her loss on Varian Saar.

It was fifteen hours before Varian roused himself to take a shower and shave. He opened his desk drawer and stared at an odd collection: a farewell ring, a floral necklace with his initials and special pictures of them, a gold birthday bracelet, an oil painting of a rare *Talia* flower, a copy of a legal bill of sale of Jana to Draco, a bank transfer slip from his account to Draco's for almost nine million *katoogas*, and three color pictures of him and Jana given to him from a fierce enemy who seemed to be winning their life-long battle.

Varian contacted the ship's historical officer and asked him to research the significance of the gold ring which so upset Jana. He sighed and rubbed his stinging eyes. Jana had left everything behind, as if wanting no reminders of their brief liaison. He grimaced at the meaning beneath her actions. *Kahala,* he missed her!

The historian responded to his ring query; the answer was self-explanatory. Varian wished he had selected a different gift.

Five long, miserable days crawled by as Varian struggled to banish Jana from his mind. He needed to concentrate on his assignment, his duty. He needed to be prepared for the current mission. But there was little to occupy his thoughts during this uneventful journey through an endless void of space. Sometimes he would stand for hours staring out the bridge transascreen. If there was a hell out there, there was also one within him!

Three more days went by and no relief or release came to

him. He craved Jana's smile, her passionate response, her laughter. No kiss had ever been sweeter than hers. No hands had ever stirred him so intensely. No body had given him such great pleasure and contentment. No woman had taken or given as she had. He was as much a prisoner of her love as she had been of his power.

Varian's dejection worried his friends and crew. Finally he realized he needed to spend less time alone in his quarters. He chose to submerge himself in work or exercise, and plotted new strategies to entrap Ryker, to make a truce with Maal and Jurad, for only then could he publicly claim Jana Greyson and marry her. As soon as it was safe for him to claim Jana, he would join Martella and speak out against the enthralling custom. Now, Martella was helping the rescued and relocated Earthlings to adjust to life on their new world of Anais. From what Tristan Zarcoff had confided to him, Martella and Tristan, too, would marry soon.

Varian's troubled mind pondered another mysterious subject: Baruch Tirana's disappearance. He had seemingly vanished from a hotel on Rigel while on leave. The surveillance team assigned to watch Baruch had seen nothing and no one suspicious. As yet there was no concrete evidence which connected him with Ryker, Moloch, or Canissia. Yet if Baruch had fled in fear, someone must have aided his escape. As far as Varian knew, the Alliance Force was still searching for the missing officer. Varian was anxious to hear why one of his best officers had betrayed him to Ryker, for Baruch had to be the guilty one. A damning microcamera had been found in his quarters. This episode had proven to him that Jana wasn't safe even on his ship, under his guard.

Varian had spoken privately with Vaiden Chaz and Daxley Prada to settle those matters involving them. Without realizing they had briefly fallen under suspicion of spying, both men accepted Varian's words and dropped the subjects completely.

Finally, Varian forced himself to spend as much time as possible with his crew. But nothing seemed to appease him. If he and the Council had believed Jana would distract him with her presence, they were all wrong; her absence was far more detrimental. The past ten days had seemed like eons to him and something had to give.

* * *

Prince Taemin of the Pyropean Federation met with one of his most trusted officers who reported on what he had learned from his spies about Jana's auction. "Commander Saar sold her as scheduled. It would seem she meant nothing to him," Captain Koch said.

Taemin laughed coldly. "It would seem, my naïve friend, that she meant far more than Father and I realized. I will be patient for a time. But I must and will have Jana Greyson, and Varian Saar's blood."

"What of this meeting with Prince Ryker Triloni to form an alliance to conquer the Maffei Galaxy?" the captain inquired.

The ruggedly handsome prince grinned. "Very soon, my friend. I shall allow Prince Ryker to help me take over the Maffei Alliance, then I shall slay him and his grandfather and lay claim to the Androas Empire. Then, my friend, you shall be the supreme commander of my new federation forces."

"Prince Ryker Triloni is sly and powerful, my liege. He possesses many evil secrets. You must be careful in your dealings with him."

"Ryker is an arrogant, cocky bastard. He will be too busy trying to defeat his half brother to notice that I am his worst enemy, not Varian Saar. I will generously help him to destroy Varian; and while he revels in his victory, I shall strike at him and destroy him. He will not suspect a thing, my friend. Once I have control of Darkar and Trilabs, I will rule the Universe."

"Your cunning and daring amaze me, my liege. I will do all you say and serve at your side always."

"Soon, Ryker Triloni will send for me to discuss our private truce; then, my friend, our secret plans will be put into action."

"What of Supreme Councilman Garthon's daughter?" Koch asked.

"She knows too much to live much longer," Taemin declared.

"What of your father, and *Kadim* Tirol, and *Kadim* Maal Triloni?"

Prince Taemin stared his loyal officer in the eye and calmly replied, "We will slay them, then you and I will rule all that exists."

"Once you have slain Prince Triloni and his brother, Commander Saar, nothing and no one can stop you from becoming supreme ruler of the Universe."

"You weren't the least surprised when Varian sold Jana Greyson, were you?"

Ryker looked up from his microscope and grinned. "I let him know I wasn't fooled by his little charade with his pretty slut. Oh, I wasn't surprised to hear he had locked her in his quarters and sated himself with her. After all, Precious, the Saar men have this strange weakness for green-eyed blondes." He smiled at his mistress, who quickly and radiantly returned it.

"I knew Varian was faking an enchantment for her to gain my attention. Now that I've unmasked Dohler and Vejar, his agents, and gotten rid of them, my brother is right back where he started from, at point zero. He must be getting awfully flustered by all of these setbacks. No way could he fool me with Jana. He would never marry an alien whore who favors my beautiful mother. Why, Jana's hardly more than a captive breeder. I talked with Baruch a few times, and he swore Varian felt nothing but lust for his captive," Ryker said, unaware of Baruch's disappearance and Baruch's lies to him.

"What if you're wrong, my love? What if Varian secretly loves this alien beauty? What if he sold her because he was afraid you would kill her?"

"I considered that point. That's why I have Moloch watching Jana and Draco. If Varian and Draco have some ruse going, I'll uncover it. Somehow I can't see my brother leaving his true love with any man, even a good friend. From what I hear, this Jana is irresistible. Besides, Varian would be afraid to leave her alone for months while he's gone. No, Precious, if he loved Jana, she would be in his quarters right now. If the Supreme Council protested, he would tell them where to go. Jana Greyson was captured as a lure for me, nothing more. But I do want to know more about this mission of his to . . . the Milky Way Galaxy, wasn't it?"

"When is that bitch Canissia Garthon scheduled to visit you again?"

Ryker laughed. "In a week or so. Come now, Precious, stop fretting over her. Soon, she'll be out of your hair for good.

Once I get all the facts I need about this curious assignment to another galaxy, I'll hand her over to Moloch or Taemin. Cass surely does make a lot of enemies.''

"You promised her to Moloch first," she reminded him.

"You should know by now that I keep very few of my promises. I might deal with Moloch in another way, when I've finished using him. Taemin wants Cass. Perhaps I'll help him obtain her, for a price . . .''

"What about Moloch? Will you leave him free?"

"Don't worry about Moloch. I'm running those new experiments in a few weeks, and I'll be needing several healthy specimens. Moloch will suit my needs perfectly.''

She rubbed her hands together in undisguised eagerness. "I can hardly wait. Why didn't you keep those two Elite Squad secret agents for our experiment?"

"And deny myself the pleasure of watching Varian squirm? I bet he was up half the night trying to decipher the deaths and placement of the bodies of his two Elite Squad agents. That's how I know Jana means nothing to him. After discovering I was onto his little plot against me and Trilabs, he would never have sold her and taken off without her.''

"And if you're wrong?" she pressed boldly.

Ryker scowled at her and shrugged. "If I am or not, they'll both die eventually.''

Jana lay in bed trying to concentrate on a book, but she couldn't. She had lived in this opulent setting for ten days, yet doubts chewed at her. Draco and his servants had done their best to make her feel at home. She should be happy and calm; but she wasn't. She couldn't be until she understood exactly what was going on. Draco had not visited her bed or sent for her to come to his. Since that day of her arrival, he had not even set foot in her suite. She was so confused. A man didn't purchase a mate, then ignore mating! Sometimes she discovered him watching her with such a disturbingly strange expression on his face. Sometimes he seemed about to speak or to touch her but would halt and shift uneasily. She needed to end this period of limbo, this ominous unknown. She needed to seal her fate as Draco's *charl,* to get their first union behind her. She could just lie in his bed and let him take what he

301

pleased, couldn't she? Perhaps she would become accustomed to his touch, maybe learn to enjoy it. She needed to prove she could live without Varian, to herself, to Draco, and everyone.

Was Draco concerned over her feelings? Was he waiting for her to come to him? Why had he seemed edgy today? Had he found her sexually undesirable now that he owned her? Was he finding it difficult or impossible to follow Varian Saar in her life? If so, he would come to resent and despise her. Insecurity and panic surged through her. She knew *charls* could be resold. . . . She didn't want to have sex with Draco, but she must! Her life here could depend on becoming his mate. Why was he avoiding her in this way?

Her taut nerves demanded release. What she needed was a long, tiring walk. She slipped down the darkened hallway toward the formal gardens. Her bare feet traveled silently through the darkened house. In the gardens she wandered down the paths, halting here and there to pluck a flower and inhale its heady fragrance. The silvery full moon offered plenty of light. Jana stopped near the huge fountain in the center of the garden and sat on its stone edge. She watched the moonlight sparkle on the cascading streams of crystal liquid. Her troubled mind returned to a day beside another waterfall.

"It would take many tears to overflow that fountain, Jana. Why not leave that chore to summer rains?" Draco teased, causing her to jump and turn. He was concerned over her obvious sadness. He knew she must be wary of her new life, yet was Varian the cause? "Is something wrong? You seem distraught tonight."

Jana felt she must confront this mystery and its truth. She bluntly came to the point. "You have not touched me since I came here, Draco. You treat me like a sister or friend. Why? Have I somehow displeased or disappointed you?"

"Why do you worry over such matters, Jana? Is there a reason you need a physical commitment from me?" he inquired. He had expected this situation to arise, but not this soon. How to deal with it properly and sensitively? His abstinence must seem irrational to her.

"I fail to understand your refusal to take what is yours. Am I naïve about men's needs and desires, or about my position here? I assumed you would claim me before now. Why haven't you?" she bravely questioned.

Draco sought his words carefully. "On the contrary, Jana, I find you more than pleasing. You've been here such a short time, and we hardly know each other. A man can sate his physical desires with any woman, but you are too special to be used lightly. There is no urgency to bed you. We must have time to adjust to each other and become close. I do not see you as a woman who yields her all to a man she does not love. You must trust him and desire him. I would never take any woman by force, Jana. Nor would I accept her submission from gratitude or from a sense of duty. I'm happy with the current arrangement between us. For now, all I demand from you was outlined on your first day here. Do you understand?"

"Does Varian's prior possession have anything to do with your decision?"

"I am not jealous nor do I fear competition with my friend Varian. Mere sexual gratification is of no importance to me. Feelings are what matter most, Jana. Take this time to enjoy life, to discover its wonders. Let your emotions heal and grow and strengthen. Forget you are a *charl*, a captive alien. Find Jana Greyson; get to know her and like her. Be my friend, my companion. If fate sees fit to change those roles later, so be it. Don't try to create feelings toward me. Remain honest with both of us."

Jana impulsively kissed his cheek and hugged him tightly. "I don't deserve such good fortune, Draco. How will I ever thank you? No other man would be so kind. I will be good; I'll make you proud of me."

Draco walked her to her room and kissed her good night. He knew his words had polished his image and darkened Varian's. It couldn't be helped. He would like nothing more than to possess Jana; he couldn't, for many reasons. He hadn't realized what a treasure and temptation she was. He prayed for time to pass swiftly.

Jana leaned against the closed door, more bewildered than before their talk. Was Draco falling in love with her? Was he afraid to press her? If he had demanded her surrender, could she have yielded? She desperately wanted to trust him, but could she? It just didn't seem natural or logical. He had spent a fortune on her; he owned her body and life. It was back to limbo. She couldn't decide if his words gave her comfort or increased her apprehensions.

303

Another week passed. Jana acknowledged her elite status in Draco's household. People were not only polite, they were genuinely amiable. She perceived no contempt from any business associates or members of his social circle. This treatment not only surprised and pleased Jana, it slowly restored her confidence and self-esteem.

Jana returned to her studies. She practiced her dancing and Draco's language. She spent hours in his library yet she was thrilled when Draco hired several tutors for her. She asked countless questions and urged them to teach her all they knew. She avidly studied his culture, his interests, his world, and his businesses. She wanted to be as helpful and satisfying as possible. She went riding every day. She explored until she knew every inch of the house, grounds, and gardens by heart. At last, she was beginning to free herself from the painful past.

Draco watched Jana carefully. He knew she was coming to trust him and admire him more each day. Her vivacity and joy in life were returning. She carried out her duties to him with a special flair. She was interesting and witty, bright and quick. She was as fresh as she was before Varian intruded on her existence. Jana fit into Draco's life as perfectly as the missing piece to an intricate and priceless puzzle.

Draco came to adore Jana. Her presence at his side became as natural as breathing. Often she was like a carefree and impish child with eyes wide and innocent. She could be a tomboy racing over meadows and hills on the back of his *esprees,* her tawny hair flying out behind her in the winds. She could be a gracious lady with the poise, elegance, and dignity of a queen. She could be a pixie whose wit and antics charmed and amused the coldest of hearts.

Jana revealed enormous intelligence and gentility. She was able to meet anyone on any level. She was always observing, questioning, and learning ways to improve herself. She was a devoted and loyal friend to Draco, a constant companion. At last she seemed at peace with herself and her new life. The old Jana had been reborn, more self-reliant, spirited, and self-controlled. She was more than any man could imagine and she showered Draco with attention.

Her hours outside quickly restored her golden tan and the silvery streaks in her hair. Her skin was smooth, healthy, and satiny. Its texture and glow was aided by hours with Draco's masseuse and her constant exercise. Her figure ripened and took on a new dimension of supple and alluring curves. Her heightened colorings and new hold on life placed a noticeable glow in her beryl eyes.

Draco surged with pride and satisfaction. Jana was his protégée, his creation. He took her everywhere with him. As he had instructed her to forget her captive role in his life, so did he . . .

Open and secret bids were issued for her. When he continued to receive such numerous exorbitant offers, Draco tried to prevent any more by suggesting to the Earthling that he and Jana feign a love match. He didn't want her constantly reminded of her *charl* rank or made to feel like a piece of property. When he would cast loving eyes on her and reply, "Jana is the center of my life. I could never part with her," his ploy worked.

In frustration and loneliness, Varian ordered the ship's speed increased to maximum. In another day, they should reach Earth to collect their six hundred captives; once he delivered them to the planet Anais, he could head for base, then Jana. He wanted, needed to complete this mission. The day he issued that command, Nigel headed to his office for a long-overdue conversation.

Varian was sitting at his desk, staring at the haunting possessions in his drawer. He slammed it shut and leaned back in his chair. The price of his duty to the Council, Alliance, and Saar name was almost too great to pay. If he had these past months to relive, he would make countless changes. The buzzer sounded at his door, drawing him from his turmoil.

Nigel was allowed to enter. Reading and weighing Varian's gray mood, he stated sympathetically, "It's harder than you ever imagined, isn't it?"

"I wonder if my sacrifices will be worth it all, Nigel. I should have let another ship take this assignment while I solved matters with Ryker. I was a fool to let things go so far; I realize it was an unforgivable mistake to auction her. At least I should have told her the truth about my feelings and her sale."

Nigel shook his head. "This isn't the time or place to worry over mistakes, Varian. You can't force this ship to reach its destination before its time. Have you forgotten the ship not far ahead of us must complete its mission first? You've got to relax and gain control of your wits."

Suddenly Tristan Zarcoff rushed to Varian's quarters and interrupted his talk with Nigel. The ship's commander listened in disbelief and rising fury as the medical chief delivered his staggering report: the decontamination chemicals from Trilabs were useless. There was no way the *Wanderlust* could carry out her assignment. If Tristan had not tested the chemicals before reaching Earth and taking on captives, the entire crew would have contracted a fatal illness.

"That lousy bastard!" Varian thundered in outrage. "How did he learn about this secret mission? He would stoop to any level to kill me. Stars forsake me! He'll pay for this offense!"

"Are you saying this was intentional?" Tristan questioned. "Could he have known about our assignment?"

"I'd bet my rank and ship Ryker is behind this evil deed. What does he care if others suffer! What does he care if the entire crew of my ship dies along with me! A war with me, I can accept and understand, but not so deadly a one sacrificing so many innocent lives! Thank *Kahala* you discovered this."

"What can we do now?" Nigel asked in grave concern.

"We have no choice but to return home as quickly as possible. It might already be too late to rescue more Earthlings before we attempt to deal with that meteor. Now that I think about it, Ryker would be a fool to tip his hand on a simple rescue mission; if he knows about the second part of this mission, he'll send his grandfather's Androas Troopers after us when our energy banks are drained. If we're to use those chemical lasers, we had better test all of them first! Let's head for base. Time is running out." The instant Varian made those statements aloud, he knew how they would affect him. This was a personal battle with Ryker, one he must confront. One he could no longer escape.

Varian ordered reports. The men pored over the facts, coming to several conclusions. Varian signaled Tesla Rilke and asked him to plot a rapid course back to Rigel. He commanded Vaiden Chaz to send *Kadim* Tirol and the Council a coded message explaining their predicament the instant they were within communication range. Secondly, Vaiden was to inform Brec Sard of Ryker Triloni's malicious deed and to have the supreme commander locate more decontamination chemicals and have them ready for pickup.

At top speed, they could reach base in nine or ten days. That would leave six to seven weeks to carry out the assault on the meteor; and if they failed, just enough time to get out of the Milky Way Galaxy before disaster struck. Thank heavens they had more time than they had believed originally, as their check on the meteor revealed its speed had decreased slightly. Without delay, the *Wanderlust* was heading home again. If only he could locate and interrogate Baruch . . .

On Karnak, Jana Greyson was being bound tighter to Draco Procyon, drawn more deeply into his world. Jana did all she could to conquer any lingering love for Varian Saar; she tried her best to inspire this same feeling toward Draco. She owed him so much. It had helped when Draco asked her to display love for him before others, to halt any further offers for her purchase. Most of the time, it succeeded; so Jana gladly cooperated. Besides, her feelings for him were warming. What did it matter if people believed they were in love? What did it matter if people assumed she was his mate in all ways? Perhaps this charade would lead them gradually toward making it a reality.

Each day, Jana would order her mind to cease all thoughts of Varian, and command her heart to slay all feelings for him. But it was impossible. In the darkest shadows of night, Jana unknowingly allowed Varian's ghost to visit her. Memories of her lost love would sneak uninvited into her slumber. She would awaken abruptly and find herself reaching out for him. Some nights her body would tremble with longing for him. She berated her submission to him, for she couldn't forget his intoxicating kisses or their blissful unions. She cursed his hold over her.

Jana came to wonder if Draco's kiss and touch could drive such agonizing feelings from her body. Could his lovemaking force Varian from her life? Could Draco release Varian's powerful hold on her body? She needed freedom and peace! She wanted this terrible emptiness and longing to go way. She wanted to feel whole again. She wanted to sate the passions which chewed viciously at her each night. She began to believe that only after total surrender to Draco could she resolve her torments. Jana used every wile she could imagine, without being wanton or shameless. Those initial fears and doubts returned during the long nights to plague her. She couldn't ignore the truth any longer; something was preventing his claim.

Two days later on Rigel, there was a large gathering of dignitaries for a dinner dance. When Draco was called away from her side for a lengthy time on business, Jana came face to face with Jurad. She didn't know how to act or what to say.

"I am pleased to see you have found a happy home with Councilman Procyon. I hope my quarrel with Commander Saar did not overly distress you. I must confess, little Earthling, I did all I could to purchase you, with or without an auction. Commander Saar made certain the Council refused my petitions. But it appears the fates were fair with you."

Jana stared at the man. "I find your words confusing, sir. Why are you and Commander Saar at war? Why did each of you think the other was trying to use me as a weapon?" she probed, hoping he might supply some answers to the questions she could not bring herself to ask Draco.

Jurad stared at her oddly. "You do not know about our conflict?" he asked incredulously. "You know nothing of Shara and Ryker?" When Jana shook her head, he added, "Amaya and Galen? *Kadim* Maal Triloni?" When she shook her head twice more, his disbelief was obvious.

"Who are they? How do they affect me? Affect how Varian treated me?" she specified. "I do know who Maal Triloni is, and I've heard the others' names a time or two. What happened to create such hatred and bitterness between you two?"

"Why did you not ask Commander Saar, or Councilman Procyon?" Jurad questioned skeptically. "He told you nothing about Shara after our quarrel?"

"Commander Saar refused any explanation. And I was not in a position to demand one. Nor did I think it wise to ask my new owner about the man who abducted and sold me." Jana didn't trust Jurad, but she wanted answers.

Jurad selected his words slyly. "Ryker Triloni is Varian Saar's fiercest enemy; they would like nothing better than to slay each other, preferably with their bare hands. If Saar could, he would destroy all Trilonis. But Ryker Triloni is a powerful man. I was surprised Ryker Triloni did not attempt to purchase

308

you, since Saar revealed such an odd interest in you," he hinted evocatively, observing her reaction to Ryker's name each time it was spoken.

Jurad searched for and used words which he knew would mislead Jana. "Commander Varian Saar has loved no woman more than Amaya Trygue, the daughter of *Kadim* Tirol. Seven years past, Shara Triloni brutally murdered Amaya, then Galen Saar, then killed herself."

At Jana's shocked and baffled expression, Jurad continued cleverly, "Perhaps I should explain who Shara is, or was. Shara was the daughter of *Kadim* Maal Triloni; she was to become my bride and our marriage was to seal the truce between the Androas Empire and the Pyropean Federation. We asked *Kadim* Tirol to select his most trusted and fearless officer to escort Shara across the Maffei Galaxy, as rival starships are not permitted to cross into another alliance's territory, and a starship was required for her protection. *Kadim* Tirol selected Commander Saar." Jurad waited to see if Jana knew he was talking about Galen Saar, not his son Varian. He must do all within his power to destroy all feelings this woman had for his bitter enemy, as his son Taemin had suggested. "Once Princess Shara Triloni met the illustrious Saar, treachery abounded. He bewitched her and she yielded to him while he was transporting her to become another man's wife. She was enchanted by him and rejected me. When he refused her hand in marriage, Shara struck out vengefully. You favor Shara a great deal, little Earthling. Like her, you surrendered to the Saar magic. I do not understand how Saar brought himself to possess you, from spite or lust."

Jana blushed profusely, then asked, "How does Ryker fit in to this puzzle?"

"Ryker and Shara are of the same royal bloodline, *Kadim* Maal's. Shara wanted to murder Varian that same day, but he was away on some glorious mission. Until all Saar blood is spilled, Ryker and Maal will continue their battle, as will I. If it weren't for the protection of Tirol, Saar would be dead this very moment. Rest assured, his defeat will come one day."

"If Ryker Triloni is an alien prince from the Androas Empire, how could he have bid on me? What would he hope to accomplish with my purchase?"

"Ryker Triloni is an Androas prince and heir to *Kadim* Maal Triloni's empire and personal estates, but he is also a Maffei citizen and ally. He owns a planetoid called Darkar which orbits Caguas. Like you, he is a chemist and research scientist. Many called Shara a witch because she knew and practiced ancient arts. Many claim she taught Ryker such powers. That is how Saar survived his treachery; he claimed she used magical potions on him.''

When the cunning Jurad refused to speak further on the matter, Jana excused herself. More shadows surrounded her. Varian had lied to her. No wonder Tirol felt an alien mate was beneath the man who had loved his daughter Amaya and no doubt would have married her. Truly the man was a clever deceiver. Perhaps this Galen was Varian's brother, one slain accidentally in his place. Now she could understand why Varian despised and mistrusted alien women. He must blame himself for those three deaths, just as Maal and Ryker and Jurad blamed him. More questions plagued Jana.

Had Varian loved Amaya, or only viewed her as a perfect mate? Why had he risked his life, career, and marriage for a brief affair with Shara? Did he have a weakness for alien women, for helpless females in his charge? Had Princess Shara been too beautiful and bewitching to resist? Had she drugged him into submission? Did he actually favor Shara? If not, why did people keep saying she did? After having his choice of two *kadims'* daughters, no doubt he felt an Earthling slave was beneath him.

Why then hadn't he allowed Jurad to buy her, to replace Shara, to end at least one bitter conflict? Had Varian feared Jurad would seek revenge on him by hurting her? It didn't make sense!

Before Draco returned, Moloch Shira cornered Jana. He lied sweetly, ''Don't be afraid, Jana, I won't hurt you or embarrass you again. I wanted to apologize.''

Jana gaped at him. ''Why are you telling me this now?''

''I wanted you to pass the word to Saar when he returns,'' he replied calmly.

''What? Why me? I hope I never see the vile beast again,'' she alleged coldly.

Moloch laughed. ''Saar doesn't often make errors, but he did in your case. Any fool can see he wants you, Jana. I fully expect him to correct it very soon.''

Provoked, Jana snapped, ''He'll be wasting his time and

energy! If you want to apologize to him and make peace, then do so yourself.''

Jana prayed Draco would return soon. She wanted to get out of this grisly situation. Before another day passed, she had to make certain Varian Saar could never get to her again. There was only one way.

Jana was too upset that night to carry out her daring plan to seduce Draco. The next day, back on Karnak, she was swimming in the large pool complete with rock islands and a small fountain, surrounded by lush greenery for privacy. When Draco came by to speak with her, Jana asked him to join her. He squatted near the pool edge and teased, ''I have more important matters to deal with than chasing sexy mermaids. You are becoming far too spoiled, my beautiful siren.''

''Really?'' Jana playfully retorted. ''You have only yourself to blame.'' She seized his shirt and pulled him into the pool, then hugged him fiercely.

''You are a mischievous vixen who needs lessons in respect.''

Jana adapted a heavy Southern accent and purred, ''Forgive me, sir. I felt so alone and miserable on this lovely morn that I forgot myself.'' She fluttered her lashes and smiled flirtatiously. ''You will join me, won't you, sir?''

Draco laughed as he stripped off his shoes and shirt. ''Indeed, I will, vixen.''

Jana hurriedly swam away as he came after her, a roguish gleam in his eye. She glided around several islands before he could catch her. ''Now, what do I have here? A slippery eel or a sultry siren?''

Jana kissed his nose and retorted, ''Neither, just a female who adores you.'' She kissed him on the lips, then quickly freed herself to swim off giggling. She climbed onto one of the flat islands and rested.

Draco joined her. He mused aloud, ''How do we get some wine and towels? Shall I order Darvellia to bring them, or fetch them myself?''

Jana laughed merrily ''Your housekeeper is always the perfect image of neatness. She will be angry if she wets her hair, crossing to the island. You'd best go for them, my love.''

''I was afraid you would say that.'' He dove in and swam to the steps.

311

While she waited for his return, Jana lay down and closed her eyes. She began to doze lightly and did not hear Draco's return. She aroused to a kiss, one unlike the affectionate pecks on previous days. This kiss was deep and long and sweet, and full of promise. Jana's arms instinctively encircled his neck and she responded to his lips. It was time for surrender.

Draco suddenly ended the kiss and pulled away from her. His gaze was filled with remorse and anger. "Not yet, Jana. It's too soon," he murmured raggedly. "I'm sorry I enticed you so rashly." Was he insane? This woman did not belong to him! He was simply her guardian. No, he legally owned her. But did he dare to refuse her return to Varian?

Jana was touched by his concern even as she sensed his desire for her. Why was it too soon if he ached for her and she was willing? She whispered tenderly, "It's all right, Draco. If you desire me, I am yours. If you but say the word, I will come to you without hesitation."

The look on his face perplexed her and his words confused her even more. "I can't take you, Jana. Please leave matters as they are," he stated sadly.

Was he afraid to touch her? Was he a timid virgin? No, he had been wed. A homosexual? No, he was too full of passion. "Is it me, Draco?"

"Don't cry, little flower. It isn't you; I swear it. There is something which must be settled before I can possess you," he commented mysteriously.

"What?" she inquired. Something to do with his deceased wife?

"I need time, Jana," was all he would say.

In bed that night, Jana mused on the pool episode. Something was troubling him deeply. She must be patient until he revealed the problem. At least one mystery was solved; Draco found her desirable and he wanted her, out of bed and in bed. She was safe from a sale, from Varian.

Far into that night, Draco sat at his desk and stared at Jana's bill of sale. Yes, there was something crucial which he must settle very soon. From now on, he must be careful not to ignite her passions. Clearly she was attracted to him, possibly even falling in love with him. Those conclusions alarmed him yet pleased him. Varian had seemingly betrayed her and in doing so had lost her love. If ever there was a prize worth risking all to obtain, Jana Greyson was it. Varian had been a fool to sell her, even with the promise Draco would resell her to Varian upon his return. True, Draco had agreed to hold her for his friend, but could he keep that promise? If he dared to refuse her sale to Varian, there was nothing Varian could do about it. The paper in his grasp was official. Varian wouldn't dare confess their illegal conduct at her auction. Varian could do nothing to prevent his retaining his exquisite mate.

Yet, Draco preferred to win Jana honestly and fairly. He couldn't betray his friend or his own word. If Varian were slain on this mission or by Ryker, Jana would be his without question. Or, if he could show Varian that he and Jana were in love, surely Varian would not demand her return. There was another facet to ponder: *Kadim* Tirol knew about the deal between Draco and Varian, and Tirol was his leader, friend, and Varian's grandfather. But if all went as Draco hoped, a bright future was before him and Jana.

Varian arrived on the planet Eire to confer with *Kadim* Tirol about Ryker's new treachery with the chemicals. "I have to stop him, Grandfather. No one is safe around me anymore."

"Can Tristan prove the contamination was intentional?"

"That's the problem, sir; there's no evidence we can use against him. But you and I know he's guilty. Considering the Milky Way Galaxy doesn't interest my evil half brother; killing me and gaining control of Maffei do inspire him. He's mad, Grandfather, dangerously insane. Perhaps I should resign from the Alliance Force and confront him as a private citizen. That way, you and the Alliance can't be held accountable for my actions."

"No, Varian!" Tirol protested sharply. "The Alliance needs you. Don't let him provoke you. Be patient and alert; he'll supply an opening."

Varian soon learned of other troubles. Baruch Tirana could not be found anywhere, and must be assumed dead. No clue or evidence had surfaced about the deaths of his two agents. How could they accuse Ryker without exposing that they planted the two spies in Trilabs? Nothing and no one could tie Ryker Triloni to any of the murders. Nor had any more Council secrets been leaked, allowing Canassia to still run free and wild. It seemed he could not get an edge on Ryker in any way.

Varian also discovered that Jurad had been frequently visiting the Maffei planets of Lynrac and Rigel, but Ryker couldn't be located anywhere. Nor could they obtain the crucial chemicals and laser gases they needed to replace the defective ones, because the combination of the vault on Darkar where they were stored existed solely in Ryker's head. Tirol cautioned Varian against rash accusations and behavior. First, it must be proven that Ryker had knowledge of the mission, and second that he had intentionally an illegally undermined it. Varian cursed Ryker's cunning, which always seemed to safeguard the snake.

"Let the Alliance search for Ryker while you take leave here. You must clear your wits and cool your temper. I will be notified the moment he is sighted anywhere. Until then, you can do nothing. According to the most recent reports, there is time to settle other pressing matters. Martella has been working with the Earthlings on Anais. As soon as the last group of them is delivered and settled, she is to return to Eire. She and I will work together to rewrite the *charl* laws. She has presented her case well. If the Council and Assembly concur, the *charls* will be given their freedom within a year. Those owners who desire marriage with their *charls* can do so; others can release their charges, and Martella will see to their adjustments where best suited."

Varian and Tirol exchanged guarded looks. *"Charls* will be free in a year?" His heart began to drum wildly. There were plans to be made. . . .

Tirol nodded, then smiled. "All *charls* will become Maffei citizens at their release. Of course, we'll send the *charls* whose owners refuse to marry them, or those who've been widowed and can't be purchased by another under the new laws, to join their fellow Earthlings on Anais. I'm sure there will also be some who will not wish to marry their Maffeian owners. We cannot coerce any marriages. Taking the alien women who don't marry Maffeian citizens to Anais will solve any problems which might arise for them and us. Too, it'll add to the Earthling population there."

Varian eyed Tirol curiously. "Something troubles you, old man," he said.

Tirol frowned and nodded. "Rumors about Draco and Jana," he hinted, then explained his knowledge of the brewing romance. "I suggest we take steps before this matter gets out of control. Jana will be as safe here with me as anywhere in the Universe. Perhaps it's time you stake your claim on the woman you love. It could favorably affect the proposed changes in the *charl* laws. Let it be known you love her and wish to marry her."

The evening of the gala party which Draco and Jana had planned for weeks had arrived. The time passed swiftly as final preparations were made and carried out by the servants. Jana leisurely bathed and dressed for the occasion. Her dress was very feminine, as were her lacy midnight-black stockings and high heels. The lines of her garment were simple yet elegant. It was black silk which clung to her body just enough to be alluring, but not overly suggestive. It matched Draco's ebony suit, which was trimmed in crimson braid, as was the zigzagged hem and neckline of her dress. They would make a striking pair tonight.

A maid wove braided crimson and black ribbons into the silvery blond curls atop Jana's head. Loose ends mingled with cascading ringlets which fell midway down her back. Jana worked until she had her makeup just right, innocence with a hint of allure. She scented herself with the heady perfume which Draco had given to her last week. Her sole jewels were black pearls in her pierced earlobes. She critically eyed her image in the tall mirror. Perfect, she decided. Tonight, she was ready and eager to face anything.

Varian stepped down from his shuttle and flexed his powerful body. His sapphire eyes sparkled with excitement and apprehension. He glanced down at his full-dress uniform in dove gray, a color which Jana loved on him. He checked the gold stripes, stars, and sunburst which proclaimed his lofty rank. The uniform fit him almost as snugly as a second skin, being only a notch or two above provocative immodesty. It did little to conceal the robust and manly physique beneath it, a stalwart frame which ignited lust in the women who gazed on him. Yet the only woman he wanted to seduce and inflame was Jana Greyson.

White teeth gleamed as he smiled to himself, contemplating Jana's surprise when he appeared unexpectedly at the party.

He could hardly wait to see her and his blood and loins flamed at the thought. His ebony hair fell casually in the windblown style which made him appear the dashing pirate straight from the sea which Jana had so often called him. That stubborn lock dangled over his temple as usual, but she liked it that way. He checked to make sure his black knee boots were shiny. For the first time in his life, he was nervous about seeing a woman and worried over his looks! He approached the front entrance, then hesitated only a moment for a deep breath before walking into Draco's home, to reclaim Jana.

Chapter Seventeen

Varian scanned the room with a deceptively placid gaze. Draco, as usual, was observing his habit of entering a room no more than one minute before the announced time for any occasion. Varian had timed his arrival perfectly, twenty minutes early. Other guests were already milling around, their laughter and conversation reaching his ears. He planned to head directly for Draco's suite to disclose his presence, but he halted momentarily to chat with an old friend.

It was at that exact instant that Jana chose to gaze out the secret peephole to see who had arrived and how things were progressing. As fate would have it, Varian had paused near the same wall and was facing it. Jana's eyes widened; her breath caught sharply. Within a few feet of her stood her heaven and hell. Her poise vanished instantly. How could she face him tonight, the very evening Varian Saar should be the farthest thing from her mind? The sight of him stirred repressed emotions to life. If possible, he looked more handsome and virile than ever.

Oh, Varian, she moaned in anguish, *why couldn't you have stayed away another day or two? Please don't make this night harder for me.*

Varian absently flashed a devastating smile at a woman guest, prodding her to anger. Jana stiffened her back and glared at her beloved tormentor, her chin lifted defiantly. Thank heavens she had seen him before entering the ballroom! By the time this party ended, Varian Saar and every guest present would know with whose heart her affections rested!

When she heard him say he was heading to see Draco to deliver some gifts, his voice vexingly warmed her very soul. She would give him a picture he would long remember! She hastily checked her appearance and crossed the hall to knock on Draco's side door. She was elated to see the door to the main hall half open. She mentally timed Varian's arrival as she pretended to adjust Draco's collar. She told him how handsome and suave he looked tonight, which was true.

To complete her ruse, she placed her arms around Draco's waist and leaned against him very intimately, just before she expected Varian to enter the room. She knew it was wrong to use her kind owner this way, but it was vital to sever all bonds to the man approaching the room. She murmured seductively, "You've made me the luckiest and happiest woman in the whole Universe, Draco. I don't know what I would do without you." She lifted her face to his and kissed him. As her mouth left his, she sighed contentedly and snuggled closer to his brawny body.

As Draco fondly embraced Jana and placed a grateful kiss on her cheek, his amber gaze fell on the stormy blue eyes and scowling face of Varian in his doorway. Draco read intense fury in those narrowed and hardened orbs. He tensed, wondering how to get out of this mess, for he knew how it must look. "Varian!" he called out, trying to sound casual. He gently released Jana from his arms and went forward to greet his friend. "When did you get back? I didn't expect your return so soon. This is quite a surprise."

Draco hastily decided this was too soon to press Varian for Jana's true ownership. Pondering his attempt and carrying it out while facing Varian weren't the same thing! Despite his own high rank on the Council, Varian wasn't a man to challenge.

"I can see it is," Varian scoffed, his tone icy.

Jana was baffled by their behavior. Varian was wearing a dark scowl; his blue eyes sent forth searing flames of fury. In fact, Varian's face was almost livid with rage. His towering body was tauter than the hide on a kettledrum. If looks could strike a person dead, Draco wouldn't be breathing! Was Varian indeed jealous and envious? How marvelous!

Jana's quizzical gaze shifted to Draco. She couldn't conceal her puzzlement at his strange conduct. He was jumpy, as if guilty of a terrible offense. Was he simply embarrassed that Varian had caught them in such an intimate embrace? Why? Varian had no claims on her. She found herself annoyed by her owner's attack of anxiety. Why should he dance attendance to this particular man, friend or not? She listened carefully for a clue.

Varian's eyes remained glued on Draco's face, ignoring Jana completely. "I presumed on our *good* friendship to arrive uninvited. I was sure you wouldn't mind."

"Of course not. You're welcome in my home anytime. Your mission is over?"

"No, there were several problems. We had to return to correct them. I'll be heading out again in a week or so." As he spoke this time, his sapphire gaze settled on Jana's seemingly unruffled poise. "I came by to deliver a gift for you, and one for Jana." He handed Draco a long, slender case.

Draco promptly opened it as he struggled to master his warring emotions. It was a hunting knife with a silver blade and agatized-wood handle. "It's magnificent. Look at the handle, Jana."

She took the knife and glanced at it. She sighed and remarked, "Yes, it's very nice. I'm sure you'll enjoy it. If you two will excuse me, I need to finish dressing for our party." She handed the knife back to Draco and started to leave.

"I have a gift for you, too, Jana," Varian reminded her, grasping her elbow.

Jana accepted the box with a polite "thank you," then tossed it on the bed to leave. "I'll join you shortly, Draco." She carefully avoided Varian's gaze.

"Aren't you going to open your present?" Varian demanded.

"Later, if you don't mind. I must see to my grooming and our guests."

"I do mind," he replied in a voice like tempered steel. "Have you forgotten your manners in such a short time? Is Karnak a bad influence on you?"

Jana bristled at Varian's stinging barb and Draco's lack of defense. Her eyes glared at Varian first, then at Draco. To end

318

the matter, she seized the box and opened it. It was a beautiful ebony gem in the shape of a heart suspended on a gold chain. She lifted fiery eyes to Varian's probing stare. "You're giving me an extravagant black heart?" She snapped the lid shut.

Varian realized his gift carried an offensive meaning for her. When Draco asked her to wear it tonight, she glared at Varian and shook her head. Draco insisted, telling her it would be perfect with her dress. He commented that Varian couldn't have chosen better if he had known what she was wearing.

"I've dressed very carefully tonight, Draco. Expensive jewelry would detract from the simplicity of my gown." Jana was surprised when Varian took her side about the necklace. But his taunting gibe rankled her.

He looked her up and down, then smiled. "You could use a little distraction tonight. You don't want your owner having to battle over you," he teased, suddenly calmed. "I'm sorry if the gift displeases you, Jana."

"You always did have a cunning flair for back-door compliments, but I no longer require your approval of my wardrobe. Nor do I care for your snide remarks about my safety and virtue."

Varian grinned wickedly. To throw him off balance, she shrugged and remarked, "Why not wear it? It is very beautiful. Would you help me?" she asked Draco, handing the necklace to him and presenting her back.

Varian took it from his friend's grasp and secured it around her neck. He turned her around and boldly nestled the heart just above the swell of her breasts. His fingers lightly brushed over her flesh, then her lips. "Exquisite. But I knew you would be. Anger causes lines on the face, moonbeam. Drop it."

Jana stared at him. How dare he talk and act like a moonstruck Romeo before her owner! How dare he give her a romantic token, a lovely heart, even if it was as black as his! Multicolored eyes clashed with blue ones. Jana easily broke the hold of his powerful gaze, visibly surprising him. She was concerned over Varian's amorous tone, more so over Draco's allowing it. He acted as if nothing unusual was transpiring so Jana hastily excused herself.

Varian waited until the door closed behind her, then turned to face Draco. "You have some explaining to do. From the reports I've been receiving for the last two days, you're playing your fake role of mate too convincingly. You have everyone believing you're in love with her. Have you forgotten who owns Jana?''

Draco sighed heavily. "You're right, Varian. I did get caught up in our little charade. I haven't been this happy since my wife was killed. Jana makes me feel alive—even whole again. Jana has a way of relaxing and enchanting a man. Please don't make any rash moves. Karnak is where Jana Greyson belongs. She loves it here, and she loves me. You're out of her life now; leave it that way. Don't hurt her again.''

Varian drilled his gaze into Draco's. "Are you in love with her?'' he asked.

"I could be soon. We're happy together, Varian. Let me buy her. You're a starship commander, an adventurer, a man who can have his choice of women. You've got too many enemies seeking you to lay claim to Jana. Your sale cut her to the soul, since she didn't know it was a ruse. She's cast you out of her heart, and turned to me. Don't devastate her for a third time: first on Earth and then on Rigel. Let her go, Varian.''

"Damn you, Draco! I thought I could trust you. Jana is mine. I love her! I would never sell her. Not to you or any man. She's leaving with me tonight.''

Draco was stunned by that announcement. "You can't take her away!''

"Like hell, I can't,'' Varian replied. "I own Jana Greyson. At least I will as soon as you release her to me. Get that document and sign it. Now!''

"I meant take her on your mission; you're heading to Earth, remember? What happens to her after you leave? She's begun a new life here. She's happy.''

"I've made plans for her safety. She's going to Grandfather's with me.''

"Do you realize what you're doing? Jana doesn't know about our deceit. You plan to drop another lie in her lap, then take off for weeks, maybe months? First you sell her and take off, then I reject her and sell her back to you? That's cruel.''

"Trying to lure her away from me is cruel, old friend,'' Varian charged.

Draco asserted defensively, "It's not like that. I feel deeply about her. I'll explain what's happened since you left.'' Afterward, Draco confessed ruefully, "I never intended to become

320

attached to Jana. She fits into my life perfectly. If I desired, I could claim legal ownership of her; my name and your seal are on her sale papers. But I wouldn't do that. I am your friend, Varian, despite your nasty charges. I'm sorry you feel you must take her away from Karnak. You'll regret it," he warned. "She doesn't love you; I doubt she ever did. Why don't you ask her about her feelings? If you care about her, for once do what's best for Jana."

Varian was pensive for long minutes. "I'll go see her right now. If you're right, Jana can remain here, permanently. If you're wrong, she leaves with me."

"Agreed," Draco replied. "She's really changed you, old boy. She would be good for you. But I think you've destroyed any hopes of a life with her."

Varian went to Jana's suite and locked the door after his entrance. Jana turned and watched his predatory approach. She began to back away from him. "Get out of my room," she warned him. "You're pushing your friendship too far."

"Draco knows I'm here, moonbeam. He wants me to question you about your feelings . . . for both of us. Could we sit down and discuss this calmly?"

"You can't be serious! What are you trying to do, Varian Saar? Are you hoping Draco will break down the door and find us in a . . . a compromising situation? Are you trying to spoil my life again? You're a cruel man." Jana glared at him accusingly. "I won't let you do this to me. Get out!"

Varian grabbed her and pinned her beneath him on the bed. "You will listen, and you will answer me truthfully, woman. Which of us do you want to live with, Jana? Whoever you select, your decision is final."

His startling question caught her unprepared to feign deception. Alarmed, Jana tried to twist out of his embrace and away from him. "Don't do this, please. I'm happy here. Draco loves me and wants me. Don't make him doubt me. This joke will cause trouble for all of us." Suspicion flooded her mind. Was Draco testing her emotions before—

"How do you feel about him?" he demanded sternly.

"I want to stay here," she stated distinctly, fusing her gaze to his.

Varian's mouth swiftly claimed hers and greedily parted her lips. She felt the heavy, rapid pounding of his heart and noted his erratic breathing. His body was fiery and tense, and his control was severely strained. He was disturbed, highly aroused, by her contact! She could see, hear, and feel the evidence of his hunger for her. He was kissing her as if trying to devour her!

Jana's control was sorely tested but she vowed not to weaken. When his lips began to tease over her face and throat, she said, sneering, "What's the matter, Rogue Saar? Do you miss your helpless victim? Did I spoil you for other women?" Jana felt her desire mounting treacherously.

Varian leaned back and replied, "Yes, moonbeam, I'm afraid you did. Now you'll have to pay heavily for your bewitchment by returning to me."

"Never," she vowed. "You should have examined your feelings months ago. I can think of nothing worse than returning to your web, space pirate."

"Can I ask you a foolish question?" he inquired, then chuckled.

"Do you know any other kind, Rogue Saar?" Jana saucily retorted.

He laughed. "Are you in love with your owner, or falling in love with him?"

"Is that against some *charl* law? I surely hope not. It's too late now."

"I take it that means 'yes'?" he pressed angrily.

"Take it any way you damn well please," she purred sultrily.

"What I please to take . . . is you, woman. And I will. You're leaving here with me tonight, one way or another," he threatened.

"You wouldn't dare abduct me again! This time, it would be a crime."

"Not if I'm your owner," he responded, smiling roguishly.

"Draco would never sell me! Certainly not to you!" she shouted.

"You think you know him so well, moonbeam?" he mocked her.

"Perhaps better than you do. I think it's time you halt this joke before you damage your friendship with Draco. Let me up, Varian, now."

"I demand honest answers, Jana, then perhaps you can join the party."

322

"To hell with your demands!" she snapped at him. Then, perceiving his resolve, she gritted her teeth and alleged, "All right, Rogue Saar. I am more than happy here. I am satisfied with my owner and my life. Why shouldn't I be happy? Draco and I are expecting a child," she blurted out a bold lie to discourage him further. Jana was too unsettled to recall she had been with Draco only three weeks, for it seemed so much longer.

Varian was stunned. He, too, forgot the shortness of their separation. "Draco would never touch you, much less impregnate you," he refuted. His expression altered immediately. His eyes sparkled as he boasted, "The child is mine, Jana, mine."

"That's impossible, Commander Saar. I haven't slept in your bed for weeks. Draco would never sell the woman carrying his heir!"

"Draco is impotent, Jana love. He can't make love to you or any woman. Don't play games with me. If you're somehow pregnant, it's mine."

"He's . . . what?" she asked in shock, then allowed those words to settle in and explain their separate rooms and beds. Compassion for Draco filled her as she berated herself for trying to pressure him into seducing her. He must have been both embarrassed and tormented. Why hadn't she left matters alone?

"He can never inflame your passions or sate them, moonbeam. Even if he could, it would never be like it is between us. Remember the two weeks we shared?"

Tears burned her eyes. "Is that why he's willing to turn me over to you again? Does he think sex is more important to me than he is? It isn't. Did you convince him I would be repulsed or disappointed by his problem? Did you tell him I was so hot-blooded I would sneak around with his male servants?"

Varian eyed her strangely. "Are you saying you love him?" he pressed.

"Yes, Commander Saar, I love him," she vowed. What did it matter if she meant a different kind of love? She couldn't allow Varian to rip her world apart. No doubt he would tire of her, then sell her to another man who wasn't as safe and gentle as Draco. Varian merely enjoyed having a helpless woman at his beck and call, one to cater to his whims. No affair with him was worth this sacrifice. "Are you so selfishly vindictive that you would ruin two lives to sate your lust for me? Please go and leave us alone. What must I say or do to end your wicked hatred for me? You know I can't hold your eye or appease your enormous craving for long. One female is not enough for you. Soon, you'd be tossing me aside again. Don't trick Draco into selling me. If you have any compassion, you won't do this to us.''

''What if I want you more than my friendship with Draco?'' he asked, his hand caressing her flushed cheek.

''It's too late, Varian. I could never love you, or desire you, or trust you, or forgive you. Never,'' she stressed dishonestly. ''Let it go, please.''

''I wish I could tell if you're lying to me, or to yourself. Before you answer again, Jana, I should explain. I did not sell you to Draco. He stood in for me at your auction. I couldn't bid on you without letting men like Jurad and Moloch know how much I wanted you. You are mine today, just like all the days since I captured you. I paid for you, moonbeam. I convinced Draco to pretend he was buying you. Draco has no claim over you; he never has. He was to be your guardian, nothing more. He was to keep you safe from my enemies until I could return for you. We couldn't tell you it was a trick and risk you behaving incorrectly. For others to believe I was selling you, you had to believe it. I'm sorry for putting you through such anguish. That's why you spent that last night with me; you were and are mine. No woman has claimed me more than you, moonbeam. I warned you not to enchant me, but you didn't listen or obey. Did you honestly think I would sell my most precious gem?''

''Everyone knows you did,'' she protested, her heart racing. This couldn't be happening! He was lying! Jana recalled the bank voucher, when Draco had said it was too dangerous to carry that much money on him. She should have known her next-day delivery was suspicious. She should have guessed something was wrong from Draco's sexual aloofness.

''Everyone was supposed to think I sold you. Just a few men know the truth: Draco, Nigel, Tristan, Brec, and Tirol. But I had to make it appear you held no interest for me; your auction accomplished that. I had every one of those bidders watched, so I knew how much your purchase would require. Legally you're mine, though I wish things hadn't gotten out of hand with Draco. I came home early, Jana, and I didn't like the rumors I was hearing about you and Draco. It seems he got carried away with this little charade. It's over, and you're leaving with me tonight. This time, you'll stay under Tirol's custody. That should keep you out of new mischief.''

All of those times when he had looked as if he wanted or needed to say something. But this explanation was crazy! ''I don't believe you or this wild story. Why send me to Tirol's? Why would I be safer there than here with Draco? Why would you go to such trouble to keep a *charl* who detests you?''

Her last remark altered Varian's response. He lied to mislead her, ''Because you haven't sated my curiosity yet. As long as you're entertaining and pleasing, I plan to keep you around. You should be flattered, Jana; no woman has held my interest half as long as you have. I enjoy you, in my bed and out. I plan to keep you as my mistress until I tire of you. So you see, it's up to you to hold my attention and to keep me contented. If you've become overly attached to Draco, I'm sorry. I didn't intend for him to deceive you. But I do understand how it happened. I'm familiar with your allure. As for the heart necklace, I'm sorry again. I have this bad habit of not knowing what to give you. And stars forsake me if bad habits aren't hard to break.''

''Don't you think it's dangerous to expose your lingering hunger for me? What happens to me and Tirol if one of your enemies attacks his home while you're gone? Why can't I remain here, if I promise to stay out of mischief with Draco?'' she said to test him.

''That wouldn't be a good idea for either of you. You're far too tempting to my friend. Besides, Tirol has excellent security precautions. He has had that for many years now,'' Varian stated coldly, pain shining briefly in his blue eyes.

Jana wisely let that statement pass. ''What if Tirol doesn't want me to stay in his home?'' she asked, playing out his game; for surely it was only a spiteful game to test her feelings.

''He suggested it. He doesn't want me worrying over my property while I'm away on a dangerous assignment. Actually, he finds you as enjoyable as I do. Nearly as enjoyable,'' he jested mirthfully, then nibbled on her neck.

''Stop it, Varian Saar. You don't think I fell for this mean joke of yours!''

Varian grinned, then casually inquired, ''You were teasing

325

about a baby? I do take precautions against such undesirable accidents, so I might be suspicious.''

"You've never—'' Jana halted her argument, then blushed.

Rumbling laughter filled the room. "I take injections every three months, and I assure you I haven't missed a single one since I came of age.'' When Jana turned a darker red, he smiled and kissed each fiery cheek. "I was wrong; you haven't changed much. Is there something I should know?'' he teased, patting her flat abdomen, then playfully cuffing her chin.

"You think you're so damn charming,'' she said at his smug expression. "Get off me, you lecherous beast, before Draco comes looking for us.''

"I suggest we head for the shuttle by the private entrance. I can send for your clothes and possessions later. Up, woman, we have lots of energy to spend.''

"If you think to trick me into appearing as if I'm trying to run off with you, it won't work. And I left the gawdy clothes you purchased on your ship!''

"I also purchased every item you have here,'' Varian told her. "I had them ordered and delivered before we arrived on Rigel for your auction. I suspected you wouldn't want to use those worn during our travels. I hope you found my choices agreeable, particularly this dress tonight. You see, moonbeam, I do know you fairly well. I have made some mistakes where you're concerned, but not many,'' he boasted cockily, then grinned at her surprise. "With your cooperation, I won't make anymore errors,'' he remarked.

"I won't leave here with you, Varian Saar,'' she informed him stubbornly.

Varian pulled an airosyringe from his pocket. "I figured as much,'' he stated in that same lazy tone. "I guess I'll have to use this on you. Tell me, Dr. Greyson, do you know that alien truth serum reacts violently to lies or defiance? Our truth drug prevents any dishonesty. Privacy is a special thing, moonbeam, and I hate to invade yours. I'll ask you once more; are you carrying my child?''

Jana's alarmed gaze went from his determined expression to the instrument in his grasp, then shifted back to his entreating eyes. Even if the timing wasn't wrong, he knew Draco was impotent, so continuing that ruse was futile. "No,'' she replied tersely.

"Do you love Draco, and do you want to remain here with him?" he asked, waving the intimidating weapon before her pale face.

If Varian wasn't lying about his hold over her, that would explain the strange episode in Draco's room. "Yes, I love him." When Varian narrowed his gaze ominously, she added, "Like a brother or best friend. Why did you have to come back and spoil things for us? Why can't you release me?"

"Do you desire me? Do you want to leave with me?" he queried insistently.

Jana went red with guilt. She pulled her revealing gaze from his. "I'm waiting, moonbeam. Do you desire me? Do you remember how it was between us?" He touched her arm with the tip of the instrument. "The truth, Jana."

Jana glared at him. The whole affair about *charls* seemed unreal, as did alien captivity. It seemed more like she had been a guest here at Draco's following a lover's quarrel with Varian! It was as if he had come after her, to win her back. The gravity and repercussions of truth and reality faded during her confusion. She knew he would keep his word, either way. "Yes, I still find you attractive and exciting. I haven't forgotten what it was like to sleep with you or to be at your side! But I'm wrong for you, Varian."

"You missed me, didn't you?" he persisted, seemingly without feeling. He tapped the cold metal object on her nose, then her chin. "Didn't you?"

Jana closed her eyes and replied, "Yes, damn you, I missed you."

When she opened them, she glowered at Varian. "I won't forgive you for what you've done to me. It can't ever be like it was before, don't you understand that? When you abducted me, I was an innocent girl who was terrified and disarmed by a cunning captor. It isn't like that now. I'm not gullible and naïve anymore; I'm not mesmerized by you. I'm not petrified by this new fate. Do you think it matters to me if you didn't actually go through with my sale? As far as I knew, you did. And I despise you for it. In fact, I despise you more because it was only a vile trick to get your way. If you think I'll become your willing slave again, you're wrong. I've seen what my existence can be like without you in it, and that's what I want. I swear to you, Varian Saar, I want to live here on Karnak with Draco."

When Varian pressed the airosyringe to her arm and emptied it, she screamed at him, ''You filthy, devious bastard! I'm telling you the truth!''

Varian's eyes chilled, as did his voice when he responded, ''I know, Jana. Curse you, woman, I do believe you! It's only a sedative. Our truth serum could be lethal to your alien system, so I couldn't risk using it, moonbeam. You see, Draco insisted you choose me over him before releasing you peaceably. According to this tape, you just did,'' He announced nonchalantly, then held up a miniature recorder. ''Of course, I only recorded those statements which suit my purpose. I'll see you when you wake up, in my quarters.''

''Damn you! He won't believe that tape. He'll know you forced me to say such things! He won't let you take me away! Damn you, Varian Sa—'' The last thing Jana saw before yielding to the sedative was Varian's victorious grin.

Jana stretched, yawned, then opened her eyes. She was curled on her left side, facing a strange wall. She rolled onto her back, then sat up on the bed. She focused her gaze and scanned the unfamiliar setting. She searched her memory for clues to this mystery. She was clad in a teal-blue satin nightgown which she had never seen before. Her tawny hair was brushed free of its curls and ringlets. She was alone, and afraid.

Jana recalled her confrontation with Varian last night. Where was she? She stood up and hurried to a window. The scenery before her revealed her location: the mansion of *Kadim* Tirol Trygue on the planet Eire! How long had she been kept drugged? Had Varian dropped her off and continued his mission? Varian owned her. . . . He had purchased her at the auction. . . .

When the door behind her opened, Jana whirled to see if her fears were justified; they were. She glanced around for a concealing robe; there was none. Varian strolled forward, his blue eyes warming as they eased over Jana's rosy face and partially exposed figure. He halted beside her and nonchalantly leaned against the panel between the windows. His sole garment was a pair of royal-blue swim trunks.

Jana wished his immense charms weren't so boldly displayed

before her troubled senses. She quickly pulled her appreciative gaze from his hard chest and shoulders. To remain so firm and supple, he would have to work out every day, and despite the time he spent on board a ship, his entire body was richly and deeply tanned. His ivory teeth and sensual lips gave him such a sense-stunning smile. Straying locks of sable hair teased the edges of his face.

"So it wasn't a bad dream. You carried out your threat to steal me from Draco. What happens when he learns you tricked him? How would you feel if someone taped your words and used them against you? How could you humiliate all of us like this?"

"Humiliate?" He echoed the word. "How so, moonbeam?"

"You don't think it's degrading to be passed between two men? You said the choice was mine. You said that syringe contained truth serum. You said you owned me. You lied. I told you I wanted to stay on Karnak with Draco."

"I said I would leave you there if you loved him; you don't. When I returned to the party and announced I had purchased you from Draco, no one thought it was strange. Surprising, but not inexplicable. I simply told everyone present that I had missed you and wanted you back. Who could argue when you're so perfectly suited to me? Everyone's had the chance to observe you; your value and appeal can't be denied." Varian watched the effect of his words on Jana. She was shocked.

Varian went on, "Draco told everyone that I wanted you back at any cost. Being my good friend, he couldn't refuse me. Besides, we told everyone that you were so glad to see me again, you chose me over Draco. Since he and I are so bewitched by you, naturally we yielded to your pleas. Actually," he added, "Draco told them you're madly in love with me and you were willing to return as my mistress just to share a part of my life."

"You wouldn't dare! He didn't!" she shrieked in outrage. "No one in his right mind would believe such trash! How did you two explain away Draco's feelings for me? I did understand you to say this charade was a secret?"

"We made no attempt to deny your or his deep affection for one another. We let it stand as is, brother to sister and vice versa. Best friends. It helps that Draco's old flame returned to

Karnak the same day, a recent widow. Right at this moment, those two probably are nestled in his home talking marriage. So you see, moonbeam, all the pieces fit together very nicely."

"What about the amorous behavior everyone has been witnessing between us these past weeks?"

"As far as people think, you and Draco gave your relationship its best shot. It didn't work; you two didn't fall in love. Because you were secretly in love with me and he was still pining for Twyla," he jested. "When she returned wanting him, and I returned for you, it all came together as it should."

"This is crazy. I can understand them accepting the tale about Draco and this Twyla, but you and me? Exactly what am I supposed to have cost you?"

He chuckled at that question. "Ten million. After all, he did deserve compensation for all the time and money he supposedly spent on you. Eight is my lucky number and I paid your sale price, not Draco."

"Just how does a starship commander come up with so much money?" she demanded sarcastically. "Your story is full of holes, Rogue Saar."

Varian laughed heartily. "Evidently no one has told you how wealthy I am. Every *katooga* for your tutors, support, and desires came from me."

"May I be so bold as to ask just how rich you are?" she asked, sneering.

"I rank in the top seven . . . in this galaxy. Why be modest?" he hinted merrily. "I'm tied for number five. Tirol is number two. One, three, and four are married. *Avatar* Faeroe of Caguas ranks at six, and Councilman Garthon at seven. What else would you care to ask about your owner? And I am your owner now, Jana, not captor. I purchased you, so you're my *charl*."

Jana stared at Varian, stunned at his imposing status. She must have seemed like a pauper to him! Garthon, Canissia's father, was a rich and powerful man whose daughter would inherit that enormous wealth and station. What was Canissia to Varian? At a loss for a suitable response to conceal her alarm and astonishment, she asked, "Who's tied with you at number five?"

Varian's eyes went as cold as arctic water. The muscle in his jawline twitched. "The owner of Trilabs and the planetoid

Darkar, a scientist and chemist named Ryker Triloni.'' As he shifted his weight to lean his back against the wall, he missed Jana's reaction.

Jana walked to the bed, an action which presented her back to Varian and hid her expression until she could mask her consternation. There was that name again: Ryker Triloni. Was he Shara's brother or cousin? Indeed, that scientist's wealth made him a powerful enemy. Jana dared not dwell on the subject which bred such hatred. She would find another way to unravel that mystery. She sat on the bed and looked at the man before her.

"When do you leave on your mission?" Jana inquired.

"Eager to get rid of me so soon after our reunion?" he retorted.

"I didn't mean it to sound that way. I was wondering what our schedule will be and how I'm supposed to behave, now that it's common knowledge I'm your prisoner again." She jumped up to pace nervously. "How does a love-smitten slave act, Commander Saar?"

"From the gossip about you and Draco, I'd say you're a superb actress in that area," he snarled, provoked by her snide query.

Jana said rashly, "It was easy! Draco was a superb actor and teacher."

Varian straightened and surged forward. Jana bounded across the bed. Varian halted his pursuit. He could see Jana needed time and a gentle hand to help her work through her anger and suspicions. He had to consider her feelings. "Come here, Jana," he ordered sternly.

When she didn't move or speak, Varian informed her, "You aren't my slave or my prisoner, you're my *charl*. Draco never owned you. I don't want you playing a phony role with me as you did with him. I was perfectly satisfied with your behavior during those two weeks we shared. You know what kind of man I am, Jana, and the kind of life I enjoy. If you can forget your resentment and conduct yourself like before, I see no reason why our arrangement can't last a very long time, become a permanent relationship. You are legally my mate."

Jana couldn't believe she was hearing him correctly. "You can't be serious?" When he nodded, she licked her dry lips. "Isn't that a bit confining for a man with your flair for life and taste for multiple liaisons? Do you intend to set me up someplace, to visit when the mood strikes you?'' she asked contemptuously.

"Unless I'm on a dangerous assignment, rules or no rules against it, you'll stay with me on my ship. When I'm on leave, which is frequent, we'll stay at my home on Altair. It's a private planetoid like Karnak, only prettier and larger. You'll love it. When I'm gone, you'll remain here with my . . . friend Tirol.'' He waited to see if she displayed any knowledge of Tirol's relation to him. He thought it wise to keep his powerful connection out of this conversation.

"Isn't that asking an awful lot from your friends? To baby-sit your mistress? What if he has to leave on business or for pleasure? He's a very important man. This doesn't make sense. It must be another ruse. Am I a prisoner here?''

"You'll be safe here, with or without Tirol. But I would imagine he'll take you with him wherever he travels. I told you, he likes you and enjoys your company. You've always under-rated yourself, Jana. I find you irresistible and irreplaceable. Our time together was refreshing. It presented me with many advantages. Contrary to popular belief, Jana, it's exhausting to live up to the role of intergalactic playboy and matchless lover. You never made any demands on me; you behaved as if all you wanted was me, not my wealth or status or power. You're good company, Jana Greyson. And you're beautiful and passionate. You're like many women rolled together. You know how to behave in all situations, public and private. Owning you makes my life simpler and happier. With you around, no female will pursue me. Who would want to compete with you for atten-tion?'' His blue gaze slipped over her.

Jana became more and more confused. Varian had paid over eight million *katoogas* to insure her safety at Draco's, then ignored the expense to reclaim her. Was he really afraid she would fall in love with Draco and forget him? Dare she hope that Varian cared for her more than he admitted?

"All right, Rogue Saar, I'll try to do things your way. What time is it? I'm famished.''

Laughter filled the quiet room. "Something tells me you don't have the same food in mind that I do.'' He extended his hand and asked, "How about breakfast on the terrace? Then we can take a swim.''

When Jana stepped around the wide bed and placed her hand in his, he pulled her into his embrace and kissed her. As their lips met, Varian warned himself she might need time to forgive him and to accept this new relationship. He reluctantly released her. "I want you very much, Jana, but I won't pressure you with demands this soon. Your belongings are in there," he informed her, pointing toward a closet.

"I am famished, but not for breakfast." Jana could refuse him no longer and she witnessed the astonishment on his face as she released the straps and allowed her gown to slide to the floor and cover their bare feet. "Well? Does the slave feed the master? Or will the master generously feed his starving slave? It's your move."

Varian lifted one brow devilishly and chuckled. "It seems to me I've heard that statement before. Perhaps the day you beat me in *Laius?* I must confess, Jana Greyson, you do make life exciting. Heavens around me, it's good to have you back. Yes, I made the right move again."

"So, you did lose that game intentionally. I suspected as much. You led me right into our cunning trap while playing the innocent prey. Alas, Sir Demon," she drawled sexily, "I shall never be a match for your wiles."

"Are you kidding me, moonbeam? We're perfectly matched in many ways."

"I hope you believe that and remember it a long, long time."

They were standing only inches apart, close enough to touch without moving. Fires danced in blue eyes; flames sparked in beryl ones. He smiled; she returned it. As if magically transformed into hands, their gazes roamed each other with stirring caresses. As if by cue, both closed the distance between them, her hands going to his chest and his to her shoulders. Their faces touched and nuzzled for a minute or two, reveling in their first contact and drawing out the moment. His lips brushed over her face, hair, and throat as she swayed her nude body against him.

Varian's mouth gradually made its way to Jana's, then hungrily claimed it. His darting tongue was met and joined by hers. Her arms lifted and encircled his neck as he drew her tighter against him. He lifted her and placed her on the bed, then quickly pulled off his swim trunks and joined her. As lips and bodies fused, an urgency consumed them to make love wildly and savagely. Weeks of hunger and anguish needed rapid appeasement.

Afterward, they lay entwined without speaking, only touching and feeling. They kissed, caressed, and aroused fiery desires again. This time they relished every instant and movement, prolonging their pleasures until passion's blaze engulfed and consumed them. The agonizing weeks of denial and loneliness vanished. They were together again, and nothing else mattered.

As Jana lay curled against Varian, her fingers toyed with the damp hair on his muscled chest. It was always so tranquil in his arms after making love.

For the next two hours, at Varian's suggestion, Jana related her days on Karnak. When she encouraged him to talk about himself and his lengthy absence, he grinned ruefully and told her he couldn't, not on this furlough. Jana teased, ''I see, you want to remain a deep and dark mystery.'' When he laughed, she asserted gravely, ''I know so little about you, Varian Saar.''

''Then why didn't you bombard Draco with questions about me?'' he jested.

Jana rolled onto her back, then to the side of the bed, and started to rise. ''I'll take a bath, then join you downstairs.''

''Jana?'' he called to her, gently capturing her wrist.

''Please, Varian, not right now,'' she entreated raggedly. ''I'll be down soon.''

Varian released his grip without forcing her to turn around or explain her sudden sadness. He wondered if it was her lack of knowledge about him and his reluctance to enlighten her which had inspired her mood change, or was it something she had learned about him during his absence. . . .

''Hear me well, Captain Koch,'' Prince Taemin warned, ''I want Jana Greyson. Get her any way you can, and without witnesses. If Commander Saar interferes, bring him to me if you can take him alive. If not . . .'' He shrugged indifferently. ''Just make certain you do not mention me or lead any Alliance officer here. Jana is not to be touched, understand?''

Captain Koch grinned and nodded. ''You have nothing to worry about, Prince Taemin. I will seize her for you. I almost hope Saar does try to stop us because we have an old score to settle. He's confiscated several of my ships, and he's been after my skin for years.''

"If you can bring me Saar alive and without anyone's knowledge, I'll double my offer of payment and you can have him after he answers a few questions for me.'' Taemin wanted to know about those Star Fleet covert voyages before he made his false alliance with Ryker Triloni. Canissia should be reporting to him very soon about those curious assignments, just as soon as she could risk a trip in this direction. Then again, Jana should have all the facts he needed. That little creature was an excellent deceiver; she had fooled him completely that day on Lynrac. Clearly she and Saar were a team, an intimate and clever team! Saar had returned for her, just as he had suspected.

Ryker was staring into Moloch Shira's eyes as the hireling delivered his news. Varian was alive and back! Had something gone wrong, or had Varian discovered the chemicals were tainted before using them? No matter, Varian could not prove any charges against him. But it would alert his half brother to his daring attempt on his life. Varian would be more alert and suspicious than ever. Rages of fate! He must resort to patience and caution again. Why had Varian purchased Jana Greyson immediately after his unexpected return?

Moloch related his observation and conclusions. "I'll tell you now, Ryker, something crazy is going on between those two. Varian arrived grinning and swaggering around, then headed to speak privately with Councilman Procyon. In less than an hour, Draco appeared acting tense and looking sad. Then Varian hung around for a couple of hours trying to behave as if he had just won the greatest prize of all time, even though he seemed angry about something. Rumor said Varian paid Draco ten million for Jana. We both know money means nothing to either of them. Varian actually bought her as his mate! I think he more than craves her in his bed. I think he's in love with this alien beauty.''

"Then why did he sell her to another man?" Ryker said, probing for more clues.

"I'm not so sure he did, not to become Draco's mate anyway. I think Draco purchased Jana to hold for Varian. I wouldn't even be surprised if Varian put up the money. If I had to venture a guess on Jana's return to Varian the other night, I would surmise that Draco and Jana were getting too close to suit Varian. He's taken her to his grandfather's home on Eire.''

"What about Jana Greyson? How did she behave?''

"That's another strange part; she never showed up that night. If I had to make another guess, I'd say she didn't like being returned to Varian. I've been keeping up with her closely, and I think she hates him. This woman is different, Ryker. She's smart and spunky. Varian might have been using her against you for some reason, but he overlooked a few angles. She's not a woman to take betrayal and degradation, and nothing would be more degrading to you than being sold by the man who pretended to love you. I doubt he planned to fall in love with a captive mate, and I doubt he realized just how perfect she is for you. You should have bought her, Ryker.''

After Moloch departed, Ryker gave this staggering turn of events deep thought. True, he would need a mate and heirs. True, Jana Greyson would have been perfect for that role, if she hadn't become Varian's whore! Now he had no use for Jana, unless it was to lure Varian into a death trap. But first there was another path to try, a path which would grant him a weapon to hold over Taemin's head. Like Canissia, that smug prince could not be trusted.

Canissia paced the elegant quarters on her ship, *Moonwind*. Her rage had been building for days. She had refused to see anyone, including the anxious Zan. Varian had taken a mate, putting him out of her reach as long as his mate lived! How dare he humiliate her by choosing an alien slut over the daughter of a supreme councilman! He would pay heavily for spurning her! And that alien bitch would pay dearly for bewitching Varian Saar!

She realized the other Council members and Varian were suspicious of her. That explained why her father had been kept in the dark on so many matters lately. If they were trying to entrap her, she could not trust any of the information given to her father to be accurate! No doubt they had passed along crafty lies to bait their snare for her. She would fool them all and take no risks! Right after she related all she knew about Varian's covert missions to the Milky Way Galaxy; first to Ryker, and then to Prince Taemin. One of them must acquire the Maffei Alliance and marry her!

Chapter Eighteen

By the third day, Jana realized she was sharing the existence of a very different Varian Saar. Their relationship was so fulfilling that it frightened her. He revealed no reservations about their new arrangement. His spirits were high and genial, most of the time. He joked with her or Tirol or the servants. He seemed at home here. The bond between Varian and the *Kadim* was strong, and it warmed Jana to see that he could display such deep affection. Jana was pleased by the changes in his personality.

Varian was playfully possessive, teasing her and keeping her with him day and night. He was gentle and thoughtful, never speaking crossly or lording his power over her; as if he were her slave, he would help her dress or bathe or would fetch her refreshments. And he was highly passionate, acting as if he couldn't get enough of her company and lovemaking. On a rare and brief occasion, he did appear slightly distracted or worried, but never appeared bored with her or anxious to depart. He was careful not to mention Draco, which would have refreshed the memory of that terrifying and humiliating auction, and spoiled their passionate reunion. He didn't want her thinking he had the power and rank to change the *charl* laws at this dangerous time, so he continued to be silent about his relationship to Tirol Trygue. And he made sure no one dropped a clue.

Jana found herself loving him and submitting to him with wild and uninhibited abandon. She experienced glimmers of hope for a lasting relationship. When she appeared to relax totally with him, he seemed to do the same. Jana recklessly decided she would live day to day, and ignore the cloudy future. She reminded herself that he hadn't sold her on Rigel.

She wondered if he ever could do such a horrible thing. For now, Varian Saar was her passion, her love, her very existence.

As for Varian, he savored these days of peace and pleasure. Life with Jana offered many glittering facets. She was like the sunshine: warm, radiant, vital, and life-sustaining. She was like the moonlight: mysterious, bewitching, and intoxicating. He had dared to yield to the emotions called love and commitment. The wanderlust in his blood was wearing thin. For the present, he was satisfied to remain with Jana. Jana was the embodiment of everything a man could desire in a woman; and she was his, almost. . . .

On the third afternoon, Varian was called to his orbiting ship about a vital matter. When he didn't return by midnight, Jana went to bed without him. She awakened near one and went to see if he had returned. As she descended the stairs, she saw Varian sitting in a chair by a fish pond in the solarium. He balled one fist and slammed it into the open palm of his other hand. He was swearing in a muffled voice.

When he said loudly enough for her to hear, ''Damn that son of a bitch! I'd better go and find him myself,'' Jana felt a surge of anguish. Was it time for him to leave her? She reminded herrself, *No pressures, no demands, no tears, no pleas, no arguments! Be only what he needs, Jana.*

Jana poured Varian a brandy and entered the glassed room. She pressed it into his hand and smiled. She stepped behind him and began to massage his stiff neck and shoulders. As she gently kneaded the muscles, she hummed very softly. She halted briefly while he downed the brandy in one gulp. She watched him close his eyes and slowly relax, the tension and anger subsiding. She continued her ministrations until he was breathing normally and leaning his head against her.

''Would you like another brandy, Varian?'' she asked, ceasing her massage. He shook his head. ''Are you all right? I was beginning to worry about you.''

His hands covered hers on his chest; he squeezed them lightly. ''You are a wonder, Jana Greyson, a sheer delight. The smartest thing I've done in my life was to come after you on Karnak; the dumbest was to leave you there.'' He lifted her hands and placed a kiss in each palm. ''I want you, Jana, now.''

"Good, because I want you," she replied. "Need some help, old man?"

Varian twisted in the chair to send her a grin. "I could use a little strenuous exercise to loosen up stiff muscles. What about you, moonbeam?"

Jana walked before him and collapsed into his lap. "Not me, I'm rag-limp."

Varian nuzzled her neck and nibbled her right ear. He buried his nose and right hand in her silky hair. He fingered the luxuriant mane as he inhaled its stirring fragrance. Varian pulled Jana closer against his body and possessively wrapped his strong arms around her torso. When she laid her head near the hollow of his shoulder, he rested his jawline against her temple. He closed his blue eyes and mentally drank in this heady nectar called love and serenity.

Jana closed her eyes. She felt so happy. Never had she experienced such sheer delight and total relaxation in a man's company. Life with Varian gave her a feeling of completeness, utter fulfillment.

Varian, too, savored this blissful episode. How strange to find rapture in nothing more than a touch, a smile, a voice, a quiet moment like this one. He shuddered to think he might never have discovered or experienced this if Jana hadn't entered his life, if they hadn't yielded to the chemistry between them, if he hadn't purchased her at the auction. From now on, Jana would be under his guard and protection, or under Tirol's. Still, he wouldn't rest easy until his foes were conquered and Jana was his wife.

"Varian, is something bothering you?" Jana inquired.

"Why would you think that, moonbeam?" he asked.

"You're stiffening up again," she remarked.

Varian's grip on her had tightened; his jawline was twitching as he clenched and unclenched his teeth. If only he could have answers to his questions about Baruch, Canissia, and Moloch. Didn't any of them realize how dangerous and traitorous the Tabrizes and Trilonis were! "I might have to leave a day early," he murmured sullenly.

"When? How long will you be away?" she questioned.

"I'll know tomorrow afternoon, late. Jana, if anything—" Varian halted.

Jana struggled to prevent herself from coaxing him to complete that alarming half statement. Varian was changing, becoming more open about his thoughts, and she realized it must be difficult for him. She had to avoid pressuring him. He wasn't accustomed to sharing his plans; no doubt that unfamiliar behavior still shocked him. He was like a wild stallion who desperately wanted to remain free and fearless and unbreakable.

"I'll miss you, Varian. Please be careful," she murmured against his neck.

Varian's arms squeezed her appreciatively. "Behave yourself while I'm gone," he teased to lighten the sudden gloom which encased them.

"With you away, it will be simple," she playfully retorted.

"Is that a fact, Dr. Greyson?" he taunted, then tickled her.

Between bursts of laughter, Jana pleaded, "Stop, Varian. We'll wake Tirol."

The two lovers didn't know Tirol had been observing them since Jana had come downstairs. How he wished Galen and Amaya were here to share in their son's happiness. Tirol wished he could roll back time and change history. He wished he could make peace between Galen Saar's two sons, for Varian's and Jana's lives were at stake.

When Jana awakened the next morning, Varian wasn't beside her. She hurriedly bathed and dressed and almost raced downstairs to find him. Time was short before his departure, and his last assignment had separated them many weeks! Jana couldn't locate either Varian or Tirol. She questioned a servant to learn that Tirol had left for a meeting on Rigel and Varian had gone to a secluded spot two miles down the beach, his favorite location during visits here, the servant confided. Should she wait for his return? Or dare she join him? Damn, how she hated this light-stepping!

Jana wandered around the house for twenty minutes as she tried to figure out what to do. Things had been progressing so well between them to risk spoiling them. What if Varian wanted privacy? What if he wasn't alone?

Jana boldly entered Tirol's private study and went to stand before the painting of Amaya Trygue, who appeared around twenty. She had been exquisitely beautiful. Thick sable curls tumbled down the back of the feminine figure with her shapely body half turned in the portrait. The face which was almost mischievously peeking over a silky shoulder was unmarred. Ice-blue eyes seemed alive with energy and joy. Her smile was radiant. Jana couldn't find a single flaw in the ravishing female. If there was such a thing as a perfect woman, in looks and personality and advantages, it had to be Amaya.

No wonder Varian had suffered so deeply and painfully at her loss. Amaya appeared to be a woman who elicited love and loyalty. If Varian had become involved with Shara Triloni, it couldn't have been willingly. What man could hurt or reject the sable-haired, blue-eyed goddess in this painting? No doubt the vain and selfish Shara had craved Varian, tried to lure him from Amaya, failed, and took her lethal revenge on those Varian loved. Why murder Varian, when leaving him alive to suffer anguish and guilt offered a better vengeance? Tears smarted Jana's eyes, for she felt she could never compete with this ghostly beauty.

Jana went upstairs and pulled on her swimsuit and a short pool robe. She headed down the beach of pinkish-beige sand. Jana was intrigued by the color of the water, a curious purplish-blue whose cresting waves flickered with hues of periwinkle beneath the sun. The shoreline was ruggedly landscaped. She weaved her way around huge rocks which jutted from the towering cliff seemingly soaring as high as the eye could see. Here and there, a contrasting and contradictory burst of greenery sprouted: stubby trees with fat trunks and large leaves, clumps of bluish-green grass, and lacy vines which hugged and decorated anything nearby.

No one was in sight, on land or water. Not even a footprint could be found. It was like being the only person alive in a strange world. Jana walked on until she found the path which rambled up the cliff and into the secluded area where Varian, so the servant had explained, should be swimming in a lagoon surrounded by unusually shaped boulders and odd vegetation. Jana moved silently. She had to make certain he was alone, and in a proper mood to see her. She came to where he had deposited his clothes and possessions; oddly, they were far from the water, concealed from the lagoon view. There was a utility belt like the one he had worn that long-ago night in

Andrea McKay's garden; attached to it were a communicator, a holster with a laser gun, and two other items which she didn't recognize. From the possessions piled near the rock, he had arrived dressed and armed, or planned to leave that way.

Jana cautiously peeked through the heavy foliage between her and the water. She saw Varian, clad in fiery red swim trunks, his body glistening with beads of water and his sable hair dripping with them. Something about his stance and expression seized her full attention. Jana leaned to her right and scanned the area in front of him. Jana froze in terror. One stranger approached Varian's right side and one swaggered toward his front; both were armed.

"Well, well," the man before Varian began scornfully, "what do we have here, Ensign Keetamon? Can it be the illustrious Commander Saar?"

"Looks like the dirty bastard to me, Captain Koch," the other man retorted.

Ominous lights danced in Koch's eyes, for it was his own hunger for vengeance he would feed today, not Prince Taemin's. He would snatch the beautiful alien for the prince, but Varian Saar must die! He grinned wickedly. "I've been waiting a long time to catch you alone and unarmed. Out for a private swim?"

"What do you want, Koch? Spit it out, or use that laser gun. This is the first and last time you'll have the advantage over me," Varian stated.

Jana's heart nearly stopped as she comprehended the gravity of this event. Her mind reeled in fear and panic as she stared at the stocky captain and his accomplice, both of whom had guns leveled on her love and sounded as if they intended to use them. Jana's gaze touched on the communicator. Since she did not know how to use it, she decided it was best to leave it alone. Pressing the wrong button might cause a crewman to respond and give away her presence. If only it had words and not symbols on it, she would know which button issued a silent emergency alert.

Her gaze slipped over the two items on Varian's utility belt and she tried to figure out their use. No luck. That left only one choice, the weapon. She soundlessly took it from the holster and hurriedly studied it. Symbols again! Which one meant "stun" and which one meant "kill"? Jana was frightened, but she knew she might not have any choice but to use the gun, for Koch was enraged by Varian's contempt for him and his dangerous position.

"Still trying to play the fearless rogue, I see," Koch snarled. "Why, you might as well be naked, Saar. No weapons, no courageous crew, no one to save your miserable hide from me. Aren't you even a little bit scared?"

Varian chuckled. "Of you, Koch, and that little flesh sucker of yours? How did you find me?" he questioned, relaxing his rigid posture.

"I was hoping to snatch that pretty piece you just purchased. I figured you'd come running to rescue her, then I'd have you by the balls. I'll get her after I finish with you. I'm giving her to my friend Taemin. He has this nasty itch for her. She must be some tasty treat to have so many men craving her. Does it make you squirm to know Keetamon and I might take our fill of her before we pass her along to the prince?"

Despite the fact she was alone, Jana blushed at Koch's lewd threats. So, the prince's intentions hadn't been honest when he had alleged his desire to obtain her for marriage! Lust and revenge had been his motives! Jana could think of nothing worse than having these two males touch her, except having them slay her love. Now she understood Varian's concern over her safety, even to the point of pretending to betray her! She comprehended his charades and her fake auction! His precautions asserted his deep feelings for her.

Like it or not, accept it or not, Varian Saar, you want me and need me!

Jana suddenly recalled the identity and use of one of the other weapons on Varian's discarded belt: a disintegrator. She had seen it at work that night in Andrea's garden. There was only one button on that lethal instrument. There could be no error in its use. Her frightened gaze shifted from one weapon to the other.

Jana made her decision, then prayed urgently for victory. All she needed was to get Koch. During the excitement, Varian could attack the second foe and easily defeat him. Jana was cognizant of one intimidating reality: while she was battling Koch and before Varian could reach the second male, one of the two villains could shoot and kill her. With Varian's life at stake, that didn't matter to her. She wrote a quick three-word message in the dirt, then rubbed it away. If she was slain saving his life, that could inspire guilt in Varian. Amaya's ghost and remorse over her were enough burdens for him to carry. During her distraction and plotting, Varian had asked Koch a question which Jana didn't hear, but which wouldn't have halted her impending action anyway, because she didn't know this frightening predicament was a trap for Captain Koch. . . .

As Koch stepped toward Varian and pointed the laser gun directly at his heart, he started to respond to Varian's evocative taunt. But Jana panicked at Koch's threatening moves. She jumped from behind the concealing vegetation and fired the laser gun at the villain, striking him in the left shoulder and stunning him. The force of the blast knocked the captain backward and into the dirt. The eerie noise of the weapon shattered the heavy silence just as a melee broke out around her: Kyle, Nigel, Ferris, and another security man leaped from hiding places. Keetamon's attention was drawn from Jana to the approaching men, and crazed, he fired wildly in several directions. Varian flung himself to the ground; Jana screamed and raced forward at the sight of her love going down. Keetamon shot and killed the man beside Nigel.

Jana halted her run so swiftly that she almost tripped and fell. Varian was getting up and casually brushing off his sandy body. Ferris was kneeling over the dead ensign. Nigel checked Koch's condition while Kyle guarded Keetamon. With a stormy black scowl on his face, Varian began to stalk toward Jana, who was frozen speechless by his grim expression. When Varian reached her, he roughly seized the laser gun from her shaking hand and glared furiously at her.

"You best get the hell out of my sight before I do something I'll regret," he warned. "How dare you follow me! And spy on me! You've ruined everything with your intrusion. I was a damn fool to retrieve you."

Jana blanched white. Her misty gaze slipped past his taut frame to the two men on the ground, one unconscious and one lifeless. There was nothing she could say or should say at this turbulent moment. All she could think about was that her action had slain a man and cost her Varian's acceptance. Jana turned and walked away, heading for the rugged cliff and beach.

Nigel joined Varian. "What was Jana doing here? She could

have gotten killed. Are you sure you should let her return home alone?'' Nigel asked.

"If I don't, I couldn't trust myself to speak wisely. Why was she spying on me? Stars forsake me, Nigel! I've got to find a way to get Jurad off my back. A few more minutes and Koch would have betrayed his connection to the Tabrizes. Once we had those charges against them, Jurad and his evil son would have been forced into a new truce, at least into backing off for a while! I would even bet Koch knows there's something brewing between those two princes. If he could have connected Ryker to Taemin . . . Damn! It's too late now. We'll only be able to hold Koch and Keetamon on lesser charges. I thought Jana would be safe here. If I keep her, I'll only get her killed, or worse. I'm a selfish man. I should have listened to Draco when he warned me to do what was best for Jana. What now, friend? Draco's getting married next week, and we've got a difficult assignment.''

"Didn't you see Jana's face?'' his first officer scolded. "She's almost in shock. You shouldn't have lashed into her like that. She needs comforting,'' Nigel advised.

"I can't go after her right now; you do it for me. I've got to decide how to handle her and our arrangement. No more rash and selfish mistakes. She risked her life to save mine. She didn't know you men were protecting me. It would have been perfect revenge to let me die. I wonder if she would have reacted the same way if she had known about that secret document which sets her free and makes her my sole heir if I should meet with an untimely demise.''

"You'd best pray Ryker doesn't discover those two secrets. But I don't think anything could have prevented her from doing what she did, thinking she had to save you.''

"I know, Nigel. Trouble is, next time, a foe could get her. *Kahala*, I'm weary of battling so many enemies. What should I do, Nigel? Keep her and risk her life every day? Or let her seek happiness and safety without me?''

Nigel grinned. "I know you really love her and want to protect her. I'm glad she's yours, my friend,'' he declared.

"Don't be, Nigel. Unless I can work things out and make a truce with some powerful men, I can't keep Jana. If she learns the reasons behind our missions to Earth, especially if I have to go ahead with that *Stardusting* project, she'll never forgive me. I can't even tell her I'm doing my best to save her planet and people! Secrets surround me like black shadows. Stardust and shadows, which is the lesser of two necessary evils?''

"You still want me to go after her?" Nigel asked.

"I'll go. Take care of matters here. See to my uniform and weapons," he added as he hurried down the path. He almost raced home, to find no Jana. He questioned the servants, who hadn't seen her return. He searched the house and gardens fruitlessly. His heart beat wildly; had there been a third assailant, one who slipped through their trap?

Suddenly Jana appeared, slowly walking toward the house from another path to the beach, having taken a long walk in the opposite direction. Sighting Varian in the walkway, Jana bravely strolled past him without stopping.

Varian whirled and started to shout for her to halt, but he let her go, then followed her to the suite they shared. When Jana turned and looked at him, Varian told her, "I'm sorry, Jana. I spoke to you in anger. I've been trying to get Koch for a long time. He was about to confess something which would have incriminated him and another enemy.''

"Your security man, is he . . . dead?" she queried.

Varian started to lie, but changed his mind. "Yes, moonbeam. But it wasn't your fault. Nigel said they were about to rush out when you did. Believe me, Jana, I think it would have gone the same way even if you hadn't been there. If fact, I think Koch or Keetamon would have gotten me. Did you realize Koch's gun fired beside me the moment you shot him? I honestly don't think it was reflexive. Accept my word or not, but you saved my life. And you were brave and generous to do so. *Kahala*, woman, don't make this harder! I'm not used to giving apologies or explanations. You could have gotten killed out there, and what would I do without my priceless treasure?''

Jana let the distressing matter pass without further discussion because she was aware of how much this apology pained him. In time, Varian might reveal more of himself to her. That night, they slept pressed against each other. Each was aware of how close death had struck.

Varian awakened Jana the next morning to give the bad news. "I have to leave for a short assignment. I might get back here for a day or two before I head out again. If not, stay close to the house and Tirol.''

Panic seized Jana; she had the terrible feeling that something dangerous was about to take place. "Don't go, Varian. I'm afraid for you."

He chuckled. "Don't worry about me. I can protect myself."

When Jana started to rise to see him off, he insisted she stay in bed and go back to sleep. As he reached the door, he stopped and turned. "I'll have a surprise for you soon, a long trip. And I won't accept any resistance. At last, we'll both find peace and our lives can be settled."

When he was gone, Jana went to the built-in dresser in the next room. She rummaged through her things until she found the ring he had given her. She stared at it for a moment then pushed it on the third finger of her left hand. Inexplicably, it gave her comfort. She went to Varian's dresser and opened one drawer at a time. She fingered his garments and fantasized about his return to her. She found a picture which baffled her: Amaya Trygue with a handsome male who favored Varian enormously. His older brother? Galen Saar? But why did Amaya look a beautiful forty? Jana examined the two images closely; Varian favored both! She called to mind every clue concerning the people involved in this mystery.

Jana dressed and raced down the steps, nearly falling in her excitement. A servant was cleaning the study when Jana crossed the room to Amaya's portrait. She asked, "Is this Tirol's daughter?" When the servant replied yes, Jana asked, "Was she in love with Varian or his brother Galen?"

At first the servant was confused, for she had returned from a holiday this morning and did not know these facts had been withheld from Jana for her protection. She explained, "Amaya Trygue was Commander Saar's mother. She was married to Supreme Commander Galen Saar, your owner's father."

"But that would make Tirol Trygue Varian's grandfather."

"You did not know the *Kadim* is Commander Saar's grandfather?"

"How were his parents killed? Wasn't it here seven years ago?" she probed.

The woman looked nervous, wary of Jana's queries. "It is forbidden to speak of that time. You must not mention it to them."

Jana examined the portrait again. His mother and father . . . She recalled her first conversation with Tirol; she reflected on the bond she had noticed between the two men. She called to mind that talk overheard between Nuala and Tarina, then sifted through the two confrontations with Jurad, whom she now suspected had intentionally misled her. Perhaps Jurad was friends with Ryker, Shara's brother or cousin.

Some facets to this mystery were still wrapped in obscure shadows. She wondered why no one had revealed Varian's relationship with Tirol. The *Kadim*'s grandson, his only heir . . . Was there no end to Varian Saar's status? When he returned she would demand some answers. The mystery had gone on for too long.

It was the next day before Tirol returned with Supreme Commander Brec Sard and Supreme Councilman Draco Procyon. It was late, and Jana should have been in her suite. She found herself trapped in the solarium until the men passed it and headed for Tirol's study. Jana shivered at overhearing part of their conversation.

"Are you sure it's safe for Varian to go to Darkar?" Draco asked.

"Yes, it's all been arranged. He's the only one who can settle matters with Ryker. After he returns from his mission, he's going to Jurad and Maal and do the same. It's time the Saar name was cleared with the Androasians and Pyropeans, if that's possible. It's been seven years. Shara can't haunt Varian forever. If it doesn't stop, either Varian or Ryker will be slain."

Brec agreed with Tirol. "You're right, sir. Only Ryker has the key to settle those matters. You both know Jana Greyson increases the tension between them. What does Varian plan to exchange for the truth and his help?"

"Varian's determined. He's willing to do whatever is necessary to end these conflicts. I've given him letters for Maal and Jurad. With luck . . ." The voice faded as the men entered the study and sealed the door.

Jana determined she wouldn't speculate on those statements. She must wait until Varian returned and clarified them. She crept upstairs, took a sleeping capsule, and went to bed.

"Varian!" Canissia called out to halt his departure from the Elysian Restaurant on Rigel.

The starship commander turned and demanded before Canissia Garthon could speak, "Have you seen Ryker lately? Or heard where he is?"

"You're searching for Ryker Triloni?" she questioned.

"It's Alliance business, and he's vanished," Varian responded cryptically.

Canissia knew about the "Alliance business" from her father and she also knew more about Varian Saar's personal plans than he or anyone could imagine. "Where's your little alien charmer? I heard you barged into Draco's and snatched her back for ten mill. Isn't that showy even for you, my love?" she teased slyly. For the first time, Canissia was threatened by another woman. Jana was a rival, to be dealt with quickly and permanently. "She isn't bad, love, but you've had better, much better, women beneath you."

"Such as Councilman Garthon's daughter?" Varian jested. He knew he had to disarm this sly witch before she would release any information.

Her seductive voice purred, "Naturally. You know we two are destined as mates. Our day will come. Tell me, love, what do you find so fascinating about this alien creature?" she quizzed, covertly taping the conversation. Later she would splice this talk, and one day soon, she would have the opportunity to torment Jana with lies! She knew Varian was trying to elicit information from her, so he would be very nice and unknowingly cooperative with her spiteful trick!

Varian knew how vain the redhead was. He must use that flaw and her craving for him against her. To do so, he must fool her about Jana. "You're a woman, Cass; you know how wily females can be. Jana's a challenge to me. She's the first woman I've ever encountered who refuses to succumb to my charms and prowess. Maybe it's that alien chemistry which makes her immune. You know how I detest defeat on any level."

"I would venture it's more your treatment of her which repels her," the flame-haired vixen suggested. "You did capture and abuse her. Even if she is of an inferior species, she does have feelings, love."

"Maybe that's why she keeps calling me all those nasty names: rogue, space pirate, savage barbarian, evil slaver, and other choice devils and ranks."

"And you allow such insults? That isn't like you, love."

"That's why I took her back. I plan to tame that clever creature. Yes, Jana needs a lesson or two in the peril of thwarting and scorning Varian Saar. Plus, I find my little battles with her amusing."

Canissia knew Varian was lying to her, but she didn't care, this time. Varian Saar would be hers, or no woman's! "It looks to me as if this Jana creature is an infection in your blood. Beware, love. You know she wants you and she's using those charms like Shara did on Galen."

"Since when did I care what a female wanted? Like you, Cass, I come first with me. Don't be so jealous of a mere *charl*," he playfully chided her.

"She seems to have a lot of mettle. Maybe that's why you're having so much trouble breaking her in to your tastes. I wonder how I would like being your amusement, your little diversion, your exquisite toy. Actually, that sounds tempting. I wouldn't mind having a handsome, virile slave to order about, one to do my every bidding. Warms me all over to imagine such a situation. I see why you men must enjoy these little breeders. If one doesn't work out, you can always sell her and acquire another one. I shall have to speak with Father about including alien males on your next slave run." Canissia eyed him strangely, then asked, "What are you doing here tonight? Why aren't you spending every available moment with Jana?"

Varian dared not expose the impending abolishment of *charl* laws. "I have some vital business with Ryker before I leave on my next assignment."

She grinned saucily. "I see, Jana doesn't know you're still around? What if someone tells her you were with me tonight? She might get jealous and cut off your honey flow. I've been missing you in my bed lately. As hard as I've tried, I can't find another man in the Universe to compare with your prowess. You know this game with Jana can't go on much longer."

"I know, love. It won't. I'm working on settling matters right now."

"Don't tell me you plan to keep her as your mate," Canissia taunted.

"Heavens, no," Varian replied, chuckling to himself. Cass would be livid when he wed Jana! But he was unaware of the pit he was digging for himself and Jana with his lies to this woman.

Canissia was serious. "Have you considered asking Tirol to free her? That way, you could marry her."

To delude this villainess, Varian laughed. "Are you insane, woman? Marry her? Come on, Cass, taking her as a mistress is fine, but as a permanent mate or wife . . ." He chuckled again. "You know me better than that. She is a valuable treasure, but she won't be my mistress much longer." He hoped that his dishonesty would appease Canissia. But he had to be careful not to offend her now, or she wouldn't tell him what he needed to know. "Since you travel around most of the time, you might know where I can locate Ryker," he probed. Varian could sense the galactic clock running out for the people of the Milky Way Galaxy. He had to find Ryker, since that bastard's evil brain possessed the laboratory combination and chemical formulas which he needed to safely approach Earth.

Canissia nodded. "I'm starving. Let's go to my ship. . ." She hesitated briefly, knowing she would clip the concealed tape there and add an erotic invitation to Jana's lover. "We can eat and talk. Why don't you find a way to end all of these nasty conflicts with rivals?"

"If all goes as Grandfather and I plan, they will. I intend to make Ryker an offer he can't refuse," Varian teased, balling his fist and waving it in her face.

Canissia relished that statement and how she would use it. "Some sacrifices are worth it for peace or truce." She wickedly added, "I suppose you'll miss Jana, but I'll be around for you. Let's go to my ship and set fire to my bed." She would end the tape there. When she saw that Varian intended to ignore her invitation she shrugged and gave in.

"Oh, well. The last time I saw Ryker, he was on Zandia. Something about jungle plants for research. You could check with *Avatar* Kael. He was suggesting several locations to Ryker. I wasn't really listening. You know how much I dislike that hateful bastard. How he ever clawed his way into our society, I'll never understand. Who cares if he's related to *Kadim* Maal!"

"Thanks, Cass. See you soon." He was gone before the woman could respond, gone to confer with *Avatar* Kael to make sure Canissia hadn't deceived him. Kael told him that Ryker was now heading for the planet Karlim, at the edge of the Pyropean Galaxy.

351

* * *

Canissia burst into laughter as she strolled into the luxurious suite on her ship. She pulled a small recorder from her purse, rewound the tape, and listened to it closely. It was perfect, or would be soon. This next trip to Ryker's for special illegal drugs would include a surprise for that bastard too! Only two males had spurned her: Varian and Ryker; soon she would have revenge on both . . . Canissia paused. Did she love Varian or hate him? Both, she admitted. He, too, would die.

Canissia decided she had just enough of the enslaving aphrodisiac to use on Varian and Ryker, although she did not know both males had been chemically immuned to such deceits by enemies. After all, she had promised Ryker she would use Shara's magical love potion on the man of her erotic dreams. Too bad Ryker didn't know he was included in those perverted fantasies. Not only would she have Varian but she would also claim Ryker!

Chapter Nineteen

Two days later *Kadim* Tirol spoke to Jana and revealed the disaster facing her world, including Varian's role in the matter. Tirol felt it was best for Jana to hear the truth. After all, he secretly planned for her to marry his grandson, and the two seemed very much in love. If Jana loved Varian, Tirol felt it was time she understood his motives and actions.

Jana had not questioned Tirol about anything since Varian's departure. She was afraid Tirol might get angry if she queried Amaya's death and Varian's puzzle. Now, in spite of her anguish, Jana listened to the leader's words. It couldn't be real; her world was doomed. "Where is Varian? Do you think he can do anything to stop this?" she asked.

Tirol partially explained by saying that the Star Fleet would do all they could. Tirol had concluded that Varian was heading for Earth. But he didn't want to tell Jana more because he didn't want to inspire questions about Varian's past today. He would grant Jana a week or so to come to grips with this tormenting news, and then would tell her more about Varian. Before he came home, Jana would know everything, and that knowledge was essential to their future happiness. The last secret was the depth of Varian's love for Jana Greyson, whom Tirol had already freed and Varian intended to marry if she would have him.

Jana tried not to think. She wanted to believe this was just another test, or evil joke. So Varian had been afraid she and others would learn about Earth's fate. No doubt he assumed she would reject him. Or blame him. Now she understood. The "*charl* raid," her capture, and how their love began as a ruse to save her world.

As the *Wanderlust* left its orbit and headed for the Pyropean boundary, Varian ordered a communications blackout. Varian was fiercely determined to find Ryker. "After I persuade him to aid our cause," he was telling Tesla, "we'll finish this mission. We've no choice but to force him, if it comes to that, to give us what we need."

"You can't go alone," Nigel cautioned. "What if Ryker lied to Canissia and *Avatar* Kael? He could be hiding from us anywhere, even in his secret lab. Varian, you'd never get out of there alive."

"We may have to try. If he's not in the Pyropean Galaxy, we'll go to Darkar. I'll need two volunteers. I'll get him. I'll take two security men. I can't risk involving or endangering my entire ship and crew. Give us three days if we don't return . . . You're in charge, Nigel."

"What about the *Kadim* and Jana? Shouldn't you send word?"

"I can't risk it. If anything goes wrong, Nigel, handle them. Stars protect us . . ."

Another day passed. Tirol took Jana with him to the planet and city of Rigel. While the leader was closeted with the Supreme Council and Alliance Assembly, Jana was sent shopping with two bodyguards. The brawny males positioned themselves outside the main entrance, after being satisfied that the back one was sealed securely.

Inside the exclusive shop, Jana walked into the dressing room. She didn't want any new clothes, but Tirol had insisted. Jana tried to force their incredible conversation to the back of her mind. All she wanted was for Varian to return, hold her and promise everything would be all right for them and the surviving Earthlings. She comprehended the actions of the Maffei Alliance Council; Tirol had said they were rescuing as many people as possible without endangering their world.

Jana wondered what Tirol had meant by his final statements: "I haven't told you everything, Jana. By tonight, you'll understand. Whatever happens and whatever you learn, please don't blame my grandson. He did save many lives. And you did present him with many problems. You have a great responsibility to Varian; please remember it and carry it out bravely."

It was the first time Tirol had called Varian his grandson! He had refused to explain further, but Jana was eager to talk more. The couturier entered the dressing room and offered Jana a cool drink, which she gratefully accepted.

"This will relax you while we're carrying out our task," the man cooed. As she drained the glass, he mechanically added, "I'm sorry, but these are Commander Saar's and *Kadim* Tirol's orders."

Jana looked at the clothes designer in confusion. A curiously sweet flavor filled her mouth. Brightly colored spots and silvery lights danced before her swiftly blackening vision. Jana reached for the wall to steady herself. Suddenly there was another voice in her ear which said ruefully, "I'm sorry, too, Jana. Varian's orders. You're to be traded for peace." The last voice she thought she heard was Nigel's.

A man quickly lifted Jana's limp form in his arms and placed her in a shipping crate after giving her a long-acting sedative. He attached an oxygen mask to Jana's face and made sure it was functioning properly. He sealed the crate and transported it to Canissia's waiting ship. None other than Zan, Canissia's captain and lover, guided the couturier into his workroom. To further baffle authorities, the shop owner was drugged. First with a syringe that contained a chemical which would neutralize the mind-control drug which had been injected earlier that

354

morning. Then with a fluid which would ensure that when the designer awoke later, he would recall nothing about today.

By dusk, the guards grew concerned. Jana had the only appointment, and the couturier should have been finished with her by now. When the man did not answer their summons, Tirol was notified. One guard remained out front, while the other went to check the back entrance, which was sealed. Neither man moved from those locations until Tirol and Brec arrived.

Brec Sard used his laser gun to open the door. It required thirty minutes to revive the designer and uncover odd facts. While the groggy shop owner vowed he hadn't seen Jana, the two guards swore that she had entered the chic salon and that they had not left their posts during this time. All three were interrogated under truth serum. They were not lying. Brec sent out an alert for Jana. The two men anxiously waited in Brec's office at Alliance Force Headquarters as that day passed without a clue or a demand for ransom. Varian couldn't be located. All Brec and Tirol could do was keep searching, and wait. Tirol knew Jana could be anywhere by now. How could he explain her loss to Varian?

An Alliance Force squad interrogated every person in the shop's area. Later they branched out to search every ship in orbit. Those who had departed were tracked and examined. A unit sent to check out each of Varian's worst enemies discovered one annoying fact: Ryker Triloni was allegedly sealed inside his secret complex, incommunicado! Before the day ended, they learned that Jurad and Maal too, had unquestionable alibis.

The next day, Brec Sard shifted his investigation to lesser rivals, only to discover that no one on the list had the means to carry out such a fearless deed. Jana's description was sent to all Alliance outposts; her rescue and return to base were ordered at any cost, by any means. Brec was stumped.

The reward which Tirol offered bore no fruit. The news of Jana's kidnapping spread quickly. Friends offered assistance; foes gloated over Varian's misfortune. Brec and Tirol fumed at their impotence as three and a half days had passed, and there was no news of Jana Greyson.

Since Varian had not contacted base in five days, the leaders assumed he was on his way to Earth, still under a communications blackout. Brec informed Tirol, "You should return home, sir. Someone might contact you there. There's nothing more we can do except wait and pray. I've never been so baffled in my life. Even a psycho makes some kind of mistake. Whoever grabbed Jana is smart and dangerous. Such perfect timing and skilled plotting."

"I wish Varian had called in before heading off to Earth. That isn't like him. Did you get any word on Ryker?" he asked worriedly. "He had to know we were trying to locate him. *Avatar* Kael saw him last week."

"I had put a surveillance team around Darkar before Jana was kidnapped. All Trilabs cargo ships have been tracked. Ryker had to have been at home during the abduction, like he claims. And he's there now. He couldn't have gotten off and on Darkar, especially with Jana, without my agents knowing."

"Why hasn't he responded to our calls, and the order for more chemicals?"

"When he's working on a new formula he refuses to answer any communication. He's totally isolated sometimes for weeks at a time. If Ryker was an accomplice to this crime, he's covered his tracks perfectly. And just like we figured, he claimed innocence about the defective chemicals. Ryker said he ordered a second supply to be shipped to the Alliance warehouse days ago. I suppose Varian got the Trilabs cargo and is now on his way out as planned. He's certainly gone somewhere, and it can't be after Ryker. But I'm surprised Varian didn't contact you and Jana before leaving. He must really be distracted; he didn't even notify me on acceptance of the cargo."

"I don't understand, Brec. If Trilabs delivered a cargo days ago, why has Varian been out of touch? Doesn't that sound as if Varian disappeared before the Trilabs cargo reached the warehouse on Thule? If he was told the cargo was en route to Thule, why didn't he contact us while he was awaiting delivery? And why take it and leave for Earth so mysteriously?" Tirol probed.

Brec frowned, then asked his squad to contact *Avatar* Feaji of Thule and Kael of Zandia for more information.

* * *

356

Brec was astonished to learn that Varian hadn't claimed the Trilabs shipment on Thule. Consternation gnawed at him when he discovered the *Wanderlust* hadn't been seen after its visit to Zandia when Kael told him Ryker was collecting rare plants in the Pyropean Galaxy! Another dismaying fact came in; Ryker came out of isolation long enough to say that he hadn't seen or spoken with Varian since their talk on Therraccus during the *charl* auction. Ryker said he canceled his plant trek to return to his complex to work. Before the day passed, he said he was surprised to learn that the Trilabs shipment was still awaiting pickup.

"A starship doesn't vanish. Why hasn't Varian contacted base? He's gone, Jana's gone, and the shipment's still on Thule! He can't perform his mission without it. What in *Kahala* is going on?" Tirol thundered angrily. Even Varian Saar didn't take such crucial matters into his own hands.

"You don't think he entered Pyropean territory looking for Ryker?" Brec asked.

"Varian wouldn't breach a truce without contacting me. Besides, Ryker's whereabouts have been known for days, there was plenty of time to alert Varian."

Tirol sighed heavily. "The timing is suspicious. Varian blacked out communication before Jana's kidnapping, before the cargo reached Thule. Where is he? Why hasn't he heard about Jana and returned to base? He couldn't head for Earth without the chemicals. And if he doesn't have the chemicals or Ryker, why isn't he looking for them? If Ryker hadn't seen Varian, how did he know to send another shipment?"

"This cargo wasn't to replace Varian's tainted one. This was part of the cargo we ordered for our second mission."

Tirol said anxiously, "I'm very worried."

"It's been three days," Kyle told Nigel. "I've got this bad feeling we shouldn't wait any longer."

Nigel inhaled deeply. He walked to the communications panel to radio base for instructions. Despite Varian's orders to maintain radio silence, Nigel was going to request permission to take a small team to search for him and the two security men who had left the ship.

Tesla shouted, "Wait, sir! A spacer just appeared on the

radar screen. It's got to be him.'' He watched the tiny blip cover the vast distance swiftly.

Nigel hurried to the screen and checked it. He sighed in relief. ''I'll be in the docking bay. Lay in a course to base and stand by to depart.''

The hatch opened but no one appeared. Nigel ordered the security man to draw his weapon and cover him as he cautiously descended into the spacer. Then, ''Get Tris quickly!'' he shouted.

''What happened, Nigel? Where are the others?'' Tristan asked as he examined his unconscious commander.

''Varian was the only one to return. He's out cold. He wouldn't have left the others behind if they were still alive. What did they do to him?'' Nigel demanded furiously, observing his friend's injuries.

''Some bastards tortured him. You'd best get us to base quickly.''

Both men crowded near the stretcher as Varian moaned in pain. A bloody hand lifted, seized Nigel's shirt, and despite his wounds pulled his friend downward with amazing strength. ''Jana.'' Varian forced out the word. ''After Jana . . . Call . . . base. Ty . . . ree . . . Lauter both dead. No Ry—Ryker. Pro . . . tect Jana. Don't . . . let Tae . . .'' Varian slipped into blackness, but his grim message was clear.

Nigel went to the communicator and ordered Tesla to head for base at top speed. He radioed Brec, grimacing at the man's responses. Nigel and Tristan exchanged anguished looks. ''We'll arrive by tomorrow night, sir.''

Jana lay on the bed in a golden cell once more. But this prison was small and almost bare. Three days ago, under ''Varian's orders,'' she had been whisked from Rigel to be presented to Ryker Triloni as a ''peace token,'' a replacement for Shara. She recalled Tirol's words on Eire and Rigel. If this deal was true, Tirol had been a party to it. Jana didn't want to believe the evidence against Varian and his grandfather, but there was so much of it.

Jana painfully reflected on the past few days of captivity. When she had awakened, she had found herself in this narrow room with only a bunk. Fears had flooded her mind as details of the kidnapping came back to her. Why had Varian ordered Nigel to steal her away? She had learned why quickly.

When the door had opened and her abductor had posed in the opening, it was Canissia Garthon. A triumphant sneer distorted the woman's beauty. "I see you're finally awake, my dear alien puss. I suppose you want to know why you're traveling on my ship." She seemed bored with the whole matter.

"Hasn't anyone told you kidnapping is a crime?" Jana scoffed.

Canissia roared with wild laughter. "You are naïve and stupid. Varian is giving you to Ryker Triloni. I volunteered to transport you there myself."

"You're lying!" Jana shouted.

Canissia had laughed coldly and confidently. "Not this time. You see this?" she waved a forged paper before Jana's nose. "It's your ownership document." She held it before Jana's wide gaze to prove her claim. "As you can see, it's signed and sealed by Commander Varian Saar himself. In case you don't recognize the other seal and name, they're *Kadim* Tirol's. I'm simply delivering a piece of cargo, Jana. Needless to say, I'm to make it worth Varian's while when he returns for allowing me this exquisite pleasure."

If Jana's hands hadn't been bound at that moment, she would have seized the document and shredded it, then slapped Canissia's smirking face. She had seen other *charl* documents, and this one looked like the real thing. "I want to see Varian, and talk to him," Jana demanded.

"He's on his way to Earth to put your people to sleep before your world goes boom, poof, and blam," Canissia purred. "You see, puss, our hands are tied. If we send enough starships to confront the meteor threatening your world, our enemies will attack us while we're defenseless. So, we're euthanatizing your people so they won't suffer during their destruction. It's called *Stardusting*; irreversible coma."

"You are in deep trouble, Canissia," Jana warned. "Varian isn't doing this to me, and we both know it. Just wait till he catches you, and he will."

"My heavens, you're dumber than I thought. Listen to these tapes, Jana puss, and you'll end your doubts." Canissia played the doctored tapes of Varian's voice made up of many prior conversations, but Jana continued to send her a look of contempt and disbelief. "Varian doesn't know I made these little gems during our talks. I wanted to give you an extra dose of reality. I took plenty of teasing over his brief affair with you. Now, I get the last laughs. Frankly, I don't give a damn whether you believe me or not. I'm sure Ryker will be only too glad to force the truth into that pretty head."

"I thought Ryker was Varian's enemy," Jana ventured, innocently revealing the narrow scope of her knowledge. "You are only a scorned ex-mistress!" Jana said insultingly.

Canissia drew back her hand to slap Jana, but didn't. Instead, she smiled wickedly. "I think I'll leave that pleasure to Ryker. Do you know what kind of man he is?" At Jana's baffled look, Canissia sent forth peals of satanic laughter. "He's a beast, little puss. He's a cold-blooded, savage misogynist. You know? A man who loathes and abuses women? He tortures them for the fun of it."

When Jana uncontrollably went white, Canissia grinned salaciously. "One good thing about this deal, there's no way Varian can change his mind. After Ryker has you for a while, no man will want you. If there's anything left after he has his fun with you. Oh, little puss, am I going to enjoy your destruction."

"You can't be so barbaric, Canissia. If Ryker is like that, Varian would never send me to him." Jana tried to control herself. She would not allow this dangerously evil woman to torment her.

"I don't have to use my time and energy to convince you of a situation which will be only too real in two days. Delude yourself, puss. I don't care."

"Please, Cannissa, don't play these games," Jana coaxed gingerly.

"Don't beg. I can't change your fate, even if I did feel sorry for you, which I don't. I detest you, and I want you out of my hair quickly. Ryker is the perfect fate for you."

"Forget it, Canissia. I'm sure Tirol and the Alliance Force are searching for me right now. As soon as they discover who grabbed me, you're done for."

"Dense, dense, dense," Canissia clucked mockingly. "Perhaps you should hear the tapes again. If you know Varian Saar at all, you'll recognize his voice." She played them once more, grinnning vindictively.

As Jana was compelled to listen, she wished she could deny that was his voice. She wished he hadn't exposed so many intimate facts about them. She could discount the first tape made during their brief affair, but not the one made a few nights ago. The tape proved Varian had been seeking Ryker. There had been such an intimate tone to his naughty words with Canissia. He had made their beautiful arrangement sound lewd and cheap, a game. Had her traitorous love made Ryker an offer he couldn't refuse? Had he spent the night with Canissia?

"Now tell me, woman to woman, what tricks did you use to keep Varian coming back for more and more? I thought I knew them all, but you Earthlings must have a secret or two. Tell me, and I'll beg Ryker to go easy with you."

Before thinking, Jana said, "You're vulgar, Canissia Garthon. You're nothing but a filthy-minded whore. If you couldn't hold Varian, don't expect help from me."

Canissia stiffened and glared at Jana. "Careful, little puss. We haven't reached Darkar yet. I just might check out your sexual talents."

"If you dare let any of your men come near me, I'll—"

Canissia cut sharply into her warning. "I do as I please. A videotape of you and Zan would offer many hours of amusement on boring nights. And don't say you wouldn't perform for us. I have drugs which can urge you to take on several men at once to appease your fierce cravings. Be nice, puss, or I'll have to break my promise to Varian. Then again, how would he find out? I'm sure Ryker won't mind if I take a tiny payment from you for my services. I'll have to think about this."

Canissia had left Jana petrified by her threats. Yet, two days had passed, and the witch hadn't even returned to taunt her. A man called Zan had appeared every so often to bring Jana food and drink, and to allow her privacy in the small bathroom nearby. On the last visit this morning, she had been left unbound. Jana's nerves were stressed and her emotions in turmoil. She was tired of denying this reality. So much evidence to condemn her love, but could she accept it at face value? No, Varian couldn't have duped her so. There had to be a reasonable explanation.

The door opened; Canissia and Zan entered. "Time to get ready for delivery, puss. You have twenty minutes to get bathed, powdered, perfumed, and dressed. In this," she informed Jana, handing her a costume which caused Jana to quiver. "Obey me, or you'll arrive stark naked," she threatened.

Jana realized the woman was serious about her donning that skimpy gold lamé bikini. "Dress quickly, or else Zan and my crew will prepare you. If they do, it'll take more than twenty minutes . . ." The threat hung in the air.

When Jana was finished, Zan held her securely while Canissia placed a cloth over her mouth and nose. Jana realized it was something like chloroform and knew it was futile to struggle. She gradually went limp in Zan's grasp. Canissia had her locked in a gilded bird cage which was placed inside a crate. After turning on a tape of bird whistles and calls, she had two other men help Zan load the box on her shuttle. On arrival, she had the three men wait.

Ryker answered the summons at the entrance to his private laboratory. He stared at the redhead as if looking through her. "What do you want, Cass?" he inquired blandly. "I'm very busy today. I told you, five minutes."

She pouted sexily and chided, "Now, now, Ryker, don't be so cold and mean. Could we talk in private?" she entreated. "You won't be sorry."

Ryker led Canissia into the sitting room of his private complex. He was repulsed by her seductive manner, but he wanted to hear what she had to say. As much as he detested this female, she did have a knack for delivering intriguing and usually valuable information. "Well?" he hinted.

"I've brought you a gift, one which I'm sure will please you immensely." She cockily related her startling actions.

Even the malevolent Ryker was shocked by her reckless behavior. "You're the one who kidnapped Jana Greyson from under Tirol's nose? You brought her here? You fool, I don't need more trouble with Tirol," he berated her. "Two Alliance Force members came here after her abduction, and Brec Sard just left. You'd better be glad he called off that sentry ship as I demanded he do. They would have searched your ship, then I would have been implicated. Why did you drag me into this crazy scheme?"

"Don't worry, love, I took extra precautions to safeguard both of us. If they even suspected me, would I still be free as a bird? Would they be rushing around interrogating people and

362

searching frantically for clues? No one followed me. The idiots already searched my ship while it was still in orbit. I have a secret compartment in my suite which only Zan knows about." She boasted casually of her evil crime. "I have an unbreakable alibi for the time of Jana's misfortune. I was having fun with *Zartiff* Dukamcea. While I kept Jana drugged and concealed, I cruised around for days without a care in the universe, just like I always do. No one on my ship has seen little Jana, except Zan. And I can trust that doting stud completely."

Ryker glanced at his timepiece and smiled, for his archrival should be dead now at the hands of Prince Taemin's men. He knew Prince Taemin would be perturbed by Jana's disappearance. After all, he had promised that insidious prince Jana in return for his help in destroying Varian. But Ryker had expected to inherit Jana when Varian's estate was settled, as he was by law the sole blood heir to all Saar holdings. With the Alliance Force seeking her, it would be too hazardous for Jana to appear in his grasp, or to ship Jana to Taemin in a Trilabs ship. If Jana was found in his possession being passed to the prince, the Alliance might get suspicious about Varian's death. He must look for another way to repay Taemin, or hold Jana until all doubts faded.

"Ryker, Ryker," she teased the sullen man. "Relax and relish your gift. I told my crew I was bringing you an exotic golden bird. No one will be suspicious. You see, love, I covered every angle," she bragged.

"I wouldn't be so smug; you're dealing with Brec Sard. He didn't become supreme commander without good reason. Why did you bring her to me?"

"You've become such an ass these days! I thought you'd be thrilled. Don't you need exotic specimens for your wicked experiments? She's a doctor and scientist. She could tell you exactly how your work is going, on her, of course. Just think, you'll have Varian Saar's priceless treasure at your mercy." Canissia licked her lips. She couldn't understand Ryker's lack of enthusiasm and pleasure. How odd.

Canissia coaxed, "Don't you want to discover why Varian found this fluff so irresistible? I wonder why another lusty Saar would be enchanted by a green-eyed, sunny-haired alien. Do you know he actually freed her and planned to marry her? Over my dead body! Father found out by accident, then I stole the information from him. Father heard Tirol telling Draco. Can you believe your brother would be so reckless? What happened to his Saar pride? How could he free and marry a common breeder? You know what's funny? Jana doesn't know she's free, nor does she know about Varian's wedding plans." Canissia savored her knowledge and the telling of it to Ryker. She went on to relate how mistaken Jana was about the two men's pasts.

"She honestly thinks she's a truce token from him to you. She'll be so hurt by his betrayal that she might cooperate with your little vengeful projects. If not, use some magical potions on her. By the way, I need more aphrodisiac myself. I've almost run out. And I'll need something to destroy Zan, the only remaining link to this secret. Only you and I will know the fate of little Jana of Earth."

Ryker thought quickly. To avoid problems, he would take Jana off Canissia's hands. Since he couldn't pass Jana to the prince, he would find some use for the alien creature. As for Canissia, her vices would be the end of her! Poor Cass, she wouldn't get any man, and certainly not his old antagonist. Indead, Canissia's gift of Jana had supplied him with the perfect way to solemnize his victory night, by destroying the one thing which Varian loved more than his heritage!

Suddenly Ryker grinned. "I've been working too hard lately. A man shouldn't be too tired to reward generosity and courage. Let's complete our exchange, then you can have my gift brought inside." He guided Canissia into a laboratory where he searched for two particular bottles. Handing her one at a time, he instructed, "You know the aphrodisiac *Jacanate* is in the blue bottle; it only takes a drop or two, Cass. You don't have to drive your victim wild. Too much, and he's raw and bleeding before he can sate his cravings. Course you probably like others to suffer at your hands. Maybe you ought to try a drop or two yourself to keep up with your partner," he teased.

He held up the yellow bottle and explained, "This is *Myozenic* concentrate. It has to be mixed with pure *Zenufian* spring water: one third of this bottle to a half tub of spring water. I haven't enough to spare, so you'll have to fetch the water yourself. Listen to me carefully, woman, substitute no other water. This liquid won't be worth anything to you if you don't follow my orders; in fact, it could be hazardous to mix it with some fluids. Only *Zenufian* spring water," he stressed firmly "I suggest you head there immediately. I want Zan dealt with before he has a chance to ruin both of us. He could crack under pressure from Sard. Besides, if Varian returns soon, he wouldn't be reluctant to use truth serum on either of you. I don't have to worry; I made myself immune to such drugs long ago."

Canissia tightly clutched the two bottles. "Anything else, love?" she interrupted impatiently.

"I want all of your evidence on this affair. I'll destroy it personally, after you've taken care of Zan. You must eliminate him immediately. That way, I can prove my innocence if you get caught. Deal?" Ryker pressed.

"Why not," she replied nonchalantly. "It is your birthday, love, so I'm sure you'll find some stimulating way to celebrate tonight. Why don't I return after I handle Zan?"

"To see if I've handled the evidence properly? Or to see if Varian's love is still alive? You needn't fret, Cass. I'll see that Jana never again competes with you. How did it feel to watch Jana get something you never could?"

Canissia scowled. "As soon as I take care of Zan, that won't be true," she asserted smugly, shaking the blue bottle containing the aphrodisiac and laughing huskily. *Right after I work you over good, my virile chemist. I wonder how a woman-hater makes love. . . .* "Rest assured, I'll take care of Varian while you take care of his lovelight. I'll have everything I want very soon."

"With Varian out of the way, so will I," Ryker concurred, misleading her. "I wonder how a captor will behave as a captive, a master of many fates as the slave of another's fate. I would love to see Varian as the cowering conquest." Ryker watched the way Canissia rotated her hips suggestively. He wanted to laugh in her face.

"Do you mind if I stop by on my return trip?" she inquired sweetly.

Ryker sighed. "If you'd like, but only for my private birthday party. Ths is my busy season for collecting plants and such. I'll expect you back in six hours, without Zan. By then, I should have prepared more aphrodisiac. You might need two bottles. Varian has an iron will and ravenous appetite."

Canissia's eyes glowed. "You are a wicked man, Ryker.

Maybe that's why I like you so much, despite how you treat me sometimes."

The crate was moved inside the laboratory and Canissia dismissed her men, telling Zan to get the shuttle ready for departure. She pried the boards free, and placing an aroma stick beneath Jana's nose, she aroused her. As Jana coughed and moved inside the gilded cage, Canissia stepped back and said, "A gift of golden intrigue and bliss, an exquisite bird to sing you to sleep at night."

Ryker's gaze traced Jana's practically nude figure. "Her pictures didn't do her justice. No wonder Varian was so reluctant to part with her. Well, well," he murmured. "It looks as if he made me a wise offer after all."

As Ryker arrogantly stalked around the cage twice, Canissia harshly commanded, "Stand up, Jana! Let Ryker examine his treasure closely."

Jana glared at the offensive woman. "Go to hell. My display days are over. I don't follow your orders."

"How about following mine, Dr. Greyson?" Ryker asked calmly. "Stand up and look at me," he stated firmly.

Jana turned to confront a savage beast, but found an exceptionally handsome man standing before her. Her wide eyes, parted lips, and intake of air expressed her surprise. Clearly he wasn't what she had expected. Jana's startled gaze roamed his face and physique. "You're . . . Ryker Tri . . . loni?"

The matchless scientist chuckled. "Is that good or bad, Jana of Earth? What did you expect, a grotesque mutant? Evil gargoyle? Fiery demon?"

There was a defiant tilt to her chin, her carriage bespeaking pride and courage. She interested him. She was a very beautiful woman. Her flesh looked as velvety as a flower petal. Her figure was arresting. But it was her blush of anger intermingled with modesty which captured his attention. At his bold scrutiny, she lowered her lashes to conceal the rage in those unusual eyes. He watched her clench and unclench slender fingers on the cage bars as he intentionally prolonged his intimate study of her. When he teased the back of one hand over her bare stomach and upper chest, she flinched and stepped backward.

Jana was only too aware of how small the cage was and how vulnerable she was to this monster's reach. Upon awakening, she had cautioned herself to patience, observation, and wisdom. Yet she felt as if Lucifer himself was scrutinizing her beneath a powerful microscope. She desperately wanted to seize her long, thick hair and cover her upper torso, or clasp her hands over her breasts to protect them from his searing gaze. She could feel the hot flush from her face creep down her throat and splash over her chest. Her fingers and jawline ached from being clenched so tightly, yet Jana remained rigid.

Ryker witnessed the rapid rising and falling of her bosom as her respiration quickened with panic. She was terrified of him, but trying to conceal it. If ever a woman had appeared angelic to him, she was in the cage in this room! He had never met a real goddess before, and here was one to dissect and study. "I must confess that Varian's timing and gift are perfect. I shall long remember this birthday." Ryker caught her wrists and pulled her against the cage near him. When Jana tried to yank free, he tightened his grasp painfully.

Jana gasped! The barbarian's strength was enormous, his voice as sharp and hard as tempered steel. His expression was like winter: cold, harsh, and forbidding. Varian's present had not softened Ryker's hostility. It appeared to Jana that Ryker was going to work out his hatred on her!

"Tell me, Jana of Earth, did any of Cass's crew enjoy you on the way here? The truth, if you value your life."

Jana was baffled by his question. Canissia spoke angrily before she could answer him. "I told you, Ryker, no one has touched her except Varian Saar."

Ryker imprisoned her hands within one of his. His other hand stroked Jana's fiery cheek, then buried itself in luxuriant hair. Ryker pulled Jana's face against the cold bars. He drilled his penetrating gaze into hers. "Don't be afraid of Canissia. I want to know the truth."

"For once, that demoness spoke it," Jana stated distinctly.

As Ryker and Jana stared challengingly at each other, Canissia yanked on Jana's hair and laughed maliciously when Jana shrieked and wrenched free of both of them. Ryker glanced at Canissia and scolded, "You can be a real bitch, Cass. How can I enjoy a gift that's wild with fear?"

"Sorry, love, but I couldn't resist. She's been a pain for months! I'd best get on my way. I'll see you later. Here's the key to delight."

Jana's eyes shifted from Canissia's hand to Ryker's as he

accepted the key to the cage and closed his fingers around it. Amid chilling laughter, Canissia and Riker departed. The door closed behind them, and Jana was alone. She sank to the floor of the cage, her legs refusing to hold her up any longer.

Ryker watched Canissia board her shuttle, a satanic grin curling the corners of his lips. He glanced at the papers and tapes in his grip. Once they were destroyed, there would be no links to Jana's location. He could envision Canissia's flaming destiny when she prepared the drugs as he had instructed. But it was too bad Canissia herself wouldn't be allowed time to comprehend her fiery fate. Before she could call for help, her ship would explode in a blaze of glorious victory. Soon, Canissia would offer no threat of discovery or defeat for him. . . . just as soon as she tried to murder Zan.

Ryker entered his private laboratory and walked over to the cage. As long as he kept Jana confined in this impregnable complex, no one would know she was here. He almost wished Varian wouldn't be dead before midnight. What sweet revenge this creature's pain could have caused in his enemy. Ryker unlocked the door and told Jana to follow him. As if knowing there was no path of escape and recognizing the folly of infuriating him with defiance, she obeyed. When it was too late to battle Ryker, she comprehended his intentions. It wouldn't have mattered if she had resisted his wishes. There was no one to stop him from doing as he pleased. Here, no one could reach him.

There was no time or enough strength for Jana to prevent Ryker from chaining her hands and feet between two posts. Nor from taking a scalpel and slicing through the material which hardly shielded much of her body. Around and around he strolled, eyeing her from silvery blond head to bare feet. Jana had never been more conscious of every inch of her shivering flesh than at this moment. She could do nothing but endure Ryker's examination.

He stopped behind her and traced his fingertips along her spine. One hand stroked the curve of her buttocks. He came to stand before her. His first action was to place his thumb against her throbbing neck pulse, then grin. After turning her face from side to side as his probing gaze explored each area and feature, his gaze and hand moved on to feel her collarbone and shoulders. His hands poked and tested the bone structure and texture of her arms and ribs. His attention and touch came to her breasts. Here, his eyes and fingers and lips did a mutual investigation. He appeared to enjoy her taste and fear.

"Please." The word came forth hoarsely and uncontrollably. Jana shuddered.

Ryker could feel the violent pounding of her heart. He grinned sardonically at his powerful position. His hand leisurely slid past her navel and over her flat, taut stomach to pause just above the thatch of whiskey-colored hair.

"Ryker, please." She tried again to reach him and stop this shame.

"Please what, little Earthling?" he asked, mocking her.

A hot tear rolled down her cheek as she replied, "Please don't do this."

"You will learn very quickly that I do as I please on my world and with my property. I am a research scientist, and you are a very rare alien specimen. Is it hard for your simple brain to realize I wish to thoroughly study the newest acquisition to my laboratory collection? You won't be injured, so relax."

Jana shouted at him, "I'm not an animal or a mindless creature! I'm a human being. I'm a research scientist too. I can answer any question you have."

Ryker chuckled. "Sorry, little alien, I prefer to make my own judgments."

Jana sneered contemptuously and said, "Do you intend to dissect me, piece by piece? Do you want skin and hair samples? Blood and organ tissue samples? Do I get anesthetized before your sadistic experiments?"

"I have never been known for my kindness or mercy, little alien, so I would watch your nasty tongue, before I remove it for testing," he threatened, tapping her lips as he spoke ominously.

"I know slavery isn't against the law in your barbaric world, but surely using human specimens for research must be," she reasoned fearfully.

Ryker laughed as if she had told a funny tale. "No one knows what happens inside this lab, little alien, nor does anyone try to control me or my work. As long as I furnish critical goods for the Alliance, it won't interfere with me." Stunned by his shocking words of self-assurance, Jana merely gaped at him as he returned to his investiga- tion of her. He squeezed the flesh and muscles of her thighs and calves. He checked out the bone

369

structure of her feet. His hands began to work upward to the last area to explore. . . .

"Are you so simple, Dr. Triloni, that you fail to realize the anatomies and chemistries of our two races are alike in almost every way? I don't believe for one minute this is scientific observation! Are you trying to intimidate me? Terrify me? Degrade me? Or is this a repulsive game to sate some perversion? You hardly appear a man to accept another's leavings, especially a crude beast like Varian Saar. I can assure you it is impossible to remove his stain from my life and body. If so, I would have carried out that deed before today," she hotly alleged, desperately trying to delude him about Varian.

To Jana's delight, Ryker did look pleased at her words. She pushed on. "How could you accept me as a peace token? That's like taking an insulting slap on the face! Since when does a smart man rid his fiercest rival of a disagreeable situation? I don't understand any of this, and certainly not you."

Ryker refuted, "That's where you're vastly mistaken, little alien. You are the only female Varian has desired for more than a brief affair. He would have been content to keep you for quite some time. You have been the talk, the envy of three galaxies. You were the perfect token to demand, the only Saarian possession which caused him enough discomfort and inconvenience to make him surrender."

"You're the one who's vastly mistaken. If you think Varian feels anything more than lust for me, you're wrong. Oh, Ryker, he has duped you badly," she asserted. "Even I underestimated his cunning."

"Explain yourself, alien," Ryker demanded, his interest piqued.

Jana craftily re-created events to support her alleged hatred for Varian Saar. She asserted that Varian had forced her to feign a romantic interest in him to avoid brutal punishments or a sale to some evil master: "If you don't believe me, ask anyone involved. It galled him to find a woman who could scorn him. He tried everything to conquer me. But he made a terrible mistake, perhaps his only one. I liked Draco and enjoyed living on Karnak; so much so that Varian couldn't stand it. Don't you see, Ryker? It was all a carefully designed charade to convince you that he wanted me. He couldn't go too far, or you wouldn't fall for his scheme. He pretended he couldn't help his attraction to me. No doubt he searched my world for the perfect woman to carry out his ploy. But he didn't expect to find one who would reject him, who wouldn't aid his plot. When you didn't bite at me during my displays or attend my auction, you left him with only one sport: my conquest. You had defeated him, and he certainly wasn't going to allow me to do so. He's won two victories, Ryker. He has you convinced you've taken his matchless gem, and he's punished my failure to yield to him and to assist his spite on you. Not only does he have a truce with you but he's made a fool of you. I can assure you, I was no sacrifice to him.''

When Jana repeated the words overheard at Tirol's, she knew she was getting to Ryker. ''If you know your enemy at all, do you really believe Varian Saar would hand over his irresistible jewel to any male, especially an enemy?''

Suddenly, Ryker started to laugh. For a moment, he had forgotten this was only a farce. He had almost gotten caught up in the delusion and been swayed by her apparent honesty. Jana's verity was enticing. Ryker regretted that he wouldn't be allowed the opportunity to use Jana against Varian. He couldn't help but wonder how Jana would react to the discoveries of Varian's love, her freedom, her criminal abduction, and Varian's death. Perhaps he would enlighten her before her eventual demise.

Ryker's thoughts were interrupted by an emergency communications signal. He went into his office and closed the door. It was a coded message from one of his spies on Rigel. Fury surged through him to hear that Varian Saar had escaped death and was hospitalized under heavy guard. Bitterness gnawed at Ryker. Why did the gods continually show favor and mercy to Varian? Still, Ryker wasn't worried, for there was nothing to connect him to Varian's misfortune.

Ryker was relieved Canissia was under radio silence and couldn't pick up a news flash about Varian's trouble. There was no way the redhead could rush to Varian's side before the chain reaction started in the fluid in the yellow bottle he had just given her. The wicked vixen and all clues leading to Jana Greyson would be destroyed within the hour. As soon as Varian regained his senses and discovered Jana's loss, Ryker would be prepared for vengeance. With the help of two rare females, Varian would be defeated for all time. The evil chemist returned to Jana's side and unfettered her hands and feet. He removed his blue laboratory coat and handed it to her. He smiled deceptively as he put his ruse into play. "That was a report from my investigator. You were right, Dr. Jana Greyson. I was allowing my hatred for Varian and the fact you came straight from his bed to color my opinion of you. This conflict between the two of us is getting old and wearisome. I don't care to make peace with him; I only want him to stay out of my affairs. I think it's about time we two stop entertaining the galaxy with our disputes. If accepting you as a token deludes him and accomplishes this desire, then let him think he's pulled a clever trick." He watched Jana slip into his knee-length coat.

"Besides, this isn't any way to treat a fellow researcher, even if she is my property. Maybe I should explain something to you. My vile reputation isn't totally accurate. I just never take the time to correct false impressions because they often work to my advantage. People fear me and leave me alone. You could say people like Cass and Varian bring out the devil in me. A wealthy, powerful single man is an object for gossip and wild tales, particularly when he has a running battle with the illustrious Varian Saar. Anyone who meets me and still believes such lies doesn't deserve to be enlightened. Of course I did make a terrible impression on you, and doubtlessly Cass filled your head with awful stories about me. I *was* trying to terrify and embarrass you."

Ryker sighed heavily and laughed genially. "I must admit, I do sometimes play out the role which fate seems determined to cast me in. It was wrong to take my enmity for another out on you. In a way, you're his victim too. My spies tell me you were speaking the truth. Now I see why Varian had to get rid of you, and swiftly. For I have just learned that Tirol and Segall are making wedding plans for Canissia and Varian on his return from your galaxy. I suppose you know all about that sorry situation. I wonder why she didn't tell us."

Jana kept staring at the handsome male of six three with sandy blond hair and eyes the color of a lush jungle after a spring rain, eyes which displayed a hint of mystery. His face boasted strong, distinct features which she attributed to his royal heritage. He was too intelliigent to be so savage and misguided, for his apology hadn't soothed her fears. The white scar which ran along his right jawline did not detract from his good looks; in fact, it gave him the look of a masterful and virile pirate. Jana tried to find Shara in his face and his personality. But those sparkling green eyes and enchanting smile prevented it. There was something about Ryker Triloni which tugged at her heart, something intangible which disarmed her. Considering her love for Varian and her present straits, such irrational magnetism distressed her.

Ryker observed the way she was looking at him and her failure to weep at his lies. "What do you say about starting our relationship anew? I'm Ryker Triloni, and I hope I'll be delighted to meet you and have you living here."

Jana couldn't decide what Ryker was attempting; she dared not query him about his enemy or dispute his words. Didn't Varian realize the danger he was placing her in by sending her here? She eyed his outstretched hand. "Is this a trick or joke?"

"No, little alien. You simply exude powerful magic and appeal. And I own you. That's what I call a splendid birthday surprise, an unforgettable gift."

Chapter Twenty

Under *Kadim* Trygue's orders, Varian was kept heavily sedated for two days while doctors treated his injuries. Lacerations were sealed; cracked or broken bones were fused together. Scrapes and bruises were tended. Blood and antibiotics were infused, as were potent nutrients. For another two days, Varian was kept under lighter sedation as he was allowed time to recover his strength and to respond gradually to the successful treatments. With Maffei's advanced medical knowledge, Varian could be healed in a week, except for a little weakness. Whenever he aroused enough to ask about Jana, the doctors would tell him everything was under control, that he was to rest and heal. Despite the narcotics, Varian sensed something was wrong, and he fought against sleep; despised the nightmares; he wanted to see Jana.

When Nigel and Tristan protested his sedation, Tirol forced them to reluctantly see his side. "My grandson was nearly killed out there. Another hour and he wouldn't—You're his best friends. You know what he'll do the moment he's awake! Go after Jana, regardless of his condition. We're doing all we can to locate her. I can't risk Varian's life. Besides," he added sadly, "if she were still alive, we would have heard or found a clue by now. There's no sense telling Varian she's lost to him, not in his present condition. Let him heal first. This will be as rough, or rougher, on him as Amaya's and Galen's deaths. Jana was such a ray of sunshine in his life. And mine. If only Brec could find her!"

Tirol sank wearily into a chair. "The doctors agree it's best to keep him sedated a while longer. That's the only way they can hold him for treatments. During that first day here, he kept trying to fight them. From what he was shouting in his delirium, his two men were brutally slain before his eyes. While they were torturing Varian, they kept telling him they were keeping him alive until Jana arrived. They told him they were planning to torture and murder her in front of him. Wild animals—"

Nigel broke in. "What is Brec doing to locate her? We sent in the coordinates of Varian's attack. If they're supposed to take her there, let me go after her. I don't give a damn if the planet Karlim is in Pyropean territory!"

"I wish it were that simple, Nigel. They were only taunting Varian about capturing Jana. No ships have headed that way since her abduction, although I personally contacted Jurad and accused him of kidnapping Jana and trying to murder my grandson. Jurad is a lot of things, Nigel, but I don't believe he was personally involved in either episode. His troops immediately surrounded the area to search for clues. We assumed the villains would have fled after Varian's escape, but when we found them they were all dead; some slow poison killed every one of them. None of them could be identified. There were no clues to Jana in the camp. Brec and Jurad don't think they ever intended to take Jana there. Her kidnapping was coincidental. The gods have a cruel sense of humor these days."

Tristan declared, "You know who's responsible for Varian's attack and those savage deaths. Ryker Triloni! I say we go see the bastard right now!" he shouted angrily.

"There are a few hitches, my friend. Ryker has an unquestionable alibi before, during, and after both incidents. He would be a fool to use poisonous chemicals which would point guilt directly at him and he's no fool, Tris. Jurad and I think it's a satanic plot to get rid of both Varian and Ryker."

"But who?"

"Probably that devil Prince Taemin."

"I'm convinced Ryker lured us into Jurad's territory," Tristan said.

"That can't be proven. *Avatar* Kael told us of Ryker's proposed trek there."

"Since Varian was almost killed, Jurad isn't pressing the matter of his breach of truce. But he should never have crossed that boundary before radioing base. Brec does have a plan in mind, but we can't use it until Varian's well."

The two men listened as Tirol related the shocking scheme.

Ryker was a great puzzle to Jana. After Canissia's departure, he was like a different man! He had taken her to a lovely suite inside the private complex. He had warned, "Don't try tricks to escape, Jana. If there are two things I detest, they're guile and defiance. This won't be an easy situation for either of us, so let's make the best of it. After a couple of weeks, I'll make a decision about your role here. From what I've heard, you're a skilled researcher. If I discover you're as intelligent as you are beautiful, I could find a place for you in one of my facilities. It's possible we can become friends. As to whether or not there can be anything more between us, I can't say. Maybe Varian will get extra enjoyment from this deed. He knows how enchanting you are, and he knows how much I'll resent following him to your bed. A cunning torment, to send me a ravishing creature who boils the blood and troubles the mind. You can rest easy on one matter, I won't kill you. But please, don't give me any reason to punish you. You'll stay in here for the next two or three weeks."

"How could I escape and to where?" she had responded. "I'm not a fool, Dr. Triloni. If you're speaking truthfully, I will do my best to carry out your orders. I've missed working; research was my life, my love."

"For both our sakes, Jana Greyson, I hope that's your only lost love," he had remarked coldly and pointedly, then left her to herself.

Jana wandered around this newest prison. It reminded her of her suite at Draco's estate. Only this time, there would be no pardon by Varian. She was trapped here. All she could do was wait. She curled up on a velvety chaise and rested her head against it. She gazed into a lush tropical setting separated from her by an impregnable glass wall.

Ryker looked at his mistress reclining beside him. Chilly laughter rumbled in his chest. "Such naïveté, such blindness, such delicious sport and revenge."

She glanced at the monitor and observed the golden-haired woman. "It's a shame such beauty must be a pawn to ensnare Varian."

Ryker pressed the button to turn off the image of Jana's room. He rolled his companion onto her back and kissed her. He teased his lips over a protruding nipple. "What do I need with a tarnished woman when I have you to care for all my needs? There are other green-eyed blondes."

As she allowed him to remove her garments and slip between her parted thighs, she reminded him, "You need an heir, a need I cannot supply."

"There is plenty of time for such a task. I just reached thirty-one. If I don't have to kill this little creature, I might consider her for such a role. The thought of entering her body disgusts me. The mating will be a difficult chore. Cease your talk and worries. It is time for pleasure."

When Ryker was sated, he observed the ravishing woman sleeping beside him. She was greedy in bed, a woman without inhibitions. He grinned sardonically, for she existed only to please him, as it should be. She owed Prince Ryker Triloni her very life! He had used her and deceived her for years; he owned her body and soul. Soon she, too, would be disposed of along with Varian.

Ryker reached up and turned on the video from Jana's room. He watched her take a bath. His gaze went from Jana's naked body to the one lying beside him. Yes, he concluded, if he didn't have to kill Jana, he might keep her once his vengeance was appeased. But let her bear his heirs, never! He hated both females, all females. Perhaps he would use her as a receptacle of his scorn. But the vixen beside him must never suspect her impending doom or his secret plans for that Earthling.

The next day, Jana dined with Ryker while an automaton

served their meal. They ate in near silence, each surreptitiously studying the other. Jana's senses were teased by a perception of evil eyes upon her. She was cold and edgy. If there was a camera or monitor of any kind in her room or this one, she could not locate it. She blamed the eerie sensation on tension.

"Tell me about your capture and training," he commanded, breaking the silence in the lush solarium.

Jana glanced at him and flushed. She thought it best to stick as closely to the truth as possible. She related everything, except her love for Vanrian and their wager. She was relieved when Ryker didn't press for more information. She waited for him to mention her relationship with his enemy; he didn't. Instead, he began to tell her about his work. Jana listened closely, for she was intrigued.

Jana didn't see Ryker again until dinner the following day. When she asked if she could tour his laboratory, he smiled and shook his head. "As much as I want to trust you, little Earthling, it's too soon."

"Trust me?" she echoed. "I don't understand."

"How do I know this isn't a scheme invented to get you inside my lab and to win my trust? Saar and the Alliance Force have tried that ploy countless times. How do I know you aren't their newest squad member? Since you are a researcher and would understand my work, it would be a stroke of genius for them to plant you here. Who would suspect an alien slave of bold treachery?"

Jana gasped in dismay. "That isn't true!" she protested. "I'm not a spy for anyone. My only crime was in being captured by that space devil. Several times he threatened to sell me to awful men or to turn me over to a public brothel. Don't you understand? There are fates worse than death to a woman. As much as I detested . . . sleeping with him, it was better than sleeping with countless men!"

Jana jumped up from the table and turned her back to him. In panic, she was crying. What if he used truth serum on her? He would know she was, and had been, lying to him! Suddenly she was frightened.

When Ryker did not move or speak for a long time, Jana sniffled and slowly turned to face him. "Don't you see how wrong and cruel it is to enslave innocent people? To steal them from their homes and families and sell them? This is an evil practice, and I do not understand how such a superior culture can be so backward and savage. Why must you abduct victims? Surely there are women who would be willing to come here and mate with your men. Your race closely matches ours in looks, anatomy, and chemistry. Why does your government allow this evil to continue?''

"Your situation is an irreversible fact, Jana. You must accept it. Are you unhappy and afraid here?''

"Yes," she answered candidly. "I'm a scientist and a human being, Ryker. I want to work in research. I want my self-respect and freedom returned. I don't want to be used by anyone. Is that so hard to understand?''

"I do understand, little Earthling, but I cannot free you. You will be safe here with me. I am your life and protection now.''

"But who will protect me from you?'' she asked bravely, almost inaudibly. "You are blinded by a conflict with the man who stole my life and honor. You won't give me a fair chance here, so why should I fool myself?''

"You are mistaken, little Earthling. I've been very unlucky where women are concerned, so don't press me. You might as well know, I have a mistress; so I don't require your services in that area. I'm sorry for the humiliation and pain you've suffered, but I have to make sure you are worthy of my trust and respect. I'm having Varian watched, so I'll know very soon if this is a trick of any kind.''

"I thought he was gone," she responded, curious to discover what she could about her love.

"He's on Rigel with his grandfather. Something is brewing, little Earthling. I surely hope you aren't involved.''

Jana tensed in dread. "Please make sure of your sources before you judge me guilty of some offense which I haven't committed," she urged.

When Jana was locked in her suite, Ryker went to his private rooms. The woman waiting there glared at him. "Why did you say such things to her? If I did not know better, I would believe you are romancing Saar's whore!''

"Calm yourself," he urged. "You know my plan. I only toy with her. After all she's heard about me, I must charm her into compliance. I want her calm and happy, so she'll do anything I wish. We might have need of tapes to lure my foe into his bottomless pit. I cannot use false ones or drug her into obedience; he would know. She must be persuaded to comply willingly, if I have need for her aid. Think how it would provoke him to see her lovingly at my side. There could be secrets inside her head which she doesn't realize are present. I shall draw them out with my charms. Don't be jealous. What would I want with my brother's whore?''

"She is very beautiful,'' the woman argued.

"No woman alive is as beautiful and as passionate as you. Don't spoil my plans with such childish emotions. Didn't you see how I have deluded her? If we have need of her help soon, she will be unable to refuse me. Have I known or desired any other female?''

She pouted her ruby lips. "She does not know the truth?''

"No one knows the truth. It's our secret.''

At lunch, Jana sat in mounting confusion. "Who are you, Ryker Triloni?'' she inquired during dessert. "I feel as if I'm not seeing the real man. You're such a private, secretive person. Your ways are so different from mine. Yet, we share one vital interest.'' "Have I just been flattered or insulted?'' he teased her.

"Neither,'' Jana responded frankly. "You are such a puzzle to me.''

"As you are to me. I've met no woman like you. Who is Jana Greyson? She fears to open herself to another alien. Don't you see, Jana? We both have needs which the other can fill.''

"What do you mean, Ryker?'' Jana gazed at his handsome features. His face and voice drew her like a bee to a flower.

"If you do not understand my meaning now, you will soon. The fates have sent you here to fill many voids in my life . . . and in my heart. I hope and pray I am not wrong about you.''

"Why do you think I'm untrustworthy?'' she inquired.

"Because Varian Saar isn't a fool. That makes me question why he would give you away. Do you realize there isn't a man in the Universe who wouldn't claim you if he could? If Varian could sacrifice you, there is a monumental reason. That is the secret I have to uncover.''

"What if it is as simple as he doesn't see me like you or

other men do? Every man alive couldn't desire me. Heavens, I'm only pretty, not beautiful. I have brains and certain strengths. But I'm not matchless or irreplaceable.''

"You are too modest, and you're wrong,'' Ryker said.

His words unsettled her. She was at a loss for a reply. Why did she feel there was always some crucial meaning in his statements which she didn't understand?

"Perhaps I should be grateful to my rival for such good fortune,'' he hinted.

"Am I your good fortune?'' Jana queried, searching for a clue.

"That remains to be proven. For both our sakes, I hope so.''

In her room, Jana pondered this strange man. Ryker Triloni was highly intelligent. His nature was mercurial, quicksilverish. Worst of all, the prince from Androas was magnetic and disarming.

Ryker's mistress peevishly chided, "Your appetite is huge these days. Is it the little alien charmer who stirs your blood and sets fire to your loins?''

Ryker laughed. "Oh, no, Precious, it is the smell and taste of impending triumph which heats my blood, and such emotions inflame my loins. I am so close to victory, I need to be reassured of your loyalty, your love. I find release and bliss only within you. I am your slave, and you are mine.''

She continued to massage his body with warm, fragrant oils. She laughed. "How can I doubt my effect on you?'' she asked, caressing his erect shaft. "Surely this fire burns only for me.''

"No female can ever please me as you do. Since that first night you visited my bed and introduced me to such wild and wonderful sensations, I have wanted nothing more than to fill your every desire, to prove my love and need for you. I can trust no one but you, and you can trust no one but me. If you doubt me, ask what you will from me to prove my love and fealty.''

"When Varian Saar is dead, let me have the Earthling for sport. That will prove you have no cravings for her. You are mine; I will never share you.''

He entered her. Time and time again he drove savagely into her receptive body. "Anything you wish, my beloved Shara.''

The moment of his climax, as always, he feasted greedily on his mother's breasts as if he were a starving baby. Rolling his sated body aside, he replied dishonestly, "You give me all I need. How could Varian's alien whore compare with Princess Shara Triloni?"

Varian stared at Tirol and Brec as they related Jana's abduction. His gaze shifted to Nigel, then Tristan. He listened to their explanation of why he had been kept sedated for days and how the investigations were proceeding. At last he spoke. "Who gave any of you the right to make such decisions for me?"

His grandfather replied, "I take full responsibility. You were in no condition to go searching for her. I'll tell you all we know."

After the lengthy discussion, Varian inquired, "How can you be so sure Jurad wasn't involved? My gut says Ryker planned this and Jurad carried it out."

"We do believe Ryker is responsible, but we need to prove it. Dammit, son, he has the best alibi possible; Elite Squad members have had him under surveillance since before her abduction. If you hadn't been under communications blackout, we could have told you where he was! That was rash to head off to Karlim without checking with base first. Why did you do it?"

Varian gazed out the window. Canissia and *Avatar* Kael had told him where to look for Ryker. He needed to question Canissia and Kael before he made any wild accusations. This time, he would go by the book to entrap Ryker! He listened as Brec told him no ships had crossed the Pyropean or Androas barriers, since Jana's capture; that meant she had to be in the Maffei Galaxy.

Weariness filled Varian and he sank into a chair. He reflected on their last days together and his harsh words after the scene at the lagoon. Despair chewed at him. He could not bear the thought of her abduction by another man, particularly a bitter foe.

"I must locate her, Brec, as quickly as possible. I must have her back. She has to learn the truth about me. When I think what I've done to her—" He couldn't finish. Agony seared

381

his heart without mercy. "I'm a bloody fool. If anything happens to her, I'll never forgive myself."

Nigel gripped his shoulder. "Don't worry; we'll find her for you."

Hours passed into days, and still no clues surfaced. Varian was like a man possessed. He was short-tempered; he found eating an annoying necessity and sleep was nearly impossible. Each time he lay down and closed his eyes, her image would haunt him.

His ship went from port to port seeking even the slightest clue to her fate. He asked questions, offered rewards, and waited for word. He felt powerless.

"Give it up, Varian. She's gone," Supreme Commander Brec Sard said after many days had passed without word of her. "I wish I could do something or say otherwise. It's over. Accept her loss and move on. I can't offer you any more hope. All I can say is she might be alive somewhere. For now, we must concentrate all our efforts on the situation developing in the Milky Way Galaxy. Our rescue operations on Earth are almost complete. Other ships have covered your assignments. We must now decide how to deal with the meteor."

"If Jana is alive, I'll find her. I'm not giving up," Varian declared, Earth's fate no longer his primary concern.

Sighing, Brec told Varian that Ryker had left Darkar for the Androas Empire shortly after Brec's last trip and queries, to seek his exotic specimens on several planets. They had been told that Ryker had left after Canissia's ship stopped briefly at that planetoid. Brec and Varian wanted to question Segall's daughter, but she and her ship had vanished completely. If she knew anything about Jana's abduction, they couldn't interrogate her until she was found. Trouble was, they couldn't connect her criminally to Ryker, or Ryker to the trap which had almost been Varian's death.

"When will that bastard return to Darkar? And where the hell is Cass?"

"I was told he'll be home in two more weeks. We can't traipse through *Kadim* Maal Triloni's territory searching for his grandson. I pulled my surveillance ships off Ryker for thirty-six hours to calm him. Presently I have three ships watching Darkar. No one can go in or out without my knowing. I just wish they had been on duty when Cass made her visit.

None of our posts can locate her. But you know Cass. When she wants to drop out of sight for an adventure, she can and does. There is one way to lure her out of hiding, if you're game.''

When the plan was put into motion, Varian headed for his private planetoid, Altair, to await news from Brec Sard or Canissia Garthon, or to see if someone else would take his bait. . . .

Altair was a relief, for there were no reminders on the planetoid of Jana. As Varian awaited news, Nigel and Tristan joined him in what appeared a genial visit. This homecoming was very different from what Varian had planned not long ago. Jana should be at his side, as his wife! Instead, he was alone and miserable. He could only hope Jana would see through the sham they had concocted and circulated about his upcoming marriage to Canissia!

Days slowly passed. The harder Varian fought to accept the possibility of her loss, the more he realized he could not. At least proof of her death offered some finality, a reason to end his search. The uncertainty of her survival and ordeal ate at his gut day and night, chewing away at his sanity. He needed to know the truth.

The Supreme Council and Alliance Assembly were meeting that day to decide whether or not to send a combined force of ten starships with chemical lasers to attack the meteor. Even with that much firepower, the staff of scientists studying the situation could not promise success! From the pictures taken by reconnaissance ships, the massive fireball threatening the Milky Way Galaxy exposed no stress points. If they decided to go after it, the perfect time to attempt this confrontation would be in five weeks, when the extrasolar body was between Jupiter and Saturn. Ten starships . . . could they risk sending that many ships to help Earth and leave the Maffei Alliance with weakened defenses?

Ryker and his mother laughed wildly as they watched the news tape. "My half brother is a genuis, Precious. But his little ruse will aid my revenge, not his. Poor Cass," he jested. "Varian has announced their wedding for next week, and she can't hear his summons."

383

"It's a good thing you arranged for her ship to explode. The bitch would sacrifice anything and anyone to marry him next week. I'll be so glad to get this matter settled. I've been trapped inside this complex for seven years. I'm strangling on privacy, my adorable son. I've taught you all I know. It is time for us to use our skills to conquer Maffei and the Saar name."

Ryker reminded his evil mother, "It was vital to keep you concealed here for all these years. You know we couldn't allow anyone to discover you're still alive. You got away with murder. Can't you imagine what Grandfather or Jurad would do if they discovered you didn't die years ago, that we duped them with a surgically altered body which lay in state at our palace in your place. When the time is right for you to venture into the world again, we'll have to alter this beautiful face so no one can recognize you. Thank heavens the Alliance didn't hold your body until it was too late for me to revive it. That was a hazardous, plot, Mother."

If Varian hadn't escaped Shara's bloody knife, Ryker thought, he would have buried his mother then and there. Instead he was forced to revive the mad Princess Shara Triloni from her suspended animation to complete her task. She alone was responsible for his being deprived of his birthright and she alone would correct it before her death.

"I am the only woman you can trust, my son, the only woman you need. When our justice is met, we will be free of the Saars. Free, as soon as the last one is dead. Then, only my son will carry the Saar blood. My son," she stressed possessively. "Soon our victory will arrive, and when my face is changed, I can live at your side as your wife. You must hire the best surgeon, and I will take the face of Jana Greyson. Then, we will have each other and all that is due us."

Ryker suppressed his contempt for this woman who had borne him. For years after her loss of Galen Saar, Shara had suffered from madness, forcing her father, Maal, to confine her. If not for Maal, Shara would have carved her son from her body or slit his throat at birth. But the years had given Ryker weapons for revenge upon the Saars: his superior knowledge and his ability to save Shara when all thought her dead.

But most of all, fate had blessed him with his father's voice and features, the physical traits which had enslaved this evil witch to him. Ryker knew it was the Galen in him which Shara craved; for without the blond dye on his sable hair and the emerald lens over his blue eyes, he was almost Galen's exact double! How clever of his grandfa- ther to mask his looks since childhood. Side by side, Ryker Triloni and Varian Saar were undeniably and immensely similar, almost twins.

Ryker knew his mother was insanely intelligent. But he had fooled her for years, using his "Galen face and voice" to master her. Shara had shamed herself and her family! She deserved to suffer, to be crushed! Every time she lay with him, his loathing increased. But as she catered to his every whim and trembled with weakness at his touch, a heady sense of power surged through him. Shara was evil and insane. She had used drugs to seduce her own son at twenty-six, the age Galen was when she met and wooed him. For five years he had allowed Shara to use his body. As long as Shara could have Galen through him, she would be his mindless slave. When she had served her final purpose, he would delight in slaying her!

Ryker turned and faced Shara. "Do you see the same allure which enslaved your senses when you looked upon my father long ago?" he baited her.

"I see more, Ryker. You have his beauty, and you are a part of me. When I failed to ensnare him with my magic potions, I could not bear his rebuffs. How dare the man to whom I chose to give myself and all I possessed deliver me to that worm Jurad! How dare he share my bed and give me a child, then return to his sickly sweet wife, Amaya! If I had not angered Father by refusing to marry Jurad and provide his conquest of the Pyropean Federation, he wouldn't have imprisoned me for years. What was Jurad compared to your father! He was lower than a slug's belly. But when Galen discarded Princess Shara Triloni, he had to pay for his crime. He forced me to slay him when he tried to save Amaya. I wanted Amaya and Varian dead so your father would come to us. When Varian is dead, I will have all that remains of my beloved Galen. I was a fool not to have wed Jurad. If I had, I would have been given the time and power to obtain Galen. As supreme ruleress of Pyropea, I could have given the order to have Amaya slain; I could have won Galen's hand in marriage. When Father died, Galen and I would have ruled the Androas Empire and Pyropean Federation. We could have squeezed the Maffei

Alliance into submission. Just think, my son, rulers of a triga-laxy . . ."

Ryker slyly ventured, "Such a dream is still possible. I am Grandfather's heir and he is old. As Jana Greyson, you could wed Prince Taemin, then slay him and Jurad. I would rule Androas and you would rule Pyropea. We could wed and form an alliance, then squeeze the Maffei Alliance into submission. All we require is time, Jana's face, and my brother's death."

Shara drifted her fingertips over his muscular frame. "It will not seem strange for *Jana* to marry a Saar, one who favors her lost love. It is perfect."

Ryker chuckled. "You are a devious witch, my Precious. First become Jana and marry Taemin, then return to me."

Shara clasped his head and brought his lips to hers. As long as Ryker lived, she would have her beloved Galen. Her son was under her control. As long as she used her talents on him, he would never hunger for another woman.

While Shara slept, Ryker went to see Jana. He observed her shock at his news. "As you see, Varian's reason for getting rid of you is obvious. He could not keep you as his mistress and marry Cass. I knew something was behind his sacrifice, more than an offer of truce. I can see why neither mentioned their upcoming marriage; they knew how I would resent being used." Ryker instantly apologized, "I'm sorry; I didn't mean to insult you. Varian wanted you out of his life, so where better to send you than here? Frankly, I'm glad he decided to leave you with me."

"Is this some kind of joke?" she inquired.

"I'll have the wedding filmed, so you can see the evidence for yourself. You've been given plenty of reasons to be skeptical of me and the Maffeians, but I had nothing to do with these clippings or that news tape. I tell you what; after the wedding, I'll take you to Rigel and you can check out this story for yourself. I promise I won't make any demands on you until our return from Rigel. That trip should convince you of my honesty. Is that fair enough?"

Jana eyed him intently. "I want to trust you, Ryker. I wish I could do so without requiring firsthand observation. I would appreciate your taking me with you to Rigel. Not to question Varian, but to see if you trust me enough to accompany you. I don't doubt this information is accurate," she told him.

Ryker escorted Jana to her suite and locked her inside. He hurried to another suite and joined Shara. "I have a new plan, Mother. I will seek the best facial surgeon immediately. Our revenge is at hand. Listen carefully."

After Ryker completed his explanation, Shara shouted, "No! You cannot marry Jana Greyson! I forbid it."

Ryker caressed her cheek. "I need her voice on the audiovideo tape and her signature on the marriage document; they must be authentic. Once your surgery is complete and she is dead, you will become Jana Greyson. Have you forgotten our plan for you to take her place and live at my side? Tirol or Brec might check out her voice print or signature. If they aren't Jana's, we could fall under suspicion. We must be cautious."

"How do you plan to explain Jana's presence here and her marriage to you?"

"I'll simply explain that after Cass caught up with me in the Androas Empire, Jana begged me to protect her and keep her. Since Jana is a free woman, there is no law against her marrying me of her own free will, which the tape and signature will prove. The Alliance Force believes I am away, so how would I know they were still searching for Jana? I'll claim that Cass told me she was only helping Jana escape from Varian and no kidnapping was involved at all. Jana and I married before returning home. When we did, I discovered the search and investigation were still in progress. Naturally Jana and I were shocked and wanted to clarify the confusion at once. Who could prove me wrong?"

"But Jana didn't run away," Shara protested.

"We know that, but we won't tell anyone. Only Jana could expose Cass's involvement. But you will be Jana by then. You will give the answers we desire them to hear. As Jana, you are a free woman. With the help of your ally Canissia Garthon, you ran away and married me. No crimes there."

"You are a genius, my son. We will arrange the wedding immediately. But you will consummate it with me, not her. I can see Varian's face now when you show him the marriage document." She laughed mirthfully.

Ryker laughed too. Yes, he would use the document, but not as Shara believed.

* * *

Jana gaped at the handsome male before her. "You want me to what?"

"Help me beat Varian at his own game. Marry me before he can marry Cass. Can't you imagine their faces when we arrive the day of the wedding already married? They wanted to dump you here and keep you hidden away. Just think how they will react to Jana Greyson Triloni. . . . Which do you prefer, Jana, to be my slave or to be my wife? The wife of one of the wealthiest, most widely known powerful men alive." He grinned mischievously. "Princess Jana Triloni . . ."

Jana couldn't believe she was hearing him correctly. Even so, what could she say? Should she say? Marry Ryker Triloni tomorrow? Appear on Rigel as his wife on Varian's wedding day? Why was Ryker suggesting this arrangement?

"Are you afraid I'll force you into my bed after the ceremony? Don't worry, Jana, I won't. I plan to keep my mistress around for a long time. I want your superior image as my wife, and eventually I'll need you as the mother of my son. As Jana Triloni, you'll be able to come and go as you please. You can return to research. No one will mistreat you again. Besides, wouldn't you like to show Cass and Varian you can't be defeated?"

"It's just so sudden and unexpected," she informed him.

"It has to be. I'll be leaving on business tomorrow afternoon. I won't return until the day before their wedding, just in time for us to surprise them."

"But I'm a captive," she protested. "You're a prince."

"I'm Androas, Jana. We have no *charl* law which says I cannot marry you. Once we're wed, I'll free you under Maffei law. I'll make them grant you citizenship. You do not understand: marriage is far more binding than *charl* ownership. Once you wed me, we own each other for life. If I should die, all I have becomes yours: Trilabs, Darkar, everything. If we have a child, it will be heir to the Androas throne and empire. So you see, Jana Greyson, it is I who am taking the greater risk in this matter. If I believed you were working for Varian, would I wed you and free you? When Varian could take all I own by arranging my demise, then marrying my widow."

"You trust me that much?" she asked.

"Yes, his marriage to Canissia proves he has no love for you. The only reason I didn't come to your auction and buy

388

you was to thwart his trap for me. I knew he wasn't going to sell you that day. You see, Canissia told me. She came here furious with him because he planned to keep you for himself a while longer. I thought it was because of some crafty scheme he was plotting against me, but it was pure lust for you. He was determined to use you as long as possible. I told you I had my men checking on the truth. Councilman Garthon told Varian to send you away and marry his daughter or else. I don't know what the 'or else' is, but I doubt it matters."

"If this marriage is so binding, don't you think you should give it more thought, Ryker? What if Varian does try to get all you own through trickery?"

"If he killed me and tried to beguile you into marriage, I doubt you would agree. If he killed me, you would know it isn't you he wants. He sold you falsely, then gave you away to marry Cass. If at my unexpected death he dropped Cass to marry my widow, would you trust him and comply? I think not."

"And I think not. What will your mistress say about our marriage?"

"I have already discussed my position with her. She could never become my wife. She loves me, and she's willing to remain in her present station. I'm not in love with her, but I am extremely fond of her and she is most satisfying. Is that why you're hesitating, because of my mistress?"

"No. Do I understand you correctly, you want me to marry you in name only? Is that legally binding?" she questioned.

Ryker laughed. "Even if we never mate, once I give you my name, you are my wife and heir. However, I do have one stipulation. It might sound unfair, but I must have your word you will never take a lover. If you find yourself in need of sex, you must come to me. Is that understood? I will give you time to consider my offer, which won't ever be repeated. I do not accept rejection, so I will return at nine tomorrow for your final answer."

Varian's laughing face and voice on the news tape left her numb. "Ryker!" she impulsively called out. When he turned, she swallowed hard and informed him, "I'll marry you and agree to all of your terms."

Chapter Twenty-One

Varian was slumped in a chair in his bedroom, sipping his fifth brandy. Nights had become worse than his days. He dreamed of Jana, of her smile and laughter, of her kiss and touch. She would come to him like a beautiful specter. She would look at him with those kalei- doscopic, mysterious eyes. Her flaxen hair would fall softly over her shoulders and move slightly as she lifted her arms to beckon him.

He would awaken with a start and expect to find her lying beside him. The dreams were so real. That last day, she had begged him not to leave, saying she was afraid for him. He had been in danger; had she sensed it? Was she summoning him this very moment?

Or was that all he had left of her, fanciful meetings during dreams? Memories? Shadows of love? "Damn you, Jana! What are you doing to me? Return to my life, or free me from your hold." He would instantly declare, "Never! You are mine; you will always be mine until all time ceases. You promised, love, you promised. . . ."

Varian flung the glass against the wall and stormed out of his room. He stripped and dove into a large pool, to swim back and forth until he was breathless. Nigel grabbed his arm and yanked on it. Varian looked up and glared at him, then grimaced. "It's this not knowing, Nigel. Where is she? A grave somewhere? Another man's home and arms? A dark cell? If she's alive, why can't we find a clue, just one? If she's dead, why can't I accept her loss? How much longer can I go on like this?" he shouted in despair.

"As long as it takes to rescue her," Nigel replied. "Somewhere out there, Jana is suffering too. She was abducted for a particular reason. I wish you hadn't gone along with Brec's crazy scheme."

"It might take a crazy scheme to entrap a crazy woman. It sounded like a good way, the only way, to lure Cass back to me. By damn, I'm sure she knows something! Just wait until Ryker gets home. I'm going to beat some answers out of both of them.'' Rage burned ominously in his steel-blue eyes.

"What if this villain used your scam to mislead Jana? Don't you realize how that news tape claiming you and Canissia are getting married will affect her? I wish you had discussed it with me.''

"Jana wouldn't believe it in a million eons. Dammit, Nigel, I feel like she's trying to reach out to me. Tonight it's stronger than ever. Could it be possible?''

At noon the next day, Brec visited Varian once more. "No word at all, Varian. We're running out of time for the primary mission. Why don't you take the *Wanderlust* and help carry out the final assignment in the Milky Way? I would prefer to have you in charge. There's nothing you can do here.''

"What has the Assembly voted?'' Varian asked.

"I have starships sneaking into the Milky Way Galaxy one at a time. If either of our enemies makes a move to strike at the Alliance, I'll recall our starships immediately. Would you rather be assigned to base to head up our defenses?'' Brec pressed him. "With ten starships gone . . .'' He halted. "As for Ryker, when the last ship picks up supplies at Darkar it will abduct Ryker. With him aboard one of the ships, *Kadim Maal* wouldn't dare attack us, and neither would Jurad risk killing Maal's grandson. As a loyal Maffeian citizen, once aboard the last ship, how could Ryker object to helping? If you'll recall, the law states the Supreme Council has the right to call any citizen into duty, without advance notice. As a Maffeian citizen, Ryker must go aboard the last ship bound for Earth to give technical advice. He has no choice . . .''

Alone in his room Varian closed the door. Brec was right; it was time to accept that he must go on with his life and, if cruel fate decre-ed, possibly without Jana at his side. Weeks had passed since her disappearance. He had to accept it; Jana was gone. He must put her behind him. He was a warrior, and death had been a part of his life for years. Dead, that was how he must view Jana. Only through death could he accept her absence and push forward.

Jana had woven her web of love around his heart and life, then vanished without releasing him. Somehow, he must cut himself free of those silky strands. He left his room an embittered and determined man. He must find the strength to put his life together again, the one which she had innocently torn asunder. He felt harsher, tougher, and even stronger. He was angered at himself and fate. He felt like a blend of ice and stone, as before Jana entered his life and changed him. Never would he love again, for it hurt too much! It was safer to remain detached and emotionless.

His plagued mind asked, *After knowing Jana and sharing such love—can you survive without it, without her? Can you allow it to end this way?*

Varian found Brec with Nigel and Tris. "All right, I'll take the assignment. I'll report to base for final instructions in the morning. Just one thing, I'll break your damn necks, if you give up the search for Jana the moment I leave. When I get back, I'm putting in my resignation to look for her. And I won't stop until I have her in my hands, alive or dead."

Nigel eyed Varian and shuddered. There was a new brittleness in his blue eyes, a cynical sneer on his lips. Varian moved like a beast stalking prey. At that moment, Nigel realized a terrible truth: Jana had made an indelible impression on his friend; as much as Varian loved her, Varian hated her tormenting hold over him. Nigel winced in dread, for he knew the tricks a man used to forget a lost love: danger, endless work, and other women.

"Be in my office at headquarters at noon tomorrow," Brec suggested.

"I'll be there, ready to leave for Darkar and Earth. Who knows," he said sneering coldly, "maybe I'll find another Jana Greyson to abduct and destroy."

Jana sat in her suite. At noon, she had become Jana Greyson Triloni. She prayed that cunning beast would keep his word, however devious. It appeared she had him fooled, just as he believed he had her fooled. She glanced at the gold bracelet encrusted with precious gems, the symbol of their legal union. She wished Ryker hadn't taken her ring, her last bond to Varian. She didn't know what mad scheme Ryker was plotting, but she did know he would have slain her if she hadn't agreed to marry him. A short reprieve, that's all this marriage meant to her. She had to pretend to be duped by him; that was the only way she could survive to escape, or to stall for a rescue.

By ten that night, Jana was lying in her bed. She had discovered how to get out of the complex and into Ryker's home, but it was too soon to try anything rash. Was that why Ryker had whispered the exit code into her ear? A test of loyalty? Getting outside this impregnable building wasn't the problem; getting off Darkar was, so she must wait until after Ryker left to check out any escape possibility. If Trilabs was nearby, perhaps she could sneak aboard a cargo ship and get away. If that proved impossible, she prayed Ryker was going to take her to Rigel next week as he claimed. Once there, she would flee him, with or without Varian Saar's help.

Jana closed her eyes and drifted on clouds of dreamy slumber. The covers moved aside and a warm body touched hers. She smiled and embraced the sable-haired, blue-eyed rogue who was lowering his shadowy face toward hers. "You won't be needing this," he murmured, playfully tugging off her nightgown.

His fiery fingers brushed over her lips and caressed her cheek. She trembled. Her breath caught as his tongue traveled round and round each nipple in turn. They responded instantly to his touch, growing taut and eager. As his fingers kneaded them, his lips covered hers. The heat of his mouth and hands seared away all reason and will. Liquid fire spread rapidly and uncontrollably throughout her body.

Jana's fingers wandered into thick ebony hair as she drew his wandering mouth back to hers. She greedily and feverishly assailed his lips, yielding her very being to her lover. As his hand slipped lower and lower, caressing every inch along the way, Jana quivered and moaned with rising hunger.

When he shifted between her thighs and gently entered her, she gasped with intense pleasure. Her hips arched upward beneath him to take all of him. There was no need for the instructions which he whispered into her ears; she had learned her lessons well. She surrendered to pure instinct and raging desire, and undying love. Her body shuddered as her passions mounted. She was devoured, possessed, and consumed by his lovemaking.

Jana writhed against the bed as his insistent hands, probing

393

tongue, and intoxicating movements stimulated and aroused her to mindless frenzy. She clung to him, responded to him, gave to him, and took from him. Yet, her lover continued to torment her blissfully. If he didn't sate her soon, she would go mad with urgency and frustration. She grasped his hand to bite him in playful warning, as that day on his ship.

Jana squealed in pain and sat up in confusion. She looked around the nearly dark room. She was alone. Her bed was rumpled, but she was clothed. Her face and body glistened with perspiration and dampened her gown. No scent of sex was in the air. She rubbed the bite on her hand. A dream, a taunting dream! *Please help me. Save me from Ryker. I love you, Varian. I need you.*

Varian jerked upward in his bed. His hair and body were damp. His covers were mussed from his tossings. He could almost smell Jana's particular fragrance. He closed his eyes and concentrated fiercely on her. *Where are you, my love? How can I help you if I cannot find you? I love you, Jana.*

The alarm system shattered the silence. Varian jumped out of bed and raced toward the nearest security post. "A small missile landed, sir. It could be an explosive."

Varian stared at the oblong rocket which was three feet long and one foot in diameter. Somehow he knew there was no danger of an explosion. Somehow he knew the answer to his destiny was locked inside that shiny object. When he started to walk toward it, the guard seized his arm and warned, "Wait, sir!"

"It's all right. It's the message I've been waiting for." Just as Varian opened the clamp and withdrew a small package, Nigel and Tristan joined him. "Get back!" Varian shouted abruptly. "It's going to self-destruct."

As all four men raced to a safe distance, the rocket disintegrated, leaving no clue as to its origin or course. Varian opened the box and grimaced. When his friends anxiously questioned the contents, Varian replied as he walked away, "Jana's alive. But I might wish she's dead after I read this message."

Nigel and Tristan hurried after him. "Who's it from? What's it say?"

Varian showed them the items inside the box; they were stunned.

Sitting in Brec's office the next morning, Varian observed the man's expression as he examined the package's contents. "They appear to be authentic, but you know this could be a trap," he said.

"Nigel ran everything through our computers on board the ship; they're Jana's. They detected intense stress in her voice and mannerisms."

"Anxiety does not prove deceit or coercion, Varian," Brec reasoned.

"I know. To look at her and hear her, you'd think she was happy." He lifted one of the items and remarked, "That's the ring I gave her, but she never wore it around me. I have no idea why she had it on when she vanished." Pointing to the jewel-encrusted bracelet on Jana's arm in the picture, he admitted, "There's no arguing that's a marriage band on her wrist, and no one can remove it except her husband. But who did she marry? Where? Why?"

"It makes me very suspicious that his name, body, and voice are blanked out on every piece of evidence here," Nigel said, concurring with Varian's doubts.

"Under the circumstances, I can see why he and Jana would want his identity kept secret. How else could they keep her location from us?" Brec said. "If I believed this was legitimate, I would drop our investigation. Jana is a free woman, a Maffei citizen. There is no crime involved in leaving Tirol's company or in marrying any man, although Canissia Garthon is definitely guilty of participation. It's my bet Jana's been forced into marrying this unknown man through drugs or threats. Or she's been tricked with lies about you. I would say that Canissia is long gone from our galaxy. She'll be of no help in locating Jana."

Tristan speculated, "You think this husband wants us to call off our search for Jana, or do you think he's using the marriage as a lure?"

Varian didn't reply. He asked Brec, "Are you sure no ships have crossed the Pyropean barrier? You sure this . . . _husband_," he said contemptuously, "isn't Prince Taemin? While I was being tortured on Karlim, I heard those bastards taunting me about Jana and Taemin."

Brec opened his desk drawer and withdrew two items. "These came in just before your arrival. I was waiting for the right moment to expose them. Last week, our Pyropean prince married another woman, a Tarterrian princess. Jurad is too smart and clever to allow his son to dupe the Tarterrians or break the Pyropean law with bigamy. The date on Jana's document prevents him from becoming her mate. I've already checked; Taemin is with his princess today."

"What about *Kadim* Maal Triloni?" Tristan ventured.

"I've had my squads patrolling both barriers. All ships have been stopped and scanned. Jana has not been slipped over either boundary; I'm sure of it. When her marriage document enters the Alliance files, it won't be a secret any longer."

"What good will that do us? According to law, registration of a marriage can take place anytime before the first anniversary!" Varian replied.

"Maybe that's his sport, to torment you about his identity for a whole year."

"I think Nigel is right. Why don't you head out on this assignment while I do some more checking around? If you stay here with hands tied, you'll be worthless to yourself and us. If you leave, he might register the marriage sooner. Whatever you decide, Varian, the marriage is legal if you can't prove coercion."

"Jana wouldn't marry another man!" he declared.

"Not even to spite you?" Brec questioned. "I may have been wrong to send out those news releases about you and Cass. Until then, Jana was invisible. If she believed those tapes, she could have been persuaded to marry some man. She could have been deluded into leaving you or marrying this man. But if he wasn't in on her abduction or deception, the marriage is binding. At least we know she's alive and well. She's his wife, Varian. Are you sure you want to continue to look for her? She doesn't belong to you anymore."

A security officer entered to deliver an urgent message for Varian. The *Wanderlust* commander read it twice then crushed the paper in his hand. "I've got to see someone. Nigel, you're in charge of the ship. Brec, you may as well drop the search for Jana."

"What's the message say?" all three men asked seemingly at once.

"It's from an old flame," he lied. "I'll deal with Jana's mystery when I return. I'll be ready to begin my assignment at noon. Leave Jana and her husband in peace. She must have known what she was doing when she married him. It's time to get on with my life. As you said, Brec, no crime has been committed. See you later." Varian stood up and reached for the items in the box. He shredded the marriage document and wedding picture, then destroyed the tape of the ceremony: none of which revealed the identify of the bastard involved! But now he knew it was Ryker! He shoved the ring on his little finger. "Have everything ready at noon to leave orbit, Nigel. Recall the crew on standby. I'll come on board around ten. As soon as Brec gives us the go-ahead, we'll be on our way to Darkar, then Earth."

At dawn, Varian leaned his buttocks against the carnelian rock behind him. Ever cautious and alert, he had placed his vulnerable blind side before a towering cliff. His penetrating sapphire gaze continually swept the open area before him. Tension put his body and mind on edge. He had left a recorded message for Nigel to go after the chemicals on Darkar and to head on to Earth for the final mission, as acting commander of the *Wanderlust*. If at all possible, Nigel was to rescue Andrea McKay and deliver her to Anais, the planet where the rescued Earthlings were being relocated. His two recordings would be heard at ten, if he wasn't back on his ship safely. . . .

Varian reflected on the first message's instructions for Nigel to take over the ship and mission. The second message explained his current actions to Tirol and his closest friends. He had sneaked away from base and traveled to this remote asteroid in a swift Spacer. He had made sure no one trailed him, to prevent complications. He couldn't afford a concealed backup team or refuse to comply with his antagonist's orders. He knew he might not come away from this place and meeting alive, but he had to take that risk. Nothing mattered except Jana's life. Others could carry out the mission in the Milky Way Galaxy; only he could save his love from death. If he survived, he could obtain the needed supplies from the new owner of Trilabs: Jana Greyson Triloni. If he was slain this morning, Ryker would return to Darkar before Nigel's arrival. Whatever happened, the mission was not in jeopardy. Only he and Jana.

Varian's ebony hair was ruffled by a crisp breeze. His arms were folded and locked over his muscular chest, implying confidence and his contempt for danger. One booted ankle was crossed over the other one. He looked as if he could respond to any threat in an instant; yet he wasn't wearing his weapons belt. He was clad in black pants and shirt; his gold Star Fleet sunburst insignia and commander's stars stood out boldly against the jet back-ground of his uniform. His roving eyes halted on the landing area before him. He had been waiting for long hours, but he refused to become jumpy and impatient. Destiny should not be confronted lightly.

"I see you came alone and unarmed, big brother," a voice remarked from nearby, causing Varian to start and whirl in that direction. "Sorry to keep you waiting, but I had to make sure you obeyed my orders." The door to a concealed cave had opened and Ryker had stepped into the morning daylight. "You don't mind my savoring this victory as long as possible?" he taunted.

Varian stared at the man who could almost be his twin, as his half brother wasn't wearing his disguise. Varian's frosty stare drifted over Ryker, then blue eyes clashed with blue eyes. "I see you're no longer ashamed to reveal those handsome Saarian looks," Varian jested to rile him.

"When I came to live in the Maffei Galaxy years ago, I didn't want everyone constantly declaring that Ryker Triloni was the bastard son of Galen Saar, until it served my purpose. It seemed best to present myself as a Triloni, son of Princess Shara and grandson to *Kadim* Maal. A prince and heir to a throne and empire do outrank you, brother dear. Since our illustrious father chose to make me an outcast, I thought it best if I didn't flaunt his looks, or yours. Our selfish, arrogant father gave you his name, love, empire, and status. He gave me nothing but this face."

"You know Shara is to blame for everything that's happened to both of us!"

"Father allowed it!" he thundered.

"You're a bloody fool, Ryker. Father wanted to raise you, but Maal and Shara refused to send you to him. All Father did was reject your mother and her evil spells. He couldn't take you without their consent. You know the Maffeian law: a bastard child must be in its father's possession to be legitimized! What did you expect him to do? Attack the Androas Empire and Maal's palace to lay claim to his second son? Did you expect Father to inspire a war between the galaxies over a baby, an Androas *prince*? Father's hands were bound by duty and obligated to peace. Would you have preferred him to become a renegade after stealing you? Your price was too high.''

"Your laws are stupid! Galen could not give me his name, yet I can inherit all he had because I am his son, his blood heir after you the firstborn!''

"Are you so bitter that you can't see the truth? This war between us has continued too long, with too much brutality. Our parents are dead and buried! Damn you, Ryker, Jana doesn't deserve this place between us! What have you done to her?''

"I married her, big brother. She is lost to you forever,'' he said coldly. "You held her and this galaxy in the palm of your hand; now, both will be mine.''

"How did you get Jana off Rigel? Your blasted marriage isn't legal. She belongs to me. Hand her over or I'll send every starship in this sector to attack Darkar. I would rather see her dead than as your prisoner.''

Ryker leaned against a boulder as Varian examined the evidence he had brought to prove Canissia's guilt and Ryker's innocence of Jana's abduction. "You see, brother, you don't have a legal foot to stand on. Jana is a free woman, free to leave Rigel and free to marry me. I had nothing to do with her kidnapping and I didn't force her to marry me. Besides, surely you don't want her to leave my bed to return to yours? If all went well, she is carrying the next Triloni–Saar. My son and heir.''

"You evil bastard! I'll kill you for this treachery! We both know she didn't marry you willingly. When she finds out she was tricked—''

"Shut up,'' Ryker warned. "Jana agreed to marry me. She can't press any charges or return to you, not carrying my child. But you see, brother, I planned for every possibility. Only one of us will leave this place alive. If you slay me, you can marry my widow and inherit all I own.''

"You're crazy,'' Varian charged. "No sane enemy would

make Jana his wife and heir, then challenge me to a battle to the death for her and all he owns!''

''Imbecile, I know that you've made Jana your heir too! Canissia has been draining her father of information for years. She was also getting facts from a traitor on your ship.'' Ryker revealed Baruch Tirana's guilt. ''No doubt Cass has disposed of him by now. And she got rid of Moloch too. You see, brother dear, they were all working for Cass, and she was working for me, providing me with all of your secrets but I've taken care of Cass, and there are no links to me. I know all about you: Jana's freedom and your plan to marry her, your upcoming mission. You see, brother, once you're dead, I will prove my paternity and lay claim to all Saar holdings and the Saar name.''

Varian observed the wild gleam in the blue eyes focused on him. He must be careful and cunning, for his half brother was dangerously mad. Varian softened his tone and expression. ''Listen to me, Ryker. I don't want Jana hurt. If she wants to remain with you for any reason, I'll agree. Just don't tell her about my feelings. I only want her safety.'' ''I bet you do,'' Ryker scoffed. ''You actually love her.''

''Jana made me feel differently. We can't alter the past, but we can build a new future as brothers. I will openly claim you as my brother and I'll split the Saar empire in half to share with you. A truce, Ryker.''

Satanic laughter shattered the tense silence. ''You offer me nothing more than I will claim legally when you are dead. Do you think I desire your affection? Or understanding?''

''You can't win this time, Ryker, too much is at stake,'' Varian argued quietly.

''Look at my face, Varian. She married both of us. Would it ease your suffering to learn she mumbles your name at a climactic moment?''

Rage thundered violently through Varian. He didn't want to provoke Ryker into an attack, not with that laser gun in his hand. He had to stall. He said sadly, ''You've won, Ryker. You possess the only thing I truly love, and I can never get her back. Killing me would be like killing part of yourself. We look alike; we carry the same blood. Why end my suffering through death?''

Ryker glowered at Varian. "I will never be free until you are dead. Until Shara . . . is avenged. Until Jana bears my son. When the Saar heir reaches age one, I will bury Jana at your side; then you two can spend eternity together."

Varian clenched his fists behind his back. He wanted nothing more than to strangle him with his bare hands.

"Did you set up that trap for me on Karlim?" Varian inquired.

"Naturally," Ryker boasted. Yet Ryker didn't expose any connection between Taemin or Jurad and that bloody incident.

When Varian probed him gingerly about Jana's abduction, Ryker told him the truth about the entire episode. "Like I said, brother, I didn't plan that crime. Although I will admit your little ruse about your wedding did inspire mine and positively insured Jana's agreement. Thanks. You see, little Cass is dead and couldn't respond." Ryker related how Canissia had vanished. "So, there is no evidence or witnesses against me. Any last words, big brother?"

"What did Jana say when she learned we're brothers?" Varian inquired.

Ryker laughed oddly. "I was teasing you. She hasn't seen me without my disguise. She has no idea who I am or that we're related," Ryker revealed.

"Can I see her one last time, Ryker? Please . . ."

Ryker glared at Varian. "So you can escape on the way to Darkar? If you slay me, you can go after her. She is confined in my private complex. The entry code is simple: my name in numbers in correct order, then reversed, then every other letter, and my date of birth. Did you know Cass gave me Jana for my birthday? The day you should have died at midnight. You see, brother, all you have to do to get Jana and all I own is to defeat me. Just think, once inside my complex you will be in possession of all my secrets."

Ryker was baiting and taunting him: tempting him with Jana's life, with obtaining all of Ryker's holdings by marrying his wife and heir, with securing some of the most powerful secrets in the Universe! "You want us to battle to the death?"

Ryker inhaled deeply and leveled the gun on Varian's heart. "No, dear brother, I'm afraid I can't risk challenging your enormous prowess. I want you to die knowing how close you stand to acquiring your every dream or wish. By tonight, I'll have mine. Anything you want me to tell Jana, next year before I plant her body next to yours?''

"The truth, Ryker. Let her hear it before you murder her. I love her.''

"I know.'' Ryker sneered. "That's why you came here alone and unarmed. Idiot! You can replace a whore, but not your life. Good-bye, my brother and matchless adversary. I shall miss our invigorating battles.''

The shrill sound of laser fire echoed over the harsh landscape. The sable-haired male in black sank to his knees, sapphire eyes glued to the bronze face of his half brother. He had fired a stun-beam. Two pairs of blue eyes clashed in lethal rivalry, as the fates had decreed. The gun setting was changed from "stun" to "kill." The laser fired a second shot, a fatal one. No plea for mercy or cry of pain escaped those lips whose grin mocked the victory. A booted toe slid beneath the limp body and rolled him onto his back in the reddish-brown dust. He leaned over and forcefully ripped the military insignia, stars, and stripes from the man's ebony uniform. He knelt to make certain the man was dead and the painful past was settled. It was done; he was free.

Jana was walking around a laboratory examining the sophisticated equipment. When the door opened, Jana turned. She grasped the arm of the chair, for she was dizzy.

She shook her head and blinked her eyes. The beautiful blonde with emerald eyes walked over to her and halted before her. The woman of fifty was exquisite. No one had to tell Jana who was standing before her. "You're . . . Shara. I thought you were dead.''

"Everyone thinks I'm dead, little alien. That wasn't me they buried.'' Princess Shara Triloni took delight in explaining how she had murdered Galen and Amaya Saar, then faked her suicide with cryonic inducer chemicals.

Jana's fuzzy brain wondered why Varian would have an affair with . . . No, it must have been Galen and Shara! Her brain struggled to reason out this clue. If Shara was the one involved with Galen, then . . .

Shara could tell from Jana's intense look that she was trying

402

to unravel the mystery. "Relax, little alien. This will explain all." She pulled a cord which drew aside a curtain to display a picture of Ryker.

Jana looked at the green-eyed blond male and asked, "Explains what?"

Shara pressed a button which caused the picture to shimmer and alter like a hologram. Jana went white. "Ryker Triloni is my son, little alien. Galen Saar was my lover. Since you are a scientist, surely you know that sons favor their fathers in our world. Do I need to say more?" Shara teased wickedly.

"Varian . . . and Ry-Ryker are bro-brothers?" she stammered.

Shara laughed wildly, almost hysterically, as she disclosed the past to Jana. But the confession only stimulated Shara's frenzied speech. The madwoman exposed the devious machinations leading to Jana's abduction, and her impending fate. "Soon, I will have your beautiful face and I will become Jana Greyson," she shouted, grasping Jana's chin and shaking it violently.

Jana's head whirled. She murmured, "You can't become a wife to your own . . . son. Varian . . . will know you . . . aren't me."

Shara lovingly stroked the picture of Ryker. "To me and for me he is Galen. We have been all to each other for five years. He cannot bear to touch another woman. I fill all of his needs, all of them." She pushed the frame aside to expose a safe. Mumbling the combination as she fingered it, she told Jana, "I have kept journals since I came of age as a woman. Here, behind my love, are all my secrets. When I become Jana Greyson Triloni, I will destroy them and begin a new one for my new life."

Jana tried to rise and flee but her body would not cooperate. Shara turned and laughed at Jana's helplessness. "Do not fret, little alien, it wasn't poison. It is only a tranquilizer in your wine to keep you under control. You poor thing. You didn't realize you married the image of your lost lover. Oh, yes, little alien, your marriage is quite legal and eternally binding; and you are my son's sole heir." Shara clarified any doubts in Jana's mind about the legality of the wedding.

"Don't you see, little alien? That's why Varian sent you here, to woo my son, his brother. After Ryker married you,

Varian planned to have him assassinated. Then Varian could marry his brother's widow and have all of this,'' she declared amid crazed laughter as she motioned all around them.

When Jana weakly refuted Shara's conclusions, the woman informed her of her freedom granted by Tirol. ''Are you a fool, little alien? Can't you see how they've all used you as the pawn in their daring schemes? The plan was always to get at Ryker through you, then at Trilabs through your marriage to Varian.''

Jana wanted to shout, You're insane. She knew that was the worst statement she could make to this madwoman. She shuddered in panic as the woman closed the safe and leaned against the portrait of Ryker. Jana's teary gaze looked at a near image of her love. Varian had freed her? He had allowed her kidnapping to carry out a clever ruse? Varian and Ryker, half brothers . . .

Jana battled to keep a clear head and her consciousness, but so many words were spinning around inside her head. Why had the relationship between the half brothers been kept such a deep, dark mystery? No doubt many, most, people knew the truth! Varian had not been betrayed by an alien lover! Had his Alliance assignment been to find a woman who resembled Shara Triloni and to dangle her before Ryker's nose, to ensnare her and trick her into stealing Trilabs from his bastard brother? It was such an ingenious, daring plan. Except for one unknown factor: Shara herself was still alive. . . .

Had Varian believed he could obtain Trilabs for the Alliance, and eventually have her as his wife? Why conceal her freedom? Why conceal his past? For certain, Varian did not trust her. He had manipulated her life for monthsl! But why? At least she now understood her strange attraction to Ryker! It was amazing how those green eyes and blond hair masked his identity, yet subtly announced it! This woman was going to kill her. How would Varian feel when he discovered ''Jana'' wasn't his Jana. . . ?

Suddenly Shara slapped Jana, then slapped her again, then again. ''Wake up, little alien. Do you think you have me fooled?'' the woman screamed.

Jana's ears were ringing. She could not defend herself or reply. She heard Shara scoff, ''I know my son craves your young body. As I see Galen in him, he sees a young Shara in you. Before his return from slaying Varian, I will prevent you from tempting him again.''

Jana struggled weakly and tried to question her horrifying words. She sneered in Jana's ashen face and said, ''Your lover is dead by now.'' As tears eased down Jana's cheeks, Shara relished the telling of Ryker's lethal trap for Varian.

Shara yanked Jana to her rubbery legs and shoved her onto a surgical table. After strapping her arms and legs securely, Shara took a syringe and placed it against the throbbing pulse on Jana's throat. ''You will never get my son,'' she vowed, then pressed the plunger. The instrument hissed as the potent liquid was forced through the skin and into Jana's jugular vein. ''Perhaps I will punish Ryker for his lust. Once he obtains the Saar name and empire, as his wife, Jana, I will arrange his demise and take everything. Everything,'' she stressed, laughing wildly as she danced around the room. ''Good-bye, little alien. Thanks for a matchless face and identity.''

Jana's vision fluctuated between shadows and sparkling dots. Shara's voice began to fade away as her thoughts blurred together. Was this how it would end for her and Varian, dying separately at the same time? As a scientist, Jana knew this was no trick; she knew her end was near. *Even in death and betrayal, I shall always love you, Varian Saar, always. . . .*

Jana's slender body gradually relaxed into black nothingness. Her ears could no longer hear Shara's crazed singing. She made no attempt to shield her eyes from the bright lights above her; she could not. It was too late. Her chest no longer rose and fell. The chemical had worked quietly and efficiently. Jana's trek into madness had ended.

Shara checked Jana, finding no pulse, no respiration, no life. She would make it appear Jana had died of natural causes or self-inflicted ones.

Ten minutes later, the blond-haired man entered the same room. Sighting Jana bound to the surgical table, he rushed to it. She was still warm, but there were no vital signs. His green gaze narrowed and hardened. He fingered the scar on his right jawline as it itched when he clenched his teeth in fury.

Shara entered the room and panicked when she saw Ryker

bending over Jana's lifeless body. When he turned and faced her, she wailed, "I tried to save her, my son. I found her too late. It doesn't matter. We planned to slay her as soon as the doctor gives me her face. Victory, my son, at last we have victory over the Saars. Remove your disguise and claim your rightful heritage." Shara hurried over to him. "Come, we must celebrate."

"Why did you kill her?" he snarled.

Shara teased her fingers over the knife scar on his face. "When the surgeon gives me her face, you must have him repair this scar from Varian's knife."

Ten fingers wrapped around Shara's throat and began to tighten. The woman fought for her life. "No, my son, you can't do this. She is dead. I must take her place. You are legally wed. How will you explain no wife? Come, let us make passionate love as never before."

"Never, you evil woman. It is all over. . . . ." he shouted.

Shara's mind snapped. She could not endure Ryker/Galen's rejection once more. Screaming horribly, her hands closed on a knife, and she lunged at him. In the struggle for the knife, they fell to the floor. It was during the ensuing battle that the knife was buried deeply in Shara's chest.

Chapter Twenty-Two

The man rose slowly. He stared at the dead woman in a near state of shock. Then he crossed the laboratory floor to where Jana lay. He studied her pale face and stroked her hair. He noticed the bottle on the shelf near Jana's shoulder. He read the label: *Drendazine*. Then he spotted the syringe.

Shocked, he rushed from the complex and issued startling orders. The security chief said, "Are you sure you want me to lower our force shields and let Commander Saar and his crew transport to the surface?"

"Follow my orders immediately. There's been a critical accident in my private lab. I need my brother's help. I've formed a truce with the Alliance Star Fleet; their officers and ships are welcome here anytime. Do I make myself clear? My conflicts with Varian and the Alliance are over as of today.''

"Yes, sir. I'll see to it right now." The man stared at Ryker Triloni as he returned to his complex. "He's gone crazy. But orders are orders."

When Nigel and Tristan were escorted inside the complex, Nigel anxiously questioned, "Any trouble fooling them?"

"None," Varian responded, "Not even Shara realized I wasn't Ryker."

"Shara?" the two men echoed simultaneously.

"I'll explain later. She's really dead this time. Tris, I hope I understand what this drug is," Varian hinted, placing the bottle in Tristan's grasp.

"Drendazine, it's a chemical substance for the first step in suspended animation," the doctor explained. Varian clasped his arm and shouted aloud.

"Shara used it on Jana. I thought she was dead, scared the hell out of me. Follow me, and we'll bring my love back to me."

Tristan examined Jana. "Step one was carried out. I wish I knew how long ago Shara injected her. Once the procedure begins, it must be completed or reversed within six hours. If not . . ." Tristan's tone indicated death. "Let's get busy, or it won't make a difference what she was given. We barely have enough time to save her as it is." He jabbered nervously as he worked.

"What can Nigel and I do to help?" Varian queried. Surely this wasn't another cruel sport by fate, to find her only to lose her?

A medical team transported to Darkar, as did a large security team to assume command of the planetoid. As the medical team searched for a life-support unit and the proper chemicals to save Jana, another drama was taking place. Two of Ryker's loyal men blew up his shuttle bay and communications room, for they had concluded accurately that the man giving orders was not their leader. As commanded by Ryker Triloni in case of an attack, those two crucial areas were to be destroyed. Ryker had not planned on anyone getting inside his complex. But he had taunted Varian with the code before his death. There was no time for the two men to sound an alert or raise the force shield before being captured by Varian's crew. Ryker's other employees were instructed to obey Commander Saar's orders.

"Varian, we've got trouble. We have to get Jana back to the ship. Shara made certain Ryker couldn't revive Jana. She destroyed the life-support units and the antidote. I can't reverse the process without returning to the *Wanderlust*. We'd best hurry. Time is critical," the doctor informed him.

Just then, Varian discovered other infuriating problems: solar flare-ups were blocking communications with his ship and the shuttle refused to start. Varian hurriedly ordered both things repaired.

In preparation for their mission, only two small Spacers had been left on board at Varian's insistence and all Darkar shuttles but one had been destroyed by Ryker's cohorts. Time rushed by, and Varian felt the strain of this dire situation. When he ranted at the men working on communications and the shuttle, they told him they were working as fast as possible.

"That isn't good enough! She's dying! I have to get her on board the ship!"

When a Spacer landed and Tesla poked his head out to say, "Communications are out, so I thought you might need something. I know you said not to—"

Varian didn't allow Tesla time to apologize for disobeying his orders not to leave the ship. "You're a lifesaver, Tesla. I'm damn glad to see you. Get Tris to the ship so he can prepare his equipment, then return for Jana. Be quick, man, her life is in danger."

Once Tristan was inside a two-seater Spacer, Tesla touched the controls and was off the ground in a moment. Varian watched the Spacer head skyward. He shifted his gaze to the woman in his arms. He gently cradled her and rocked her. "Hold on, love. I can't lose you again. Hurry, Tesla," he prayed aloud.

"What's taking so damn long?" Varian snapped.

"Tesla will return soon. Dockings and takeoffs are time-consuming."

"All I know is Jana is slipping away from me with each passing minute, passing beyond my power to save her. If she doesn't survive this—"

"Get hold of yourself. She'll make it. You two will live long and happy lives," Nigel vowed, squeezing his friend's shoulder.

Tesla returned and Jana was placed inside the Spacer. "Hurry, Tesla. I'll be waiting for you." Again, the spacecraft lifted off and flashed skyward.

Varian sighed in relief. If anyone could save Jana, it was—A blinding flash of light was followed by a thunderous boom as a massive explosion seared across the sky above their heads. "My God, Nigel, the Spacer . . ."

"Communications are still out, Commander. Too much interference."

"Keep trying, Kyle. I have to know if she made it to the ship before . . ."

Nigel worked with his small communicator, but only static reached his ears. The men on the surface waited and watched tensely. And prayed.

On the ship, Braq Volsung took over the helm. "Get those communications working fast! The commander will be frantic. Any news on the Spacer?"

"Read-outs indicate she was destroyed. Tesla didn't make it back, sir."

"What happened?" Braq shouted. "The commander said not to send anyone down unless . . . Forget it, just get that last Spacer to Darkar. Something's wrong, and I'll take full responsibility for disobeying orders."

Tristan connected the facial mask to the adapter by Jana's ears. He turned on the safety valve and pre-set the regulator for one liter. Jana's lungs instantly expanded with the sudden rush of enforced oxygen. The automatic resuscitator kicked on, forcing her lungs to inhale and exhale ten times per minute.

Varian arrived at that moment and shouted, "She's breathing, Tris!"

Tristan shook his head. "It's the unit, Varian. It breathes for her."

Varian stared at the cardiac monitor. There was a flat white line traveling steadily across the screen. Tristan followed his tormented gaze. "I can't restart her heart until she's received one-fourth liter of Isoprenaline and one hundred cc's of *Ambazine*. The *Ambazine* will counteract the drug Shara gave her. The other one is to stimulate her vital signs. All I can do is wait and work carefully. *Kahala!* We're following the same process which saved Shara."

Time seemed as endless as space. Its passage was a merciless tormentor. Varian was too aware of the waning time schedule which Tristan had mentioned, yet he coaxed his friend to hurry.

"I can't rush these drugs or this procedure. That could be just as fatal as the *Drendazine* if not treated properly. We've got three hours. With luck, she'll make it." Yet, Tristan wasn't sure of his timing.

"Luck? Where was luck when I needed her the most! The fates be damned!"

Tristan scolded, "Consider it damn lucky Shara gave her *Drendazine*, and not some poison! Fates be blessed for giving us this chance to save Jana! Go get something to drink. Better still, get some sleep. You'll need it later. Even if I pull her through this critical period, she'll be out for another day."

"Sleep? I can't sleep until Jana is out of danger."

"You could try! At least get out of my way," Tristan said.

Varian moved aside, but refused to leave the laboratory. When the Isoprenaline container was empty, Tristan ordered another one to replace it. He picked up the cardiac stimulator and attached it to Jana's chest. He ordered his technician to set the control voltage for four hundred millivolts of electrical current. She pressed the switch. Nothing. Varian's heart thudded as he watched the unchanging flat white line. Had he come so close to a miraculous second chance only to be denied it? Fear gripped him.

"Increase the current output to five hundred millivolts. Hand me a cardiosyringe," Tristan ordered, his own tension mounting.

Varian watched in horror as Tristan inserted the long needle directly into Jana's heart. "What the hell are you doing?" he shouted in alarm. Beads of perspiration formed on his brow and upper lip.

"Direct cardiac puncture . . . I've got to get this straight into the aortic valve," the older man mumbled. He was worried, and it showed.

410

Varian winced as the needle was withdrawn. Blood followed its exit and pooled between her breasts. The technician pressed the switch again. The line dipped and jumped spasmodically. Within minutes, Jana's heartbeat was sending out a rhythmic pattern which the machine forcibly continued.

"No respiratory distress. Vital signs steadily improving," was Tristan's encouraging report.

The waiting was nerve-racking. Varian paced and sat, to jump up and pace again. Braq Volsung called him to say all ships systems were now functioning properly. There was no explanation available yet for the Spacer explosion which claimed Tesla Rilke's life. Varian ordered a full inquiry. He gave Nigel Sanger command of the bridge while Kyle Dykstra reported that all was under control on Darkar, and an Alliance security force had arrived to keep it that way.

Tristan Zarcoff and Varian Saar talked quietly while they waited to see if the treatments would save Jana's life. "You know it was crazy to meet Ryker alone. He could have killed you," the doctor admonished his friend.

"What good am I as a leader if I can't defend myself, my crew, and my ship? Ryker didn't know about our new weapon which would fit unnoticed down a man's sleeve. He was insane, Tris. He was wearing a uniform just like mine. You should have seen the look in his eyes when I shot him. I was going to stun him. But when I realized Ryker could only be freed through death, I ended his madness and misery. It was like killing a part of myself. This scar itches like mad. Can you laser it off as easily as you put it on?" He returned Tristan's smile. "He wanted me to get inside his secret complex. He knew Shara would be waiting to slay me, if he failed to do so. That's why he revealed the release code. He never imagined I would use his deceitful disguise. I nearly stumbled when I saw his mother there."

Tristan inhaled deeply. "I feel as if we've been traveling through the past."

"Dr. Zarcoff?" his assistant called to him.

"What is it?"

"The timer has lapsed, sir, and the patient has not stabilized."

411

Varian surged forward to Jana's side. "Come on, Tris, please . . ."

"Stay calm. We could have miscalculated the time and amount of drug."

"What if it was sooner, not later?" Varian speculated in dread. When Tristan continued to examine Jana, Varian repeated his question.

"I heard what you asked. I'm doing all I can! If she had been working in my lab, this wouldn't have happened!" Tristan snapped nervously. "I'm sorry. This woman is special to me too. I hate to see her life end like this. By damn, she deserves better! She'll stabilize soon or . . . it won't matter."

Varian dropped into the nearest chair. He covered his face with his hands. His mind was numb, his heart heavy. Nearly one hour had passed when Tristan slapped him on the back. When Varian eyed him strangely, Tristan smiled and reported that all vital signs had stabilized. Jana would survive.

Varian jumped up and shouted with relief. He went to stand over Jana and watch her face slowly return to its natural glow. The oxygen mask had been removed and she was breathing on her own. He gazed into her serene features with intense longing and deep love. He needed to hold her, to kiss her, to speak with her. "How long before she arouses, Tris?" he inquired.

"Can't be certain. *Drendazine* is a very perplexing chemical. Probably hours," Tristan said, dismissing his assistant.

"I'll wait here. I need to see her the moment she opens those lovely eyes. I have a question to ask her. Stars above, I love this woman."

Tristan chuckled. "You need rest. I'll let everybody know she's going to pull through. Looks as if we have a wedding on the horizon."

"Only if Jana agrees. I'll never control her life again. I'll tell her she's free, then ask her to accept me as her husband."

"After you clear up her bond to Ryker, what if she says no?" Tristan teased.

"I'll use my infamous Saar charms on her," Varian replied. "Just as soon as we complete this mission to her world, I'm going to persuade her to marry me. She can wait for me at Grandfather's on Eire. With Ryker dead, we can have all the supplies we need for our assignment, and Jana's world can be saved. We have just enough time to load the supplies and take Jana to Grandfather before leaving.''

Tristan departed as Varian stretched out on the nearby bunk to rest and wait. His muscles ached from the tension of the last hours. He was near exhaustion. The green lenses had been removed, but his blue eyes were streaked with red. The darkened shadow of his unshaven face scratched the hand which lay across his mouth. He realized he must be a fearsome sight, but he didn't want to leave Jana's side even for a quick shave and shower.

Varian wanted to see her the instant she awakened. He must confess his love and propose marriage. He must put all the lies between them to rest. He rested his arm over his heavy eyes to shield them from the overhead glare. Fatigue took possession of Varian Saar.

Tristan smiled when he came in later to find his friend in deep slumber. Varian had been through a terrible ordeal with Ryker, Shara, and Jana. Tristan returned every thirty minutes to check on Jana's vital signs and condition. Several hours had passed since her crisis and she was holding her own. He was pleased when Jana moved and sighed. It wouldn't be long now. He left again.

Jana slowly opened her eyes and blinked in confusion. She yawned as if arousing from a nap or night's sleep. Her baffled gaze took in the life-support unit and the medical laboratory . . . of the *Wanderlu-st*. She winced in discomfort at the soreness in her limbs. She was so groggy. She lifted the clear lid of the unit and forced herself to a sitting position. She hesitated while her spinning head settled itself.

Shocked, Jana saw Ryker asleep on the bunk not far away. What was he doing here? Where was Varian? She wanted her sable-haired love, not that blond monster! Why wasn't he in chains? Where was Shara?

Tristan entered to find Jana swaying beside the unit attempting to stand. ''What are you doing up? You scared ten years off my life. I'll wake Varian.''

''He's alive?'' she murmured. ''Then why is Ryker here?''

Tristan rapidly related the facts of the past few weeks, especially her near call with death only hours before. "I think we should awaken Varian and let him finish this explanation, he's been out of his mind since you vanished. He never gave up hope. You lie down."

"No, Tris. Let Varian sleep. We're both out of it right now. We can talk later. If I don't lie down, I'll be on the floor shortly."

"He'll be furious if he learns you came to and I didn't wake him. Your face should be the first thing he sees when he opens his eyes."

Jana grinned weakly. "How about I join him over there?"

Tristan chuckled. "That's a damn good suggestion."

He helped Jana over to the bunk where she eased down beside Varian and gradually snuggled close to him. She winked at Tristan and closed her eyes. Varian was sleeping on his left side, as usual. His arms automatically embraced Jana and he sighed peacefully. She rested her head in the hollow between his chin and shoulder. She inhaled his familiar manly scent and smiled.

Tristan dimmed the lights and pressed the music button to low volume. He grinned and whispered softly, "I'll lock the door until you two send for me. I think I'll get Nigel to join me for a drink." Tristan left humming softly.

Tristan ran into Nigel in the passageway. "How is she?"

"They're both fine, or will be soon." Tristan told Nigel he left Jana nestled in Varian's arms. "He'll be mighty surprised when he wakes up. I sealed off that lab. I believe they'll need a little privacy. . . ." The men exchanged smiles.

Varian's warmth radiated to Jana. The security of his arms soothed her. She smiled as her left arm went around his waist while his legs imprisoned hers. Soon, she too was fast asleep.

Hours passed. Varian stirred from his slumber. He gazed down at the silky head resting on his shoulder, her hand across his side and her legs captured between his. He feared he was dreaming. He glanced from the life-support unit to Jana to the sealed door. Varian grinned. Tristan was very wise indeed.

Varian assumed the doctor had placed Jana on the bunk as soon as she was free of danger. He wondered what she would think when she awakened at his side. As her hand fell over his chest, he looked at the marriage bracelet which had bonded her briefly to his half brother. How would Jana feel about Ryker's death? How would she react to being a free and rich widow? Fear gnawed at Varian, for he had no hold over Jana if she didn't want to stay with him.

Varian tenderly brushed aside a few straying locks of silvery gold. What had Ryker done to her? He gingerly touched the bruises on her cheeks. "Oh, Jana love, how can I make you understand I love you?"

Jana shifted and moaned. Her eyes slowly opened, her gaze joined with his. "You look terrible, Varian Saar. Is this any way for a starship commander to dress? No shave. Wrinkled, dirty clothes. Blond hair?"

Varian didn't ask, *How did you know it was me and not your husband, Ryker?* He smiled and informed her, "I've been rather preoccupied with saving the life of the woman I love. You gave me the scare of my life, woman."

"Shara told me you were dead. I'm damn glad you aren't," she replied.

"You're free, Jana, a Maffei citizen. I can't hold you by force any longer. I can even understand if you don't want to stay with me," he said.

"But I'm not free, Varian," she refuted.

He misunderstood. He lifted her arm with the marriage band and grimaced. "You're a rich and powerful widow; Ryker is dead. You own Darkar and Trilabs."

Jana's eyes teared, for she felt a surge of anguish for Varian. "That isn't what I meant. Your hold over me doesn't require legal papers. I only married Ryker to survive long enough to escape back to you. I was praying it was a ruse and you wanted me. I love you, Varian Saar. Does that matter to you?"

"You're serious? Don't tease me, woman," he warned.

"Surely you don't believe I'm immune to the Saar charm?"

"I need you, Jana Greyson of Earth. Can you forgive me for being so obstinate? I know I have plenty of explaining to do, but it can wait a while. Right now, all I want to do is hold you and give thanks that you're alive and beside me."

"Where else would I be, Rogue Saar?" she teased, cuffing his chin. "By the way, I know the combination to Shara's safe.

415

From what she said before trying to dispose of me, there is evidence inside to clear your family name and honor with Maal and Jurad. I'm sorry about your brother's death.''

"You never cease to amaze me, woman," he murmured.

"I hope I never do," she retorted with a sultry smile.

Varian's lips claimed Jana's and painful shadows receded. His strong hands closed possessively around his golden moonbeam, vowing to never allow her to slip through his fingers again. "This is how it should be for us, my love, magic and rapture in each other's arms. We've been assailed by the forces of moondust and madness, but the gods and fates have taken pity on us."

Varian felt a joy and contentment which he had feared were lost forever as Jana snuggled closer to him. Their lips met; their hungry bodies joined; their minds united with love. The storm was over, all but for the rising storm of raging passion. Tonight, the gods smiled on Jana Greyson and Varian Saar. Time seemed to cease for the Earthling beauty and the alien starship commander as they succumbed to the intensity, magic, and power of a love which reached beyond the planets and stars themselves.

Moondust Rapture

As the sated Gods gather to watch mortals below,
The Fates laugh joyfully, for only they know:
Two hearts joined by love, Aliens no more.
Light conquered Shadows; fiery passions soar.
Moondust has settled, Madness has fled;
Magic and Rapture rule in their stead . . .